The Book of Lexis

One

Liam

A.J. Ford

To Rachel, Jessica and Joe.

*Without the three of you,
I wouldn't have dusted off
this 20 year old project.*

Thank you.

Prologue

Snow blanketed the winding path that led toward the Glacier Kingdom. Jagged rocks jutted from the slope like broken teeth, their silent warning clear: one misstep could be fatal.

Five weary travelers climbed steadily, their breath fogging in the frigid air. The cold bit through their battle-worn clothes, and hunger churned in their stomachs, but reaching the summit didn't ease the weight in their chests.

Above them, the palace emerged from the grey peaks— its pale stone facade carved directly from the mountain. Spires rose like frozen spears into the clouds. Long, narrow windows broke the walls, too slim for entry, designed to limit any weakness in the structure. Below them, white flags fluttered above carved balconies. From within the main archway, a faint warmth spilled out into the snow.

Tylak, tall and dark-haired, ran a gloved hand over his black felt coat and signaled for the group to halt. "Get down," he murmured, gesturing toward a boulder thick with snow.

They dropped behind it, pressing close to the rock.

"The path's clear," he said, "but that doesn't mean it's safe."

His hazel eyes locked on the front gate. The palace walls stretched to meet the surrounding cliffs, offering no way in except through that single entrance.

Meltek crouched beside him, his deep blue eyes scanning the windows. "No sign of movement," he said, voice low. "But they're in there. And I'd wager they already know we're out here."

He flicked a frozen twig from his boot tread and let his hand relax over the hilt of the silver sword strapped across his back.

"Well?" Scythe asked. She rose slightly, dark hair stirring in the wind. "What are we waiting for? I've always wanted to fight a Crosser."

Meltek caught her wrist and yanked her back down. "Don't be reckless," he snapped. "It'll take all of us to bring one down. You rush in alone, and someone's going to die."

He let her go and softened his tone. "We need you focused."

Scythe frowned, rubbing her wrist. Her eyes stayed fixed on the gate. "Fine. Come up with a plan, then."

Tylak slammed his fist into the snow-covered rock. "Damn it," he muttered. "I've run scenarios like this a hundred times—palace breach, hostile takeover, unknown threats—but I never thought we'd actually need them. Not without knowing what went wrong first."

He sat back, drawing in a slow breath and exhaling a plume of mist into the wind.

Behind him, Purge stared down the path they'd climbed. Her voice was barely audible. "Those poor people…"

They all knew the sight she couldn't forget—dozens of bodies scattered at the base of the mountain, uniforms still bearing the crest of the palace. Servants. Slaughtered and discarded.

"They were defenseless," she said. A single tear tracked down her cheek. "I just hope the three of them made it out."

Eulis drew his green coat tighter and stared into the snowy expanse, hoping to find clarity in the white. Eventually, he spoke, voice firm. "They weren't among the bodies below. That means they're still inside." He looked to Meltek and Tylak. "What do we do?"

Meltek nodded slowly, face set. "It's not much to go on,

but it's all we have. Tylak?" He glanced to him, then back to the group. "If they're alive, we might still shift the odds. But once we enter, we don't get to walk away."

He scanned each of them, searching for doubt. If anyone wanted to back out, this was the time.

Scythe snorted. "We've faced worse. You really think we're leaving now?" Her excitement cut through the cold like a blade—not with thrill, but with fury. She didn't just want to fight a Crosser. She needed to. Someone had to pay.

Meltek allowed himself the smallest smile as the others nodded their agreement.

"Alright then," Tylak said, rising. "None of us have fought a Crosser before. Don't hesitate. Don't let your guard drop. And don't waste time if someone falls—we move. The throne room is the goal. If we get separated and you see a way forward, take it. No heroics."

He turned to Scythe and gave her a half-smile. She rolled her eyes and laughed.

Together, they rose and advanced. The path broadened as it neared the entrance. The snow was thick, slowing them down, but the walls began to shield them from the worst of the wind. The massive doorway loomed just ahead.

Then a figure dropped between them and the gate.

He was pale, slender, and dressed in dark clothes. Black hair whipped about his face, and his coal-black eyes locked onto them with unsettling calm. He folded his arms, a twisted smile curling his lips.

"Well, well," he said, voice smooth and mocking. "An honour to meet you at last." He bowed theatrically. "Welcome to the palace. Shall we begin the tour?"

They froze—just for a heartbeat—watching the figure's stance, reading the terrain.

Then they moved.

Tylak lunged toward Meltek, gripping him with practiced precision—one hand on his collar, the other at his belt—and hurled him forward like a spear. It was a technique they'd rehearsed countless times.

Meltek didn't resist. He twisted mid-air, sword flashing from its sheath as he flew toward the Crosser.

The blade came down fast.

The Crosser flicked his hand—once, effortlessly—and the sword was knocked clean from Meltek's grip. Its point drove down through the snow and punched into the stone with a dull, final sound.

Meltek landed hard, tumbling through the snow and into the palace threshold. He rolled with the momentum and caught himself low on the thick red carpet just inside the hall, boots skidding across the plush surface. The rug bunched beneath him, dragging slightly as he slid. He glanced down. The edge was no longer flat. Noted. Something to watch if they had to move fast.

He looked up—and felt the absence in his hand.

No one had ever knocked the sword from his grip before. Not like that. Not with a flick.

They'd believed the opening would work. It was a move they'd drilled to perfection—fast, coordinated, overwhelming. A tactic meant to unbalance a Crosser before he could react.

Instead, it had separated him.

He was disarmed, exposed, too far from the others to support him—wasn't he?

The Crosser turned to face him. No flourish. No mockery. Just the stillness of a predator ready to finish the stray first.

He stepped forward, hand beginning to rise—

—when Eulis crashed into his side.

He hadn't been seen. Not by Meltek. Not by the Crosser.

It wasn't a clean hit—more of a full-bodied lunge—but it was enough to stagger the Crosser mid-step.

The retaliation was instant. A backhanded strike drove straight into Eulis's ribs, folding him in mid-air. He flew backward, hitting the snow with a choked breath and tumbling into Tylak, who caught him by the coat, braced hard, and shoved him back onto his feet—just as Scythe and Purge closed in.

They moved like a pair of blades—fast, honed, precise. The Crosser pivoted, parried Scythe's first strike, ducked Purge's follow-up, and weaved between them like smoke. His laughter echoed—sharp, almost delighted.

Scythe pressed forward, slashing low, then high. Purge mirrored her, their timing tight, their rhythm clean—but the Crosser didn't break. His movements were faster than they should've been, each motion fluid, each counter exact.

Purge suddenly dropped into a roll, narrowly avoiding a strike aimed at her head. She popped up just behind him and lashed out with a high kick. Her boot grazed his nose—not meant to strike, but to blind. That had been the intent all along.

The Crosser flinched.

Tylak didn't hesitate. He charged shoulder-first and slammed into him with full force, launching the Crosser sideways through the air.

Across the threshold, Meltek reached out.

The sword tore free from the stone and snapped back into his hand.

In one fluid motion, he turned and brought the blade across the Crosser's path—clean, fast, and final.

The strike landed.

There was no scream. No blood.

The Crosser unraveled, his form dissolving into dark smoke that scattered into the cold.

"We did it!" Scythe shouted, voice sharp with adrenaline.

Tylak straightened. "We got lucky."

Meltek didn't take his eyes off the smoke. "He was holding back. If we stay in these fights too long, they'll start learning—our patterns, our footwork, even our timing."

Together, they moved swiftly and silently into the palace hall.

Meltek's gaze swept across the wide chamber, checking corners, watching shadows.

Light from a crystal chandelier spilled across polished

floorboards and a long red carpet. Portraits lined the white walls—noble faces frozen in moments of joy, their eyes seeming to follow the group as they passed. Marble pillars rose on either side, their reflections stretched across the lacquered floor, and at the far end stood the staircase. Two iron beasts crouched at its base—broad, sculpted things with claws curled tight and eyes fixed on the entrance behind them, as though still watching for intruders.

They climbed fast, boots thudding against stone and carpet.

At the top, the corridor bent sharply to the right. They turned the corner—

and saw him.

A Crosser, waiting at the far end, leaning casually against the wall. His eyes drifted over them, pausing on the narrow walls as if measuring how tightly they'd be forced to bunch.

He didn't get to speak.

Scythe lunged. Her daggers flashed into her hands as she closed the distance—low, high, fast—but the Crosser blocked each strike with ease, then stepped forward and slammed her into the wall. The stone cracked on impact, swallowing her in a cloud of dust and broken brick.

"Scythe!" Eulis shouted, taking a step forward.

"Keep it down, Kimmak," came a voice from behind.

The second Crosser strolled forward, popping a grape into his mouth. He gave the hole in the wall a glance, then turned to Eulis with a smirk.

"Missed a spot, didn't you?" he said. "I thought the interior was supposed to be your specialty."

He flicked a knuckle against the corner wall, chipped the plaster, and sighed like a disappointed critic.

They still had the numbers—five against two—but it didn't matter. The Crossers had the power, and every one of them could feel it. The corridor forced them into a line, nullifying any advantage of formation or teamwork.

Another crash split the corridor—Scythe burst through the

far wall, catching the second Crosser off guard with a solid punch to the jaw. He staggered, barely catching himself.

Purge followed without pause.

Mana surged beneath her skin, lighting her limbs with a soft blue glow. She struck fast, no windup—just a sharp hook to the first Crosser's guard. He stepped in to intercept, but his arm shattered under the force.

Smoke poured from the break. He retreated, clutching the ruin of his limb. "Impossible," he spat.

Eulis reached her side, eyes wide. "Purge, that's too much—"

"I'm fine," she said—and launched a kick that cracked the wall beside her.

Kimmak ducked, slipped inside her reach, and slammed a foot into her chest. She gasped, but grabbed his leg and pulled. Together, they crashed backward down the corridor.

Tylak moved to catch her, but Eulis yanked him aside at the last second.

Meltek didn't pause.

He grabbed Scythe, dropped low, and kicked off the wall, sliding them both clear.

Ahead, Kimmak's eyes gleamed as he raised a hand toward Purge.

Then the corridor detonated.

A blast of blue light ripped through the walls. Cracks raced outward. Dust poured from the ceiling. The group hit the floor as the shockwave rolled over them.

"NO!" Tylak's voice cut through the ringing. He scrambled to the edge of the crater, scanning the rubble. Smoke still rose. There was no sign of Purge. No sign of either Crosser.

He turned, rage overtaking him, and grabbed Eulis by the throat. "Why did you stop me? I could've caught her!"

"She did it on purpose," Meltek said quietly.

Tylak didn't move.

"She released everything she had."

Meltek stepped forward and took hold of his wrist.

"If you'd touched her, it would've killed you. Eulis saved your life."

Tylak's grip tightened—then slowly let go.

The silence that followed sat heavy in the wreckage.

"She… she sacrificed herself to defeat them both… I… I couldn't…" Scythe murmured, her voice thin and uneven. Her expression twisted—first with grief, then anger. She shook her head, jaw clenched. "We did nothing," she said sharply. "We just stood there."

"Enough!" Tylak's voice cut through across the corridor like a whip. He locked eyes with Eulis, then looked away as he loosened his grip. Eulis collapsed to the ground, coughing, dragging in ragged breaths.

"We barely managed to deal with one at the entrance," Tylak said, his voice steady but weighted. "The corridor nullified our numbers." He extended a hand to Eulis and pulled him to his feet. "But we're learning."

The group—now four—moved together, slower, tighter. No one rushed ahead. The weight of what they'd lost followed them like a shadow.

It wasn't long before they found the next pair of Crossers standing on either side of the double doors to the throne room. Neither moved. One looked up, brow furrowed in faint confusion. "What do we have here then?" he asked. Not mocking. Almost curious.

The other Crosser twitched, his body glitching with small, uncontrolled jolts. "They made it this far?" he said, disbelieving. "Well. No witnesses, right?"

He pushed off the wall, slow and lazy—then vanished into a black blur.

Eulis didn't even see the hit coming. A fist slammed into his gut, folding him in half and launching him down the hallway. He smashed through a wooden door and disappeared into the splinters.

Meltek turned to react—too slow. A hand grabbed him

from behind and yanked him to the floor. He hit hard, pain exploding through his shoulder as something cracked deep. The sword flew from his hand as if struck by lightning, his fingers forced open by the shock. It was the second time now he'd lost it—twice, in front of Crossers. His scream tore through the corridor. He rolled onto his side, gasping, and struggled up onto his knees, just in time to feel the pressure of fingers closing around his throat.

The gaunt Crosser, watching it all unfold, barely moved. "Let's not make this worse than it has to be," he said.

Scythe was already circling, daggers drawn. But she was boxed in. Her eyes locked with Meltek's. One Crosser had him by the throat, lifting him steadily off the ground.

Eulis had managed to sit up, still dazed. He saw the scene and froze—one wrong move, and Meltek would be dead. The balance of the entire fight tilted on that one held breath.

"Let him go," Tylak said, his voice tight with fury.

The Crosser holding Meltek tutted and gave a little shake of the head. "You're not going to deprive me of this, are you?" he said, lifting Meltek higher. "One of the King's lapdogs... ah well. Let's end it properly."

Scythe moved.

She rolled, snatched the sword from where it had fallen, and whipped it around—not at the Crosser, but through Meltek.

The blade shattered on impact, fragments exploding outward. For a second, it seemed like madness. Then the shards reversed course—pulling back, reforming mid-air, and slicing clean through the Crosser.

He disintegrated on the spot.

Scythe was already at Meltek's side, catching him as he sagged. She gave him a smile, soft and sharp at once—until her expression shifted.

Her eyes went wide.

Meltek's stomach dropped. He didn't have to look.

The words echoed in his head—"Angel's magical blade,

hey? That must make you Meltek." But they meant nothing now. All he could feel was the cold, the stillness.

The Crosser had driven his hand straight through Scythe's chest.

He felt her weight go slack in his arms. Her eyes, wide and full of light only moments before, now stared through him, empty.

"Why?" Meltek whispered. "Why did you leave yourself open? I wasn't worth it."

The Crosser tilted his head. "Touching," he said. With no ceremony, he slid his hand free and let her drop.

He looked around the corridor, wiped the blood on his sleeve. "Didn't know we were dealing with Royal Guards," he muttered, almost amused. "Weren't there five of you?"

An outburst of raw fury echoed through the corridor as Eulis found his strength, pushing himself up from the wreckage. With a surge of energy, he thrust his arm forward.

The Crosser, poised and ready to intercept what he expected to be a physical attack, was caught off guard. His eyes widened at the green energy surging toward him. "Wha —?" he started, but the beam struck him before he could finish. It tore through him with lethal precision, and his body disintegrated into swirling black mist. The dark cloud lingered only a moment before it scattered, leaving nothing behind.

Meltek, still cradling his shoulder, stared at Eulis. "Eulis… how did you—?" His voice trailed off, caught between awe and disbelief.

Only their breathing filled the corridor. Not long ago, they'd been on a boat from Saddul, sharing laughter. Now, they stood among silence and ash. Two friends gone.

Eulis approached slowly, each step dragging under the weight of what they'd lost. Meltek bent, wincing, and retrieved his sword with his good arm. Words had no place here. Once a solid five—now a broken three.

Tylak knelt beside Scythe. He took her hand, jaw clenched, holding back the tide behind his eyes. Gently, he set her against the wall and closed her eyes. For a fleeting moment, she looked at peace.

A shout echoed from below. Then explosions. Tylak's head snapped up.

"What's that?" he asked, rising.

Meltek shook his head. "I'm not sure."

"Servants fighting back?" Eulis guessed.

"Maybe," Meltek said. "But we can't wait to find out. They'll be on us any moment." He turned toward the door.

"Let's finish this."

He pushed it open and led them into the throne room.

CHAPTER ONE
Awakening in Shadows

I found myself aboard the Under Caper, its belly lit by flickering crystal-lamps and lined with carved symbols that shimmered faintly whenever the hull creaked. The vessel pitched and rolled beneath my feet, each movement a reminder that I was trapped on one of humanity's most ingenious forms of prison: a ship. There's nowhere to run when you're surrounded by endless ocean, and few places more effective at making you feel like you're going nowhere while in constant motion.

My first conscious moment struck like lightning—sharp, sudden, and disorienting. You might think you understand what I mean, but imagine this: you exist, and then you simply are, with nothing before. No childhood memories, no yesterday, not even the ghost of a dream. It's as if someone had taken a book and torn out every page except the one you're reading right now. The sensation is less like waking up and more like being thrust into existence mid-sentence, your mind scrambling to find the beginning of a story that isn't there.

I came to awareness in a chamber that seemed designed to crush the spirit. Both walls and floor were fashioned from dark wood, knotted and rough, each grain a reminder of the tree's former life—probably more free than I was at that moment. As I tried to shift my weight, what began as a dull numbness in my arms erupted into white-hot agony. My wrists were bound by rope to an iron grate overhead, the metal coldly indifferent to my discomfort as it remained steadfast in its connection to the ship's skeletal framework.

The room swayed with the ocean's rhythm, and though I couldn't remember my own name, I knew with bone-deep certainty that I was at sea. It wasn't just the perpetual motion or the creaking of timbers that gave it away—it was the air itself. Each breath brought the sharp tang of salt and seaweed, mingled with the musty undertones of damp wood and stale air that could only belong to a vessel's belly.

Through the deck above, thin spears of light pierced the gloom like searching fingers. They illuminated lazy spirals of dust, each mote dancing to the thunder of footsteps overhead. Shadows regularly eclipsed these meager beams, accompanied by the muffled cadence of voices. The words themselves were indistinct, but their tone carried clearly enough—a particular kind of cruel amusement that needed no translation.

In such circumstances, a sensible prisoner would have immediately begun plotting their escape, counting guard rotations, or testing their bonds. But when you wake up without so much as a name to call your own, the mind rebels against practical concerns. Instead, I found myself transfixed by the most useless of questions: not "how do I get out?" but "who am I, and why can't I remember?"

The worst part wasn't the physical discomfort or even the amnesia itself—it was the maddening sense that knowledge lurked just beyond my grasp. Like a word perched on the tip of your tongue, my identity felt simultaneously foreign and familiar, as if I were a stranger in my own skin. Each attempt to recall anything before this moment was like trying to catch smoke with bare hands—the harder I tried, the more it slipped away.

In a surge of raw desperation, I let out a piercing cry for help, my voice ascending towards the deck above. Frantically, I tugged against the iron grating, oblivious to the shackles that bit cruelly into my wrists. "Is anyone there? Can anyone hear me?"

"'Ello…"

That single word sent my heart into a tumultuous race. Inarticulate sounds, striving to become words, tumbled from my lips as I whirled around. There, crouched beside me, was a man. I yelped, instinctively recoiling against the wooden wall. His skin bore a lustrous grey hue, a sparse scattering of hair atop his head, bushy eyebrows, and lips painted a vivid red, curling into a gentle, almost disarming smile. His worn brown trousers draped loosely over his slender frame, and from his shoulder hung a small, dark leather bag. As he began to rummage through it, I realized with a jolt of unease: that this being was an enigma, distinctly separate from the realm of humanity.

He fumbled with his words, clearly ill at ease in the situation. "I, um, fort youse might be needing a drink, sir," he uttered, as I intensified my struggle against the iron grating. He held up a small, intricately designed green vial, extending it towards me with a hesitant hand. "It's jus' water, I'm 'fraid," he chuckled nervously. "Ain't often I get to chat with folks down 'ere, so I fort I'd try to make a good first impression… err… are youse okay?"

Panic surged within me. "Don't kill me!" I pleaded desperately. "Please, just let me go!"

His chuckle carried a hint of unease. "Don't youse worry, sir, I ain't gonna harm youse," he assured, edging the vial closer to me. The vial itself presented a stark contrast to him— a thing of beauty and refinement, almost alien in his rough, weathered hands. It was akin to finding a gleaming jewel in a bed of coarse earth. How much water could such a small, yet exquisitely crafted vessel hold? Doubtful, I averted my gaze. His smile slowly faded. "Ah, okay… I understand. Youse don't know me, so it makes sense. I'll leave youse to whatever youse was doin' before."

"No, wait!" My voice echoed in the dim room as he began to shuffle away, his gray face turning back towards me. "What am I doing here, and where exactly is 'here'?" I hesitated, a wave of embarrassment washing over me as I braced myself for the next question. "…Who am I?"

This void within me was profoundly unsettling. Desperately, my mind clawed for any fragment of memory, any anchor in this storm of oblivion, yet found only an expansive, engulfing darkness. The most peculiar aspect? It wasn't as though elusive memories were dancing at the fringes of my consciousness. Rather, it felt as if there was simply nothing there to grasp at all. I looked down, engulfed in confusion. How could I mourn a loss when I had no inkling of what was missing?

"Don't worry," he chuckled. "Youse'll understand what youse need to in due time."

"But you know something, don't you?" I pressed as he moved to leave once more. "You could tell me, right?"

He scratched his sparse hair, his gaze wandering pensively before settling back on me. "No, sir. Can't tell youse," he admitted, his voice carrying a hint of reluctance.

Exhaling a frustrated sigh, I persisted. "Then, can you at least tell me who you are? What's your name?"

"Name? Nah, sir, never needed one," he replied, his grin revealing a row of uneven teeth.

"So what do people call you?"

He raised a finger, pointing towards the deck above. "Around dees parts, people on dis ship, dey calls me Dingersby."

"Dingersby?" I echoed, the name hanging in the air like an enigmatic riddle. As I tilted my head, sifting through the abyss of my memory, a solitary thought emerged. "Isn't that the name of a sea creature?"

His eyes sparkled, igniting with a starry glimmer. "Ah, youse remembers dat, do ya?" His tone was a mix of astonishment and joy, akin to uncovering a long-lost relic.

"Isn't it a creature known for consuming its waste…?" I muttered, my gaze averted, dreading the notion that this might be the source of his nickname.

"Yup, dat's da one," he affirmed with a grin, which quickly morphed into an expression of sheepishness. "But no, I'm not a Dingersby! I don't eat my own... well, youse know!" He gestured with his lanky hands, then resumed his habitual head-scratching. "Honestly, I don't quite know why dey call me dat."

"Alright then," I responded, clearing my throat in an attempt to dispel the awkwardness. "If it's all the same to you, I'd prefer to call you 'Ding' instead. Is that agreeable?"

His eyes lit up, gleaming with a sense of newfound dignity. "Oh, yes, sir. Youse can call me whatever name youse fancy."

Relieved, I exhaled a deep sigh, grateful to have navigated past the awkward terrain of names. "Good, I'm glad that's settled. Now, about that drink you offered." My words trailed off as the reality of my situation reasserted itself. "Why exactly are my hands tied?" I queried, giving another tug at the rough rope binding my wrists above me, its texture starkly contrasting with the iron shackles I had envisioned. "Ding!" I called out as he began to drift away again. He promptly returned, his face etched with confusion. "I'd appreciate that water, but as you can see..." I inclined my head towards my bound wrists, an unspoken invitation for him to observe the obvious.

Ding's eyes suddenly widened, a light of comprehension dawning. "Oh, dears me," he chuckled, a robust, resonant laugh that seemed disproportionate to his slender build. "I completely forgot 'bout dat. I fort youse didn't want any. Here, let me assist youse."

He deftly placed the vial between his lips and reached for the ropes. Despite my initial trepidation, a single, firm pull from him, and my hands were liberated. I gingerly rubbed my wrists, half-expecting to find them raw and inflamed, but they showed only faint impressions of the ropes. The numbness swiftly receded, giving way to a prickling sensation as I tentatively flexed my fingers.

Ding carefully retrieved the vial from between his teeth, extending it towards me. I paused to examine the container. The vial, a work of art in emerald green, boasted intricate designs. Curiosity once again stirred within me, wondering how such a disheveled figure came to possess an item of such refined beauty.

Gently uncorking it, I took a tentative sip. The water tasted unexpectedly sweet, almost as if infused with a subtle fragrance, unlike any water I could recall—or thought I recalled. My thirst, however, overrode any hesitation, welcoming the refreshment.

Suddenly, Ding's demeanor shifted. His eyes narrowed, his previously cheerful expression evaporating in an instant. He crossed his arms over his chest, head bowed, fists tightly clenched. "What's happening, Ding?" I inquired, noting the abrupt change. His eyes darted towards me, wide and urgent, conveying a silent, yet unmistakable warning.

Before I could further ponder Ding's cryptic gesture, the room was jolted by the sound of a metallic thud. A door, unnoticed until now, swung open across the dimly lit chamber. The deliberate creak of footsteps descending a wooden staircase filled the space, and a large, robust figure materialized at the bottom, his face veiled in shadows. I could feel the intensity of his gaze, appraising me, weighing the implications of my presence. A nervous itch crawled up my wrists, and I found myself longing for the familiar timbre of Ding's voice to break the heavy, looming silence.

The figure lingered momentarily in the shadows before venturing into the dim light, revealing himself. He was clad in bright, intricately crafted armor, his long, pure white hair cascading over the metallic sheen. As he moved closer, his white, mirror-like full plate glinted with a golden luster, refracting and distorting the sparse light in the room. The armor's dazzling effect seemed to captivate me, yet it was the peculiar crest on his chest that seized my attention. Composed of five distinct colors, the emblem was mesmerizing. The outer ring, segmented into thirds of blue, red, and green, encased a black circle, which in turn framed a pulsating white core, appearing to ebb and flow in and out of existence. An inexplicable pull drew me towards it, a deep urge to touch it, as if such an action might somehow restore balance, making everything right again.

"So then, it appears you're finally back where you belong," the man spoke, his voice carrying a softness that contrasted with his imposing presence. Snapped out of my reverie, I scrutinized him more closely. His face, etched with the lines of experience, retained an unexpected youthfulness, and his eyes, a vivid shade of green, seemed to hold a depth of wisdom tempered with caution. His smile was enigmatic, not entirely reassuring; it hinted at an eagerness as if he was keenly anticipating my next move.

"I see our hudder custodian has been tending to you, even going so far as to free you from your bindings," he observed, his gaze briefly resting on the remnants of the rope that had confined my wrists. It dawned on me then that Ding had snapped the rope, not simply untied it. Out of the corner of my eye, I noticed Ding shifting uneasily, his discomfort palpable. "Regrettably, I must hasten this reunion. We have anchored at port D'wan Ma'hal, your designated destination."

I found myself intermittently locking eyes with his penetrating gaze, unable to maintain constant eye contact. He tilted his head, a faint frown creasing his features. In that instant, I felt an unnerving sensation, as though he were delving into the depths of my thoughts. Confusion and unease swirled within me, and I involuntarily flinched as he reached out, grasping my shoulders to hoist me to my feet. Once upright, I promptly averted my gaze to his polished metal boots, no longer daring to meet his intense stare. A sense of imbalance washed over me, though the ship itself had ceased its gentle sway upon the waves.

"Hudder, kindly assist this young gentleman; he seems to be struggling with his balance," the man instructed. Ding's arms encircled me from beneath, providing a steadying support, and he guided me forward in the wake of the man, up the stairs, and through the metallic door.

Stepping into the outside world, I was momentarily blinded by the brilliant light. My hand instinctively rose to shield my eyes, struggling to adjust to the stark brightness. I waved my arm in front of me, searching for something tangible, yet grasping only the chill air.

A silhouette materialized, its hand firmly grasping my wrist, guiding me closer to the luminous outdoors. As my vision slowly adapted, the scene before me unfolded in breathtaking clarity. The first elements to capture my awe were two majestic snow-capped mountains nearby, their grandeur perfectly mirrored in the tranquil sea. My eyes traced the path of a large wooden walkway descending from the ship to a cobbled stone floor below. Still entranced by the mountains, I stumbled slightly, bumping into a man busily securing a rope around a metal structure, anchoring the ship to the shore. He shot me a look of irritation, but my attention was already enraptured by the surrounding spectacle.

Spanning the distance between the quiet port and the towering mountains was a bustling city, its buildings crafted from grey stone, encircled by walls dozens of feet high. Wisps of smoke curled from occasional chimneys, collectively weaving a dense fog that lingered in the sky. Based on the heavy snow blanketing the mountain slopes, it seemed I had arrived in D'wan Ma'hal in the heart of winter, yet curiously, snow was absent elsewhere. At that moment, however, such anomalies escaped my notice; I was utterly engrossed in absorbing every sight, smell, and sound surrounding me.

A loud, droning noise suddenly captured my attention, drawing my gaze to a towering factory at the town's core, its stacks belching black smoke. It was undoubtedly the source of the relentless hum, churning out some sought-after machinery. Further into the city's heart, a colossal structure dominated the view—a grand building capped with a vast glass dome, casting a formidable shadow over its surroundings. My eyes then wandered, following the throng of people meandering along the docks and streets.

"Follows me, sir," Ding beckoned, gently releasing my arms and navigating through the crowd, leading the way towards the city. It struck me then how little I had seen of Ding's form. Tall and slender, almost awkward in his movements, he was an enigma—how could such a lanky figure have effortlessly snapped my bindings? I might have contemplated this longer, but my train of thought was abruptly interrupted by a firm hand gripping my shoulder.

The man in armor stood behind me, his gaze piercing through the dense city. "Right-oh, then. Here we are. Lovely morning, isn't it?" he remarked, stepping beside me and stealing a glance from the corner of his eye. "Does my city evoke any memories for you?"

"Your city?" I queried, taken aback.

"Yes, did I fail to mention? I am the Tekka of this city, which, incidentally, means," he leaned in, his voice a whisper near my ear, "...While you are here, what I say, goes." His words were sharp, resonating in my skull and sending a shiver down my spine. "Now, would you kindly accompany me..."

I cast a final glance at the large ship, noting the crew bustling about, readying for another voyage. Turning, I followed the cobbled path where the armored man and Ding waited. The town was a whirlwind of activity; everyone moved with a sense of purpose. Stalls flanked a prominent stone building, each offering unique wares. One featured a genial, albeit portly, butcher expertly carving meat while engaging in cheerful conversation with a customer. Adjacent was a stall manned by a stern woman in green, her demeanor shifting from gentle to reprimanding as she tapped a young boy on the head – the nature of her goods was ambiguous. Nearby, a man with rosy cheeks, clad in striped red attire, displayed a cornucopia of fruits, his demeanor radiating warmth. Down the path, stalls brimming with ornaments and jewelry caught the sunlight, though they held little appeal to me. My initial impression of D'wan Ma'hal was that of a lively and generally welcoming city, with the notable exception of the formidable lady in green, whose offerings I instinctively knew to avoid.

I pivoted back towards the Tekka, catching him in hushed, rapid conversation with Ding, who occasionally grunted in response. Their exchange ceased abruptly as I approached.

"Right then, your companion, Ding," he said, accentuating the name, "will guide you to your destination. I have pressing matters to address, but rest assured, I will seek you out when necessary."

"Wait, hold on," I interjected, stepping forward, an arm raised in protest. "Aren't you going to answer any of my questions?"

He offered a sly smile, tilting his head slightly. "You haven't asked any."

"But… I don't even know who you are," I said, a note of frustration in my voice.

He dismissed my concern with a laugh and a casual wave of his hand. "My name is of no consequence to you at this moment."

"And what if I need to find you?" I pressed.

"As I have already stated, I will find you when the time comes," he assured, before disappearing through a nearby doorway.

I moved to follow, but Ding's grip on my wrist halted me. "Here youse go, sir. Youse need to take dis to the Conveyer." He handed me a rolled-up scroll, its paper aged yet immaculate, sealed with red wax shaped like a crown. I traced the seal, then looked up at Ding, offering a grateful smile, before heading towards the same door the Tekka had used. "No, no, sir. We's heading through dis door," Ding corrected, gesturing towards a beautifully ornate door, adorned with swirls of gold and green, leading into a grand building adjacent to the Tekka's. The emblem I had noticed on the armor was replicated on it, with 'Conveyer's Office' inscribed above. Ding held the door open for me. "I'm not allowed inside. Youse'll have to go alone. I'll be waiting on da other side, so don't take too long, okay?" he said, his smile not quite reaching his eyes.

As I stepped through the door, I couldn't shake the feeling that Ding was concealing his concerns. What could the Tekka and he have been discussing so intently before my approach?

CHAPTER TWO
Reflections of a Forgotten Self

"Oh yes, indeed, splendidly timely. Marvelous, in fact." As soon as the door had gently closed behind me, a man with strikingly golden hair, dressed in a bright green cloak, approached swiftly. His arm extended, and his slightly clammy fingers enveloped mine in a vigorous handshake.

The Conveyor's Office was a study in over-decoration and confined space. Despite its grandiose exterior, the interior was surprisingly small. A modest, somewhat unstable bed was squeezed against one wall, while an old wooden desk and chairs occupied another. Opposite me, five imposing mirrors stretched from floor to ceiling, each framed in a different hue. Golden drapes, intended to embellish, instead added to the clutter. My attention returned to the man, his teeth a dazzling white.

"How was your journey?" he asked with a buoyant tone. Before I could respond, he quickly added, "Oh, forgive me, what a thoughtless question. Those detention ships lack style and comfort, don't they?" A giggle escaped him, self-amused. "Now, how may I be of assistance?"

I hesitated briefly, then spoke, "I was told to give this to you." My voice carried a hint of nervousness as I extended the scroll to him, which he took with an elegant motion, his grin widening.

He peered at the scroll, eyes widening. "Oh, a Royal

seal," he murmured, more to himself than to me. His observation was new to me, revealing an aspect of the scroll I hadn't noticed. He ran a fingernail across the red wax seal, breaking it open.

Something about this man felt unsettling. His demeanor seemed perpetually cheerful, a notion that persisted until he perused the scroll. Gradually, his eyes grew wide and his once-beaming smile subdued. He tilted his head as he read.

"Oh... oh dear... well then." In a fluid motion, he rolled the scroll, raised it, and with a sudden whoosh, it burst into flames, disintegrating into ashes on the floor.

I gasped, stepping back in alarm. "Oh my goodness, are you alright?" I blurted out, kneeling to gather the burnt fragments. "I apologize; I had no idea this would happen." Looking up, I paused, observing his expression, and slowly rose to my feet. "Is everything... are you alright?" His smile, now strained and unconvincing, did little to mask the concern in his eyes.

"No, no, no, no problem at all." He sauntered over to his desk, and pulled open a drawer, revealing its emptiness. A laugh, more of a forced chuckle, escaped through his teeth as he quickly slammed it shut. Then, moving to the opposite side of the desk, he opened another drawer, this time retrieving a document. With a casual slide, he pushed it across the desk towards a wooden chair, where a quill rested in a pot of black ink. "If you could be so kind as to sit down and fill out the questionnaire in front of you," he motioned with a wave of his hand towards the chair. Circling the desk, I settled into the chair, my eyes scanning the document. I cleared my throat, drawing the ink pot closer, and grasped the long-feathered quill.

The first question read simply - 'Name'. A sudden pause overtook me. All this time, I had the chance to inquire about my name, yet I hadn't. My identity was a blank slate. A nagging sensation teased at the back of my mind, but as I strained to grasp it, it seemed to slip further away. My memory was a void, extending no further back than my conversation with Ding minutes earlier. Confusion swirled within me – why hadn't I been more inquisitive? Why hadn't I resisted when I was bound? And, pertinently, why didn't I know why I was bound in the first place?

I set the quill down, turning towards the man, who still wore a dazed expression, his gaze fixed on me. "Excuse me… uh…"

"Se'Jam…" he cut in swiftly. "Se'Jam Ruped's the name! How may I assist you further?" he said, shaking off his reverie.

"Se'Jam… that's a nice name," I responded, a forced smile playing on my lips.

"I… suppose it is. Thank you…" He regarded me now with a look mirroring my own, though I sensed my discomfort outweighed his.

"Yes, well, about this first question," I tapped the paper lightly. "What am I to put here, exactly?"

His giggle, slightly higher pitched than before, broke the brief silence. "The first question asks for your name."

"Yes, I understand that," I replied, a hint of exasperation coloring my tone. "But what do I write here… precisely?" I emphasized the word, tapping the paper again.

Se'Jam's eyes widened once more, his gaze shifting to the charred remains of the scroll I had handed him earlier.

"Oh, of course. Wow! You can't remember anything at all? Well, apart from the obvious, like being able to talk, and understanding what things are," Se'Jam mused, his finger thoughtfully tapping his chin. "This is intriguing… Let me ask you something else. Do you recognize this?" He gestured towards the top-right corner of my document, where I noticed the same crest I had seen earlier on the armor and door.

"Not… really…" I responded, a bit unsure. "Could it be some kind of royal symbol?" I looked up at Se'Jam, offering a tentative shrug.

Se'Jam seemed genuinely intrigued as he slumped back into his chair. "This is the 'Crest of Nations'," he explained.

"Each color here represents a nation, or, more recently, a faction. Blue for the 'Gouds'," he said pointing to the upper left third of the outer ring before sliding his finger to the bottom. "Red for the 'Minors'," his finger moved to the upper right third. "Green for the 'Eulis'," he tapped the middle section. "Black for the 'Crossers', and the white in the very center is for the 'Guardians'." He looked back at me. "Does any of this seem familiar to you?"

I shook my head in response to Se'Jam's question, feeling a bit adrift. "I assume it's meant to?" The concepts of nations and factions, as he described them, seemed like they should be foundational knowledge, perhaps something learned in early childhood alongside one's first words. However, despite a vague sense of familiarity, they held no significant meaning for me.

Se'Jam offered a kind smile, not seeming perturbed by my lack of recognition. "You, at the moment, are one of these," he said, his finger coming to rest on the red section of the circle. The implication that I belonged to a specific group within this unfamiliar societal structure added another layer to the mystery of my identity.

"So I'm a miner?" I said, feeling a hint of pride for even slightly grasping what he meant.

"Exactly. Every newborn starts as a Minor, and some remain Minors for their entire lives."

"Miners at birth?" I asked, frowning, now less certain. Did he mean they belonged to a family of miners, or did they work as miners in some manner? I decided not to ask more questions to avoid appearing even more foolish than I already felt.

"Well, newborns have unknown skills, so they are immediately marked as Minors. In the future, they can choose their path. You see, if we labeled them as Gouds at birth, we'd have issues if they weren't strong, or if they had an affinity for magic."

"Magic?"

"Yes, magi—" he began but instantly stopped, his

attention shifting back to the scroll's ashes. "You don't know anything about magic, do you?"

I slowly shook my head. "Sorry."

Se'Jam smiled and gave a soft shake of his head. "Fascinating!" he chuckled. "Don't worry about it... we'll have you back up to speed in no time."

"Are you going to teach me magic?" I pointed to the ashes on the floor. "Was that you? Did you do that with magic?"

Se'Jam's eyes twinkled with a hint of nostalgia. "Seeing your expression takes me back," he mused. "I remember my first encounter with magic. As a child, it was just parlor tricks— dancing lights, simple levitation. But oh, how things have changed..." He leaned back, his gaze drifting upwards as if pulling memories from the drapes above.

"How do I begin? Ah, suggest something... something... impossible," he prompted.

I frowned, puzzled. "What do you mean?"

"Just speak! Something you want me to show you!"

"Anything?" I hesitated. "Can you make water? Food? Drink?"

Se'Jam's expression faltered, his enthusiasm dimming. "Well, no. Some mana users might, but..." He paused, tapping his fingers together thoughtfully. "Magic has long been elusive for us. Our history speaks of great mana users many generations ago, but now it's... a lost art, in many ways." His smile was tinged with a sense of regret.

"And this God faction you mentioned, they're not good with magic?"

Se'Jam corrected gently, "Not god, Goud. 'Goo-add'."

"Okay, Goud... what about them and magic?"

Se'Jam sighed, a brief shadow of weariness crossing his face before he regained his composure. "Forgive me. Explaining this is new to me. It's common knowledge, like teaching someone how to walk. But I'll do my best." He stood up, cleared his throat, and then perched on the edge of his desk, resting his hand next to the crest on the paper. "I am a member of the Eulis faction but am stationed here as the Conveyor. The Eulis are the green faction," he pointed to the upper-right section of the outer circle. "We're mainly magic users." His finger slid to the upper-left section. "Gouds are fighters, soldiers, guards, and the like." His finger shifted to the bottom. "Minors are civilians. Your butchers, builders, teachers." He glanced up at me, likely checking I was keeping up with him. "There are also two others, the Crossers, and the Guardians," he added, pointing to the inner ring and center circle respectively. "These are both very rare. However, I believe you've already met a Guardian. The Tekka of each city is a Guardian."

I pointed at the white circle on the crest. "Each city has its own Guardian?"

"Well, not exactly. Our Tekka, for instance, is just for this city, but another Tekka might oversee multiple smaller communities," he explained, nodding at me, checking if I was following along.

"Who are the Crossers? Why are they rare?" I asked, looking at the black ring that outlined the white.

Se'Jam sighed. "Honestly? The Crossers are considered rare because we don't know who they are. They could be anyone, even someone sitting next to us at the local tavern. They're very dangerous," he said, twirling the document around and tapping the black ring almost absentmindedly. "They're still somewhat of a mystery, and it's not fully understood how one becomes a Crosser."

"So they're bad? Then why include them on your crest?"

He smiled knowingly. "One must be aware of both the light and the dark in life. Focusing only on the good leaves us vulnerable to the darkness," he said dramatically, his tone serious for the first time. "Oh, wonderful!" he suddenly exclaimed, breaking into a smile. "I've been waiting months to say that line!" His laughter rang out, slowing down as he noticed I wasn't joining in. "Anyway… where was I?"

Turning back to the crest, he continued, "The Eulis

mainly deal with magic, potions, scrolls, and so on. But, like everyone outside these walls, I too started as a Minor." He rolled up his right sleeve to reveal his inner forearm, where the crest was faintly imprinted. All the colors were dim, except for the green, which shone brightly.

"The Crest of Nations," I said aloud. "So everyone is born with this? Or is it something they receive later?"

"At birth, the crest is fused into the skin. It's a straightforward application of illusion magic. We Eulis can modify it by simply touching one of the symbols. For instance, if I wanted to masquerade as a Minor..." Se'Jam tapped the dim red section of the crest, and it began to pulse, replacing the green's glow. "But, a person can only feign belonging to another faction for a short while before it reverts to its true color." He tapped the green section again, restoring its natural light, and rolled down his sleeve.

"Why does it revert? How does the crest know your true faction?" I inquired, intrigued despite the deluge of information.

"Blood," Se'Jam replied tersely. "To join a faction, one must attend the academy. There are academies for both Goud and Eulis factions in every city across Lylackia." He paused, noticing my puzzled look. "Lylackia is our country's name." With a snap of his fingers, he opened another drawer, retrieved a large scroll, and unfurled it across his desk.

"A map!" I exclaimed, leaning in with eagerness.

"The known world consists of four continents. Here's Lylackia," he said, tracing a long, curved island on the left side of the map. "We're allied with Tal-Set, a smaller island to the north, but our relations with the other two islands, Saddul and Mayat, are strained." He sighed, his hand hovering over the large island to the east and a smaller one to the far north.

"Why the strained relations?" I asked.

Se'Jam gave a slight smile and rolled the map back up. "I think we're veering off-topic. It's been ages since I left this office, so the world outside might have changed significantly," he chuckled, giving my shoulder a playful tap.

As my mind raced to absorb each detail, trying to commit the names of factions and countries to memory, I finally asked, "The Gouds, you haven't explained about them yet." It was a query I might have overlooked, given another chance to revisit this conversation.

Se'Jam's jaw clenched and his eyes narrowed. "Forgive me, but being a Eulis, I fear I might bias your opinion about factions. The Eulis faction, still quite new, tends to be looked down upon by the Gouds." I was about to probe further, but Se'Jam seemed to anticipate my curiosity. "Let's just say I've had some bad experiences with them, and leave it at that," he said, shifting to face me directly. "Please understand, I'm not trying to deter you from joining them. Our ways are just different from the Gouds', which sometimes leads to... disagreements. And disagreements can lead to..." He paused, suggesting a change of topic. "Shall we just leave it there and get back to your paperwork?"

Though it was phrased as a question, his tone indicated it was time to move on, so I turned back to the document. I looked at the first question again and sighed. "I still don't know my name." Se'Jam simply smiled and suggested we return to that question later. Relieved, I moved on to the next question: 'Age'. I put my head on the table with a groan.

I could hear Se'Jam giggling to himself, which seemed out of place to me. His demeanor was a puzzle – one moment reserved about his personal experiences, the next laughing. I wondered about the wisdom of appointing someone like him as the Conveyor for alleged criminals.

His laughter gave way to a sigh of sympathy. "Don't worry about the age question, that's an easy one. Roll up your sleeve and show me your crest." At first, I was confused, then realized that I, too, must have a crest on my arm. So, I rolled up my sleeve, turned my arm over, and there it was: a vivid array of black, hollow circles with dimly lit colors filling them, the red section glowing prominently. "The crest is directly linked to your blood, which, as you hopefully know, is your life source," he explained, pausing to ensure I was following.

"This crest reveals more about you than just your faction. Watch."

He tapped the glowing red part of the crest and waited. Initially, it seemed as if nothing had happened, but then the red began to seep out from its defined area, tracing along my veins toward my hand. When it reached my palm, it ceased its flow and reshaped itself into…

"Sixteen!" I exclaimed, my voice tinged with excitement. The red from the crest had formed a perfect '16' in my palm. "Does this mean I'm sixteen years old?" I looked up at Se'Jam, my face lit with a newfound joy, then back to my hand. It felt like a significant revelation, to have some knowledge about myself at last.

Eagerly, I filled in the 'Age' section of the form, but the next question halted me. "Criminal charges." Scanning the remaining questions, I realized I couldn't answer them either. With a sense of resignation, I slid the paper across the desk. "I can't answer any more of these. I doubt my crest can help either," I remarked, glancing at my palm where the faction color had returned to its place within the crest.

Se'Jam, with a gentle smile, placed a small object in my hand. It was a tiny glass jar, containing shriveled, blackened curls. I looked up at him questioningly as he pulled the document closer.

"You needn't worry about that," he reassured. "Honestly, I just wanted to truly see how affected your memory is. I gathered all the information I needed from that jar you're holding, or rather, from the scroll you gave me earlier that's now inside it."

I raised my eyes to him. His face was split by a broad smile, and I glanced down at where the scroll had burnt to ashes. It was no longer there.

"But you haven't moved," I said, puzzled. "When did you manage to collect every piece from the floor?"

His familiar giggle filled the room. "I asked them to collect themselves while we were talking. Just a little nudge towards you considering the Eulis faction," he said with a wink. "Who knows, maybe you'll be able to recombine them one of these days."

His demonstrations were impressive, showcasing the abilities of the Eulis. Yet, my thoughts kept drifting to the Gouds. Perhaps it was because I knew so little about them. I resolved to ask Ding about them once I left the office.

"But now," Se'Jam announced, "our time together must end. I've got all I need from you, and it's getting late. Please, follow me." He rose and guided me away from the desk, towards the mirrors on the wall.

The moment was surreal, almost dreamlike. There I was, standing close to mirrors, about to confront a face I had never seen – my own. As I drew closer, my heart throbbed with anticipation and anxiety. The surface of the mirror shimmered as if anticipating my arrival. I knew what a mirror was, I understood the concept of a reflection, yet why did my hands tremble? Why did my breath catch in my throat? With a deep breath, I stepped forward, eyes closed for a moment, then opened them.

The person staring back at me was a stranger in every sense. I stared, mouth slightly agape, as my reflection mimicked my actions. Dark blond hair, untidy and spiked at the front, framed a face with wide, ocean-blue eyes. My attire was simple: a torn white shirt, black trousers, and boots. But there was no mark of identity, no sudden rush of memories. I was, indeed, a stranger to myself.

"You're quite the looker, aren't you? Bet you've broken a few hearts," Se'Jam jested, nudging me playfully.

"I wouldn't know," I murmured, feeling a sense of loss wash over me. Here I was, confronting a person I should have known best, yet feeling utterly disconnected. I leaned against the golden frame of the mirror, which shimmered into blackness. A myriad of questions about my past – my imprisonment, my origins, my lost memories – swirled inside, rising to the brink of expression but never escaping my lips.

"Don't worry, young man. Look at me," Se'Jam said, his voice soft. I turned, and he embraced me, offering a surprising comfort. "Listen," he urged, stepping back to meet my gaze. "Three things before you leave. First, as far as I'm concerned, you've done nothing wrong." A wave of relief washed over me. "Second, your name is Liam." I froze. "And third…" He placed his hand on my chest and winked. "Goodbye."

With that, he pushed me, sending me soaring towards the mirror. I braced for impact, expecting the glass to shatter, but instead, Se'Jam's image stretched away, replaced by a silvery ripple. Silence engulfed me, a sense of weightlessness prevailing.

Abruptly, a brick wall materialized before me, and a cacophony of voices erupted around. Stumbling, I landed hard on my back.

"Sir! Sir!" Ding's concerned face appeared above me, framed by the night sky. "Sir, what youse doing on the floor? Are youse okay?"

"Liam," I replied, smiling. "My name is Liam."

CHAPTER THREE
Through the Eyes of Outsiders

"What's dat youse say, sir?" Ding's voice echoed, imbued with a sense of humble curiosity.

Propping myself up to a sitting position, my elbows pressing against the cold, cobbled stone, I faced Ding's luminous, grey-skinned countenance. "My name… it's Liam," I said, a wide smile unfurling on my lips. A flutter of pleasure stirred in my stomach; the revelation of my name, though simple, was a precious anchor in the sea of forgotten identity. "So, Ding," I pressed on, a newfound warmth in my tone, "would you mind calling me Liam instead of 'Sir'? That is if you're accompanying me."

"Oh yes, sir. I have to do dat anyways. I am now your Overseer…" Ding paused, his gaze reading my puzzled expression. "Dat means I have to look after youse…" A smile stretched across his face, bushy eyebrows arching high. "…Sir."

I chuckled softly. "Thank you, Ding." It was clear; his intention to adhere to formality over-familiarity remained steadfast.

"No problem, sir," he replied. Shaking my head gently, I listened as he added, "Right den. We better find a place for youse to rest." Ding took my hand, helping me to my feet. "Youse were in der for an awful long time, sir, but I kept thinking dat if I stayed, youse would eventually come back, so dat's what I did."

"I wasn't in there for that long," I countered.

Ding's smile widened, a twinkle igniting in his eyes. "I might be mistaken, sir, but I think we got 'ere early in da morning, and well, it doesn't look much like morning anymore, does it?"

Lifting my gaze skyward, I observed clouds drifting past the luminous moon, stars glittering like diamonds in the encompassing blackness. How long had I been in that room? A frown creased my brow as I ran a hand through my hair, replaying the events in Se'Jam's office in my mind. For me, it had seemed a mere ten or fifteen minutes, but for Ding, who had waited outside, it had been almost an entire day.

"How long was I in there?" I asked, rising to my feet and rotating my shoulder. The awkward landing had left it initially sore, but the discomfort was swiftly subsiding.

Ding responded with a shrug. "Time don't mean much t' me, sir. But I fink quite a few hours. Maybe... six? Seven?"

"What?!" My exclamation echoed in the alley.

"Dat's what 'appens in da Conveyor's Office." He gestured over his shoulder towards the wall. "Time's different for Se'Jam. Some magic or sumfin'."

"But... Is that possible? Time's slower for him than outside?" The concept of magic still seemed almost fantastical to me.

"Yup!" Ding affirmed with a smile. "It was 'is idea, I fink. Means he always 'as sumfin' to keep 'im busy!"

I shook my head, awestruck. "That's incredible..." I glanced at Ding, then surveyed our surroundings. We were in a small alleyway, and the path behind Ding appeared to lead back onto a main street. "So, what do we do now?"

"Dat's up t' youse, sir. I've been asked t' let youse explore for a bit."

* * *

Ding and I aimlessly wandered the streets. D'wan Ma'hal was impressively clean and orderly for its size. At the time, my attention was preoccupied with the echoing taps of a pebble I was kicking across the stone pavement, barely registering the city's details. The streets we traversed were open and brightly illuminated by blue lamps hanging from tall metal poles, well above the buildings. I couldn't help but notice how Ding consistently guided me away from dimly lit alleyways with a gentle touch on my shoulder, either distrustful of the common folk or cautious of me slipping away into the darkness.

The modest family homes seemed almost dwarfed by the larger buildings, their small, curtained windows still aglow. The factory I had noticed earlier that morning was now silent, suggesting that most of the town had retired for the night.

Above us, dark blue clouds drifted lazily, casting shifting shadows in the half-moon's light, which bathed the large, snowy mountains. I heard a soft cough beside me and turned to see Ding, who had been attentively following my gaze. I realized then that we had been walking in silence for quite a while.

I cleared my throat to break the lingering silence. "So, Ding," I began. Ding jumped slightly before turning to face me, his expression inquiring. "Yes, sir?" he asked.

"What were you doing on the ship? You worked there, but why did you come off with me? And why do I need an Overseer?" I glanced at my feet, feeling a bit awkward about bombarding him with questions.

"I don't work on da ship." Ding stopped abruptly and eyed me with suspicion. "Youse didn't read any of dat scroll I gave you dis morning, did youse?" he asked, his hand gently guiding my shoulder to turn me towards him.

I placed my hand on his. "Don't worry, I didn't open it. Only Se'Jam did."

"And what did Se'Jam do wiv it, sir?" he queried, eyebrows raised.

"He burnt it," I responded.

"Ah, good," Ding exhaled a sigh of relief.

"And then…" A memory flickered, prompting me to reach into my pocket. "He gave it back to me," I revealed the jar with the curled-up fragments inside. Ding gasped, reaching out to take it, but I quickly pulled my hand back, keeping it close. "What's written on this scroll?" I demanded. "What aren't you telling me?"

"Sir mustn't look at da scroll unless he must," Ding replied swiftly, skillfully transferring the jar into his bag. "I don't know what dat man was finking giving it to youse."

"What?!" My eyes widened in disbelief as I stared at my now empty hands. Just seconds before, I had watched Ding secure the jar, which I had kept from his reach, into his leather bag.

"How did you do that?" I asked, my mouth agape. "I didn't even see you take it!"

"Never youse mind, sir," he said, his gaze returning to me with a head shake. "What youse should be finking about now is sleep. Youse may not have felt like youse was in dat room for very long, but time still treats youse da same."

Ding was right. Exhaustion was rapidly overtaking me. He began leading me toward a tavern, explaining that a friend of his owned it. I remember smiling at Ding's fond reminiscence as he guided me deeper into the heart of the city. Finally, we reached a large building, contrasting sharply with the surrounding grey stone buildings. The inn's walls were made from spherical wooden chunks, each about the size of a fist, compressed to form blocks and bound by shiny brown paste. Above the door, the Crest of Nations adorned a large wooden sign, its red section vibrant in the moonlight.

Ding caught my gaze towards the symbol. "Se'Jam told you a bit about dis, yes?" I nodded in response, and he elaborated. "Dis means my friend is a Minor," Ding explained with a touch of pride, pointing at the sign. "He owns da whole building, so he's bound t'have somewhere for youse to sleep. If a building has all of da crest on it, it means anyone is allowed in." He then gestured towards another nearby building, its sign displaying only a green and red section, the green part glowing conspicuously. "See dis one? It says Gouds aren't welcome."

"What about the Guardians or Crossers?" I inquired, my eyes scanning the various signs around us.

Ding chuckled at my question. "People learn not to tell strong people what dey can't do," he replied with a knowing smirk.

He then pushed open the door to the tavern, and we stepped inside.

Immediately, a cacophony of music and conversation washed over us, the din almost palpable. The air was thick with the heady scent of ale. Amidst the noise, I struggled to maintain proximity to Ding as he navigated towards the bar.

The tavern was a hive of activity. People crowded around aged wooden tables, engaged in games and revelry, their laughter mingling with the clink of glasses. Others stood, swaying to the music or simply enjoying their drinks. The red tiled floor, sticky underfoot from spilled alcohol, contrasted with the yellowed walls, which hinted at a former pristine whiteness in certain patches.

My attention was drawn to a small table where humans and members of Ding's race mingled, their laughter vibrant as they conversed and drank. Each wore a hint of blue – be it headbands, armbands, or even a simple silver ring adorned with a blue gem. Their communal cheers and the clatter of glasses on the table punctuated the air.

"Gouds..." I whispered to myself, intrigued.

These were the first Gouds I had ever seen. My knowledge of them, limited to Se'Jam's cryptic remarks, left me keenly observing their every gesture and interaction.

Across the tavern, a band played on a modest stage opposite the main bar. Their music, characterized by stretched, soothing notes, merged beautifully with the soft, melodious voice of a red-headed singer. She appeared to struggle slightly to project her voice above the rising din of laughter and conversation.

As I tried to keep pace with Ding, who navigated the crowd with ease, I accidentally bumped into a table. After a swift apology to its occupants, I quickened my steps to catch up with Ding, who had already made his way to the bar.

"I thought you said we were going to sleep here. Don't you think it's a bit loud?" I shouted over the noise.

He laughed in response. "Did youse hear da music when we's were outside?" He rapped his knuckles on the bar. "Made with good, strong materials. We're gonna be upstairs," he explained, gesturing towards the stairs near the band. "It's a lot quieter der." Despite the din, Ding's voice carried clearly, his words distinct amidst the noise. "Oh, der's my friend."

"I fort I cud 'ear you," came another deep voice, remarkably similar to Ding's. The two were nearly indistinguishable in appearance – the same facial shape, hair, height, and skin color. The only discernible difference was Ding's slender build compared to his friend's muscular physique, evident even beneath the friend's red top. "So I s'pose you be lookin' for a room, right?"

"Yeah, dat's right. Can I have da one I usually 'ave?" Ding inquired.

"Course'ya can. You neva fort I would let anyone else der, did ya? That's for m'special guests only," his friend replied, and they shared a laugh marked by their synchronously similar chuckles.

Ding then turned back to me, resting his hand on my shoulder. "Now I'll only be a bit, okay? I'm gonna go sort out ya room for youse." Unsure what he meant by 'sorting out the room', I nodded, and he made his way upstairs.

There I stood, alone at the bar, amidst the bustling atmosphere, feeling a peculiar sensation as if all eyes were upon me. I nodded my head in time with the music, my gaze wandering. Ding's friend remained opposite me, stationed behind the bar, his gaze fixed on me through his bushy eyebrows.

"Hello," I ventured, breaking the silence.

Startled from his reverie, he offered a smile reminiscent of Ding's. "'Ello," he replied.

A brief, awkward silence ensued, during which we both found ourselves absentmindedly caressing the sticky surface of the bar. Eventually, I broke the lull. "So, what's your name?"

"I don't 'av a name. Never needed one," he stated matter-of-factly.

I nodded in understanding. It seemed Ding wasn't the only one in his race without a personal designation. Reflecting, I realize the wiser choice might have been to follow the same conversational pattern I had with Ding, which had proved to be somewhat successful. But my curiosity got the better of me.

"How come you don't have a name? Everyone needs a name," I pressed.

He tilted his head, a curious grin playing on his lips. "Why would I needs a name?"

"Well… how is anyone meant to know what to call you?"

"I'm da bartender," he responded flatly, his shiny red lips parting slightly. "Nope, I've got a job n dat's all dat matters."

"Oh, yes, I heard. You're a miner, aren't you?"

"Dat's right," he confirmed with a nod.

"But you're also the owner of this tavern?"

"Dat's right too."

"So, how often do you go to the mine then? It must be hard having two jobs."

"I…" He paused, his expression shifting to a frown. Then, as if a realization had struck him, his face lit up with amusement. He looked at me again, grinning. "I get youse, very funny. I now knows why youse is his friend." With that, he turned away, chuckling softly to himself as he attended to other customers.

I took a seat on one of the many high wooden stools by the bar, a strange mix of pride and confusion swirling within me. I was proud of having seemingly endeared myself to members of Ding's race – having met two and made them both laugh within minutes of conversation. Yet, I was also bewildered because on neither occasion had that been my intention.

"You're not from around these parts, are you?" a rough voice inquired beside me. I turned to find its owner seated on an adjacent stool. He appeared to be in his forties, sporting large tinted glasses and long black hair that parted in the middle. His face bore numerous scratches, among them a relatively fresh cut on his bottom lip. "I heard your conversation," he said, his voice raised to compete with the surrounding clamor. "You didn't tell a joke, did you?"

Although I was slightly uneasy conversing with someone who eavesdropped, I replied, "No, I didn't, and no, I'm not from around here. Why did he think I was telling a joke?"

The man took a swig from his glass, filled with some amber liquid, then sighed deeply. Pushing his glasses up his nose, he clarified, "You're confusing 'Minor' with an 'o' and 'miner' with an 'e'. They sound the same but mean different things. It's odd to think a Minor..." he stressed the 'o', "...could work in a mine, but such thoughts don't occur to locals."

"Well, like I've already mentioned, I'm not from here. But the bartender didn't seem to pick up on that."

The man let out a husky laugh that ended in a loud cough. "Of course he did! He's a hudder. They make the smartest humans look stupid."

This statement caught me off guard. "Smart? They can barely pronounce the word," I remarked skeptically. The thought of Ding, or the bartender for that matter, being classified as one of the planet's most intelligent beings seemed implausible. I glanced over at the bartender, who was struggling to take an order, then turned back to the man, unconvinced.

His eyebrows furrowed as he studied me intently. "You really aren't from around here, are you?" he observed, an air of surprise in his tone. "Gods, the world's changed a lot. Outsiders mixing with locals..." He trailed off, raising his glass again for another sip, then gestured it towards me. "You need to learn more about this place. A lack of knowledge makes for an easy prey."

I observed the liquid sloshing in his glass, my unease growing. Something about this man set me on edge – perhaps it was his dark glasses, the rasp in his voice, or even his slick hair… though, admittedly, not the last one. But the first two, definitely.

"Hudders don't talk using their voice," the man elaborated. "They can transmit thoughts instead of words, to any living being if they choose, and they move their mouths in sync so we humans aren't too bewildered."

I stared in disbelief, my mouth agape, and glanced back at Ding's friend. He was simultaneously engaging in three conversations while his hands adeptly prepared multiple drinks. "They don't… talk?"

The man smiled knowingly. "When communicating among themselves, they don't even bother with the pretense of speech. Why spend hours explaining something when you can instantly share your thoughts or memories? They usually refrain from using this ability on humans, though. We tend to panic, thinking we're going mad when we hear a voice in our head that isn't our own."

"But… his speech. Why does he omit so many letters?"

"You know what? I've never thought to ask," he responded with a chuckle. "Spend more time with your hudder friend, and you'll soon realize how intelligent they are." He gestured towards the bartender. "For him, speaking isn't just learning a second language, it's adapting to a completely foreign form of communication."

"I guess I see your point," I admitted, though I still found it hard to reconcile this with my perception of Ding.

The man laughed softly, drained his glass in one long gulp, and stood up. "I'm relatively new here myself. Hope to see you around." He slid the glass across the bar and turned towards me. "What's your name, lad?"

A sense of pride welled up in me as I could finally introduce myself. "Liam."

He paused, studying me intently. "A rare name," he noted with a smile, placing a hand on my shoulder. "Have a good night." He gave a slight nod towards Ding, who had just returned, and greeted him with a respectful, "Hudder," before walking across the room and exiting.

I faced Ding, who greeted me with one of his broad smiles. "I sorted out da room f'youse. Hope I wasn't too long. Shall we go now?"

As Ding 'spoke', my attention was drawn to the movement of his lips. They synchronized flawlessly with the sound of his voice, which felt as though it was emanating from in front of me rather than inside my head. The idea that hudders communicated through thought swam through my mind. Was the man at the bar teasing me because he saw me as an outsider, or was there truth to his words? These thoughts swirled in my mind as I nodded in agreement, following Ding through the lively atmosphere of the tavern towards the staircase. The weariness from the earlier time distortion was intensifying, making the prospect of rest increasingly desirable.

Ascending the stairs, we arrived at a long hallway, markedly cleaner and less sticky than the tavern below. The walls were adorned with an unappealing green wallpaper, speckled with black flowers, and framed by wooden skirting. Ten numbered doors lined the hallway, five on each side, leading up to a highly ornate door at the end. Decorated with gold and silver, it stood out ostentatiously. I speculated whether it was an overly extravagant bathroom or perhaps the sleeping quarters of Ding's friend.

"We's in room nine," Ding informed me as we progressed down the hall.

The door to room nine appeared somewhat dilapidated, its white paint flaking away in places. Ding inserted a large golden key into the lock, and with a click, the door swung open.

The interior was a stark contrast to what I had anticipated. "Was this what you meant by 'sorting out the room', Ding?" I asked, taken aback. The walls were lined with an array of large weapons, all pointed menacingly toward the centrally placed bed. Draped in sheets that mirrored the hallway's wallpaper, the bed seemed less offensive in this context. A solitary pillow sat at the head, ominously aligned with the weapons. I counted about twenty different types, from broadswords to darts, each poised as if threatening any who dared to sleep there. On the opposite side, a large sliding window opened onto a balcony. Ding entered, turned to me with a proud smile, and spread his arms wide.

"What do youse fink?" he asked, his eyes gleaming with satisfaction. I was at a loss for words, baffled by the idea of sleeping amidst such an arsenal.

Ding's smile faltered slightly as he noticed my hesitation. "It's very nice," I lied, masking my discomfort. "But why all the weapons?"

His smile returned to full force. "I fort youse might like it," he beamed. "Well, da bed's 'ere, so youse can get in now if youse like."

"Only one bed?" The idea of sharing a bed with Ding, whom I had only met that morning, was far from appealing. "Where will you be sleeping?" I inquired, hoping for a preferable arrangement.

Ding chuckled softly. "Don't youse worry, sir. I won't be sleeping. I'll be staying up tonight." He moved a chair to the window, sat down, and crossed his arms, resembling a vigilant guardian.

I stood there for a moment, pondering the sleeping habits of hudders, but Ding's unwavering, statuesque smile redirected my focus. "You're not going to just sit there, are you?" I asked, somewhat incredulously. Ding's nod, still beaming, left me with little choice. I retreated to a small adjoining room to prepare myself for the night.

Soon, I lay in the bed, struggling with the coarse and

itchy mattress. The knowledge of Ding's watchful presence only added to my discomfort. However, the exhaustion from the day's events eventually overtook me, and I silently drifted off to sleep.

CHAPTER FOUR
The Parade of Factions

Clasping my eyelids tighter, I tried to shield myself from the intrusive light that seemed to seep into my consciousness. For what felt like an eternity, I grappled with the futility of my efforts, before finally surrendering to the inevitable. With reluctant caution, I cracked open my left eye, surveying the room around me. A slender shaft of sunlight, a traitor to my rest, had slipped through a minuscule gap in the curtains, its trajectory perfectly orchestrated to spoil my morning tranquility. To my surprise, Ding was absent. A surge of urgency propelled me out of bed, only to discover another absence — my clothes.

"Wonderful," I grumbled, as my fingers combed through my hair in exasperation. My gaze drifted towards Ding's chair, where a note lay atop a neatly arranged pile of clothes. "New clothes for you, sir," it read, penned in remarkably tidy script.

Curiosity piqued, I picked up what I assumed was the shirt. It was unexpectedly cool against my skin, shimmering faintly in the sliver of light sneaking past the curtain. Upon closer examination, I realized it was crafted from fine chain mail, composed of intricately woven, tiny silver rings. Beneath it lay black trousers, tailored from a sturdy fabric, adorned with an array of pockets along the legs — both front and sides. A smile tugged at my lips as I quickly donned them.

I lingered a moment, letting my thoughts drift to Ding. Where could he be this early? The mystery tugged at me as I slowly made my way to the door, each step heavy with concern and curiosity. My hand halted on the handle as the sound of music drifted through the window behind me. Intrigued, I walked back across the room and drew back the heavy curtains, unleashing a deluge of light that flooded in, filling every corner of the room. Behind them were double doors leading to a balcony. Sliding them open, I stepped out, greeted by a soft, caressing breeze. Above, the sky boasted a brilliant blue, marred only by a solitary, wispy cloud. Other balconies were populated too, some with young children who bubbled with excitement, craning to peer over the railings. Leaning slightly over my balcony's metal railing, I looked down towards the source of the music.

Below, two rows of musicians, about a dozen in number, clad in light cream suits and armed with trumpets, marched down the road's center. Their music, lively and synchronized, reverberated through the street, unexpectedly coaxing a rhythmic tapping from my foot.

"It's only just started," a man's voice drifted from a neighboring balcony, tinged with excitement. I glanced over to see him addressing a child, "So the factions haven't arrived yet. See! I told you it was worth waking up early!" My gaze followed the street's length, catching sight of a swelling mass of red. Squinting, I endeavored to discern the details. "Oh, here they come! Here come the Minors." The group was now in clear view, some fifty individuals dressed in red, marching in formation two stories below me.

'This must be some kind of parade!' I mused, captivated by the spectacle unfolding before me. The five lines of Minors marched with an almost hypnotic precision, their steps echoing a rhythm that resonated with the very heart of the street. My hand involuntarily tapped against the railing, my senses fully immersed in the vibrant atmosphere.

My attention was suddenly drawn to a voice to my left. On the adjacent balcony, three boys, noticeably younger than myself, were perched on their toes, straining to peer over the edge. One, clad in blue and black, his blond hair catching the sunlight, had hoisted himself up for a better view. As he leaned precariously over the railing, I opened my mouth to caution him but stopped abruptly. With a quick, mischievous motion, he spat down into the throng of Minors. The spit landed with unerring accuracy on a red-clad man below, who, startled, touched his head in bewilderment. Realizing the nature of the assault, he glanced upwards, searching for the culprit. Finding none, he continued, shaking off the insult.

The boys' laughter pierced the air, a stark contrast to my rising indignation. "Why?" I asked, my voice a blend of disbelief and anger. Their carefree mischief clashed violently with my sense of respect for the parade below.

My grip on the railing tightened, knuckles bleaching with tension.

"Here come the Eulis'!" another boy exclaimed, his voice tinged with anticipation. The ringleader, still perched precariously, readied himself for another disgraceful act. As the Eulis approached, the music subtly transformed, its melody shifting indescribably. The new tune no longer evoked a desire to tap my feet; instead, it beckoned me to stand in silent reverence, swaying gently to its rhythm. The Eulis moved as a singular entity, their green robes flowing like a tranquil river, their movement almost ethereal.

I glanced nervously at the boy to my left as he leaned back, preparing for another despicable act. He spat once more, his aim true, striking a Eulis. My eyes widened in shock, and I felt the urge to hide as every member of the Eulis contingent turned their gaze upwards, pinpointing the offender with an unnerving precision that the Minors had lacked. The boy quickly retreated behind the safety of the railing, his laughter mingling with that of his friends. The targeted Eulis simply wiped his head and shook it in a gesture of resigned tolerance before continuing, undeterred by the disrespect.

The commotion from the crowd below crescendoed, a symphony of gasps and shouts painting the air with excitement. It was then that the music morphed once more, adopting a more abrasive, urgent tone. I peered down, curiosity piqued, as a wave of blue approached. "The Gouds," I whispered to myself, a smile unfurling as a rush of exhilaration pulsed through me. There was something about their presence that electrified the atmosphere, quickening my heartbeat.

"The Gouds are coming!" echoed the voice of one of the boys. The blond troublemaker resumed his mischievous stance. Exasperated, I called out, "Oh, come on! Grow up!" His response was a pointed ignorance, a dismissal that spoke volumes of his childish intent.

The Gouds, in stark contrast to the other factions, bore no semblance of order. Their expressions were those of boredom and disdain; it was clear none wished to partake in the parade. As they passed below, my gaze drifted to the boy, resigned to witness yet another act of disrespect. He spat, his aim unerring as always, targeting a Goud clad in dark glasses. But then, in a moment that defied belief, the spit never found its mark—it plummeted to the ground as the Goud blurred into nothingness.

My jaw dropped as the man in glasses materialized atop the railing, the boy's collar clasped in his hand, dangling the offender precariously in mid-air. The Goud's voice was a study in calm restraint, "Don't spit on people. I don't even want to be here, so I don't need young fools like yourselves making things worse." With a release, the boy dropped heavily back down to the balcony before scrambling back to his room with his friends in tow.

The Goud's gaze turned to me, a silent reprimand in his eyes. "Maybe next time you might think to stop them." His words weren't a query, but a command veiled in disappointment. I was left speechless, managing only a stunned "Wow."

Then, with a grace that belied his stern demeanor, the Goud crouched and sprung away from the railing, executing a flawless twist and landing precisely in his original spot, twenty feet below. The display was nothing short of miraculous. He had not only evaded an unseen attack but also pinpointed and confronted the assailant in a span that defied time. I stood there, awestruck by the prowess and agility of the Goud, a spectacle that once again transcended the bounds of what I thought possible.

The melody of the parade dwindled into a distant echo as I lingered by the railing, my gaze tracing the thinning crowd below. A tangle of thoughts ensnared my mind, mysteries of my own life that seemed as elusive as shadows. The most appropriate would I could find to describe my situation was simply 'Odd'. I could recall every tiny detail about the Dingersby from my childhood books, but the Crest of Nations, so pivotal in our history, remained a blur. It's like my past was locked behind a door, and I'd misplaced the key. The gaps in my memory were voids, unfathomable and deep. Why was I on that prison ship? What reason did Ding have to stay by my side? And the Tekka – why had he ordered my release? The weight of these questions bore down on me, heavy with the unknown. What could a sixteen-year-old possibly have done to merit confinement on a prison ship?

A shroud of melancholy enveloped me as I retreated from the balcony, stepping back into my room and then out into the corridor. The door had barely closed behind me when Ding appeared, his approach one of weariness and cheer.

"Ah good mornin', sir," he greeted with a weary smile, his eyes betraying a night devoid of rest, dark circles and bloodshot whites painting a picture of exhaustion. "Did youse sleep well?"

"Yes, thank you," I responded, mustering a smile. "Oh, and thank you for the new clothes, Ding, they're great." My stomach grumbled loudly. "Is there... any food I can eat?" I realized I hadn't eaten the previous day and couldn't recall my last meal.

Ding, his heavy nod conveying a mixture of fatigue and eagerness, smiled. "Oh yes, sir. Don't youse worry. I've gone ahead and made sure food is prepared for us. It's ready downstairs now." Grateful, I followed him to the main bar.

The tavern was deserted, save for Ding's friend, who sat at a table dressed in a pristine white cloth. I joined him, pulling up a chair. The table was a cornucopia of foods, a feast for the eyes and stomach. Small loaves of bread nestled in a bowl, a variety of cheeses in another, and a platter of colorful meats artfully sliced and presented.

"I hope da meal's to your likin'. I'm no chef, but I tried to make somefin' special," Ding's friend apologized, his concern evident.

A slightly maniacal laugh escaped me, "No, no, this is wonderful, thank you!" I sliced two pieces of bread, then layered some meat in between, creating a makeshift sandwich. As I raised it to my mouth, I noticed Ding and his friend watching me, their faces mirroring smiles. Pausing, I lowered my sandwich. "What's wrong?" I asked. "Aren't you two eating?"

They exchanged a look, a silent understanding passing between them, then both picked up their bread. At that moment, we all began to eat, a companionable silence enveloping us as we savored the meal together.

After breakfast, with parting words still lingering, we left the tavern. The door sealed our departure, and Ding, with a determined turn to his right, set a brisk pace down the street. I hastened to match his strides, curiosity bubbling within. "Where are we headed?" I inquired, interspersing my steps with short jogs to keep pace.

"Today, sir, is da start of examinations," Ding revealed.

"Examinations? Which ones?" I probed, perplexed.

"Dis examination," Ding elaborated, "is a chance for youse to change status from a Minor. And today, youse are taking it." I opened my mouth, but his words quickly silenced me. "Has sir forgotten?" He halted, facing me squarely. "As

Overseer, I must see youse do what I say." Ding laughed a booming laugh and continued on his journey.

I sprinted to catch up, my mind swirling with questions and doubts. "So, I have no choice? But I don't know what the exam is about... I haven't prepared!"

Ding's chuckle resounded again. "Dat's precisely da point. Da nature of each year's exam is a secret. Youse saw da parade earlier, yes? I saw youse from da crowd below. Our destination is da same as ders – da main academy." He navigated another turn, not breaking stride.

Anxiety quickened my heartbeat. "Is deferring it an option?" I ventured hopefully.

"Of course," Ding conceded, igniting a fleeting spark of hope within me. "But I wan' youse to take it now." My spirits deflated once more. "Your chances are da same, now or in da future." He paused, gripping my shoulders, his gaze firm yet reassuring. "Sir, youse will be fine."

Desperation gripped me, and I seized his elbow. "But my memory is... broken! How am I possibly meant to take an exam?"

Ding's laughter soared, perhaps louder than ever, a clear delight in my consternation. "Youse will understand in due time," he responded, dismissively yet not unkindly. He maintained this stance, a mentor guiding a reluctant protйgй, all the way to our destination, the main academy looming ahead.

The Academy loomed before me, a colossal cylinder of white that dwarfed the Tavern to mere insignificance. Its stature, towering over a hundred paces tall and spanning about a thousand in diameter. I stood at its base, craning my neck to absorb its grandeur. Blackened windows peppered the walls, and a vast glass dome crowned its upper half, under which the Crest of the Academy shimmered and pulsed with an array of vibrant colors.

'Ah, this is the monumental building I glimpsed when disembarking from the boat,' I realized. Around me, people bustled towards the entrance, some with eager strides, others with reluctant steps that mirrored my apprehensions.

"Right, let's go in," Ding announced, his tone brimming with an almost mischievous glee. "After you, sir," he added, his grin broad and unyielding, a clear indication of his amusement. "Don't worry... once inside, you'll feel much better," he assured.

However, the interior of the Academy only intensified my unease. Before me stood three distinct doors, each marked by a different crest – the Gouds to the left, the Eulis to the right, and the Minors in the center, before which stretched a daunting queue of dozens of entrants. The diversity in age was striking, ranging from my peers to individuals seemingly in their forties. At the head of the queue, a tall man in blue attire scrutinized each candidate against his clipboard before granting entry.

Ding's voice whispered, "Good luck, sir," but when I turned, he had vanished. In my hand, I found a crumpled note. Unfolding it, I read, "Don't let anyone know about your memory or lack of it. This is of the utmost importance. Good luck!" Ding's penchant for leaving surreptitious messages was less surprising now, yet no less frustrating. Abandoned at an unfamiliar place, I joined the queue, Ding's cryptic message replaying in my mind, sparking a torrent of questions. Why the secrecy? Why this exam? Should I stay or leave?

"Name?" The sudden query jolted me back to reality. I had reached the front of the queue without realizing it, lost in thought. The man in blue looked up from his clipboard, his expression tinged with impatience at my hesitation.

"Liam!" I exclaimed, louder than I had anticipated, quickly turning to face the others in line behind me. Hoping to lighten the mood, I quipped, "First exam question correct!" The response was a sea of unamused faces, so I awkwardly turned back to the man, who had already begun searching for my name on his clipboard.

"Family name?" His inquiry, simple yet loaded, hung in the air.

Family name? The concept hadn't even crossed my mind. Panic and frustration began to intertwine within me. Why had nobody mentioned this? Ding had assured me I'd manage, yet here I was, floundering over basic personal details.

As I stood there, a thought struck me like a hammer – family. The idea was as foreign as it was absent from my mind. My frustration swelled. 'What's the point of all this?' I thought, the absurdity of the situation gnawing at me. "You know what? I guess I don't have a last name," I retorted, a mixture of resignation and defiance in my tone. In my mind, this was a ticket out, an excuse to evade the exam due to a lack of identification.

But as I turned to leave, a wave goodbye already forming, the man's grip on my wrist halted my escape. He tapped my red crest, which transformed into the number 16 on my palm.

The man's smile carried a hint of recognition. "Should have figured it was you, young man. Your Overseer has informed us about your situation. Please, proceed."

For a moment, a surge of defiance rose within me, a fleeting thought to turn back. But then, a deeper resolve settled in my chest. This was a chance, perhaps the only one, to unearth my past. With a steadying breath, I pushed open the door, stepping into the unknown but ready to face whatever lay ahead.

CHAPTER FIVE
Alliances Amidst Uncertainty

I drew a sharp breath, caught off guard by the sight ahead. A wire fence stood between me and the forest inside. The trees rose tall, their branches reaching up to brush the glass of the dome overhead. It was strange, almost unsettling—like the forest had kept growing without noticing, or maybe just didn't care, that it was sealed in.

The others were already gathered near the fence. I recognised some of them from earlier, standing in small groups, talking quietly. Their voices wove together into a soft, scattered murmur I couldn't make sense of. Every now and then, a phrase reached me, but it was too faint to follow. A few people seemed familiar with one another, laughing in that easy way friends do. I felt a flicker of envy but kept moving, slipping between them, focused on getting to the front.

A sudden hush swept through the crowd, halting the movement and chatter around me. I rose onto the balls of my feet, craning my neck to see past the heads in front. My eyes found a raised platform where three men stood, each one wearing the colours of a different faction.

There was a short silence before the man in crimson stepped forward. "Welcome, everybody, to this year's examination. For those who are new to this, I will explain each section of the exam." His gaze moved across the crowd, then stopped—just for a moment—as his eyes met mine. It was sharp, deliberate, like he'd singled me out. A shiver ran through me. And yet, as he looked away, I wasn't sure if it had really happened or if I'd just imagined the whole thing.

His voice was clear, resonating over the now-stirring audience. "What you see behind me is where the first exam will take place. Now, I will require you to arrange yourself into groups of four." The crowd stirred, a growing murmur accompanying their movements as they began to form alliances. The man's voice rose once more, slicing through the burgeoning chaos. "But before we start doing that, I would like you to move to the faction of your choosing!" he declared.

Voices engulfed the room again.

A wave of panic engulfed me as I realized the gravity of choosing a faction. I had naively underestimated this moment, not grasping how this choice would define my alliances, strategy, and perhaps my very survival in the examination.

As eyes glossed over me, I sensed the factions were more than mere teams; they were embodiments of distinct philosophies and skills. My decision now would not only determine my allies but also mark me in the eyes of rivals.

My thoughts churned, once again tinged with frustration at Ding for thrusting me into this ordeal unprepared and anxious over the possibility of making a misstep. My ignorance, already betrayed by my earlier admission of not knowing my family name, weighed heavily on me.

"I'm sure many of your friends or family have influenced what faction you will be belonging to, so if you intend on becoming a Goud, can you please step over to my right, and if you intend on trying out for Eulis, can you stand to my left." The man's words spurred movement, a renewed chorus of muttering and footsteps filling the space.

I watched as the crowd began to divide, a sense of impending isolation creeping over me. In a moment, I would be left exposed, a lone figure amidst a sea of decisiveness. With a hesitant glance at each faction, I took a tentative step toward the Goud group, a choice born of necessity rather than conviction.

A voice, soft yet distinct, interrupted my thoughts. "Excuse me?" The unexpected interjection felt like a lifeline in an ocean of uncertainty. I raised my eyes to meet hers, finding myself momentarily lost in the arresting beauty that greeted me. Her golden hair cascaded like liquid sunlight, framing a face illuminated by eyes as blue and bright as the summer sky. The casual elegance of her purple shorts and pink t-shirt seemed at odds with the tense atmosphere around us. My reaction was instant and visceral - a cocktail of nerves and awe. My palm grew damp, my throat parched, and my thoughts clouded in a disorienting haze.

Realizing I was gawking, I hastily closed my mouth, offering a contrite smile and stepping aside to let her pass. Her light laugh, tinged with friendliness, broke through my daze. "No, I'm also unsure of what faction I'm going to choose, so I just thought I'd introduce myself," she said, her voice a melody that eased my anxious heart.

A wave of relief washed over me. "Oh, thank goodness!" I exclaimed. "I was afraid I was going to be the only one. I have no idea which faction to choose!"

As I voiced my uncertainty, another voice chimed in from my left. "Me neither." I turned to see a young man, about twenty, his timid demeanor evident in the way he nervously bit his lip. His dark hair contrasted sharply with his pale complexion, and his attire mirrored mine, though his trousers were a distinct brown, and his chain mail was complemented by a black jacket.

"I don't see what all the fuss is about really. Why can't we just get it all over and done with?" he said, his voice carrying a hint of impatience.

Before we could converse further, the examiner's voice boomed, calling for silence. "Ah, so it looks like we have one of our groups already," he announced. "Can I have your names please?" He motioned to the Eulis faction member, who promptly prepared to record our names.

"Naya," the girl said confidently. Our eyes met, and her smile sparked a connection that felt both new and familiar. "Nice to meet you," she whispered.

The young man to my left introduced himself as "Lammat," his name drawing snickers from some in the crowd. Unperturbed, he retorted under his breath, a touch of defiance in his tone.

Encouraged by Naya's gesture, I stepped forward. "Liam," I declared. The crowd's murmurs subsided quickly, and I turned to Naya with a smile. "Nice to meet you, too."

As I exchanged a smile with Naya, moving a step closer to forge a new bond, another voice cut through the air.

"Tyran," it called, drawing the room's attention to the entrance. There stood a figure exuding an aura of nonchalance, leaning against the wall, hands in the numerous pockets of his black trousers. His attire was a study in shadows, all black, accentuated by his pitch-black hair that spiked rebelliously. brown bag hung at his waist, completing his unique appearance. He did not move to approach, as if he were a spectator rather than a participant in the unfolding drama.

The sudden eruption of whispers from the crowd was like a storm breaking the silence. Naya's grip on my arm tightened, her voice tinged with disbelief. "Tyran? The son of Tylak? Why isn't he with the Gouds?"

I felt a pang of ignorance at her question. "Who's Tyran?" I whispered back, feeling increasingly out of the loop.

Naya's eyes widened in astonishment. "What? Tyran!" she emphasized. "You not from D'wan Ma'Hal? He's the son of one of the four Legendary Gouds, heroes from the war six years ago. Why isn't he joining the Gouds?"

The examiner's voice cut through the murmurs, beckoning Tyran to join us. With a heavy sigh, Tyran detached himself from the wall, his body language exuding a blend of reluctance and arrogance.

I couldn't help but feel a twinge of jealousy as Naya brushed her hair aside, her smile widening for Tyran. "He's quite cute, isn't he?" she muttered, seemingly to herself. At that moment, my opinion of Tyran soured. Despite his apparent aloofness and disinterest, he still drew admiration effortlessly.

Standing beside me, Tyran folded his arms, emitting an air of disinterest that only seemed to enhance his appeal to the onlookers. I couldn't help but glare at him, mentally adding his height advantage to my growing list of reasons for disliking him.

As the examiner urged the rest of the participants to form groups, Naya eagerly approached Tyran, "Hi, my name is Naya," she said. "It's nice to meet you!"

Tyran's reaction struck a cold note, his eyes briefly meeting Naya's before flitting away indifferently. His aloofness was evident, creating an invisible barrier that distanced him even as he stood among us. This brief interaction revealed more than mere disinterest; it spoke of a deeply ingrained sense of superiority and detachment. As I observed this, I felt a mix of resentment and curiosity. "I know your name. I heard you call it out a few seconds ago," he retorted. "Just don't slow me down."

Naya's laugh faltered as she took in his stern demeanor. A surge of indignation and protectiveness welled up within me. His vague comment about us slowing him down left no doubt – he viewed us as mere impediments, an unspoken challenge that stoked the fire burning inside me.

Lammat leaned in closer to me, "Takes after his father with his manners, doesn't he?" His observation about Tyran drew a slow nod from me, a silent agreement to his implicit criticism. "The least he can do is cut us some slack," Lammat continued, a trace of bitterness in his tone. "He's probably had all the training in the world." His words painted a stark contrast between Tyran's privileged preparation and my own untested skills. "I bet some people here can't even fight to save their lives. That wouldn't suit these exams, would it?" His laugh, though self-derisive, did little to mask the underlying unease.

His words struck a nerve, sending a ripple of fear

through me. My body began to tremble, a physical manifestation of the dread that swirled within.

The notion of fighting for my life, a concept so alien and petrifying, crystallized into a terrifying reality. My heart raced, and a cold sweat broke out on my forehead as I grappled with this newfound fear. Images of unseen dangers lurking in the forest's depths haunted my thoughts. This was no longer a mere competition; it was a battle against unknown threats and, more frighteningly, against my untested courage and resolve. A bead of sweat formed at my temple, and my heart pounded with heavy, foreboding beats.

Glancing at Naya, I noticed the change in her demeanor. Gone was the buoyant, lively spirit that had introduced herself to me. Now, she looked downcast, her gaze flickering around, lost and unsure. Her earlier exuberance had dissipated, perhaps weighed down by the gravity of our situation or Tyran's dismissive attitude.

Despite my instinct to reach out, to rekindle that spark of cheerfulness in her, I couldn't shake off my feelings of irritation. Tyran's arrival had shifted the dynamics, and I felt an unjust sense of dismissal from her, so instead my frustration manifested as a scowl, my arms folding across my chest in a defiant posture.

The examiner's voice cut through the murmurs of the divided room, bringing our attention to the daunting task ahead. With twenty groups of four formed, the air was thick with a blend of anticipation and uncertainty. Seven groups aspired to join the Gouds, twelve aimed for Eulis, and then there was us – the one group seemingly adrift in purpose.

"As I have said already," the examiner's voice boomed, capturing the room's focus, "the first section of the exam will take place in the forest. You will be required to locate three, I repeat, three of these per team." He held aloft a red orb, pulsating with a luminous glow, about the size of a fist. Its eerie light cast dancing shadows across his face, underscoring the seriousness of his words.

"These have already been distributed randomly throughout the forest for you to find," he continued, his tone imbued with a hint of warning. "But be warned... that is not all we have placed." A murmur of traps and wild animals rippled through the groups. He slid the orb into a brown, leather bag at his side, his movements deliberate and measured.

The oblique mention of traps set my heart pounding with apprehension. The forest, once an enticing riddle to solve, now harbored untold perils deliberately scattered among the trees and shrubbery. Locating the orbs was no longer a straightforward endeavor but a hazardous undertaking where every step could potentially trigger an unseen snare or pitfall. The tantalizing mystery had morphed into a foreboding gauntlet of hidden dangers.

Turning to Lammat, I expressed my concern. "They wouldn't do traps, would they? I don't know how to deal with traps." But he was too engrossed in the examiner's words, waving me off to listen more intently.

"The second exam will take place tomorrow, but I am afraid that not everyone will be able to pass today. There are eighty people here at the moment, and sadly only a maximum of forty will be able to get through this first round." The announcement sparked a chorus of protests and arguments among the participants, a sense of unfairness rippling through the crowd.

A member from the Eulis group, his attire a unique ensemble of thin brown vines intricately wrapped around his body, stepped forward with a question that echoed the collective curiosity. "How are you going to ensure that only forty people will be able to get through?" His query was followed by a thoughtful click of his tongue and a nod, "I see... There are only thirty of those orbs in there, aren't there?" A smile played across his lips as he confidently crossed his arms.

His teammates, evidently familiar with each other, were engaged in hushed strategizing. Two boys, dressed in green with brown patches, whispered fervently, likely plotting their approach for the impending challenge. The team's fourth member, a girl with short blond hair dressed in blue shorts and a shirt adorned with a red floral pattern, seemed momentarily distracted, her gaze fixed dreamily on Tyran. Catching my eye, she shot me a brief, sharp glare before refocusing on the examiner.

"You are correct, young...?" the examiner prompted.

"My name is Kai," the vine-clad youth announced boldly. A tense moment unfolded as the girl in his group reached towards him, only to retract her hand swiftly when he turned sharply towards her. Her ducking motion suggested an anticipation of conflict, but Kai's rough "What?" was met with only a silent shake of her head.

The examiner, unfazed by the brief altercation, confirmed Kai's deduction. "Young Kai is correct. There are only thirty orbs within the forest, meaning that only ten teams can advance. There will be a three-hour time limit. If at any time your team collects three orbs, proceed immediately to the forest's opposite end, where an exit awaits. You may only pass through with your entire team. Understood?"

The room absorbed this information, the gravity of the task and the competition for the limited orbs sinking in. He then requested a volunteer from each team. Without much thought, I almost raised my hand, but Lammat was quicker. Not only did he signal his willingness, but he also began moving towards the examiner. Similarly, representatives from other groups emerged, forming an orderly line at the front.

The tension in the air was heavy as we awaited further instructions, the forest's unknown challenges looming large in my mind.

The scene at the front of the room was a diverse array of individuals stepping forward, a mixture of genders and expressions. Among them, a particularly frightened boy caught my eye, his body trembling visibly. For a fleeting moment, I found a sense of solace in knowing there were others more terrified than myself. But this comfort was short-lived as my mind began to speculate on the reasons behind his fear. My gaze involuntarily drifted towards the forest, its unknown depths sending a shiver through me. The realization dawned on me that, unlike the others who might have some inkling of what awaited us, I was stepping into this challenge utterly blind.

The examiner, whom the Minor referred to, instructed the group leaders to take a bag each from a table laden with small black bags. A curious instruction followed, directed at a boy in the line. "Oh, and pass me a spare one, would you?" The boy complied, handing one bag to the examiner before rejoining his group.

"These black bags must not be opened," the Minor announced, his gaze sweeping across the room, pausing pointedly at the Goud group where some had already begun to untie them. These are to be used only if you find yourselves in great danger. I do not want any deaths today."

His mention of death, following the earlier revelation of traps, sent a jolt of fear through me. I turned to Tyran, my voice tinged with alarm. "Deaths? First traps, now there's a chance I could die?" Realizing to whom I was speaking, I quickly faced the examiner again, my expression darkening.

The Minor resumed his explanation. "I will demonstrate what these bags are for," he said, casually dropping it over the stage's edge. The resultant 'bang' as it hit the ground was startling, followed by the dramatic launch of a massive red flare that soared upwards and attached itself to the domed ceiling. The suddenness of it made people recoil, but the flare glowed and hummed, drawing all eyes to its intense radiance.

"This is a beacon," the Minor clarified. "As soon as we see this, an examiner will come to help." With a snap of his fingers, the Eulis examiner extinguished the beacon, eliciting a silent laugh from me at the evident disdain on the Goud examiner's face.

The revelation of the beacons' purpose added another

layer to the complexity of the task ahead. They were a lifeline, a call for help, but also a symbol of vulnerability and potential failure.

"Let's hope we don't need to use it, hey?" Naya said with a soft smile. Her optimism was a small beacon in itself amidst the uncertainty. I chuckled in response, my gaze shifting to Lammat, who was nonchalantly flipping his black bag from hand to hand.

"Hey, be careful with that!" Naya's cautionary nudge caught Lammat off guard, causing him to fumble and almost drop the bag. We collectively held our breath, watching its descent with wide eyes. In a swift move, Tyran's hand darted out, snatching the bag mid-air. His silence as he stowed the bag in his side bag was as notable as his quick reflexes.

The examiner's voice brought our attention back. "I think that's all there is to explain." He scanned his fellow examiners for confirmation, receiving nods in response. "Very well then, we shall begin. The group in the middle will enter first."

This decision didn't sit well with everyone. A protest erupted from the Goud faction, led by a woman with long brown hair tied back, clad in orange. "That's not fair," she objected loudly. "If they get to enter first, that means they have more time to gather the orbs. We should all enter at the same time." Her words stirred a chorus of agreement from both sides, escalating the room into a hum of dissent.

The examiner, attempting to restore order, gestured emphatically for silence. "It seems this wasn't as clear as I had assumed," the examiner murmured, his gaze drifting downward, a tangible note of frustration in his tone. "Under normal circumstances, everyone would enter simultaneously, each from their distinct entrances." The girl, poised to interject, was promptly silenced by the examiner's raised finger. "Consider this scenario," he proposed, his voice laced with inquiry. "If you were to encounter a band of Gouds and a gathering of Eulis in the forest, whom would you challenge for their orbs?"

The girl's lips sealed shut, her eyes reflecting a newfound understanding.

"The Eulis are likely pondering the same quandary," he continued, pointing at us with deliberate emphasis. "Would any of you hesitate to confront this team?" His smile tinged with sympathy. "In my view, their head-start is justified, given their pronounced disadvantage." The air hung heavy with unspoken objections, yet I couldn't shake off a sense of unease, feeling scrutinized by every surrounding gaze. "Very well, let us commence. This team shall enter forthwith through this entrance, while the others will be guided to alternative entries." His eyes lingered on Tyran, his head tilting slightly as if mulling over an unspoken thought. "Two minutes," he declared with a grin, "is what I'll grant you."

Lammat nudged my shoulder gently. "Two minutes, huh? Barely a head-start."

Behind us, the colossal metal gates groaned open, gradually revealing the forest beyond. They moved ponderously, scraping against underbrush and displacing the foliage. "The first team may proceed."

CHAPTER SIX
Strategy and Survival

Tyran led the way, hands nonchalantly buried in his pockets, and we trailed in his wake. As we crossed the threshold, the examiner's voice faded, swallowed by the forest's dense canopy. The woods were eerily silent, save for the soft crunch of twigs and grass beneath our feet. The air was still, yet the scent of dry grass and bark pervaded effortlessly. Occasional rustling betrayed the presence of unseen animals, prompting me to crouch repeatedly for a better look, though success eluded me each time.

Breaking the oppressive silence that enveloped our group, I quickened my pace to align with Naya, who was striding briskly, seemingly lost in thought. Her indecision about whether to accompany Tyran was apparent, but she greeted me with a warm smile as she noticed my approach.

"Is this your first attempt at the exam?" I inquired, curious.

"Yes," Naya responded, her voice tinged with trepidation and excitement. "Today's my sixteenth birthday, and my father wasted no time in enrolling me for this exam. Honestly, I'm still warming up to the idea." Her laughter, tinged with nerves, momentarily filled the space between us. "I have two brothers who've previously taken it. They also said they did a forest, but didn't mention any orbs."

Glancing back, I saw Lammat, his gaze darting through

the forest, vigilant for any sign of an orb. Turning back to Naya, I shared, "Each year the exam is altered slightly, so there's no surefire way to prepare. That's what my Overseer mentioned, at least."

Naya's expression shifted abruptly. "Overseer? Why do you have an Overseer? Were you in prison?"

Her question caught me off guard, revealing my ignorance about the term 'Overseer'. Naya's understanding seemed far more concrete. "Ah, sorry... 'Overseer' is just a nickname for a friend," I lied. "I've grown so accustomed to it, it tends to slip out." Her gaze still bore a hint of skepticism, so I continued, "Why would an Overseer permit someone to participate in an exam?" I responded with laughter.

Lammat, his vigilance momentarily abating, drifted closer to our huddle. "What are we talking about?" he inquired, bluntly.

"Liam has an Overseer," Tyran interjected, his voice steady, not bothering to glance back.

Lammat's reaction was immediate; a jolt of surprise flashed across his face, his eyes darting in rapid succession among us. For a fleeting moment, he looked as if he might bolt, but he quickly regained his composure, fixing me with a blank stare.

"Don't worry, Lammat," I hastened to clarify, throwing a sharp look at Tyran. "He misheard and misunderstood my words." Tyran halted his stride and pivoted to face us, seemingly unconcerned by my glare.

Brushing aside my comment, Tyran took command of the conversation. "We have roughly a minute before the others enter. Our objective is to reach the exit swiftly and set up an ambush about a hundred paces out."

"And then?" Naya interjected.

"We ambush another team and seize their orbs. It's the most straightforward strategy for us," Tyran explained, his voice carrying an implicit assumption of authority.

I bristled at Tyran's natural inclination, about to voice my objections, but Lammat preempted me. "Hold on," he challenged, "who decided you're in charge?"

Tyran exhaled a weary sigh, his gaze locking onto Lammat's. "You heard the examiner. Every team will be targeting us. Without an orb, we're still a threat in their eyes. They'll want to eliminate us to prevent us from acquiring one."

Naya, her expression tinged with confusion, posed a question. "How is waiting at the exit the fastest way for us to get other orbs?"

"There are only thirty orbs scattered throughout this forest," he began, turning and resuming his march. "This scarcity is by design, compelling teams to confront each other for the orbs."

"But the Goud and Eulis groups will mainly oppose one another, right?" I said.

Tyran glanced back, at me. "You may see one or two teams join forces, but that won't last. If a team of eight only managed to find five orbs, do you honestly believe they'll separate amicably?" He didn't wait for an answer. "The separate entrances are a tactic to prevent immediate conflicts, while the forest serves as an unpredictable battlefield with threats potentially emerging from any direction."

As Tyran spoke, the pieces started to fit together in my mind. Despite my reluctance to embrace such tactics, I had to admit, that Tyran's analytical prowess was impressive. He had been piecing this together from the very outset, his mind working like a seasoned strategist from the moment he'd stepped through the gates.

Lammat, still grappling with the plan, posed another question. "But why position ourselves a hundred paces from the exit rather than right at it?"

Tyran exhaled a long sigh, his stride unbroken. "We'll be waiting there because that's where the other groups will inevitably converge. Some will perceive three hours as insufficient and will opt for a direct route to the single exit to ensure timely completion. This means they'll pass right by our ambush point."

"Oh, gods… I forgot about the three-hour time limit." I heard Naya mutter under her breath.

As he cast another glance over his shoulder, a smile crept onto Tyran's face, revealing a hint of confidence in his strategy. "And one last thing," he added, his tone shifting slightly, "if any of you happen to spot an orb, you must ignore it, understood?" The directive was clear, yet it underscored the complexity and challenge of the task ahead.

"Can you believe this? We're in a race against time to collect orbs, and yet, if we come across one, we're supposed to just walk past it?" I questioned Lammat, my tone laced with disbelief.

Tyran, overhearing our exchange, pivoted towards us, gesturing emphatically. "This is exactly what the other groups will be thinking," he countered. "The journey from the entrance to the exit in this terrain is roughly twenty minutes. The three-hour limit is merely a psychological tactic to incite panic." His arm fell to his side as he scanned our faces. "Can any of you disarm traps?" he called out. The silence that followed was his answer. "Neither can I."

Lammat, undeterred, pressed further. "How do you know the time it takes to cross the forest? Have you taken this exam before?"

A smirk played on Tyran's lips. "Did you not see the building from the outside? It's a perfect cylinder, less than a thousand paces in diameter. It won't take nearly three hours to cross it…"

His explanation was abruptly interrupted by a loud 'BANG'. We all whirled around to see a red flare ascending toward the domed ceiling. It seemed someone was already facing trouble, alarmingly near our entrance point. Yet, Tyran, undisturbed by the sound, continued walking as if nothing had happened.

We followed him, the sound of dry leaves crunching underfoot. I strained my ears for any sign of other teams, but the forest remained eerily silent, save for the rustling leaves. Looking up, I saw the blue sky, partially obscured by tree branches, the sun struggling to illuminate the forest floor through the dense canopy.

Turning to Naya, I offered a wry smile. "Not the friendliest, is he?" I commented, nodding subtly towards Tyran.

Naya's response was surprisingly defensive. "He's incredible! Haven't you been paying attention? We're lucky to have him on our team." With that, she hastened her steps to catch up with Tyran, leaving me to ponder the complexities of our group dynamics.

A while later, Lammat and I found ourselves trailing behind the others, engulfed in a contemplative silence. I couldn't help but feel a sense of dissonance with what I had expected these exams to entail.

The forest enveloped us in its otherworldly embrace, a symphony of nature's beauty and mystery. Each step took us deeper into a tapestry woven from the vibrant greens and earthy browns of the dense foliage. The air was rich with the scent of damp earth and decaying leaves, a raw perfume indeed. The soft murmur of a distant stream played a soothing background melody, occasionally punctuated by the call of an unseen bird. Shafts of sunlight pierced the canopy in scattered beams, casting dancing shadows that played upon the forest floor, transforming ordinary rocks and fallen branches into ethereal sculptures. Here, deeper in the forest, every sense was awakened, drawing us into a world that was at once alien and intimately familiar.

I froze, my eyes darting back a step. Backtracking slightly, I regained my line of sight through the trees. Urgently, I tugged at Lammat's arm, drawing him back.

"What?" he questioned.

I raised a pointed finger. There, near a decaying tree stump, large, oddly angled fungi clustered, among which nestled, "An orb."

Lammat's eyes lit up with excitement. We glanced towards Tyran, then back at the orb. "I'm going to get it," he declared.

As he moved forward, I grasped his arm again, my caution resurfacing. "Wait, what about traps?"

"Maybe there aren't any," he reasoned, slipping off his jacket and handing it to me. "It's noisy, and any traps could be sound-activated. Can't be too careful." With that, he advanced slowly towards the orb.

"But Tyran explicitly said not to touch any orbs," I protested.

Lammat halted, turning to face me. "So, you're calling him leader now?" His question hung in the air, heavy with implication.

I hesitated, weighing the decision. Looking back, I saw Tyran and Naya vanishing into the dimness of the forest. I turned back to Lammat, my resolve firming. "Do it," I urged.

Lammat's grin was a mixture of excitement and relief as he cautiously approached the orb. The faint sounds of twigs snapping and dry grass being compressed underfoot heightened my awareness of the potential danger. In response, I opted for what felt like the safest course of action – albeit not necessarily the most helpful – by concealing myself behind a nearby tree. Peering out, I watched Lammat's every careful step.

As Lammat neared the orb, his pace slowed to a crawl. With just a single pace separating him from the orb, and no sign of any trap being triggered, he knelt gingerly. His hand, trembling slightly, extended towards the orb. The moment his finger made contact, he instinctively recoiled, bracing for an outcome that never came. The orb merely wobbled slightly before settling back into place.

Realizing I had been holding my breath, I exhaled

slowly, watching as Lammat cautiously uncurled from his protective huddle. He hesitated for a moment longer, surveying his surroundings, before finally grasping the orb. Standing up triumphantly, he held it aloft, a look of vindication on his face.

"I thought so," he said, turning towards me. "The examiner hinted that not all orbs would be booby-trapped."

Emerging from my hiding spot, I watched as he confidently strode back towards me, orb in hand, dispelling the fear and uncertainty that had gripped us moments before.

At that moment, the air was pierced by a sound, a sharp 'whipping' that erupted from behind him. He became a statue, every muscle tensed in sudden stillness. The branch of the tree, animated with a sinister life of its own, swung in a wide arc, hurling what seemed to be slender, wooden needles straight at him. My voice tore through the silence, a desperate warning, but he remained an unmoving silhouette against the danger. Compelled by urgency, my feet pounded the earth as I surged forward, arms reaching out as if I could somehow bridge the distance with sheer will.

Lammat stood there, a captive of shock, while the needles danced through the air toward him with deceptive grace, almost mockingly in their arc. I pushed my body to its limits, every muscle straining, but the space between us yawned like a chasm. I was too far, hopelessly so, and the needles were a whisper away from his vulnerable neck. My hand stretched out, fingers splayed in a futile attempt to alter the inevitable…

In an instant, a blur, swift and sudden, flashed before my eyes. My feet halted their desperate race, and I watched, breath caught in my throat, as Tyran intervened. With a swift motion, he thrust his arm in the path of the deadly needles. His teeth clenched in a grimace, eyes squeezed shut against the pain, the needles embedded themselves into his flesh. His legs wavered, a momentary buckle under the strain, and his arm dropped heavily to his side.

"Woah!" Lammat's voice, a mixture of shock and awe,

broke the tense silence. He leaped back to life, his eyes wide. "How did you do that?" he sputtered, his words tumbling out in a rush of disbelief and admiration.

I turned to face Lammat, my gaze lingering on Tyran, still grappling with the shock of his swift intervention. "It was the tree," I replied, my voice threading through the confusion with a deliberate slowness. My mind was racing, not just with the immediate danger, but with a grudging respect for Tyran. Despite my aversion to him, he had managed to leave an impression, twice now. First, with his tactical foresight, planning our moves even before the examination had fully unfolded. And now, his speed — it was almost surreal, reminiscent of the Goud I had glimpsed from the balcony.

As I watched, Tyran, with a grimace, gripped his wrist and raised the injured arm, bringing it closer to his face with a wince. He scrutinized the needles briefly before his eyes found mine. "You, Liam. Pull these needles out," he directed with a surprising calm.

His request caught me off guard. "What? Me?" I blurted, disbelief coloring my tone.

Tyran met my gaze, his voice tinged with a casual air. "What, am I supposed to do it myself?" His arm dropped, hanging limp and defeated. "I think they're laced with some sort of toxin. I should regain feeling soon, but it would be safer and easier for…"

His words were cut short by a harrowing scream, slicing through the air and sending an icy shiver down my spine. Tyran's eyes darted toward the source of the sound, then back to me, a genuine concern etching his features. "Naya," we uttered simultaneously, and in the next instant, I was sprinting, propelled by a surge of adrenaline, with Tyran at my side. His injured arm flailed uselessly as he ran. He turned to me, worry written all over his face, but I didn't meet his gaze. All I could focus on was Naya. She was in trouble, and we had to reach her. Fast.

CHAPTER SEVEN
Kai

"Oh, hello there. Tell me, does this belong to you?" Kai, garbed in his ensemble crafted entirely of intertwining vines, stood over Naya's still figure. A smile, mocking and sly, played on his lips as he narrowed his eyes with a hint of mischief.

"What have you done to her?" The words escaped my lips in a growl, laced with threat and concern. Beside me, Tyran's breaths were heavy and labored, his chest heaving from exertion. For a fleeting moment, my eyes darted to a rustling in the trees, but I quickly refocused on Kai, knowing the importance of not losing sight of him.

"Me? Oh, worry not, she's simply unconscious," he retorted, the smirk on his face growing. "It was her misjudgment, really. She saw me alone and thought it an opportune moment to strike. I suspect it was more an effort to impress…" His gaze subtly shifted, resting on Tyran with an insinuating linger, "…someone."

"You're lying," I countered, my voice seething with heat. "Naya wouldn't attack someone without a valid reason!" Yet, as I spoke, a thread of doubt wove through my words. Although I was fond of Naya, the truth was that I didn't know her all that well.

Kai's smile widened, brimming with a knowing arrogance. "Oh, she had her reasons." He casually brandished an orb, tossing it from hand to hand with a nonchalant flair. "I was en route to check on a little 'surprise' I've left for someone. She must have spotted me with this." His gaze drifted downwards to Naya, his expression morphing into an exaggerated, feigned sorrow. "Poor girl. It does make one wonder why she was left all alone." His eyes then flicked back to Tyran, a pointed glance at his dangling arm, mirrored by tapping his own. "Ah, now I understand. Someone's already stumbled upon my surprise, and they've even taken the trouble to bring it back to me."

With a fluid motion, Kai swept his hand through the air. In response, needles ripped through Tyran's arm before embedding themselves into the floor beside Naya. Tyran's outcry of agony sliced through the tense air as he crumpled to one knee, beads of sweat adorning his forehead like a crown of distress. He clenched his teeth, a silent testament to his battle against the overwhelming pain.

I stared, disbelief etching my features as I observed the needles, now quivering slightly from their abrupt halt. Kai had manipulated them with a startling degree of control, a revelation that sent my mind reeling back to the moment I first witnessed him. He had entered the examination to become a Eulis, and his mastery of such advanced techniques left no doubt as to his qualifications.

Gritting through the pain, Tyran forced himself upright, casting a dark, piercing gaze at Kai. "So, what do you intend on doing now then?" he asked, his voice trembling with pain and underlying dread, echoing the thoughts swirling in my mind. He wiped the sweat from his brow with his sleeve, swaying slightly as he fought to maintain his balance amidst labored breaths.

Kai, wearing a grin that danced with mischief, regarded Tyran. "Hey, are you okay?" His eyes briefly flickered to the needles near his feet before he snapped his fingers with a casual air. "Oh, of course, you might be feeling some of the side effects from the poison."

The word 'poison' struck me like a physical blow,

widening my eyes in shock. "Poison!? You poisoned him? But… why?" My voice rose in volume, a tumult of disbelief and accusation, drawing Kai's attention. He turned towards me, feigning surprise with a theatrical jump as if my presence had just registered in his mind.

"I didn't intentionally poison him… in particular. He, unfortunately, was simply in the wrong place at the wrong time. And as for the 'why', I decided to look at the examiner's rules in a different way. You see, my logic suggests that if there are fewer people to pass this stage of the exam, then there's more chance I will pass the others." As these words slithered from Kai's lips, a chilling, almost psychotic smile unfurled across his face. His eyes, alight with a wild intensity, bore into us. "The examiner did say that a team can't pass if anyone is missing, so…" His gaze drifted downwards, ominously settling on Naya.

In a sudden blur of motion, Tyran launched himself towards Kai. His injured arm trailed behind him like a forgotten shadow, while his other arm, driven by fury and desperation, arced towards Kai's face. With an unsettling calmness, Kai simply folded his arms, almost as if he were welcoming the assault.

But then, as if nature itself conspired against us, a colossal root erupted from the earth, a living barricade that shattered under the force of Tyran's strike. In the aftermath, the root receded as swiftly as it had appeared, leaving an open path for Tyran's renewed attack. Yet, Kai was a step ahead. His fist, a lightning bolt of force, connected with Tyran's jaw with such staggering impact that it seemed as if invisible hands had swept Tyran's feet from beneath him. A cry of pain escaped as he crumpled to the ground, landing awkwardly on his already injured arm.

Amidst this chaos, I stood frozen, a silent spectator to the maelstrom of violence unfolding before me. The instinct to flee warred with a deeper, inexplicable compulsion to stay. They were my team, and despite feeling like a burden, something bound me to this place, to them.

Kai's laughter, a sound both jarring and ominous, boomed as he crouched predatorily over the fallen Tyran. "By now, the poison should have worked its way through most of your organs, slowly sapping your strength. I'm amazed you were able to move that fast... but I imagine that strength's all used up now," he taunted, his voice a chilling mix of mockery and malice. Tyran, in a display of defiance, reached upwards towards Kai with a trembling hand.

Observing this feeble attempt with a mixture of amusement and contempt, Kai chuckled darkly. "Nevertheless, we'd better be safe than sorry, eh?" In an instant, dozens of sinewy roots erupted from the ground, ensnaring Tyran in a relentless grasp. They coiled around his hands, anchoring them firmly to the earth, while others entwined his waist and chest in an unyielding embrace. Tyran, now a prisoner to the roots, had no means of escape.

"Oh dear," Kai murmured with a feigned concern, his voice dripping with insincerity as he leaned closer to Tyran. "I hear your father was meant to be some important hero. What would he think, seeing you like this, hey? You're bleeding!" With a callous gesture, he touched Tyran's nose, then lifted his hand to show the blood smeared on his fingertips. Rubbing them together, he sighed theatrically, as if mourning a tragic scene in a play. "It appears that only one more thing remains."

My heart lurched in my chest as Kai rose to his full height and turned towards me, his intentions as clear as they were terrifying. He was going to fight me, and the stark realization dawned that there was nothing I could do to stop him.

I found myself retreating instinctively, each step a silent echo of my growing apprehension. Yet, Kai's voice halted my retreat. "Where are you going? Don't worry, I'm not going to waste energy trying to fight you. I'm more interested in that orb you and Tyran here found back there." His eyes narrowed, like the focused gaze of a predator. "I am correct to assume one of you brought it with you?"

Amidst this grave situation, Tyran's laughter, tinged with pain, cut through the tension. He coughed, turning towards me, his smile a grim display, his teeth stained red with blood. "I don't have it," he said. "Do you, Liam?" I slowly shook my head. Tyran's laughter echoed once more, a sound both defiant and despairing.

Kai's gaze flickered down to Tyran, and without warning, he delivered a brutal kick to his ribs. The sharp sound of impact was followed by Tyran's gasp and cough, a stark reminder of his vulnerability. Kai, momentarily lost in his cruel satisfaction, ran his fingers through his hair, as if rearranging his composure, before his icy stare settled back on me. "Well, seeing as neither of you two have it, that can only mean that your fourth member does." He glanced in the direction from which we had come, a calculating look in his eyes. "Let's bring him out."

The air was suddenly filled with a rumbling, scraping noise, drawing my attention. I spun around to witness a startling scene. Lammat was being propelled towards us, ensnared at the waist by a long, thick root that snaked through the ground. My eyes involuntarily shut, a gesture of despair, as I saw the orb, radiating a bright glow, firmly grasped in Lammat's hands. "Thank you," Kai said, his smile laced with triumph. A smaller root elegantly rose from the ground, coiling around the orb with a precision that seemed almost sentient. It delicately plucked the orb from Lammat's powerless grip, cradling it in a slow, deliberate motion towards Kai's lazily outstretched hand.

Lammat writhed in a desperate struggle against the roots that ensnared him, his cries for release piercing the tense air. "Let me down!" he yelled, his voice a testament to his futile resistance.

Kai, with an air of annoyance, sighed heavily. His gaze shifted from Lammat to Tyran, then back again, as if weighing his options. "Hold on a moment, will you?" he said dismissively. With a nonchalant gesture, another root surged from the earth, this time ensnaring Lammat's neck and effectively muzzling his protests. "Ah, silence, much better." His words were laced with a cold satisfaction. With three of my teammates now incapacitated, I stood alone, acutely aware of my vulnerability. Kai's disregard for me was evident; he knew of my limitations and seemed content to leave me as a spectator to his malevolence.

Kai sauntered back to Tyran, brandishing the two glowing orbs with a triumphant flair. The orbs' luminescence cast eerie shadows across Tyran's defeated face. "That's it now. My team already have two and now so do I. I think I'll hide this one up a tree or something. I'll make sure it's never found. That means that another team will be unable to pass." Tyran, weakened and bound, could only muster a feeble attempt at resistance, his efforts swallowed by his overwhelming exhaustion.

Looking down at Tyran with feigned sorrow, Kai's voice dripped with mockery. "Aww, don't worry, …you've been a huge help to me, but consider this a learning experience. You can't win every battle!"

In response, Tyran coughed and offered a weak, yet defiant smile. "I never intended to win," he whispered, his voice barely audible.

Then, unexpectedly, another voice resounded behind Kai. "No… but I do." In an instant, a second Tyran materialized, delivering a staggering blow directly to Kai's jaw. The force sent Kai spiraling through the air, his body contorting grotesquely as he crashed onto the forest floor. I stared in disbelief at the Tyran still bound on the ground, who met my gaze, smiled, and then dissipated into a cloud of black smoke, whisked away by the wind.

The roots that held Lammat slackened, releasing him. He collapsed, gasping for air, his hand pressed against his chest in a bid to steady himself. The real Tyran approached me, placing a reassuring hand on my shoulder. "Are you okay?" he asked with a calmness that belied the recent chaos. "You look drained." I turned my gaze back to where Kai lay motionless, a victim of his hubris.

'How did Tyran manage that? A clone of himself! Ingeniously devised to intercept the needles aimed at Lammat.' My gaze returned to Tyran, now tinged with a newfound respect and awe.

Tyran, with a purposeful stride, made his way to where Naya lay motionless. He crouched beside her in a gentle yet efficient manner, scooping up the two orbs and securing them in his bag. "We'd better move. He'll wake any minute, and he isn't going to be happy when he does. Liam, pick up Naya. Lammat, just leave her alone." Lammat, who had been tenderly tapping Naya's face and checking her pulse, quickly obeyed Tyran's command and stood back. I approached Naya, carefully lifting her. To my relief, she was surprisingly light, a small mercy considering my reluctance to bear any additional burdens after the day's events.

We began our journey anew, with Tyran leading our small, beleaguered group. My mind relentlessly replayed the battle, each detail vivid and astonishing. The first act of Tyran after the tumult was to check on my well-being – an unexpected gesture of concern that left me quietly perplexed. The extraordinary abilities we had witnessed – Kai's command over the roots with mere gestures, and Tyran's uncanny ability to create a decoy for strategic advantage – were still fresh in my thoughts. It dawned on me that Tyran had anticipated the conflict, crafting his illusion to protect Lammat while safeguarding Naya. This revelation cast Tyran in a completely different light. Whether I was ready to admit it or not, I found myself reevaluating him, inching towards the realization that perhaps, he was a genuinely decent person after all.

CHAPTER EIGHT
The Orb Ambush

Not ten minutes had elapsed when an enraged roar shattered the forest's tranquility, signaling Kai's revival. As we moved, the trees around us seemed to respond to his fury, leaning ominously towards the source of the roar, their trunks groaning and creaking in a symphony of natural distress. Kai's power was undeniable and fearsome. Tyran's foresight in hastening our departure was justified.

As we quickened our pace, delving deeper into the forest's embrace, a question escaped my lips, weighted with urgency. "Where are we going now?" I asked, struggling to keep up with Tyran, all the while feeling Naya's head bob against my shoulder with each hurried step.

Tyran cast a glance back at me, his face etched with seriousness. "I was hoping we could avoid doing this, but Kai slowed us down too much. We're going to have to wait by the exit itself."

Lammat, trailing a few steps behind, caught up to us and questioned Tyran with evident confusion. "Why are we going there? We haven't finished yet."

"I know we haven't," Tyran responded, his voice tinged with a hint of resignation, "but too much time has already passed, meaning that there's a chance that a lot of others will have finished, and where will they be heading?"

His words fell into place in my mind, forming a strategy I

hadn't considered before. "We're going to take an orb from another team just before the exit…" I trailed off, a realization dawning on me. "Then why were we originally going to wait a hundred meters from the exit?"

"Well, as much as I'd like to take credit for the idea," Tyran began, his voice tinged with a hint of laughter, "…I don't think I'm going to be the only person thinking to wait by the exit." He cast a meaningful glance back at me. "There was no guarantee we'd be the ones to make it there first."

His words slowly began to weave together a clearer picture in my mind. The danger of our situation gradually dawned on me, an uncomfortable realization settling in. If we had chosen to wait at the exit, we might have walked into a trap laid by others with intentions similar to ours. It was conceivable that, like Kai, they were planning to gatekeep the exit – a strategic move to reduce the number of successful teams, thereby easing their path through subsequent stages of the exam. This predatory strategy carried a dual advantage: in the face of confrontation, they could either retreat into the safety of the forest or, if they already possessed the requisite number of orbs, make a swift escape through the doorway.

This insight into the cutthroat nature of the exam and the lengths to which others might go to succeed cast a new light on our predicament, adding layers of complexity to our decision-making process.

I was on the verge of sharing my newfound understanding with Lammat when Tyran abruptly raised his arm, signaling us to halt. He cast a cautious glance over his shoulder into the dense forest. "Can you hear that?" he asked, his voice barely above a whisper. The sound was unmistakable - a deep, ominous rumbling that grew steadily in volume, an approaching threat that seemed to vibrate through the very ground beneath our feet. "Both of you hide, quickly!" Tyran urged, swiftly concealing himself behind a nearby tree.

Lammat remained motionless for a moment, as if straining to discern the source of the noise. Urgency overtook me, and I nudged him with Naya's feet, jolting him into action. He quickly darted behind a tree, his earlier obliviousness to the danger now apparent. I, too, found refuge behind a large bush, and as I settled into my hiding spot, an eerie silence enveloped us.

Time seemed to stretch, each second an eternity as we remained hidden, our bodies tense and our breaths shallow in an effort to remain undetected. Minutes ticked by - five, maybe ten - I couldn't be sure. Just as a false sense of security began to creep in, the rumbling resumed, louder and more threatening than before.

Then, breaking through the tense quiet, Kai burst into view. He rode atop a massive root, its surface coated in dirt and debris, a testament to its subterranean journey. With an agility that belied his earlier fury, Kai leaped from one root to another as they erupted from the earth, propelling him forward in his relentless pursuit. He was almost upon us, the distance closing rapidly, when...

With a sudden, jarring 'CRACK', the precarious stillness shattered.

Kai halted abruptly, his previously swift movement ceasing as the massive root beneath him swayed unsteadily. Slowly, with an almost predatory deliberation, it turned him toward our direction. My eyes darted to the source of the noise, and my heart sank. It was Lammat, pulling a broken twig out from beneath his boot, his face a picture of horror. Tyran, emerging slightly from his hiding spot, glared at Lammat with an intensity that spoke volumes of his frustration. Lammat's eyes met mine, cringing with apology. "I'm sorry," he mouthed silently.

I shook my head in resignation, my gaze drifting down to Naya in my arms. At that moment, her fragility struck me anew, and the realization dawned on me that escaping with her in tow would be an almost insurmountable challenge.

Meanwhile, Kai, balancing atop his colossal root, leaned forward slightly, his movements cautious and calculated. He peered around, his eyes scanning the area, hunting for any sign of us. Then, with a dramatic gesture, he stretched out his hand, palm open. In response to his unspoken command, the broken twigs in Lammat's hand tore themselves free, soaring through the air straight toward Kai. He caught them effortlessly with one hand, his smile widening as he examined the twigs. "I know you're there, so you might as well come out," he called out, his voice echoing through the forest, directed towards our hiding place.

Crouching lower, I pulled Naya closer to my chest, closing my eyes as I felt my heartbeat thundering with a crescendo of fear. 'He's going to find us,' the thought echoed relentlessly in my mind, a mantra of impending doom.

"Very well… if you're not going to reveal yourselves…" Kai's voice trailed off, only to be replaced by the ominous sound of trees groaning and creaking once again. Lifting my gaze, I witnessed the massive trunks leaning ominously towards him. My eyes flicked to Tyran, who had slid down to his knees, his back pressed desperately against a tree stump that was bending unnaturally, threatening to snap under the immense pressure. The tension was palpable – the tree's breaking point was imminent. We were on the brink of being exposed.

Suddenly, the bush concealing me rustled noisily. I flinched as three figures walked past, pushing aside branches that rebounded to strike my head. "Okay, okay, we're coming!!!" a girl from the group exclaimed, her voice laced with frustration. Kai let out a sigh and shook his head, a gesture that seemed to release the trees from his invisible grip. They gradually straightened, and I turned to Tyran, exhaling a silent sigh of relief. He was already peering around the tree, surveying the scene.

Gently, I laid Naya back on the ground and looked up to see Kai's team. "Why do you always go over the top? You know simply shouting would have been easier than breaking trees in half!" The group must have been heading in the direction we were taking. It felt like a miracle that they hadn't discovered us in our hiding places.

"Oh," responded Kai, a hint of surprise in his voice. "I thought you were… never mind. You still have the other two orbs, right?"

"Better than that, Kai. We now have three. Junz was able to take one from a group without them noticing." He draped his arm around Junz' shoulder, his hand casually hanging down.

Junz beamed with a self-assured grin. "It was nothing. I think they were about to ambush someone and took their mind off one of their orbs. They were easily persuaded."

Kai's smile broadened with satisfaction. "Lucky us. On my way here I happened to run into a group too." My eyes shifted to Tyran, who returned a confident smile, evidently eager to hear how Kai would spin his recent defeat.

'Maybe his group won't find him so great after he tells them how easily he lost two orbs,' I mused silently, a flicker of amusement igniting within me.

Kai delved into the tangle of vines that surrounded him and, with a flourish, produced an orb. The girl from his group gasped in excitement. "Another?" she exclaimed. "That means that we now have four!"

"Yes," Kai affirmed, his smile unwavering. "I met up with a group only a few minutes ago. They appeared to be tracking another group in front of them." I glanced back at Tyran, whose smile had vanished, replaced by a look of self-reproach. It seemed he hadn't realized we were being followed, and now, the evidence of our oversight gleamed in Kai's hand. He tossed the orb between his hands before throwing it to the girl. "Leana, dispose of this."

Leana's expression shifted to one of surprise. "Why don't we just keep it?"

Kai's gaze was sharp, an unspoken rebuke in his eyes. Leana hesitated, then stepped back. "Can you not remember what the examiner said? We must have three and only three. Hide it somewhere."

"So what do we do now, Kai?" Junz inquired, breaking

the brief tension.

Kai exhaled a sigh, his gaze inadvertently drifting in our direction. "I've had more than enough time in this forest. We have what we need, so let's just get out of here." He turned back to Leana with an impatient tone. "What are you waiting for? Get rid of that thing. I don't want anyone else to find it."

A jolt of panic surged through me as Leana turned, her steps leading directly toward our hiding place. The thought struck me like a thunderbolt – she was going to discover us. Desperation clouded my mind as I scanned our surroundings for an escape, but with her approaching and Kai's group nearby, our options were bleak, especially given Kai's command over the forest itself. I glanced at Tyran, who pressed himself even closer to the tree in a futile attempt to vanish.

As Leana walked past us, my heart pounded in my ears. Miraculously, she seemed oblivious to our presence. I risked a glance at Kai and his group, who had resumed their departure, the sound of their footsteps crunching on the dry grass.

"Any ideas where I should..." Leana began, glancing over her shoulder. Her movement faltered as her eyes landed on Lammat, crouched by his tree. Her gaze flicked rapidly between him, me, Naya, and finally settled on "Tyran!" she whispered, a smile creeping onto her face.

The sound of Kai's footsteps abruptly ceased. "What was that, Leana?" His voice carried a note of suspicion as he halted his group, looking back.

Leana quickly averted her gaze from Tyran and called out, "No, nothing. I've just found the perfect place to hide this thing." As Kai's group moved on, she leaned closer to Tyran, who met her gaze unflinchingly, neither blinking nor looking away.

As I hoisted Naya up once again, my muscles tensed, ready to bolt. I could see Tyran's eyes widening, bracing for a confrontation. I was on the verge of standing...

"Here!" Leana's soft voice cut through the tension. I

nearly lost my grip on Naya, shocked by the unexpected gesture. She was extending the orb – an offering, not a threat. Tyran's gaze shifted from her eyes to the orb, a flicker of surprise in his expression, but he made no move to take it. "How many of these do you have?" she whispered.

"Two," Lammat responded without hesitation.

"Well, then this is perfect!" Leana paused, her eyes still locked onto Tyran's, who remained silent. She exhaled, a hint of frustration in her sigh. "Look, I can either give it to you or bury it somewhere. Either way, you're going to get it, and besides…" Her voice trailed off, her cheeks coloring slightly. "…I'll admit I wouldn't mind seeing more of you." She grinned, flashing white teeth. "It would be a shame for you to fail this early in the exam." Tyran seemed to weigh her words, then finally accepted the orb from her. Leana's blush returned, accompanied by a light giggle. "My name is Leana, by the way."

"I know," Tyran replied, his tone even. Leana's delight at his acknowledgment was evident, but she quickly composed herself and stood up. "You'd better catch up with your group." She nodded, took a few steps backward, still holding Tyran's gaze, then turned and jogged after her team.

In the wake of her departure, a profound silence enveloped us, broken only by Tyran's laughter as he rose to his feet, leaning back against the tree. He opened his bag, revealing all the orbs.

Lammat joined the laughter, "That's insane! You realize we managed to get all three orbs from the same group?"

I let out a short laugh, but it soon faded as a sobering thought crossed my mind. "Does it concern you how easily that team seemed to gather six orbs? Do we stand a chance against them in future exams?"

Tyran's expression shifted to one of grave seriousness as he carefully stowed the orbs away. "That Kai seems to be the only one with any real power. I've heard of people being able to control elements and such, but have never seen it being done. I hear it's a genetic ability… and not something you'd usually find in Lylackia." His words lingered in the air, hinting at a world of possibilities far beyond the ordinary. The concept of people controlling elements seemed like a fantasy to me, but after witnessing today's events, my skepticism was wavering.

"Oh, that reminds me," Tyran said abruptly.

In a swift movement, he had Lammat pinned by his collar against a tree. Lammat's protest was immediate. "Ow! What are you doing? Get off me!"

"Do you realize how close you came to giving away our location?" Tyran's voice was sharp, his grip tightening as Lammat struggled for air. "We were hiding perfectly fine for ten minutes, but the moment Kai appeared, that's when your ability to stay still falters?"

I intervened, grasping Tyran's arm. For a moment, we locked eyes in a silent standoff, each unyielding in our gaze.

Eventually, Tyran exhaled deeply and released Lammat, who collapsed to the ground, gasping for breath. "I promise you," Lammat pleaded, "it was an accident. I was just trying to push myself closer to the tree. I didn't even see it there!"

"You ALWAYS check your surroundings when taking cover! Always!" Tyran's admonishment was fierce, his voice resonating with a growl.

"I'm sorry! Like I said, it was an accident! Look, things worked out, didn't they?"

"We got lucky!" Tyran retorted, punctuating each word, his fury was evident, but beneath it, I sensed an undercurrent of sadness.

Deciding to defuse the tension, I intervened. "Come on, let's get to the exit." I bent down to pick up Naya, her unconscious form a reminder of the ordeal we had faced and the challenges yet to come.

We cautiously trailed Kai's team, their footprints guiding us through the dense forest towards the hoped-for exit on the far end, opposite the main entrance. My heart leaped as I caught sight of it through a labyrinth of trees and vines. "Finally!" I exclaimed. The exit was unassuming, just a simple wooden, white door set within a wall of intertwining vines and plants – a stark contrast to the grandeur of the entrance. Evidentially, Kai's team had already passed through.

Relief washed over me, and I quickened my pace, but Tyran's hand on my shoulder halted me. We crouched down together, Lammat following suit, as Tyran leaned in to speak.

"Remember what I said about the exit?" We nodded in unison, our eyes fixed on his. "There is bound to be at least one ambush planned, so we have to keep a lookout at all times."

Rising slowly, we resumed our cautious advance toward the exit, maintaining proximity and vigilance. Our ears pricked at every distant sound – a rustle, a snap – but each time, it was just an animal or the forest's natural symphony. Paranoia seemed to heighten with every step closer to the exit, our senses acutely aware of the potential dangers lurking around us.

'BANG'

The sudden, explosive sound sent us sprawling to the ground. I awkwardly maneuvered myself to cover, hindered by Naya's unconscious form. Peering up, I saw a large red flare illuminating the sky, its origin unsettlingly close. "It's very close to us. Someone has just fallen for a trap, now's the time to move whilst they're all focused on that," Tyran whispered urgently. Without hesitation, we scrambled to our feet, propelling ourselves forward in a desperate sprint towards the exit.

As the exit loomed tantalizingly close, just a few dozen meters away, an inexplicable shiver coursed through my body. Reality seemed to warp, time stretching into a surreal slow-motion, with me as the sole exception. My instincts roared to life, commanding my actions with an urgency I couldn't ignore.

Surrendering control, I watched as if detached, while my body reacted with a mind of its own.

Swiftly, I set Naya down and raised my eyes to Tyran and Lammat. They were still sprinting towards the exit, but their movements were agonizingly sluggish. In a flash, I lunged at them, hitting their backs with all the force I could muster, driving them downwards. My palms pressed their heads into the earth as I too hunkered down, locking eyes with Tyran. His wide eyes mirrored my shock and confusion.

Abruptly, a searing pain erupted at the back of my head, forcing my face into the dirt. Dazed, I lifted my gaze just in time to see a massive log, suspended by thick ropes, swinging away. It reached its zenith, hesitated for a moment in mid-air, and then began its menacing return arc towards me. Struggling to my feet, I tried to focus on the looming threat, but shadows crept at the edges of my vision, a darkness threatening to engulf me. I battled against the encroaching blackness, fighting for clarity, but it was a losing struggle.

A wry smile crossed my lips as reality snapped back to its normal pace. The log hurtled towards me, and in that final moment, as the world regained its speed, everything went black.

CHAPTER NINE
Medical Attention

Gently, my eyes fluttered open, revealing a world hazily coming into focus. A sense of urgency gripped me as I abruptly sat up, only to be greeted by Naya's presence. "Hey, calm down… you're okay," she soothed. Her visage, pale as moonlight, hovered above me, her eyes brimming with concern. A dull, persistent throb pulsated at the back of my head, drawing my hand instinctively to the source of discomfort, only to find it swathed in bandages. "The medical team wrapped your head," she explained softly.

"Medical team?" My voice was laced with confusion as I surveyed the surroundings. The room, shrouded in shadows, was faintly illuminated by the silvery glow of moonlight streaming through a window above. I lay in a soft bed, an island amidst a sea of ten other empty ones. To my side, a bed lay bare, its covers now serving as Naya's makeshift shroud against the chill.

Her hand, cool and reassuring, rested upon my forehead. "They said you lost quite a lot of blood. I…" Her gaze, intense and searching, met mine. "I was worried about you." A surge of warmth blossomed within me, manifesting as a grateful smile.

"And you? How have you been feeling?" I inquired, my concern genuine. "You were unconscious for quite some time."

Her lips curled into a smile, a spark of life igniting in her eyes. "I woke a few hours ago. Already had visitors," she chuckled, her fingers intertwining with mine. "Tyran... Tyran mentioned how you've been shouldering the burden of carrying me." She raised her eyebrows, glancing away before returning with an embarrassed smile. "I just wanted to thank you... and to apologize."

I shook my head, dispelling her worries. "There's nothing for you to apologize for."

She averted her gaze, a shadow of regret crossing her features. "The last time we spoke, I stormed off. I just wanted to say I'm sorry." I couldn't help but laugh, her words bringing a lightness to the air, and she looked back, perplexed. "What?"

"I'd completely forgotten about that. Don't worry. I'm just sorry that your birthday had to be like this." Our laughter mingled, a brief respite from the uncertainty that lay beyond the walls. "But what happened to you? What did Kai do?"

Naya's gaze drifted away, a distant look clouding her eyes. "It was my fault, really," she admitted, her voice tinged with regret and self-reproach. The smile on my face dissolved, giving way to a more solemn expression as I listened intently to her words. "Moments after I stormed off, I realized you weren't behind me. I was about to tell Tyran, but he urged me to hide. He disappeared into the forest, but I... I was too slow. That's when Kai appeared, holding an orb, alone and seemingly vulnerable."

Her narrative piqued my curiosity. "So you attacked him?" I asked, unable to hide my surprise and a hint of admiration for her boldness.

She returned her gaze to me, a flicker of frustration in her eyes. "I figured it would be two against one. But when I charged him, Tyran didn't show up and Kai just stood there, smiling at me. A flick of his wrist, and then..." She tilted her head, revealing a faint mark on her neck. "Tyran said I collapsed within seconds. But why didn't he help?" She shrugged with a shake of her head. "He evades the question, saying it's not important anymore." Her sigh echoed her deep-seated bewilderment.

My thoughts drifted back to the forest, and my hand instinctively touched the bandage on my head. "Are Tyran and Lammat alright? They weren't hit by that log, were they?"

Her laughter broke the solemn mood. "No, you were the only one hit. They're fine, thanks to you. Funnily enough, they visited earlier, but I suspect their concern was more for you." A yawn escaped her lips, and she offered me a sleepy, tear-tinted smile.

"Haven't you slept?" I inquired, my gaze following the path of her tear.

She managed another laugh, brushing the moisture from her cheek. "Besides the four-hour unconscious stint?" She shook her head lightly, a wry smile on her lips. "Nope, and yet I feel completely drained."

My laughter mingled with hers, understanding her sentiment all too well. Despite the forced rest from being knocked out, a profound weariness clung to me. A yawn escaped me, prompting me to cover my mouth. "I think we'd both better try to get some real sleep. We've got the second exam soon..." Mid-sentence, a sudden realization jolted me upright, narrowly avoiding a collision with Naya. "We did pass today, right? We had three orbs and made it to the exit... didn't we?"

Her laughter was a reassuring sound as she gently coaxed me back onto the pillow. "I was wondering when you'd remember to ask that. Yes, we passed." My body relaxed as I exhaled deeply, a wave of relief washing over me. My heart still raced from the sudden panic.

Naya yawned again, her voice laced with fatigue. "You're right, sleep is what we need." I offered her a contented smile and let my eyelids close. Sleep began to take hold quickly, a comforting blanket of darkness. As I drifted off, Naya's voice reached me from afar. "Goodnight, Liam... and thank you again." In that half-dream state, I sensed, more than felt, what seemed like the gentle pressure of her lips on my cheek.

* * *

I awoke abruptly, a sharp gasp and a wheeze escaping my lips. Glancing down, I found Naya, cocooned in her covers, nestled half across me with her head resting gently on my chest. Carefully, I leaned to the side, affording myself a better view of her face. In her slumber, she radiated a serene beauty, a tranquil aura enveloping her. Admittedly, a small droplet of drool adorned my covers, but at that moment, such a trivial detail seemed endearingly inconsequential. A peculiar sense of closeness enveloped me as if our souls had been intertwined for a lifetime. I entertained this thought for a fleeting moment, only to dismiss it with the realization that had we shared a past, recognition would have sparked in her eyes.

Gently, I ran my fingers through her hair, lost in the peacefulness of the moment. My gaze then wandered to the window opposite, where the early morning light painted a breathtaking scene. The two snow-capped mountains stood guard in the distance, with the sun just beginning to crest above them, bathing the world in the soft hues of dawn. The sky, a canvas of light blue, promised the start of a new day.

My gaze returned to Naya, her presence beside me stirring a gentle curiosity. Why had she chosen to sleep here, rather than in her own bed? A glance towards her untouched bed confirmed my suspicion – the pillows lay just as they had been the night before, indicating she hadn't slept there at all. It seemed she had stayed by my side since I had fallen asleep.

Continuing to softly run my fingers through her hair, I found a comforting rhythm in the motion. My eyes drifted back to the window, watching the clouds meander lazily across the early morning sky, carried by the gentle breeze. There was a moment of serenity, a calm before the day's inevitable activities.

I didn't feel it was right to disturb her peaceful slumber,

especially considering the ordeal we had both endured. Her hair, soft and soothing under my touch, provided a simple yet intimate activity, anchoring me in the present while my mind wandered. This quiet time, with Naya resting so trustingly against me, offered a rare opportunity for reflection and connection, a moment of stillness in a world that was otherwise in constant motion.

I let my head sink back onto the pillow, eyelids fluttering closed as I surrendered to the tranquil rhythm of the morning. Time seemed to drift by lazily, marked only by the soft rise and fall of Naya's breathing against my chest. This persisted undisturbed for several minutes, until my fingers, previously gliding effortlessly through her hair, suddenly found themselves entwined in a small tangle. With cautious movements, I endeavored to extricate them, only to find that each gentle pull seemed to weave them deeper into the spiderweb that was once her hair.

My brief moment of panic was suddenly punctuated by the sound of Naya's laughter. She lifted her hand, effortlessly gliding her fingers through her hair, skillfully unraveling the knots that had ensnared mine. "I'm sorry," I blurted out, hastily withdrawing my hand. A tinge of embarrassment colored my voice as I struggled to articulate. "I don't know why I..."

Naya lifted her gaze to meet mine, her soft smile illuminated by a glimmer in her blue eyes. "No... It was nice," she murmured, her voice a soothing whisper. Gently, she closed her eyes again and resettled her head against my chest. With a tender gesture, she took my hand and guided it back to her hair. "It was relaxing," she added. I resumed the motion of running my fingers through her locks, now acutely aware of each strand shimmering in the light, but a sense of unease crept over me.

It's difficult to articulate, this sudden shift in dynamics. Before, it was an absent-minded action, like when one mindlessly fiddles with a small twig, a scrap of paper, or any trivial object. It was a simple, thoughtless act of keeping my hands busy. But now, with her awake and acknowledging it, the act took on a new weight, an intimacy that I hadn't anticipated. It felt strangely invasive, and as I voice these thoughts, I'm hit with a wave of self-consciousness. The simplicity of the action has been transformed, leaving me feeling exposed in a way I can't quite explain.

It seemed my internal turmoil did not go unnoticed. Only moments later, Naya gently grasped my hand once more, her gaze lifting to mine. Her expression had transformed; the softness was replaced by a look of profound seriousness, as if a sudden realization or memory had dawned upon her. Delicately, she guided my hand to her cheek, the warmth of her skin against my palm. Gradually, she raised herself, diminishing the space between us to a mere whisper of distance. Her face hovered just an inch from mine.

The moment between us was shattered abruptly as the door to the room swung open. Startled, Naya lost her balance and tumbled off the bed with a startled yelp. In a flurry of motion, she scrambled back to her bed, her movements a blend of haste and embarrassment. Her eyes darted to the door from which Tyran strode, his approach marked by a purposeful frown directed unmistakably at Naya.

I looked over at her. "Are you okay?" I asked.

"Yes, yes," she responded briskly, her hand dismissing the concern with a quick wave. She avoided meeting my gaze, her voice carrying a hint of feigned nonchalance. "I'm still a bit tired, I think." With that, she rolled over, turning her back to me, a clear signal of her desire to retreat from the sudden awkwardness.

Tyran lingered in his stance, his gaze fixed on Naya with a trace of suspicion. After a brief, tense silence, he spoke, his voice firm. "Naya, move to another bed, please…" Naya sat up abruptly, her demeanor shifting to one of indignation. "I want to talk to Liam in private," Tyran continued, turning his expressionless face towards me. I cast a glance at Naya, noting her cheeks flushed a vivid shade of crimson.

In a flurry of movements, Naya stood up, her actions

brisk as she gathered her sheets. Her bed was made in a hurried, almost frantic manner. Clad in her purple shorts and pink t-shirt, her feet bare, she moved with a palpable sense of discomfort. Crossing the room to a bed on the opposite side, she lay down, pointedly ignoring the covers.

My gaze shifted back to Tyran as he hooked a finger around the post of Naya's former bed, dragging it nearer to mine before taking a seat.

Attempting to break the heavy silence, I offered a smile. "I heard you came in to see if I was okay," I said, hoping to lighten the mood.

"You heard wrong." The abruptness in Tyran's response extinguished my smile instantly. He leaned forward, scrutinizing my face and the bandaged head with a piercing intensity that lingered for a few uncomfortable seconds. Then, standing up, he closed the gap between us, his presence imposing. "I want to know something," he said, his tone hinting at the gravity of his inquiry.

Tyran's movements were deliberate, his hands reaching out to deftly find the end of my bandage. With a careful yet firm touch, he began to loosen it, gradually unwrapping the layers from around my head. The bandage, once securely encasing my injury, came free in his skilled hands. He then placed the unraveled bundle into my hands. I stared down at the blood-stained dressings, a jolt of shock coursing through me. The dark, crimson stains spoke volumes of the injury I had sustained — far more severe than I had initially realized. Naya's words echoed in my mind, confirming the extent of blood loss I had endured.

Tyran's fingers gently probed the back of my head, his touch surprisingly light. After a moment, he pulled his hand away, examining his fingertips with a critical eye. "Right, as I thought," he murmured, more to himself than to me.

Puzzled, I tilted my head slightly. "Sorry? What did you think?" I asked, seeking clarity.

His gaze met mine, searching. "Did that hurt when I

touched it?" Tyran inquired, his tone laced with a hint of curiosity.

"No, it didn't. Why? Is there a problem?" The concern in my voice was evident.

Without a word, Tyran turned his hand, revealing his fingers to me. They were clean — devoid of any blood. "I think we need a little chat," he said calmly, retaking his seat on the bed. "Beyond having matted hair, there's nothing wrong at all. Your wound has healed."

A wave of confusion swept over me as I regarded Tyran. "Surely… that's a good thing," I remarked, the perplexity evident in my tone. The idea that we needed to have a serious conversation about my wound healing was baffling. In the back of my mind, I had harbored the expectation that Tyran's visit was to express gratitude for my actions in the forest.

Tyran inhaled deeply, a sense of solemnity settling over him. "Liam, do you know what caused you to lose a lot of blood?" I shook my head in response, my curiosity piqued. "It was a giant log that split your head open. Then do you know what I saw?" Again, I shook my head, a sense of foreboding building within me. "I saw you stand up, with the back of your head pretty much caved in." My expression morphed into one of confusion, the usual indicator of my lack of understanding.

Tyran exhaled a heavy sigh, then said, "Let's go through each stage separately." I nodded, indicating my readiness to listen. "If that log hit me instead of you, I would have died. The trap was set up so the log was low to the ground and hit people in the legs, but you knew that the only possible way for us all to dodge it was to duck; which very smoothly takes me to my next point." He leaned in closer, his gaze piercing. "Tell me, how did you know to duck something that was behind you?"

I was momentarily paralyzed, my mind grappling for a coherent response. My mouth opened and closed repeatedly, a mute testament to my struggle to vocalize an answer.

Observing my dilemma, Tyran's smile broadened, his

eyes narrowing with a keen, analytical gaze. "One more point," he interjected, prompting me to halt my futile attempts at speech and focus on him. "How did you create that copy of me?"

My response was a slow, involuntary shake of my head, the gesture embodying my confusion. "I didn't," I managed to articulate. "You... did. I tried to save Lammat, but you got there first, or your copy did."

Tyran leaned back, his smile returning, tinged with an odd hint of enjoyment. "No, Liam, I was watching Naya being attacked by Kai from behind the trees, waiting for a chance to attack. But then, imagine my surprise when I see you and a copy of me dash in and join the fray."

I shook my head firmly, adamant in my denial. "I didn't do it. If it wasn't you, then maybe it was Lammat."

Tyran, however, was not convinced. He shook his head in frustration, his patience wearing thin. "Oh, give it up, already! What's a 16-year-old, who clearly knows advanced magic, doing taking a public exam? With your skills, you could easily opt for a private exam."

"What's a private exam?" I asked, genuinely perplexed.

Tyran's expression darkened. He reached back, pulling the bed even closer, before sitting back down and leaning forward. "You're not who you pretend to be. Naya mentioned in the forest that you were unaware of who my father is. Unfortunately, that's common knowledge these days."

I felt a slow burn of embarrassment creeping into my cheeks. "That doesn't mean anything!" I protested, a defensive edge in my voice.

"Okay then, let's consider the moment at the exam's entrance when you couldn't recall your family name," Tyran pressed on.

I was taken aback. "I... how did you know about that?"

Tyran's smile held a hint of triumph. "I was standing right behind you in the line, and besides, you practically announced it to everyone there." He paused, nodding as if piecing together a puzzle. "And about your Overseer? You let that information slip to Naya, then quickly changed the subject."

"So?" I shot back, a hint of defiance in my tone.

"Again, I was there, right behind you. The examiner realized you had an Overseer just from your first name and age. He your friend, too?" My heart sank as the memories of the encounter with the Goud at the door resurfaced. Despite my efforts to deflect, Tyran's relentless questions bore down on me, his suspicions growing with each answer I failed to give convincingly. It was becoming increasingly clear; he knew I was hiding something.

All I could muster in response was a faint, "Oh..." Ding's note had been clear — to keep my memory loss a secret. At this moment, I felt a keen sense of having failed him.

Yet, Tyran's smile persisted, an indication that his line of inquiry was far from over. "Now then, having an Overseer usually marks one as a criminal on parole. But if that's true in your case, why has he allowed you to take part in this exam?" I shook my head, the implications of his words eluding me. "Overseers are assigned to criminals who were either exceptionally dangerous..." His gaze bore into me, assessing, "...or powerful."

His words sent a cascade of questions through my mind. Was Tyran piecing together the answers I couldn't find myself? The idea of being imprisoned for excessive power seemed far-fetched; I couldn't consider myself as anything more than a Minor. Yet, both Kai and Tyran were Minors too. Had I, in a moment of desperate need to save Lammat, unconsciously created that duplicate of Tyran? The questions multiplied, but it seemed Tyran was methodically reconstructing the fragmented puzzle of my past.

"How many spells do you know?" Tyran pressed, his tone insistent.

I shook my head with forceful denial. "I'm telling you, I don't know any spells!"

Tyran's skepticism was palpable. "Oh, don't give me that!

Nobody can heal a head wound like that so quick-" His words abruptly halted, a realization dawning in his expression. "Are you suggesting it's passive magic?"

His barrage of questions felt relentless, each one hitting me like a battering ram. How could I maintain the secrecy Ding had instructed without revealing my ignorance to Tyran, who likely perceived these as straightforward inquiries? Would admitting my lack of understanding about passive magic only deepen his suspicions? The tightrope I was walking between concealing my memory loss and not arousing further doubt seemed to narrow with each exchange.

At my noncommittal shrug, a spark of realization flickered in Tyran's eyes. "When's the earliest you can remember?" he probed.

He had me. Feeling the weight of his gaze, I lowered my head, only to raise it slowly, meeting his intense scrutiny. "Two days ago," I mumbled with resignation, my voice barely above a whisper. "I was on a prison ship..." The admission seemed to strike Tyran like a bolt of lightning. In a swift motion, he seized my wrist and yanked up the sleeve of my chainmail, his eyes scanning the crest revealed beneath.

"What are you doing? What's wrong?" I asked, bewildered by his sudden urgency.

Tyran abruptly released my wrist, a storm of emotions playing across his face. He stood up, taking cautious steps backward, as if distancing himself from a revelation too immense to comprehend. Without uttering another word, he turned on his heel and exited the room, the door closing with a resonant thud behind him.

CHAPTER TEN
Whispers and Revelations

Naya, hearing Tyran depart, immediately stood up as he made his abrupt exit. She opened her mouth to say something to him, but he was gone before she could get a single word out. She quickly made her way over to me, her expression etched with concern. "What's happened? Did you two argue?"

I shook my head, still trying to process the swift turn of events. "I don't think so," I admitted, my voice reflecting my confusion at Tyran's sudden and inexplicable departure.

Naya's eyes widened in alarm as she noticed the bandages on my lap. "You've taken your bandage off?!" she gasped. Quickly scooping it up, she began to rewrap it around my head with a bit more urgency than comfort. "What were you thinking? The medical team said it could take weeks to fully heal."

I gently caught her arm to stop her. "Tyran told me that it's already healed," I said calmly.

She let out a laugh, tinged with incredulity. "Don't be ridiculous, they said it's a miracle that…" Her words faltered as I turned my head, exposing the back to her view. There was a moment of stunned silence. "…you've… healed. That's impossible; they said the blow had cracked your skull."

I turned back to face her, offering a reassuring smile. "Well, apparently they were wrong."

Naya, however, remained unconvinced, holding the

bandage aloft as evidence. "Look at this! See how much blood there is? And your pillow!" I glanced behind, noticing the red stains that I had overlooked. "This isn't the aftermath of a wound that heals overnight, Liam. This is from something nearly fatal." She set the bandage back on the bed, her tone laced with concern. "They weren't going to let you take the exam unless you kept it on at all times…" She paused, mulling over something. "Quick, let's put it back on," she urged, reaching for the bandages once more.

I instinctively moved away. "Look, I don't need it on if it's healed, surely."

Naya paused in thought for a second, before offering a sly smile. "Just think of the tactical advantage you'd have if everyone believed you were handicapped!" Her tone was borderline patronizing. I tried to envision such a scenario, but nothing concrete formed in my mind. "Look, if you just…"

The conversation was abruptly interrupted as the door swung open again. Two men entered, wheeling in a trolley laden with fresh bandages and a large bowl of water. "Good morning," the younger man greeted us. His eyes then snapped up, widening in alarm as he caught sight of the scene before him. In a flurry, he rushed toward me, his expression one of concern and reprimand. "Young lady, what do you think you are doing? Do you realize how dangerous it is to take his bandages off?" His stern gaze flicked to me. "You could easily get an infection with it exposed like this." I glanced at Naya, who, under the weight of their scrutiny, nervously slipped off my bed onto her own.

"What is this?" the older man exclaimed, his voice booming in the quiet room. "Why is your bed over here?" Naya muttered an apology and began the laborious task of dragging her bed back to its original position. I couldn't help but laugh, recalling how effortlessly Tyran had moved it. Naya, in contrast, was visibly struggling with the task.

"This is no laughing matter," the young man scolded sternly. "Removing the bandages prematurely is extremely risky. If it weren't for my intervention, you might not have survived. And yet, here you are, rendering all my efforts..." His voice trailed off as his eyes locked onto my head, his mouth agape in disbelief. Hesitantly, he reached out to touch my head, his fingers gingerly exploring the area where the log had impacted.

His colleague approached with a new set of bandages, but upon seeing my head, he too was struck by astonishment, the bandages slipping slightly from his grasp. For a moment, he stared, mirroring his partner's expression of utter disbelief, before his eyes narrowed. "Saved his life, did you?" he said.

"But, Sir, his head really was... I mean, I'm certain it was..."

"You dragged me down here to, what, pretend you had healed this boy's skull?"

"No! It was fractured!"

"You'll have to forgive my student," said the older medic, tossing the bandages back onto the trolley with a sigh. "Sometimes this job breaks a person. Come along, let's leave them to it."

"But I..." His words cut off as he locked eyes with his teacher, and he quickly turned to me. "Yes, well... things are looking good. Things are coming along fine," he stammered, his professional demeanor faltering in the wake of his astonishment. "I guess you don't need any more bandages after all." He then pivoted towards Naya, gesturing somewhat absently towards the trolley they had brought in. "Young lady, are you well?"

"Yes, I am," she answered.

"Well then, if it's not too much trouble, would you mind tending to the..." He faltered once more, eyes inexorably drawn back to my head in disbelief. "...the injury? We have others who require our aid."

"Oh... erm, yes, Sir!" Naya responded, her voice laced with surprise and uncertainty.

Both men offered us a strained smile before hastily

exiting the room, the door closing briskly behind them. Their hushed, urgent whispers to each other were just audible as they departed, leaving an air of bewilderment hanging in the room.

I furrowed my brow, turning to Naya, who was still observing the medical team's hasty retreat. "What was that about?" I queried, my confusion evident.

Naya maneuvered the trolley closer, gently setting the bowl of water on the bed. She reached in, retrieving a small yellow sponge soaked in water. "Just so you know, I have no idea what they expect me to do, so I'm just going to clean off the blood." Sitting beside me, she looked at me with a questioning frown. "So, you know healing magic?" she laughed, her tone a mix of skepticism and curiosity.

I rolled my eyes and let out a resigned sigh. "Naya…"

"Oh, don't give me that," she chided playfully, her smile betraying a hint of amusement. "It's obvious you're keeping secrets." The reality of my situation was becoming increasingly clear—I had managed to keep my secrets for only two days before people started noticing things about me that I wasn't even aware of myself. "Are you going to tell me?" she pressed, her grin widening in anticipation.

Deciding it was better to tell her myself than let her hear it from Tyran, I gave a confirming nod. Naya gently wrung out the sponge above the bowl, then carefully dabbed it at the back of my head. I was still trying to make sense of her sudden care and attention. All I had done was carry her through the forest for a short while. Granted, that might have been significant, but her sudden closeness felt unexpectedly swift.

"I don't know how to say this, so I'm just going to say it, okay?" I began, bracing myself. Naya gave a nod, her grip on my hand tightening in anticipation.

"I've lost my memory." Naya's reaction was immediate; she gasped, her hands flying to her mouth in shock. "Not all of it, though…"

"How much?" she cut in, her eyes wide with concern.

"I can only remember the past two days."

A frown creased Naya's forehead as she lowered her hands. "I... don't understand. So, hitting your head made you forget everything except the last couple of days?"

"What?" I shook my head to clarify. "No, the log didn't cause my memory loss."

"Then how did you lose it?" Her questions came rapidly.

"I... don't remember," I admitted.

"Then maybe it was the log."

I smiled gently, trying to ease her rapid-fire questioning. "Look, Naya," I said, placing my hand reassuringly on her arm. "I can promise you, it wasn't the log. I arrived in D'wan Ma'hal just a couple of days ago on a... ship." I decided to omit the detail about it being a prisoner transport. "Since then, I have all of my memory intact. But everything before that is a blank. I didn't even know my name, age, or what I looked like."

Naya reached out, gently taking my hand in hers, her touch conveying empathy. "What about your family?" she asked softly.

The question struck a chord. "My family? I... hadn't..." My words trailed off, my mouth lingering open as the realization hit me. A lump formed in my throat, and I slowly closed my mouth, overwhelmed by the sudden wave of emotion. It dawned on me then — in the past two days, my thoughts had been solely focused on myself, my predicament, the mystery of my incarceration, and the nature of my supposed crime. Beyond the concept of having a family name, I hadn't spared a single thought for my actual family. The realization was jarring. I had no images of my mother or father, no recollection of their professions, their voices, their faces. Overcome, I lay down and turned away from Naya, my chest constricting with a poignant mix of sorrow and guilt as tears began to well in my eyes.

Naya's movements were gentle as she shifted closer to me on the bed, her proximity offering a sense of solace. "Liam, I'm sorry," she said, her voice imbued with genuine concern. I heard the soft sound of the sponge being dipped and wrung out in the water before she resumed dabbing at my head. I closed my eyes, a lone tear escaping in response to her kindness.

"I know we've only known each other since yesterday, but..." Her chuckle was soft, a light note in the solemn atmosphere. "Let's just say I owe you one for carrying me during the first exam. And for saving Tyran and Lammat." Her voice became a whisper, "Just know you're not alone, okay?"

Turning slowly, I looked over my shoulder to meet her gaze. Naya's eyes, filled with understanding, met mine. "I trust you, Liam. I want you to feel you can trust me, too."

In that quiet moment, Naya and I simply held each other's gaze. Her words, offering trust and seeking it in return, resonated deeply with me.

"What's going on here, then?" The unexpected voice made Naya startle, causing her to tumble off the bed once more. I looked up to see Lammat standing there, a broad grin on his face. "It's good to see you're feeling better, Liam. I knew a smashed skull wouldn't slow you down!"

Naya quickly got to her feet, a frown crossing her features. "What's wrong?" Lammat asked, his smile fading into a look of realization. "Oh, I'm sorry, have I interrupted something?"

Naya shot him a glare before settling back down at the end of the bed. Lammat, undeterred, redirected his cheerful smile towards her and took a seat as well.

"I didn't hear you come in," Naya remarked, her tone edged with irritation.

Lammat gestured towards the door. "It was open," he replied before turning his attention to me. "Tyran's taken off for some reason, leaving me the task of delivering the good news to our wounded hero here." His comment elicited a slight chuckle from me; Lammat's blunt humor had an oddly appealing quality, though Naya seemed less than amused, likely still irked by the interruption.

Clearing his throat, Lammat announced with a booming voice, "The second exam is set to begin in twenty minutes," he quickly returned to his normal tone, "so we should all get ready and meet with the examiner." Naya and I exchanged a quick glance, a shared sense of concern passing between us. "This one's overseen by the Eulis, so brace yourselves for a challenge," he added with a boyish grin.

CHAPTER ELEVEN
Shadows and Flames

Fifteen minutes, and a very long staircase later, I found myself in a vast room, buzzing with the low hum of conversations among the gathered examinees. However, my mind was too gripped by anxiety to even consider engaging in any chatter.

Scanning the room, I counted twenty-eight desks, all arranged to face the Eulis examiner. His dark hair contrasted sharply with his pale complexion. He paced methodically back and forth, arms folded, his demeanor exuding a quiet authority. Small, rectangular glasses perched on his nose, and a modest tuft of hair adorned his chin, an attempt at a beard. Every so often, he would halt his pacing to survey the room with a penetrating gaze, only to resume his restless movement moments later. As I placed my hand on one of the wooden desks, a shiver ran down my spine, intensifying the sense of foreboding that filled the air.

'What kind of exam is this?' I pondered, my thoughts racing. 'Is it a written test? Will I be expected to answer questions?' The sound of the desk quivering under the tremble of my hand drew curious glances from several participants. Embarrassed, I quickly withdrew my hand and shoved both into my pockets, offering a sheepish smile to those who glanced my way until their attention shifted elsewhere.

Once I felt the weight of their gazes lift, I allowed myself a moment to take in the room more thoroughly, taking deep breaths to steady my nerves. The wooden floor beneath me was marred with signs of age — cracks and dents marking its long use. The walls emitted a warm, inviting yellow hue, bathed in the soft sunlight filtering through a large window that framed a view of the bustling city streets outside.

My eyes eventually drifted upwards to the ceiling, where a large Crest of Nations symbol was painted, glowing subtly. It struck me as different from the one on my arm; the green segment was absent, and the black and white parts seemed altered in some way.

The sound of the doors being nudged open startled me, and I quickly turned to see the Minor examiner entering, the Goud following closely behind, their expression stern. A few of the examinees greeted the Minor warmly, though the Goud seemed to go largely unnoticed. The Eulis examiner ceased his pacing immediately, and the three convened in a huddled discussion.

Their voices were low, just whispers floating in the air, drowned out by the soft murmuring of my fellow examinees. I briefly entertained the thought of eavesdropping if only the room were quieter, but then dismissed it, reasoning that their conversation was likely related to the exam details, which would be revealed soon enough.

True to my prediction, the three broke away from their discussion after a short while. The Eulis stepped forward, addressing the room with a booming voice. "I'm glad to see so many happy faces today." I rooted my feet firmly to the ground, fighting the urge to tremble. The Eulis took a seat in a chair ornately decorated in gold and green. "So then," he began, casting a brief glance at the Minor examiner before returning his focus to us, "...are you all looking forward to this exam?"

A collective, somewhat listless "Yes" echoed through the room. I opened my mouth to join in, but a sudden dryness in my throat reduced my attempt to a silent choke.

"Excellent! I'm looking forward to it, too! Now, your first

task is to find a single partner from your current team. You have thirty seconds," announced the Eulis.

As the Eulis examiner's words settled in the air, the room burst into a cacophony of chatter. The phrase "Can I be with you?" reverberated across the room, bouncing from one corner to the other. Amidst this flurry, I heard those very words directed at me. Turning around, I found Lammat standing there, his smile wide and inviting. I was just about to respond affirmatively when I felt a sudden tug on my arm.

"Sorry, Lammat, but I'm with Liam this time," Naya declared, her eyes locking with mine as she offered a warm smile. "We medical patients have to stick together." Her words drew a laugh from me, and I turned back to Lammat, who responded with a subdued smile and a subtle wink.

Lammat's gaze then drifted across the room, eventually landing on Tyran. He was seated near the door, his hands clasped together, seemingly indifferent to the task of finding a partner. I figured Tyran was either leaving his partnership to chance, given the unknown nature of the exam, or perhaps he simply didn't care. Either way, his detachment stood in contrast to the rest of the room's frantic pairing efforts.

The examiner rose to his feet, his voice cutting through the chatter. "Time," he announced, and the room promptly quieted down. A few individuals hastily scurried to their last-second partners, and then a hush fell over the room.

"Right, from now on your teams of four are history, I'm afraid. Those you've just parted from are now your competitors," he declared, a hint of amusement in his tone as he let out a snort of laughter. I glanced back at Tyran, noticing he had stood up and was now leaning casually against the wall. His eyes briefly met mine, an eyebrow raised in a silent query, before shifting his attention back to the examiner.

"I would like you to take a seat, somewhere away from your partner, please," the examiner instructed, signaling the next phase of the examination process. As the examiner's instructions were given, the room once again erupted into activity, with examinees swiftly finding their seats. Already positioned at a desk towards the back, I simply stayed put. I noted Lammat choosing a seat a few desks to my right. My gaze then drifted to my left, where I saw Leana, a member of Kai's former team. She was rhythmically tapping her fingers on the desk, a soft hum accompanying her movements.

Catching me observing her, Leana abruptly ceased her humming and looked in my direction. "Oh, sorry," she said, her smile revealing a row of white teeth. She swept a strand of blond hair from her face and quickly redirected her attention to the front of the room, where the examiner was busily arranging his chair and desk.

I was mildly taken aback by Leana's sudden halting of her rhythmic tapping due to my presence, but she soon resumed the habit. My chuckle drew her curious gaze once again. Realizing why, she joined in with a light laugh. "I'm sorry, I guess it's just a nervous habit," she admitted, then consciously clenched her hands into fists, stopping herself from tapping the table. "I'm Leana, by the way."

I nodded in recognition. "Yeah, I know. We kind of met in the forest," I replied, recalling our brief encounter.

Her expression shifted to one of puzzlement. "I... don't remember seeing you," she said slowly, pausing as if trying to place me in her memory.

I leaned in slightly. "You gave us an orb right before the end," I reminded her.

Leana's eyes widened with sudden realization. She cast a quick, furtive glance towards Kai, then leaned in closer to me. "Shhh... Kai has very good hearing! He doesn't know I helped you," she whispered conspiratorially. Sitting back up, she flashed a smile, relief and mischief in her expression. "So, you're on Tyran's team, huh?" Stretching slightly, she casually observed Tyran, who was sitting a few rows ahead. He appeared relaxed, leaning back in his chair, his gaze fixed on the ceiling.

A girl seated next to Tyran attempted to strike up a conversation with him, but he responded with a pronounced yawn and a deliberate turn of his head.

"I was on his team," I explained, "...but I'm paired with Naya for this exam."

Our conversation was cut short by the Eulis examiner's booming voice. "All right, is everyone ready to begin?" he called out across the room. A smattering of 'yes' responses echoed back, though most examinees simply nodded in acknowledgment; Tyran, true to form, responded with another exaggerated yawn.

"Very well. Let me explain what you're going to be doing," the Eulis continued, drawing the room's attention. He extended his hand, palm facing upward. To the collective amazement of the room, a small, transparent green orb materialized in his hand, hovering and gently bobbing up and down. "Upon request, you will all need to do this," he announced, presenting the magical demonstration as the exam's first challenge.

"Magic⁉!" My exclamation escaped before I could stop it, my voice ringing with surprise and disbelief. Around me, a few chuckles broke out, including from Lammat and Leana. Turning, I caught Naya's gaze a few rows ahead. She had swiveled in her seat and was now looking back at me, her face etched with deep concern. I could easily interpret her expression; it mirrored the growing apprehension I felt. How was I to navigate this part of the exam with my limited knowledge of... well, everything?

I glanced toward Tyran, hoping for some hint of reassurance or guidance. He met my gaze briefly before turning away. It seemed he had been watching me, perhaps sharing Naya's concern, though his demeanor was less overtly worried.

The examiner's gaze shifted towards me, the orb still floating above his palm. "I'm glad you recognize magic when you see it," he remarked with a hint of amusement, "but next time, try not to announce your epiphany to the entire room." His comment drew more laughter from around us, and with a simple closing of his hand, the orb vanished into thin air.

Leana glanced at me, her tone light and oblivious to my growing distress. "Condensed mana, eh? I had no idea they were going to include an actual magical test." She gave a soft whistle. "That's a pretty tricky spell. Honestly, I've never tried it before, but we'll see how it goes. Strange they'd include it in an entrance exam." My glare sharpened, silently envious of her apparent lack of concern. "My father couldn't do magic, but he loved it. He spent hours teaching spells to my brother and me whenever he had the time..." Her voice trailed into the background of my thoughts. While I continued to gaze at her, my mind was elsewhere, ensnared in a whirlpool of anxiety about the daunting task ahead and my profound lack of preparation for it.

The examiner's commanding voice drew my attention back to the front. "I will begin by explaining the rules to you all," he declared, ensuring he had the room's full attention. "Your pairing at the start is crucial, as you will be working together on this task. Both you and your partner must successfully create the orb for either of you to pass. If one of you fails, unfortunately, both will fail. I will select who attempts the spell at random and will grant only one opportunity to succeed."

Hearing we had just a single chance sent a heavy thud of dread through my chest, though I realized that even a hundred attempts wouldn't improve my odds. Naya's choice to partner with me now seemed like a grave miscalculation, and I had a suspicion she was aware of it.

As the examiner continued, I noticed Naya's gradual descent, her head finally resting on her desk in apparent dismay. "Each time a pair fails, both participants will be removed from the exam," the examiner concluded, his words final and uncompromising.

Nervous energy coursed through me, manifesting in a

restless tapping on the desk, mirroring Leana's earlier action. My gaze drifted back to Naya, and a heavy realization settled in. 'If I fail, Naya fails too. I must succeed. There's no other option.'

"The test will now begin," announced the Eulis, snapping me back to the present. A sudden dryness constricted my throat, and my stomach twisted into knots as he clapped his hands, signaling the start. "Oh yes, one more rule. If you speak out of turn, you will be immediately disqualified."

As I resumed breathing, a glance around the room revealed that I wasn't alone in my reaction; faces etched with shock and fear reflected my own emotions.

The Eulis' finger roamed over the crowd, finally settling on a small, brown-haired girl from the Goud group I recognized from the previous exam. "You," he pointed.

Tentatively, the girl asked, "Can... can I speak?" The examiner gave a kind nod, and she continued, her voice tinged with apprehension, "I can't do this... I'm here to become a Goud, not a Eulis."

"I'm sorry, but these are the rules for this year's exam. If you refuse to try, I'll have to fail you right now," the examiner replied, his tone firm.

"But how am I supposed to do it?" her voice wavered slightly.

He chuckled, "Just hold out your hand, feel the mana within you, and push it from your palm while shaping it into a ball. It's quite simple, really."

With a resigned sigh, the girl extended her hand, palm facing upward, mimicking the Eulis' earlier demonstration. She concentrated intently on her hand, but after a few moments... nothing happened.

The Eulis examiner's expression was one of disappointment as he shook his head. "Too bad... I'm going to have to fail you." Suddenly, his hand ignited with a startling orange flame. With a swift flick of his wrist, he hurled a ball of fire across the room. It hit the girl squarely in the chest, and in an instant, her body was engulfed in flames, collapsing onto her desk before disintegrating into ash.

I stifled a gasp, my eyes wide with shock at the horrifying spectacle. Without a moment's hesitation, the Eulis turned to the girl's partner. Another fireball flew from his hand, fast and unerring. The boy attempted to evade, but his reaction was a fraction too late. He vanished in a burst of flame, mid-leap from his desk. A cloud of ashes drifted across the room, some reaching Tyran, who ducked, his face etched with disbelief.

"There we go," the Eulis examiner remarked casually, his voice starkly contrasting the gravity of what had just transpired. He effortlessly snuffed out the flame in his hand. "Two down, twenty-six to go."

A sudden commotion broke out as a boy from Kai's team sprang to his feet, his voice trembling with outrage. "You just killed them! This isn't failing, this is..." His words were abruptly cut off by a horrific scream as he too was engulfed in flames. Desperately, he clawed at the fire consuming him, but it was futile. Within seconds, he too collapsed, his body reduced to ashes.

Before the room could even process this second shock, another scream pierced the air. The Eulis had targeted the boy's team-mate, enforcing the rule he had laid out: 'Each time one of you fails, I will remove both you and your partner.' The examiner's words, once seemingly metaphorical, were being executed with literal and lethal seriousness.

The Eulis began to wave his hand once more, ominously selecting the next candidate. The room was steeped in fear and uncertainty, the reality of the consequences brutally clear.

The urgent need to flee, to save both myself and Naya from this twisted exam, consumed my thoughts. There was no conceivable way I could perform the spell required; four individuals had already perished for their inability. 'This is unjust,' I thought frantically. 'Why would they subject us to this? Are we truly expected to master these spells? So many here are trying to become Gouds, not Eulis'…'

Meanwhile, the Eulis' finger ominously settled on Kai, who glanced around with an uneasy expression. As he slowly rose from his seat, the unexpected happened — a massive root erupted from the floor. It surged upwards, ensnaring Kai, and hoisted him from his desk. In a swift motion, the root wrapped around him and propelled him towards Leana, knocking aside desks in its path. He grabbed her roughly by the collar, dragging her upward with him. Abruptly, another root tore through the floor, ripping open the ceiling above me, and together, Kai and Leana were catapulted toward the newly formed opening in a whirlwind of chaos.

A deafening roar filled the room as the root holding Kai and Leana burst into flames, sending them plummeting to the floor. The Eulis examiner rose from his seat, the sound of wood scraping against wood echoing through the room as he approached them. In each hand, a fireball materialized, and he lifted them high, poised to strike. Suddenly, a smaller root shot up from the floor, entwining around his hands and pinning them to his sides. The Eulis merely laughed at this attempt to restrain him, effortlessly shaking off the roots before callously dropping the fireballs onto Kai and Leana's prone forms.

The heat from the flames was intense, especially from my nearby seat. The acrid smell of burning filled the air, overwhelming my senses. Mere moments ago, I had been conversing with Leana, and now… I lifted my gaze to meet Naya's. Her eyes, brimming with tears, were fixed on me. In the space of these few, terrifying moments, six people had lost their lives.

The Eulis examiner returned to his desk with unsettling calmness. Seated once again, he began a slow, deliberate sweep of his hand over the remaining examinees, ominously selecting the next participant. The entirety of Kai's team had been obliterated in mere moments, a grim reminder of the potential fate awaiting my team. My heart pounded with dread as his finger finally halted, pointing directly at Lammat.

I swallowed hard, my gaze shifting between Naya and Tyran. Naya's reaction was one of sheer terror; her hand clamped over her mouth, her body shaking visibly. The fear in her eyes mirrored my own – neither of us wanted to witness Lammat's demise. Tyran, however, displayed a different demeanor. His eyes were narrow, focused, and his hand rested tensely on his desk, as if prepared to spring into action at the first sign of Lammat's failure.

Lammat's confident gaze met mine across the room; he offered a reassuring smile and a wink. "Don't worry," he said with a hint of bravado, "...I've been able to do this spell since I was a kid."

With an air of confidence, he extended his hand, palm up, and focused intently on it. He swirled his hand in a practiced motion, but to the shock of everyone, nothing materialized. As he looked up, perhaps to voice his confusion, a fireball from the Eulis struck him squarely in the face, instantly igniting into flames.

Time seemed to crawl in those horrific moments. Lammat's arms flailed wildly as he staggered to his feet, overturning his desk in a desperate attempt to extinguish the fire. But it was too late. His body went limp, and I watched, frozen in horror, as he disintegrated into ashes, scattering across the floor.

Snapped back to reality by the imminent danger, I turned my gaze towards the Eulis examiner. He was now facing Tyran, who was still fixated on Lammat, a look of horror etched on his face. A new fireball materialized in the Eulis' hand, and with a swift, merciless motion, he hurled it toward Tyran.

Driven by instinct, I leaped from my seat, shoving my desk aside in a desperate bid to intercept the fireball aimed at Tyran. It was a race against the deadly flame, and I was determined to reach Tyran first, to save him from the fate that had claimed Lammat.

But just as I closed the distance, mere seconds from my goal, Tyran's figure shimmered unnaturally, like a mirage dissolving into thin air, leaving behind nothing but an empty desk. A confused grunt escaped me, a vocal expression of my utter perplexity. Time, which had seemed to slow in those tense moments, abruptly resumed its normal pace. My momentum carried me forward uncontrollably, and I collided with the now-empty desk with a resounding crash, shattering it into pieces before tumbling into the wall.

I spun around, my gaze snapping back to the Eulis examiner. There, I saw Tyran, his fist raised towards the examiner's face, halted by a glowing red sphere that encased the Eulis, protecting him.

"But Tyran, none of this is real," the Eulis calmly stated. His words sent a wave of confusion through me. I turned back to the room, only to find a scene starkly different from what I had just witnessed. The other examinees were all in their seats, unharmed and very much alive. Some craned their necks to get a better look at me, perplexed by my position on the floor, while others sat frozen, their expressions showing variations of surprise.

"Wha...?" I stammered, struggling to grasp the situation, but the Eulis cut me off.

"Not yet, Liam... we still have to see who else reacts," he said, eyes still locked onto Tyran's.

I opened my mouth to question the Eulis further but then thought better of it, suspecting he would only repeat his previous statement. His words lingered in my mind – what exactly did he mean? Slowly, I stood up, still processing the unfolding events, and turned my attention back to the other examinees. The scene before me was bewilderingly normal; Lammat was calmly seated at the back of the room, and Kai appeared unharmed.

As I observed, a root suddenly erupted from the floor, coiling swiftly around Kai's waist. The room tensed, but only for a moment. Seconds later, the root gently unwound itself, withdrawing back into the ground. Kai was left sitting there, his face a blend of confusion and mild embarrassment.

As I tried to make sense of the situation, my eyes found Naya. She was sitting still, her gaze unfocused as if lost in a trance. Then, almost as if sensing my observation, she blinked rapidly, her awareness returning. She looked around the room in confusion before her eyes met mine, and she offered a small, uncertain shrug. Nearby, Lammat casually stretched, giving me a quick wave, seemingly unbothered by the strange events.

The tense silence in the room was punctuated by the soft sounds of a few more individuals gradually snapping out of their daze. After a few minutes of this unsettling stillness, the Eulis examiner sighed, a note of disappointment in his voice. "Very well… it seems this is everyone." With a snap of his fingers, half the room instantly slumped forward, heads gently colliding with their desks. A collective gasp filled the room, followed by the examiner clapping his hands sharply. "Congratulations to all of you still awake… you pass."

CHAPTER TWELVE
A Mirrored Past

I was momentarily stunned, convinced I had misunderstood. "Sorry?" I managed, my voice tinged with disbelief.

The examiner's smile broadened as he surveyed the room. "You have all passed," he reiterated, his gaze sweeping over us. As his words sank in, my mouth dropped open in astonishment. "This exam was never about your ability to cast spells."

Around the room, expressions of disbelief mirrored my own. Tyran, Lammat, Naya, Kai, Leana, and several others sat in stunned silence, grappling with the unexpected announcement. The notion that we had all passed, despite the harrowing illusions we had just experienced, seemed almost unfathomable.

Breaking the silence, Kai finally voiced what many of us were thinking. "I don't understand... You put us through that... for no purpose?"

The examiner leaned against his desk, his gaze fixating on Kai. "Ah, not as sharp as you were before yesterday's exam, Kai," he remarked with a touch of dry humor. He then addressed the rest of us, his expression becoming more serious. "We are seeking students that we can effectively train, and for that, it's crucial to select the right candidates. Our aim isn't to find those who will passively stand by in critical moments. We need individuals willing to risk themselves for others, to act decisively when needed."

His words carried a weight of solemnity as he continued, "Those who are now asleep failed to demonstrate this willingness to act. They either chose not to risk themselves for their peers or couldn't think of a way to evade the perceived danger."

The room's focus shifted as Tyran spoke, his voice carrying realization and accusation. "So you put us all under a hypnosis spell?" His fist remained pressed against the shield. "You just wanted to see if any of us would react to the sight of others being seemingly killed... to test whether we were willing to sacrifice ourselves for another." His words hung in the air, capturing the essence of the examiner's ploy – a test of character and bravery rather than magical ability.

As Tyran turned to face me, the Eulis responded with a knowing smile. "You are only partly correct, Master Tyran. However, you are quite astute in pointing out the individual who has demonstrated remarkable willpower." His gaze then shifted back to Tyran. "It seems Liam was willing to jeopardize his own safety, even to the point of self-sacrifice, for you—a former teammate," he stated, the emphasis on 'former' hanging heavily in the air.

In response, Tyran lowered his hand, and with this gesture, the red shield that had separated him from the Eulis dissipated into nothingness. "The next exam will commence soon. After that, there will be a social gathering for all participants of this year's exam," the Eulis announced, settling back into his chair. "No further details will be provided at this time. You are all free to go about your business until then."

Leana's voice, laced with concern, cut through the room's newfound silence. "What about our friends?" she asked, her gaze sweeping across the room to her former teammates, who were still slumped over their desks, unresponsive.

The Eulis examiner replied with an air of nonchalance, "People will be here to wake them shortly," assuring her, "Please don't worry about them." He then gestured casually towards the exit, signaling that the session was over. Turning his attention away from the examinees, he engaged in a conversation with the Goud and Minor examiners, effectively dismissing us.

"That's it?" I blurted out, my voice tinged with irritation. I pushed aside the remnants of Tyran's desk, which lay scattered around me as I stood up. My outburst seemed to surprise the Eulis examiner, who turned to me with an expression of mild astonishment. "I watched seven people 'die', just to see how I'd react?" My frustration was palpable.

The Eulis' gaze settled back on me, his expression shifting to one of concern. He shook his head slowly. "No, Liam, the test wasn't just about your reactions. The only way to pass this exam was to break free from the hypnosis spell," he explained. "It was designed to be broken either by attempting to save someone else, successfully escaping, or by openly challenging the morality of the scenario."

My voice rose. "But you made me watch people die... I watched Lammat burst into flames!" I tried to block out Lammat's sarcastic comment from the background, focusing my ire on the examiner. "What you did to us was reprehensible."

As I strode towards the examiner, his composure wavered, and he instinctively retreated a half step. He glanced towards the Goud for support, but the Goud only offered a nonchalant smile and crossed his arms.

"But you passed," the Eulis stammered, his previously calm demeanor now unsettled. "This test was designed to identify those worthy of our training. We can't invest in those who are weak-minded," he said, gesturing towards the still-unconscious examinees. "It was a straightforward exam – one of mental strength."

"You're missing my point," I countered, closing the distance between us. "How can you justify subjecting students to illusions like that?"

Rattled, the Eulis fumbled for words, his retreat more pronounced this time. "Liam, please calm down..."

My laugh was tinged with irony. "And to think... all you wanted us to do was..." With a hint of sarcasm, I extended my arm and opened my palm, fully expecting nothing to happen. To my utter shock, a large green orb materialized in my hand, many times larger than the one the Eulis examiner had created, gently bobbing up and down.

Behind me, I heard a series of gasps from the other examinees. In a reflexive motion, I clenched my fist, and the orb dissipated into a wisp of smoke. With all eyes still fixed on me, I made my way back to my chair, righting it before sitting down somewhat awkwardly, still processing the unexpected manifestation of my magical ability.

The Eulis examiner's gaze shifted to the Goud, whose previously nonchalant expression had now given way to something more pensive. Turning back to face me, the Eulis let out a loud, bemused laugh, a grin spreading across his face. "You definitely pass, Liam," he declared, his eyes sparkling with amusement and surprise. "All of you are to return to your rooms now. Those who failed will wake up shortly and be guided to a separate area."

With a casual flick of his fingers, the Eulis vanished before our eyes in a shimmering display. The Goud gave me a nod of acknowledgment before he too blurred out of sight in a swift, enigmatic departure. The Minor examiner, seemingly caught off guard by his colleagues disappearing, blushed slightly and promptly strode from the room, leaving behind a sense of relief mixed with lingering astonishment.

As the examiners vanished, the room instantly burst into a cacophony of animated discussions. Lammat, turning towards me with an expression of pure awe, exclaimed, "That was incredible!"

Before I could respond, a voice from my left chimed in. I glanced over to see Leana, her eyes wide with astonishment, a smile playing on her lips as she brushed her hair aside. "I thought you were worried about that spell," she said, her tone laced with amazement. "Was that your first time doing it? To maintain a controlled amount of energy in your hand like that... you're almost at the level of producing a condensed beam..."

Her words added to my bewilderment, not just at my unexpected ability to produce the orb, but also at the level of skill it indicated, a skill I hadn't even known I possessed.

As the room buzzed with conversation, I noticed a figure standing near me. Looking up, I saw Naya shifting uneasily, rocking back and forth on her heels. She crouched down, leaning in close, her voice barely above a whisper. "I, uhh..." she began, then paused. After a moment, she lifted her gaze to mine, her blue eyes sparkling. With a gentle smile, she said, "Well done."

I returned her smile, my attention then drawn to Tyran. He still stood where the Eulis had been, his intense gaze fixed on me. A whirl of questions about his actions during the exam spun in my mind – the red shield, his confrontation with the examiner.

Breaking the moment, Tyran approached me. "Liam," he spoke softly, glancing briefly at Naya and Lammat before focusing back on me. "Can we talk in private?" he asked, his tone unexpectedly courteous.

Taken aback, I nodded. "Oh, okay," I replied, rising from my seat. I offered an awkward smile to Naya and Lammat, then followed Tyran out of the room, curious and slightly apprehensive about the nature of our impending private conversation.

As we stepped through the door, a man clad in green robes hastily stopped leaning against the corridor wall and hurried towards us. He zeroed in on Tyran, his voice high-pitched and rapid. "Oh, hello there! Congratulations on passing. Your sleeping quarters remain as they were last night. Tomorrow you'll begin your third exam, after which there's a dance where you can reconnect with those from the previous exams and unwind before the final test."

Tyran, cutting to the chase, asked, "What's the next exam going to be?"

The man in green shook his head, "I'm sorry, but that information is only disclosed on the day." With a nod of understanding, Tyran moved to walk away, but the man turned his attention to me. "During these days, you cannot leave the grounds, but visitors are welcome."

I offered a polite smile and hurried to keep pace with Tyran, who was striding ahead briskly. "So," I ventured, "where are we heading?"

Without glancing back, Tyran replied, "We're going to our quarters. I need to escort you there since you spent last night in the medical wing."

The walk to our quarters was marked by a heavy silence, with Tyran leading the way. He eventually halted in front of a door and turned to me. He paused, his eyes darting between mine, as though contemplating.

"Everything okay?" I asked.

"Just..." he sighed. "Avoid eye contact." He leaned against the door, pushing it open and gesturing for me to enter. The room that greeted me was unexpectedly inviting. Its walls were painted a calming sky blue, adorned with whimsical green swirls. Four neatly made beds with thick, white bedding lined the walls, promising comfort and rest. At the far end, a small fireplace crackled cheerfully, casting a warm glow over the room. Seated in front of it, in a large, cozy chair, was a familiar figure.

"Ding!" I exclaimed, a wave of relief washing over me.

Ding turned, his face breaking into a warm smile. "'ello, sir," he greeted me enthusiastically, quickly closing the distance between us and placing his hands on my shoulders.

"It's so good to see you, I have so much to tell..." I began, eager to share my experiences.

But my reunion was interrupted by another voice. "I'm afraid that will have to wait, Liam." I turned to see the Tekka rising from a second chair beside the fire. His gaze shifted to Tyran. "Could you shut the door, please?"

As Tyran closed the door, the Tekka gestured subtly, and

I heard the distinct click of a lock engaging. The Tekka, no longer in armor, was now dressed in a long, flowing white robe. The garb, though matching the color of his stark white hair, added a sense of solemnity to his appearance. He brushed his hair back from his face, his smile serene yet unnerving.

With a growing sense of unease, I turned to Ding. "What's going on?" I asked, my voice tinged with apprehension. The atmosphere in the room had shifted rapidly.

The Tekka's response was prompt and direct. "Take a seat, and I will explain everything to you." I glanced at Tyran, who had already made his way to one of the beds near the fire, settling himself down. Turning back, I saw Ding giving me a reassuring nod, gesturing towards an empty chair by the fire. With a moment of hesitation, I walked forward, touching the chair's soft cushion before finally taking a seat.

The Tekka, now seated comfortably in his own chair, let out a heavy sigh. "I am the organizer of this exam, and as such, I'm privy to everything that transpires here. I'm fully aware of the events in the forest and what occurred in the second exam just moments ago." He paused briefly, his gaze shifting to Tyran and then back to me. "It seems Tyran has uncovered your secret — a secret that Ding specifically instructed you to guard."

A wave of regret washed over me. "I'm sorry. I tried. I really did."

Ding offered a reassuring smile, his words tinged with understanding. "I know youse did, sir. Master Tyran has already informed us of dat."

My eyes flickered to Tyran, then back to the Tekka, a maelstrom of confusion swirling within. "Tyran's come to talk to you about me?"

The Tekka, eyes closed, exhaled another profound sigh, as if releasing the weight of untold stories. "Listen to me, Liam. There's a reason for your lost memory, and why we've remained silent about your true identity." His gaze shifted to Tyran. "However, it appears Tyran has not just requested, but rather, insisted vehemently, that we unveil everything to you… now."

My heart leaped, a frantic rhythm pounding against my ribcage, while a whirlpool of anxiety churned in my stomach. The moment I had been waiting for, the revelation of my past and the reasons for my presence on the prison ship. With a heavy swallow, I braced myself for the truth.

The Tekka rose, his movements deliberate, and stationed himself beside the flickering flames of the fire. "Six years ago, a war tore through our lands. Our forces were divided into two primary factions: the Minors and the Gouds." He paused, his eyes briefly meeting Tyran's, laden with unspoken words, before continuing. "In the heart of this conflict, five elite warriors emerged, now enshrined in history as the Legendary Gouds."

"Yes, Naya mentioned that earlier," I interjected, my mind racing. I glanced at Ding and added, "…but I was under the impression that there were only four."

A knowing smile played upon the Tekka's lips. "Indeed, few have chosen to recognize the fifth as Legendary… for he was the sole survivor."

That revelation lingered in the air, heavy with implications. After a moment of contemplation, realization dawned on me with startling clarity. I turned to look at Tyran; his father was revered as one of the Legendary Gouds. That meant Tyran's father…

"Yet it remains an undeniable fact that without the combined strength of all five, the war's tide would surely have turned against us." His gaze drifted into the middle distance, as he recounted the heroes. "Meltek and Tylak stood as the pillars of the group, each a paragon of strength and wisdom in equal measure. They shouldered the mantle of leadership, their actions steeped in selflessness." His eyes briefly met Tyran's, who diverted his gaze.

"Additionally, two women, Scythe and Purge, graced their ranks. The newest and, admittedly, the least battle-hardened, they possessed a raw potential that Meltek saw surpassing his own one day." A momentary cloud of reflection passed over his face, punctuated by a small, rueful shake of the head.

"And then, there was the fifth." He paused, his voice lowering a shade. "Initially, he was less adept in the arts of physical combat. Yet, as time unfurled, his gaze shifted, drawn inexorably towards the arcane mysteries." His own eyes followed the intricate, green-swirled patterns adorning the walls, tracing their sinuous paths before settling back on me with a furrowed brow.

"Certain forms of magic are frowned upon, you see, especially by the majority within the Goud faction. They view such practices as shortcuts, unworthy of their proud heritage." He sighed, a hint of frustration coloring his tone. "A pride that, at times, borders on excess, obscuring their judgment."

The intricate tapestry of history and conflict he wove was undeniably fascinating, yet I couldn't help but wonder how it related to me. That was, until a sudden realization dawned, prompting my question with a surge of eagerness. "What was the final Goud's name?"

"The fifth Legendary Goud was known as Eulis." There was a brief, almost imperceptible pause as I processed the name, feeling the pieces of a long-unsolved puzzle clicking into place. The enmity between the Eulis' and the Gouds suddenly made a harrowing sense. It was Eulis, the lone survivor of the legendary five, who had not only outlived the war but had also founded his own faction, giving it his own name.

"Many among the Gouds harbor the belief that it was Eulis himself who betrayed and slew his comrades on the battlefield," he continued, a note of regret threading his voice. "But such thoughts stem from ignorance of the deep bond that united them. Both the Gouds and the Eulis' are inherently good people. Yet, it is the swirling rumors and misunderstandings that have sown the seeds of animosity between them."

I slowly shook my head. "But what has this to do with

me?"

The Tekka frowned, then pinched his eyes before turning to Tyran. "This is taking too long."

"I don't care," replied Tyran flatly. "If you don't tell him, I will." He looked at me. "He has a right to know why he lost his memory."

"The rest of your team will be back any minute."

"Then I suggest you get to the point quickly."

My mouth opened in surprise. How was Tyran able to talk to the Tekka in such a manner?

The Tekka glanced toward the door, before returning his gaze to Tyran. The two stared at each other for several silent seconds, but the Tekka finally sighed. His eyes flashed once more to the door before he turned to me. "Okay, Liam. Sorry about this, I'll be with you shortly…"

"Hm?" I uttered, looking at him.

Tyran stepped forward, "What? No!"

As I met the Tekka's eyes, his pupils stretched, growing into infinity. The world around me filled with darkness as I lifted from my chair and tumbled head over foot. I screamed as the sensation of falling engulfed me, a void where time and space lost their meaning, my voice echoing into the nothingness that surrounded me.

With a sudden lurch, my feet found solid ground, and I stumbled on the spot. I was no longer inside our quarters. Instead, I was standing in front of a large lake, framed by trees and mountains. A soft trickling sound beside me caught my attention, and I turned to find a small stream winding its way through a lush meadow, its waters sparkling in the light of the sun. The air was filled with the scent of wildflowers and the distant call of birds, creating a sense of peace that starkly contrasted with the chaos of the moment before.

Far in the distance, I caught sight of a waterfall, its cascading waters a brilliant silver against the backdrop of dark, forested cliffs. The sunlight caught in the mist, creating a spectrum of colors that danced through the air. The sound of the falling water, though distant, resonated deeply, adding a majestic rhythm to the serene landscape before me.

Where was I? I assumed the Tekka had somehow transported me here, and honestly, at this point, I started to just assume that anything that seemed impossible was just magic I didn't understand. However, my biggest concern at the moment was the whereabouts of the Tekka. He said he'd be right with me, yet I was entirely alone.

CHAPTER THIRTEEN
Beyond the Waterfall

I spent the next few hours sitting on the smooth, surprisingly sandy beach at the side of the lake. After a while, I searched the area for a flat stone to skip across the water's surface, before stumbling upon a large pile at the bottom of the stream.

I scooped up a few handfuls and carried them back over to the indentation I'd left in the sand throughout the day, settling down to continue my wait for the Tekka.

After another hour, and a personal best of 20 skims, I lay down on the sand and let out a sigh, shielding my eyes from the sun. "Where are you?" I asked, loudly. I shook my head, taking note of how far the sun had traveled across the sky since I appeared here. While it had started far behind me, high above the waterfall, it was now across the lake, threatening to fall behind the mountains in the distance.

Coming to a decision, I stood up, brushed the sand from my hair and clothes, and then started walking along the stream toward the waterfall. If the Tekka truly was planning on joining me, he'd be here already. If he was running late, then he would just have to come looking for me. Besides, I felt it was past time to figure out where I was. I needed to find civilization, and to do that, I needed higher ground.

'What a bizarre thing to do,' I thought to myself. 'Why would he send me here in the middle of our discussion?'

Several minutes later, I was climbing the rocky edge of

the waterfall, feeling strangely comforted by the cool mist. Although the weather wasn't what I'd call hot, the droplets were a welcome addition. They clung to my skin, refreshing me with each step I took upwards. The rocks were slick with moisture, demanding careful navigation, but there was an inexplicable sense of familiarity in this climb, as if my body remembered the motions even when my mind did not. The sound of the waterfall grew louder, a constant roar that seemed to drown out the concern that had gripped me moments before.

I reached the top feeling somewhat invigorated. My muscles felt as though they hadn't had any real exercise, and where I expected aches and pains, I felt energy and strength. I stretched my arms out to my side, before resting them behind my head and having a good look around the area.

Expecting to find D'wan Ma'hal in sight, my heart dropped when I saw nothing but forests and more bodies of water stretching endlessly before me. I dropped to my knees, letting out a laugh that lacked any humor. It was a sound more of resignation than amusement, echoing slightly in the vastness around me. "Guess I'm missing the next exam," I mumbled to myself, shaking my head. The absurdity of my situation – lost in an unknown landscape, far from where I intended to be – struck me with a bitter-sweet irony. I sat there for a moment, taking in the surreal beauty around me, feeling both lost and oddly at peace in this strange, tranquil world.

I started to rise to my feet when something suddenly caught my eye. Out from the forest before me, smoke wisps were curling lazily into the sky, thin but unmistakable. My heart quickened at the sight, and hope surged within me as I considered the possibility of finding others.

I turned away from the waterfall, its roar diminishing into a distant hum as I followed the river upstream, heading towards the forest where the smoke had originated. The journey was serene yet tinged with an undercurrent of anticipation. As I walked, the river beside me was a constant companion, its waters gurgling and splashing over rocks. The sun filtered through the trees, casting dappled shadows on the ground, and the air was alive with the symphony of nature.

Birds flitted from branch to branch, their songs a complex chorus that filled the air. I paused occasionally to watch small creatures scurrying in the underbrush, each absorbed in its own world. Squirrels darted up tree trunks, their bushy tails flickering, while a deer, elegant and poised, glanced my way from a distance before vanishing silently into the thicket. The diversity of insects was astounding – from the iridescent dragonflies hovering over the river to the myriad of butterflies that danced in the sunbeams. Each step revealed new wonders, and I found myself lost in the simple beauty of it all.

As the journey stretched on, I realized it had likely been another hour since I left the waterfall. Hunger began to gnaw at me, reminding me of my last meal in the Tavern with Ding. Just as the pangs became more insistent, I stumbled upon a cluster of bushes laden with berries. They were plump and dark, glistening invitingly in the sunlight. Cautiously, I picked one and tasted it. The berry was sweet and tangy, bursting with flavor, a welcome relief to my hunger. I ate eagerly, the juice staining my fingers. Their deliciousness prompted me to gather as many as I could. I filled my pockets, conscious of the uncertainty of my next meal.

As I circled the bush, searching for more, I looked up to find a young red-haired girl looking right at me. "Uhh, hello!" I said, giving a small wave. She couldn't have been any older than eight.

"Marneev?" she called out cautiously over her shoulder, her eyes still locked onto mine. She was wearing a long brown skirt and a white shirt stained with blues and purples.

I looked down at my hands, noting my fingers matched her stains. I took a step closer to her, hands held up in front of me, trying to look as non-threatening as possible. "Can you tell me where I am?" I asked.

The girl suddenly took off at a run, deeper into the forest, shouting "Marneev!" over and over again.

Not wanting to lose sight of her, I jogged behind her. "I'm

sorry, I'm not trying to scare you!" I called out. "Do you know where I can find an adult?"

My chase ended at the top of a hill, where I paused and finally found the source of the smoke I'd seen from the top of the waterfall. A small settlement lay before me, approximately seven wooden shacks surrounding a large bonfire, atop which rested a comically large cooking pot. People went about their business. Some sitting on benches, mid-conversation, others sawing logs, and others tending to the cooking pot.

All eyes, however, turned to look at me, while the little girl continued to yell "Marneev!" at the top of her lungs. A woman shifted a curtain leading to one of the small shacks and poked her head out. She laughed as the child ran into her, wrapping her arms around her waist.

"Marneev, look! Someone new!" the child turned and pointed at me, causing me to once again give a small wave.

Marneev bent over at the waist, returning the child's hug before turning to me, approaching confidently. "Welcome!" she called out loudly, giving a subtle gesture toward the settlement. "It's been a while since we've seen a new face!" She looked to be in her late forties, but her bright, friendly smile gave her a timeless aura. She wore a yellow dress that draped elegantly over her frame, the color complementing her cheerful demeanor. Tucked into her hair, which was styled in a simple yet graceful manner, was a white flower—a subtle touch that added to her charming appearance. As she stepped closer, she looked around me, back the way I had come, her expression turning to one of confusion. "Where's the Tekka?"

A flicker of hope I didn't even realize that I was nurturing instantly extinguished. "I was hoping I'd find him here," I said, feeling my body deflate somewhat. "He sent me here, and I thought he was going to be joining me… but he never appeared."

Marneev frowned, increasing her look of confusion. "That's unusual. He never brings a person here without introducing them to us. How long have you been here?"

I glanced up at the sky, searching for the sun. While I could no longer directly see it, the shadows from the trees indicated it was approaching late afternoon. "I'd say about seven hours or so."

"Well, I'm sure he'll turn up shortly. In any case, come! Let me show you to your house." She started walking back into the settlement, waving me forward.

"House?" I repeated.

"Don't worry, you won't be living with anyone unless you choose to." She laughed. "It's so nice to have you join us. I'm sure everyone is looking forward to hearing your story." She looked at me from over her shoulder and offered a kind smile. "When you're ready, of course."

"Sorry, but can you tell me where I am?" I asked, watching everyone in the settlement smiling and waving at me as I passed them.

Marneev stopped outside one of the shacks and turned, taking my hands. "My name is Marneev," she said with a grin.

"I'm Liam," I replied.

"It's so nice to meet you, Liam." She then released my hands and pulled aside the curtain blocking the doorway. "Welcome to your new home!" she said and ushered me inside. "I'll come get you once dinner is ready. Feel free to settle in."

Upon entering the wooden shack, I was immediately struck by the stark contrast between its humble exterior and the elaborate interior. The space was small, almost cramped, but every inch was utilized with careful consideration. The two pieces of furniture within the shack were impossible to overlook; both were ornate, almost out of place in their intricacy.

To my left stood a bed, its frame carved from dark wood that gleamed in the dim light filtering through the small window. The headboard was an exquisite piece of craftsmanship, adorned with intricate patterns and designs that depicted scenes of nature - trees, birds, and flowing rivers. The bed's covers were richly colored, adding a splash of warmth to the room.

Directly opposite the bed was a chair, equally elaborate. Its high back was adorned with delicate carvings of mythical creatures, each scale and feather rendered with astonishing detail. The chair's legs were curved, ending in clawed feet, and the seat itself was cushioned with a velvet-like fabric that looked both regal and inviting.

The floor was a curious sight. Scattered around were wooden swords and shields, each crafted with care. They were toys, but they seemed unused, more like pieces of a collection. The shields bore different symbols, none of which I recognized.

Along the back wall stood a large library. Shelves, not as intricately made as the bed and chair, but still beautiful, were filled with books. They ranged from well-worn tomes with cracked spines to newer volumes that still held the crispness of rarely turned pages. The collection was eclectic – from histories and tales of heroism to treatises on strategy and combat.

I turned to Marneev, "Why am I being given a house?" But she had already walked away, and now stood next to whom I assume was the chef, stirring the large cooking pot with what looked like a paddle.

I stepped further inside, allowing the curtain to close softly behind me. Drawn to the bed, I ran my fingers over the headboard, tracing the intricately carved shapes of trees and birds. Their textures were smooth and detailed under my touch. Beside my feet lay the wooden swords. I picked one up, examining its well-crafted form before carefully propping it against the wall.

Curiosity then led me to the bookshelf. I browsed the titles, their spines whispering tales and knowledge of ages past. Selecting a book at random, I carried it over to the bed and sat down. The bed was comfortable, yielding softly under my weight. I opened the book, anticipating the words and stories it might hold, only to find blank pages staring back at me. Puzzled, I closed it and returned it to the shelf, replacing it with another. But, to my surprise, this book was the same, each page as blank as the last.

I picked up a handful, then returned to the bed. Kicking off my boots, I lay down and started thumbing through each book in turn. As before, each was perfectly blank, including those with the worn spines.

"I drew pictures in mine," said a voice.

I quickly looked over to the doorway, to see the young red-haired girl poking her head through the curtain. "Yours are blank, too?" I asked.

"Yup!" she said, walking in and picking up one of my boots. "Well, they were at first, but they're slowly filling up with stories! You have big feet!" she said with a smile. "Mine are small."

I laughed, "Yes, but you're still growing." I said, sitting up. "Hey, I'm sorry if I scared you earlier. My name is Liam."

"I'm Jessara!" she replied, placing down my boot and picking up one of the wooden swords, swinging it around. "You didn't scare me! I was happy to see you! I'm no longer the newest person here."

I leaned forward slightly, lowering my voice to just above a whisper. "Can you tell me where 'here' is?"

Jessara opened her mouth to answer, but the curtain on my doorway once again parted, and Marneev stood in the doorway. "Dinner's ready, you two!" she smiled at me, "Looks like you arrived just in time."

"Yeah," I said, giving a forced smile.

I followed her out to find the other members of the settlement already gathered outside, many already sitting down, arranged in a semi-circle. I took a seat on one of the small chairs at the end.

The man to my right, with broad shoulders and a rugged beard, handed me a bowl of stew. "I'm Tharol," he said with a hearty laugh. "Hope you've got an appetite. My stew's famous around these parts."

Next to him, a woman introduced herself as Elara and leaned over to shake my hand. "And I'm the one who makes sure Tharol's cooking is edible," she quipped with a grin. "Nice to meet you, Liam."

The elder of the group sat with a calm and steady presence, yet merrily joined in the laughter. "Greetings, I'm Grevin. We're glad to have new company."

Beside Grevin was a young girl, perhaps a few years older than me, her youthful face framed by curious eyes. "I'm Liora," she said, her voice tinged with a hint of excitement. "It's good to have someone new to talk to."

At the end, a man with a quiet aura and observant eyes gave a brief nod. "Kael," he introduced himself simply, yet his gaze was penetrating.

"And of course, you've met Jessara and me," Marneev added. "We're all curious about the latest from D'wan Ma'hal."

As I sipped the stew, they all turned expectantly towards me. "Well, I'm quite new to the city myself. I was in the middle of the Crest exam when the Tekka brought me here," I explained.

"A Crest exam, eh?" Tharol mused. "That's a big deal. Shame to be pulled away like that."

Elara nodded sympathetically. "How did you find the exam? Which trial did you get to?"

"The second one," I said with a shrug, looking up at the darkening sky. "But I guess I won't have a chance at the third one."

Grevin stroked his beard thoughtfully. "I'm sure the Tekka did his best for you."

Liora leaned forward, her eyes full of curiosity. "What's it like in D'wan Ma'hal? I don't suppose anything interesting has taken place in the last few days."

Kael, who had been quietly listening, finally spoke. "The Tekka does visit us, but he rarely has news to keep us entertained."

The group nodded in agreement, each sharing fond

memories of the time in D'wan Ma'hal. As the night deepened, so did our conversation, drifting from earnest discussions to light-hearted banter. Tharol and Elara playfully bickered like an old married couple, while Grevin offered wise words, often punctuated by Liora's bright laughter. Kael spoke less but listened intently, his comments were always insightful.

"Have any of you considered returning to D'wan Ma'hal?" I asked.

The mood seemed to shift, but Jessara spoke up. "The Tekka brings my family here now and then, but..." she paused, sighing. "No, I don't want to go back."

"How about you and I talk about this tomorrow, Liam..." said Marneev with a gentle smile.

Grevin cleared his throat, "I've been thinking of going back the past few months." A few objections broke out, but Grevin simply chuckled. "Calm down! Like I said, I was only 'thinking' about it. I've spent too many years away from my real home. I've always said, I was born in D'wan Ma'hal, and I'll die in D'wan Ma'hal." No protests followed this, but he turned to me with a smile. "When you've lived as long as I have..." he paused, searching for the words, before shrugging, "Well, each person has a time, you know? And I know I'm reaching the end of mine."

The conversation swiftly took on a lighter tone, as Elara once again teased Tharol about his cooking, who responded by refilling my bowl to cheers from the others.

Eventually, with a second empty bowl of stew and the fire dwindling to embers, I excused myself. "Thank you for the company and the meal," I said, already feeling a sense of camaraderie with these strangers.

"Hopefully the Tekka will be here in the morning," said Marneev, who approached and gave me a brief hug. I returned her hug, surprising myself, and then offered a smile and a nod.

"Goodnight, Liam," they chorused, their voices a comforting blend in the cool night air. I walked back to the shack, their laughter and the crackling of the fire lingering in my ears.

CHAPTER FOURTEEN
Ghosts

Lying there, restless on the unfamiliar bed, my gaze was fixed unblinkingly on the ceiling, which merged imperceptibly with the shadows cast by the night. The day's weariness clung to me, yet sleep danced just beyond my reach, as elusive as tendrils of mist. Memories of the day just passed replayed in my mind, unfurling with the vividness and ceaselessness of a dream.

There was an undercurrent of unease about this place, a subtle stirring of disquiet that nestled uneasily in the depths of my stomach. The people here, with their gentle smiles and easy laughter, held an air of mystery that I couldn't quite decipher. They were welcoming, yes, but in their eyes, I sensed depths untold, secrets that lay beneath the surface of their serene existence.

As I shifted in bed, the sheets rustled softly against my skin, a constant reminder of how out of place I felt. The darkness of the room seemed to press in on me, amplifying my racing thoughts. Should I have asked more questions?

My mind wandered to the interactions of the day – Marneev's nurturing presence, the innocent curiosity of Jessara, and the communal spirit that seemed to permeate the air. Yet, beneath the apparent tranquility, I felt an undercurrent of something else, something almost... unnatural.

My spiraling thoughts were suddenly interrupted, not by

a voice, but by a sensation – an almost imperceptible pulling at the edges of my consciousness. It was as if some unseen force was beckoning me, tugging gently yet insistently at the strings of my mind, drawing me towards something unknown.

I sat up, the sheets falling away from me, and my feet found the cold floor. With cautious movements, I edged towards the curtain, peering out into the night. The settlement was cloaked in darkness, the homes of the inhabitants like silent sentinels under the moonlit sky. It seemed everyone had fallen asleep a while ago.

Yet this inexplicable sensation, this pulling, continued to resonate within me, growing stronger the more I focused on it, almost as though it knew that I was aware of it. I glanced back at the bed, contemplating the safety and warmth it offered. A part of me yearned to dismiss this strange compulsion as a trick of my restless mind and return to the futile pursuit of sleep, but I knew I couldn't, and reached for my boots.

Stepping outside, the cool night air brushed against my face, a stark contrast to the stifling atmosphere of the room I had just left. The ground beneath my feet was damp with dew, the grass seemingly whispering with each step I took. The moon hung low in the sky, casting a silvery glow over the landscape, transforming the surroundings into a realm of ethereal beauty.

As I ventured into the forest, the sensation in my mind became more pronounced, guiding me like a compass needle drawn to an unseen north. The trees stood tall and majestic, their leaves rustling softly, as if in hushed conversation. The sounds of the night – the distant hoot of an owl, the gentle rustle of small creatures in the underbrush – seemed to accompany my journey, a symphony of the nocturnal world.

The deeper I went, the more the forest seemed to change. The air grew heavier, charged with an energy I couldn't explain. The pull in my mind was now a constant presence, an invisible thread leading me forward. I couldn't say what I was searching for, or what I expected to find, but the need to discover the source of this sensation was overwhelming.

The path I followed twisted and turned, the moonlight casting elongated shadows that danced alongside me. My heart beat faster, not from fear, but from anticipation, from the sense of approaching something extraordinary. And so, I continued, deeper into the heart of the forest, towards the unknown, driven by a curiosity that seemed to transcend my understanding, a curiosity that promised to unveil the mysteries of this enchanting and enigmatic world.

The forest gradually thinned, and the ground began to slope upwards. With each step, the pull in my mind intensified, guiding me inexorably forward. The trees gave way to a clearing, and before me, the landscape transformed dramatically. Rising from the earth was a colossal cliff face, a monolithic guardian standing against the backdrop of the starry sky. Its surface was rugged, scarred by the passage of time, illuminated by the moonlight in a display of haunting beauty.

As I approached, a sense of awe washed over me. Embedded within the cliff were numerous caves, their entrances like the gaping mouths of an ancient beast. Each cave was sealed off with metal bars, meticulously crafted, and embedded deep into the stone. The bars were thick, their surfaces etched with age, suggesting they had been part of this landscape for generations. They seemed to serve a dual purpose – keeping something in, or perhaps keeping others out.

The air around these caves felt heavier, charged with an almost tangible energy. The silence here was profound, broken only by the occasional rustle of wind against stone. The scene was eerie yet captivating, a forgotten place hiding secrets in plain sight.

One cave, in particular, drew my attention. It was not the largest nor the most distinct, but the sensation that had led me here was centered on this very spot. The bars guarding this cave were just like the others, yet they held a significance that made my heart race.

Peering through the bars, the darkness within was nearly impenetrable. However, as my eyes adjusted, I discerned a figure in the shadows – a young man with hair as dark as obsidian, his clothing blending seamlessly with the darkness around him, yet his skin shone in the moonlight. He sat perfectly still, his legs crossed, and his posture one of deep contemplation. The air itself seemed to ripple around him, and pulse like a heartbeat, as if his very presence was a force of nature.

Compelled by an inexplicable connection, I found myself moving closer until I stood right before the bars. The man remained motionless, an extension of its ancient mystery. The silence was overwhelming, the only sound was my shallow breaths and the distant call of nocturnal creatures.

Hesitantly, I reached out towards the bars, my fingers grazing the cold metal. The sensation was jarring, a stark reminder of the barrier between us. It was then, in that moment of contact, that the man's eyes flew open. His gaze was intense, penetrating, as if he could see right through me. The speed of his movement was startling – one moment he was a statue, and the next, he had lunged forward with astonishing agility, his hand reaching through the bars to grasp my arm with a grip that was both alarming and electrifying.

As I recoiled, the man studied my face with an intensity that felt like it could pierce through the very fabric of my being. For a fleeting moment, his eyes softened, revealing a glimmer of something akin to disappointment. Then, releasing me, he uttered, "You're not him."

I stumbled backward, my heart pounding against my ribcage. My hand instinctively cradled my wrist, expecting a searing pain from his iron grip. Yet, to my astonishment, there was only a faint tingling sensation, no sign of bruising or injury.

Gathering my wits, I managed to stammer, "Why are you behind bars?" My voice echoed slightly, sounding foreign in the stillness that surrounded us.

The man leaned back into the shadows of his cave, his figure becoming part of the darkness once again. His eyes, however, remained fixed on me, glowing faintly in the dim light. "Where's the Tekka?" he asked, almost to himself, his gaze drifting past me as if searching for something – or someone – in the distance.

I felt a pang of confusion. "I... I don't know. I was brought here by the Tekka, but..." My voice trailed off, uncertainty creeping into my words.

He waved his hand dismissively, his attention already waning. "Just another ghost," he muttered under his breath, a note of resignation in his tone.

But his words only fueled my curiosity further. "Where is this place?" I pressed on, my voice steadier now.

The man paused, turning his gaze back to me. He regarded me with a peculiar look as if seeing me for the first time. "Nowhere," he answered cryptically, his voice echoing the emptiness of his response.

His answer hung in the air, unsatisfying and enigmatic. I pushed on, "How can this be nowhere? What is this place?"

A flicker of surprise crossed his features. "You don't know?" he asked, skepticism lacing his tone. He studied me more intently, his brow furrowing. "How did you die?"

His question hit me like a physical blow. "Die? I didn't die," I responded, confusion and defiance in my voice. "I was teleported here. By the Tekka."

At this, his demeanor changed abruptly. His eyes widened, a sudden spark of interest, or perhaps hope, igniting within them. "You're alive?" he exclaimed, his voice laced excitement. "A living person in this world..."

His image blurred, and he was once again at the bars, gripping them tightly, his knuckles whitening. "Listen closely," he said urgently. "In D'wan Ma'hal, at the docks. The large guarded warehouse to the east—"

He paused, his gaze flickering with a haunted look. "This world... it's a cruel illusion. It's not real. We're trapped in the

Tekka's mind. It's a realm of endless torture, designed to extend our lives beyond natural limits."

His voice dropped to a fervent whisper. "Here, you can't die. You can't starve. You can't even hurt yourself. It's eternal torment, an existence without end or escape."

My mind whirled with confusion. What was he talking about? A world where death was a wish ungranted, where suffering had no end – it was a concept too horrific to fully grasp.

His expression contorted with desperation. "Please," he pleaded, his voice cracking. "If you truly are alive, if you have any power here, kill me! KILL ME!" His shout echoed through the night, a cry of anguish in this unending nightmare.

His words hit me like a wave, leaving me reeling with their implications. But before I could process them, before I could ask for any semblance of clarification, the world around us began to ripple and distort.

The cliff face and the caves elongated, stretching away into the distance as if being pulled by an unseen force. I spun around, disoriented by the sudden shift in reality.

The figure of the man, still grasping the bars and shouting for release from his endless torment, faded into the distance. His plea for death hung heavy in the air, a stark reminder of the hellish reality of this place.

Two hands gripped my shoulders and steadied me. "Calm down, Liam." The Tekka stood before me, his form shimmering and imposing in the moonlight. I turned back towards where the cliff had been, but it was gone, swallowed by the rapidly changing landscape. The man, his urgent message, and the revelation he had just shared – all were lost in the transformation.

I faced the Tekka, my mind racing with the horror of what I had just learned. "What is this place? Why did you bring me here?" I demanded, my voice filled with a mix of fear and determination. My mind raced back over the evening's conversations. Grevin speaking of his own death so casually.

"Am I… dead?"

The Tekka's expression was a mixture of sympathy and regret as he looked at me. "No, Liam, you are not dead," he assured me, his voice imbued with a calming presence. Sensing the need for a more intimate conversation, he gestured with his hand, and two chairs materialized beside us, seemingly woven from the night air.

As we both took our seats, the Tekka leaned forward, his eyes meeting mine. "This place you find yourself in," he began, his voice laced with a touch of sorrow, "is a sanctuary I created. It's a realm for those at the twilight of their lives, those who are gravely ill in our real world. I developed a magic that allows their consciousness to reside here, where time is dilated. A single second in the real world can be hours, even days, here. It's like a prolonged dream, where a lifetime can be lived in what is merely a night's slumber outside."

His voice took on a pained tone, conveying the weight of his guilt. "You've been here far longer than you should have been. I was meant to join you instantly, to speed up our conversation in the real world, but…" his eyes glanced away and a look of mild frustration flashed on his face. "…I was interrupted." He gave a small chuckle. "I am sorry, Liam. Truly sorry."

I sat there, trying to process everything he said. "So, the people in the village, the settlement I found…" my voice trailed off, grappling with the reality of this revelation.

"Yes," he nodded. "They are real people, living their final days here in tranquility. My magic gives them the chance to live full lives, to experience joy and fulfillment in ways their physical conditions in the real world wouldn't permit. They find happiness and contentment, a final chapter written with joy rather than sorrow."

Leaning back in the chair, I felt a mixture of relief and confusion wash over me. I was alive, not dead, but trapped in a world that wasn't mine, a world of extended goodbyes and dreams turned reality. The realization brought forth a myriad of questions, each one painting a complex picture of a world crafted from profound magic, beauty, and unintended consequences.

"But Jessera… she's only 8…" My voice broke a little as I thought of the cheerful, innocent child I had met.

The Tekka nodded, his expression reflecting a deep, quiet sadness. "Jessera, yes. Just an ordinary day, playing outside, and a simple misstep changed everything. She fell and hit her head quite badly. It was just a tragic accident, but it left her in a coma."

He sighed softly, looking down for a moment. "Her parents were beside themselves with grief. When I told them about this place, they were torn. But ultimately, they decided to let her come here, hoping she could at least have some semblance of the childhood she was missing."

I struggled to imagine what her parents must be going through. "So, she's been here all this time? Just like she was before the accident?"

"Yes," he confirmed. "To her, she's just a little girl playing, making friends, living a life she can't have in the real world. Her parents, they come to see her, sitting by her side, even though she's not really there. They've watched her grow up here, in a way."

"And she can leave this place?" I asked, trying to grasp the reality of her situation.

"Everyone here can, at any time. But for Jessera, and others like her, this world offers something they can't have elsewhere. Here, she's happy and carefree. It's a difficult decision, but many find a kind of peace in this existence."

I nodded, trying to process it all. Jessera, living a childhood that spanned decades, her parents holding onto hope in both worlds.

"Then why didn't you let Jessera's parents come here with her?" I asked, trying to understand the complexities of this decision.

The Tekka nodded, his expression showing a deep

understanding of my question. "It's a reasonable query," he began. "The truth is, death and loss are intrinsic parts of life, and I've learned that the hard way. There was a time when I allowed a healthy person to live in this world. I even gave them the power to use magic, to create fictional representations of those who had passed. But it became clear that it's hard for people to let go. Given the chance, many would choose to live in a dream indefinitely."

He paused, reflecting on his words. "This world is for those who can't live their lives in the real world due to their conditions. It's not an escape for the healthy or a place to avoid the inevitable truths of life."

"The hope," he continued, "is that one day, a magic might be discovered that can heal Jessera's wounds, or perhaps she'll wake up on her own. But if I had done nothing, her parents would have lost her completely. Here, at least, she has a life. And I speak with her parents every week, telling them about her adventures, her joys. It comforts them, knowing she's still experiencing a kind of childhood, even if it's not under the normal circumstances."

His voice was tinged with melancholy. "It's a delicate balance, Liam. This world offers a semblance of life to those who have been robbed of it. But for those who are still part of the living world, they must face and embrace its realities, no matter how painful."

Sitting there, listening to the Tekka, I began to understand the bittersweet nature of this world. It was a place of refuge and continuation, yet bound by the necessary limitations of life and death. Jessera's story, though tragic, was a testament to the delicate balance between holding on and letting go, a balance the Tekka strived to maintain.

"What about the man who begged me to kill him?" I asked, recalling the desperation in his voice. "He described this world as a place of torture."

The Tekka's expression hardened, his demeanor shifting to one of stern resolve. "That man," he began, his voice firm, "was a Crosser, a mass murderer who took many lives without remorse – men, women, and children."

He paused, letting the gravity of his words sink in. "This world, Liam, is indeed intended for those close to death, but death is not always physical. That man's soul was as near to death as one can be while still living. I will release him one day, but not before he has existed here for the length of every life he took, doubled for the children he killed."

I felt a chill at the Tekka's words, the justice in them severe yet seemingly fitting. "There were multiple cells," I pointed out, recalling the line of barred caves.

The Tekka nodded, a hint of sorrow in his eyes. "Creating those cells... I cannot help but feel sad. Many in this world are sick in the mind, like the man you encountered. I made several cells in advance, as a place of atonement for such individuals. It's a grim task, but necessary. This world is a haven for those denied a fair chance at life, but it also serves as a place of reckoning for those who have grievously wronged others."

He looked directly at me, his gaze unwavering. "I must warn you, Liam, do not try to approach him again. His existence here is to be one of solitude, at least for the next hundred years. It is part of his atonement, part of the balance this world must maintain."

"You say people aren't meant to be brought here if they're still healthy in the real world... so why did you bring me here?" I asked, my confusion evident.

The Tekka sighed, his expression becoming introspective. "The time dilation here serves more than just the sanctuary's purpose. It allows for swift communication, handling this world's complexities efficiently. However, your case was an unfortunate error. I inadvertently kept you here much longer than intended. It's a mistake I deeply regret and a practice I'll need to reassess."

"Before you brought me here... what was it you wanted to say?"

"I was worried that your friends would enter, so…"

I smiled, giving a short laugh. "I understand. Don't worry. By the sounds of it, we now have more than enough time for you to say what you wanted."

After a brief pause, he cleared his throat, his voice taking on a reflective tone. "Eight years ago, there was a conflict between Lylackia and a country called Saddul. Saddul is a stark contrast to Lylackia. Here, we live simply, believing that overreliance on technology can obscure one's clarity of thought. Lylackia, small as it is, relies on the simplicity of movement, the reliance on our own capabilities."

He glanced around as if the surroundings reminded him of this principle. "Saddul, however, is at the other end of the spectrum. They're deeply entrenched in technology, so much so that there are even rumors of them aiming to explore beyond our planet. Their path has led them to feats we wouldn't dare dream of."

He looked at me again, a hint of pride in his eyes. "But the opposite is true for us. In Saddul, they've lost touch with the abilities that define us – crests, powers, magic. They might have had these once, but technology has shifted their existence. They no longer understand or possess the powers we hold dear, the magic that is woven into the fabric of our lives."

The Tekka, sensing my growing understanding of our world's complexities, extended his right arm towards me. With a deliberate motion, he rolled back his sleeve, revealing the skin of his forearm. "We, however, have used magic to preserve our way of life," he said, his tone embodying a blend of pride and solemnity.

He pointed to the crest on his forearm; an intricate pattern of interlocking circles, with the center section pulsating in a soft white light. "This," he explained, "is the Crest of Nations. At birth, it is sealed into the skin of a child, connecting directly with the user's bloodstream to provide vital information."

I nodded, my eyes fixed on the crest. "Yes, the Conveyor told me about this." I pulled back my chain mail sleeve, revealing my crest. Curiously, I tapped the red section and watched as it flowed up towards my hand. As I did so, something caught my eye, something about my crest that looked oddly unfamiliar.

The Tekka observed my reaction, a knowing look in his eyes. "Each crest is unique, Liam. They're not just symbols; they're a part of us, a connection to our heritage and to the magic that flows through Lylackia."

"But why is my crest so different?" I asked, looking up at the Tekka. "Compared to yours, mine looks brand new."

The Tekka nodded slowly. "Yes, well we'll come back to that," he replied with a dismissive wave of his hand.

I glanced back down at my crest, noticing the stark contrast in the vivid colors and the sharp, black outlines that framed them, compared to the Tekka's more subdued mark.

"The people of Saddul slowly grew suspicious of us over the years," he continued, "yet still considered us relatively primitive." He paused, cleared his throat, and then added, "An attack on their capital city was wrongfully attributed to us, leading them to believe we were a threat. Eventually, they tried to take Lylackia for themselves." Standing up, he walked a few paces away and a man with dark hair appeared before him. The Tekka stood face to face with him, his jaw clenched. "Our intelligence indicated that a man named Zeipher was behind the destruction of many homes and businesses in Saddul, resulting in hundreds of deaths."

He looked back at me over his shoulder. "Zeipher was a fallen Guardian, once the right-hand man of Lexis the Fourth, the King of Lylackia." Then, turning back to face me, he continued, "Zeipher murdered the King and anyone in the Glacier Kingdom who refused to submit to him. Dozens of innocent servants and soldiers were mercilessly killed, their bodies discarded in the streets."

"I'm sorry, but I don't follow... what is the Glacier

Kingdom?" I asked, my curiosity piqued.

The Tekka gestured, and a ghostly image of two majestic mountains appeared before us. "You have seen those mountains, correct?" As I nodded, he continued, "Within those mountains is our Kingdom, once the home of generations of Royalty. But now, he lives there."

"Zeipher?" I queried, watching the shadowy figure of Zeipher appear within the vision, his presence dark and foreboding within the grandeur of the palace.

The Tekka nodded gravely. "The attack on Saddul was more directly aimed at Lylackia. He attacked them, blamed us, and then, while we were occupied, he seized the throne." The scenes shifted to show the chaos and destruction of Saddul, and then Zeipher turning his sights on Lylackia.

"So, he's now the King?" I wondered aloud.

"No, he never wanted that," the Tekka replied, his tone reflecting the complexity of Zeipher's motives.

The Tekka continued, "After the King's death, the Legendary Gouds returned from Saddul. Seeing the state of the town, they went straight to the palace." The scenes changed, showing the Gouds, determined and brave, marching towards their destiny.

"The five of them fought their way into the palace," the Tekka narrated. The vision played out the battle, the fall of Purge, then Scythe, each moment laden with heroism and tragedy.

The Tekka's voice grew heavier. "Meltek, Tylak, and Eulis reached the throne room where Zeipher awaited." The spectral figures of Meltek, Tylak, and Eulis appeared, confronting Zeipher in a showdown.

"They knew they couldn't defeat him in direct combat," the Tekka explained. "They planned to subdue him long enough for Eulis to cast the 'Time Constrict Charm'." The vision froze, showing the figures locked in an eternal stalemate, the charm's effect spreading throughout the palace.

The Tekka rubbed his eyes, the burden of the tale

evident. "They are still there, frozen in time. A testament to the lengths they went to stop Zeipher, even if it meant their own eternal confinement."

Confusion enveloped me like a thick fog. "But you mentioned Eulis survived... how is that possible if he was part of the charm?" I asked, trying to piece together the fragmented history.

The Tekka's expression held a blend of sorrow and understanding. "Eulis fled, Liam," he said softly. "That decision haunts his legacy. Many label him a coward, not for surviving, but for abandoning his comrades in their final stand."

The weight of the Tekka's words seemed to fill the air around us. "You need to decide if you're ready to believe what I'm about to tell you," he continued, his gaze intense. "And it must remain between us. Do you understand?" I could feel my mouth go dry, my lips sticking together as I nodded.

He inhaled deeply, preparing to reveal something momentous. "This might shock you," he said solemnly. "The last battle against Zeipher had another survivor. You, Liam."

A smile unconsciously spread across my face, but it was empty, devoid of understanding or recognition. In the silence that followed, I half-expected someone to jest about my lack of shock.

My smile morphed into a perplexed frown. "I don't understand. What was my role in the palace?" The Tekka remained silent, his eyes revealing nothing. My mind spun with a whirlwind of questions. "That battle was years ago... What have I been doing all this time?"

"Liam..." the Tekka began, his voice heavy with unspoken truths.

"What was my purpose there?"

"Your father was King Lexis, Liam."

CHAPTER FIFTEEN
Royalty

I felt as if the ground beneath me had given way. My entire being felt numb and cold. "What?" I managed to croak out, my voice barely a whisper.

"King Lexis was your father."

His words hit me like a tidal wave. "Lexis was the King… and my father… that means I am…"

"…the Prince. Our future King," the Tekka finished for me.

A slow nod was all I could muster. "Ahhh… I see." I stood up, my mind racing, yet strangely calm.

"Liam, please sit. I haven't yet shown you the proof," the Tekka said, urging me to reconsider.

I shook my head, a half-smile still playing on my lips. "How can I believe something so… extraordinary?" I gave a loud, uncontrollable, booming laugh. "I understand I've lost my memory, but this…" I trailed off, my mind grappling with the enormity of the revelation. "If I can recall minor details like Ding being named after a fish, shouldn't the knowledge of being a prince, the son of a King, be something I'd remember?" My skepticism was a thin veil over the turmoil of emotions and questions swirling within me.

"But that's what I'm trying to explain… you won't be able to remember any of it," the Tekka said, a tone of resignation in his voice. I looked down at him, still frowning, struggling to grasp the full meaning of his words. "Sit down, and I will explain," he urged gently. Reluctantly, I sat back down, clasping my hands together, and leaning back in the chair.

As he spoke, the world around us subtly shifted. Ethereal images began to materialize, mirroring the Tekka's narrative. "Whilst Eulis was escaping from the throne room, he found a young boy among the dead, you, surrounded by bodies." A ghostly vision appeared before us, showing a young boy - me, lying amidst a scene of chaos and destruction.

"Eulis thought you were a servant, given your appearance. Dirty, dusty, and charred clothing, weak and barely conscious." The vision shifted, showing Eulis, his face etched with concern, picking up the young me and hurrying away from the palace as it began to be enveloped by the charm's effect.

"He took you to the tavern," the Tekka continued, the vision changing to show the interior of the tavern I had recently stayed in. "There, you collapsed and didn't wake for two days. The tavern keepers cared for you, and one in particular…" The vision shifted to show Ding stood by my side. "When you awoke, you were deeply troubled," the Tekka's voice brought me back to the present. "Your speech was fragmented, full of fear."

"Ding… knows?"

"You mentioned witnessing your father's death," the Tekka said solemnly. "It's unclear whether you understood what you were saying, or if it was the shock speaking." The visions around us now showed a young me, speaking in hushed, broken sentences, a look of horror and confusion on my face.

The Tekka stood and walked toward a vision of a fireplace, the fire casting dancing shadows around us. "What was wrong with me?" I asked.

He turned, his face glowing in the firelight. "As a Guardian, my hair is always white. It's a sign of our faction. When we use our powers, we emit a slight glow." A soft luminescence surrounded him, illustrating his point.

"But Crossers..." he continued, "they have black hair and emit a black aura when using their powers." He seemed to lose his train of thought momentarily, caught up in the complexities of factions and powers.

Regaining his focus, he looked at me. "You gradually calmed down but couldn't make sense of what had happened. You knew your father had been killed, but the reasons were beyond your comprehension."

As the Tekka spoke, the air around us seemed to ripple with the power of his memories, bringing forth spectral images that intertwined with his words.

"Ding attempted to establish a telepathic link with you, to reorder your fragmented thoughts," the Tekka explained, his hand resting gently on my shoulder. "Dingersby still carries the weight of that decision, but it was I who commanded it. In my eagerness for answers, I overlooked the potential harm to you." His eyes, full of regret, met mine.

"What does this all mean?"

The Tekka gave a weary sigh and resumed. "You were in denial about your father's death. But as the haunting images of his demise infiltrated deeper into your mind, something unprecedented occurred..." Around us, faint visions began to materialize, showing fragmented scenes of chaos and a young boy amidst it all – me.

"What happened?" I urged, captivated by the unfolding images.

"You transformed, Liam." The Tekka's voice was heavy with significance. The visions around us sharpened, showing a young boy with golden curls. Suddenly, his hair darkened, turning as black as the night sky. "Your memory triggered a profound change. You became a Crosser."

I stopped him, disbelief in my voice. "A Crosser? But I was just a child!" His nod confirmed the implausible truth. "I must have been ten or eleven; how is that even possible?"

"You are the youngest ever recorded to undergo such a

transformation," he said solemnly. "It's never happened before, not at such an early age."

"So, what happened next?" My frown deepened as I tried to comprehend this revelation.

"That's when we lost control," the Tekka answered. The visions around us grew more tumultuous, showing a young me unleashing a destructive force within the tavern. "Your newfound power was overwhelming. Not even trained Guardians could restrain you."

I struggled to grasp the reality of his words. The air shimmered with scenes of chaos – the tavern in ruins, people injured, and Guardians being repelled.

The Tekka's voice brought me back. "It took five Guardians to finally subdue you, and that's when they signaled for me. There were few with magical abilities back then, but I was known for being the best at the time… and I did the only thing I could think of… I removed your crest." The vision showed the Tekka, surrounded by other Guardians, as they struggled to contain me.

I shook my head, still unable to believe what I was hearing. "You removed my crest?"

The Tekka leaned forward, the weight of his words evident in his posture. "Liam, when a person's crest is removed, they enter a coma-like state. Upon awakening, they lose all memories related to their crest and its powers. It's an effect of a charm embedded in the crest at its creation." He paused, his hands rubbing his eyes, betraying a discomfort with the subject.

"This procedure… we've had to use it before, but only in extreme cases. Typically, it's applied to low-level faction members, criminals, or those who have suffered traumatic experiences linked to their crest. The person can only be awakened by inserting a new crest. But it's a delicate process." His voice was tinged with regret and resolve.

"Please understand, we've been trying relentlessly to restore you. Every month for years, we attempted to give you a new crest, but each time, your hair would turn black, indicating the transformation back into a Crosser." The visions around us flickered, showing scenes of these attempts – a comatose figure, me, being given a new crest, only to react violently each time.

"We had to perform these attempts over the ocean, to minimize the damage from your inevitable outbursts. You'd wake up, lash out, and then we'd have to restrain you once again." The images showed the grim routine of these efforts, the frustration and desperation evident in the actions of the Guardians involved.

"But a week ago," he continued, a hint of hope in his voice, "something changed. Your hair remained its natural color. You didn't awaken immediately this time." He chuckled dryly. "I guess you didn't notice the other Guardians on the ship, or question why I was clad in full armor. We were prepared for the worst, but for the first time, there was no violent awakening."

The visions slowly faded, leaving me sitting there, trying to piece together the fragments of my past. The revelation that I had been lost in a cycle of comas and awakenings, each time reverting to a Crosser, was staggering. The lengths to which the Tekka and others had gone to try to bring me back, only to be met with failure each time, spoke of a determination and hope that was hard to comprehend.

I blinked, my mouth closing as the pieces began to fall into place. The last few days, once a blur, started to make sense. I'd never fully realized my lack of memory regarding the crest; it explained why I knew the names of creatures and foods, but not my own family. I looked up at the Tekka, a dawning comprehension in my eyes. "That's why I was on a prison ship? I was essentially unconscious for five years?"

"Back then, our orders were to kill Crossers on sight. I... we... we couldn't just kill you..."

The realization hit me hard, a flood of emotions I had never truly felt before – sadness, loss, a sense of being adrift. I glanced down at my crest. "This is why my crest looks different to yours, Ding's, probably Tyran's… it's new, isn't it?" A hollow laugh escaped me as I looked out the window, mourning the loss of my memory, my crest, my entire past. "That's why he called you after seeing my crest."

The Tekka nodded, "He was very insistent. He knows something happened to you that demanded we remove it, but not exactly what."

"My father… he was the King?" I asked, the words barely a whisper. He nodded once again. "And my mother?"

The Tekka's eyes held mine, heavy with empathy. "She died when you were born, Liam."

I stood up, feeling weak, and unsteady. The realization that I had no memories of my parents, that they had never been a part of my life as I knew it, was overwhelming. "I'm sorry, but I need to leave now. I need to be alone. I need to… walk, or something."

The Tekka stood as well, and the chairs and visions vanished. "I understand. I'll be at the village when you're ready."

"No, the real world, I…" I started.

"Do you think you're in the right state of mind to see your friends?" he gently interjected.

I paused, shaking my head slowly. "Take your time," the Tekka assured me. "I'll take you back to the real world in the morning… give you a chance to say goodbye to Jessara."

I offered a faint smile and began walking back towards the village.

"Liam…" The Tekka called out, and I turned to face him. "I was the only Eulis capable of removing your crest at the time… I hope one day you can forgive me."

I nodded, acknowledging his words, and continued on my way. As the minutes passed, a sudden realization struck me – something the Tekka had just said. My eyes widened as it dawned on me. "The only Eulis capable at the time? The first Eulis! The Tekka is Eulis!"

* * *

As I wandered aimlessly through the forest, the twilight shadows stretching long and thin, I noticed something peculiar. Despite the emotional turmoil and the miles I had covered, my body felt no fatigue. It was an odd sensation, as if the physical constraints I should have been subject to were absent. The realization slowly dawned on me – this must be a result of living in the Tekka's created world, a place where biological limitations like exhaustion didn't apply.

Eventually, I found myself drawn back to the village. The familiar sights and sounds were oddly comforting, grounding me in a reality that felt increasingly fluid and uncertain. As I approached, I saw the Tekka sitting in the center of the village, a calm presence amidst the villagers who had gathered around him. They seemed to be waiting, perhaps for me.

Marneev, with her kind eyes and gentle demeanor, was among the first to approach me. Her presence was a balm to the chaos of my thoughts. Then came Jessara, the innocent eight-year-old whose story had touched me deeply. With the unreserved affection only a child could offer, she hugged me tightly.

"I'm sorry we all thought you died during the exams," she said, her voice muffled against me. The simplicity of her apology, devoid of the complexities of the adults around us, was surprisingly comforting.

I knelt to her level, a smile breaking through the confusion and sadness. "It's okay, Jessara. I'm just glad to see you're doing well here," I replied, my voice gentle.

The villagers, their faces a mix of curiosity and concern, watched our exchange. Among them, the Tekka's gaze met mine, full of unspoken understanding and empathy. At this moment, surrounded by the villagers and with Jessara's warmth against me, I felt a flicker of something like peace, a brief respite from the storm of revelations and memories that had upended my world.

"The Tekka explained the confusion. We must have

sounded so odd to you," said Marneev, also moving in for a hug. "You must have thought 'Why are these people giving me a house?'."

I laughed, "Yeah, admittedly, that was a little strange."

Jessara pulled on my sleeve, "When new people arrive in the village, a house is created just for them. The Tekka's magic makes it just right for the owner."

The Tekka stood up and approached. "What did you think of your house, Liam?"

"Ornate," I replied with a shrug.

He cocked his head, a curious expression crossing his face. "Mind showing me?"

I gave a smile and gestured toward my house. "Be my guest!" I said with a laugh.

We both moved toward the house, shifting the curtain aside, and stepping in. The Tekka's eyes went wide, and his mouth opened slightly. "Liam, this..." he laughed and ran his hand across the chair. "This is your father's chair..."

"My... father's..."

"These swords, you would play fight with him every day." He picked one up, examining it closely. He moved to the bookshelf, taking one out. "Just like Jessara's..."

"Yeah, why are they blank?"

"They're not your books, Liam. These are your father's personal collection. You didn't ever read them!" He closed the book and turned to me, beaming. "Liam, this means you remember him. He's still in your memories, somewhere."

I couldn't help but smile back at him. "Is it possible to fix... can you do anything to get them back?"

"I don't know," he said, still smiling, eyes racing from side to side as though already planning things out. "But the fact that my magic has already tapped into part of it means it should be possible, in time."

* * *

An hour later, feeling both replenished and reflective, the Tekka and I shared heartfelt goodbyes with each villager. Embracing each person, I found an unexpected strength in Kael's hug, his arms tight around me. "Stay away for a good while, okay?" Kael said, grinning broadly. "Experience the real world to its fullest while you've got the chance!"

Liora, ever the optimist, chimed in with a chuckle, "No way! Convince the Tekka to let you visit us again soon. We'll keep your house ready for you."

"We'll see about that," the Tekka replied, his eye roll betraying a hidden amusement.

As I was about to turn away, I felt a small tug at my leg. Jessara, her eyes bright and earnest, looked up at me. "Liam, can you do me a favor?"

I bent down to her level. "Anything for you, Jessara."

She reached for my hand, pulling me down to her height to whisper in my ear, though louder than she probably intended. "Can you visit my parents when you get back? Tell them I love them, and I miss them?"

A lump formed in my throat as I glanced at the Tekka. His face was serious, but he gave me an affirming nod.

"Of course, Jessara," I replied, managing a smile. "I'll make sure they get your message next time they visit and I'll be sure to give you a big hug in the real world, too."

Her face broke into a beaming smile. "You promise?"

"I promise."

Standing back up, I felt the Tekka's hand on my shoulder. "Farewell, everyone," he announced to the villagers.

Their collective voices rang out with goodbyes as the village scene faded into darkness. When I opened my eyes again, I was back in the dormitory.

"Put me down!" Tyran's voice broke the silence. He was being held aloft by Ding.

"Sorry, I didn' want youse to get hurt!" Ding apologized.

"He deserves it after what he did to Liam!" the Tekka

retorted, striding towards Tyran. "Do you understand the impact of your actions? How many hours you delayed me from reaching Liam?"

Tyran shrugged off Ding's hold and shot me a look. "I warned you not to look him in the eye!"

Confusion swirled within me. "I don't understand what's happening..."

Tyran turned to the Tekka, frustration evident. "I told you that spell shouldn't be used on people!"

"And I argued one mistake doesn't mean we abandon a powerful, necessary magic," the Tekka countered.

"One mistake?!" Tyran's voice rose in anger. "One...?" His fists clenched, hinting at a brewing storm within him, but he held back, instead walking past us towards the door, only to find it still locked.

"Let me..." the Tekka began, but Tyran, stepping back, unleashed a small blue beam towards the lock. The door's handle, part of the lock, and a chunk of the wall shattered under the force. He then stormed out of the room without another word.

"Sorry, Sir," Ding muttered.

The Tekka gave a loud sigh and shook his head. "No, Dingersby, I'm sorry. Do you mind patching that up before their teammates return? I have to take Liam somewhere."

I stood up as Ding gave a short bow and started toward the door. "Where are we going?" I asked.

"We're keeping a promise," he replied with a weak smile, before taking hold of both shoulders and pulling me close to him. I momentarily thought he was offering a hug, before he muttered "Hold your breath."

I had a moment to react before the air around me rippled once again, but this time I wasn't thrown into darkness. The world twisted before reforming in a large open room with orange walls. "Where are we?" I asked before a loud horn sounded from outside. I stepped towards one of the windows and looked out at the docks.

"I thought you might like to see your new friends." He gestured to a row of beds along one wall.

Walking past the row of beds, I couldn't help but notice the stark contrast between this clinical setting and the vibrant village I'd just left. Each villager, now lying motionless, was hooked up to a network of tubes and feeding devices. It was a jarring sight – the machinery ensuring their survival while their minds wandered in the Tekka's created world. The tubes, some attached to their arms, others discreetly tucked away, made me feel a bit uneasy, but I understood their necessity.

Medics in soft-soled shoes moved quietly between the beds. They checked and adjusted the tubes with practiced ease, their presence a silent yet constant reminder of the delicate balance between the two worlds these villagers inhabited.

As I neared the end of the row, I paused at a smaller bed, where a young girl lay. It took me a moment to recognize her as Jessara. She looked so different in this dormant state. Beside her, a man and a woman were deeply engrossed in reading a story aloud from a book. Their gentle tones and the loving way they turned the pages or brushed her hair away from her face spoke of a deep bond. I didn't need to be told – these were Jessara's parents, sharing stories in the hope that some part of it reached her.

I stood there for a moment, watching them. This scene, so full of love and quiet sorrow, was a powerful reminder of what the Tekka's magic had created: a lifeline for some, a tether for others. The medics continued their rounds, a silent dance of care and vigilance, while Jessara's parents remained lost in their story, their voices a soft lullaby in the hushed room.

As I stood by Jessara's bedside, lost in my thoughts, I was jolted back to reality by her mother's voice. "Can we help you?" I realized I had been staring, absorbed in my reflections about Jessara and her other life.

I cleared the lump in my throat. "I'm sorry, I didn't mean to disturb…"

"This is Liam," the Tekka introduced me with a warm smile. "He's just come from your daughter's world."

Jessara's mother stood up slowly, her eyes reflecting a sea of emotions. "You've seen our Jessara? Today? How is she doing?" Her voice trembled with a mixture of hope and longing.

A smile broke through my emotions, but it was quickly accompanied by tears. "She's absolutely perfect," I managed to say, surprised at my emotional response. Despite my brief acquaintance with Jessara, seeing her like this—so still and silent—so different from her vibrant self in the Tekka's world. She deserved more than this suspended existence; she deserved the laughter and warmth of her parents' embrace.

Jessara's father then stood, extending his hand toward me. His handshake was firm and full of gratitude. "Thank you for visiting her. Any friend of Jessara's is always welcome here," he said, his voice warm yet laden with unshed tears.

Taking a deep breath, I relayed Jessara's heartfelt message. "She asked me to tell you both that she loves you and misses you very much." A vivid memory of Jessara proudly talking about her books came to me. "She also mentioned her books are filling up with words, thanks to your stories. Seems like your reading is making its way to her, even here."

Upon hearing this, Jessara's parents shared a tight embrace, their tears mingling in a bittersweet moment of shared sorrow and joy. It was a poignant reminder of the power of their love, reaching across the boundaries of consciousness.

Catching the Tekka's nod of encouragement, I added somewhat hesitantly, "I know it might sound odd, but I promised Jessara I'd give her a hug in the real world…"

Her mother laughed through her tears, a sound full of love and heartache. "That sounds just like Jessara. She's always been one for hugs." She gestured towards Jessara, encouraging me to fulfill my promise.

I stepped closer to Jessara's bedside, feeling a sense of

reverence and responsibility. Gently, I wrapped my arms around her, delivering the hug I had promised. It was a simple act, yet one laden with profound meaning—a tangible connection between her two worlds, a promise kept, and a message of love conveyed. Jessara's small body remained still, but in that moment, I hoped she could feel the warmth and affection that her parents, and now I, held for her.

As I stepped back from Jessara's bedside, the Tekka spoke up, his tone gentle but firm. "Are you ready?" At first, I thought he was addressing me, but his gaze was fixed on Jessara's parents.

They looked at each other, their eyes still glistening with tears, and nodded resolutely. "We're ready," they said in unison, their arms wrapped around each other in a supportive embrace.

Confused, I turned to the Tekka. "What's happening?" I asked, a hint of worry creeping into my voice.

The Tekka offered a reassuring smile, noticing my concern. Jessara spends just one day a week in the world I created. We need to take her out for the rest of the week to slow down her mental aging. The time dilation in that world would make her grow up too fast otherwise."

Her mother, holding Jessara's hand, added softly, We want to preserve her childhood as much as possible. Even if it means bringing her back to this state." As she spoke, a medic approached the bed and began gently removing the feeding tube with practiced hands.

The Tekka placed his hand lightly on the bed, his expression one of quiet resolve. "Alright, I'll go and bring her back." As he said this, a subtle ripple disturbed the air around him. He turned to me, "She was excited to hear you'd already been to visit her." He chuckled, "She…"

"Liam…?" It was barely more than a whisper. I looked down to see her eyes fluttering open, focusing on me with a frail smile. "You're still here!"

CHAPTER SIXTEEN

The Burden of Unseen Powers

I stayed back when she opened her eyes. Her family was already around her, and something in the way they moved—quiet, focused—told me this was their moment, not mine. It didn't feel right to be part of it. I wasn't asked to leave, but I felt like I should have been.

Later, I said nothing about it to the team. Some moments aren't meant to be shared. Whatever passed between them in that room belonged to them alone. Still, it left an impression—joy, relief, and something harder to name. It's stayed with me in a quiet way, difficult to shake.

Soon after, the Tekka guided me back to the dorm. The sudden shift—from the weight of that moment to the calm of familiar walls—left me a little unsteady.

Ding, rising from his chair, saluted the Tekka with respect. Caught in the lingering tide of emotions, I impulsively embraced him, my arms encircling his figure. "Thank you, Ding," I murmured into his chest. As I stepped back, our eyes locked. "You aren't to blame for what happened to me. Don't carry that burden." His posture softened as if a colossal weight had been lifted from his shoulders. He didn't smile but responded with a firm nod and a salute, identical to the one he had offered the Tekka moments before.

"Thank you, my Prince," echoed Ding's voice in my mind.

"Do me a favor, Ding? Don't salute me," I chuckled, embracing him once more before turning to face the Tekka. His presence was a comforting testament to the journey between two worlds I had just traversed. A surge of deep gratitude filled me. "Thank you for allowing me to be part of that... for everything," I said, my voice saturated with heartfelt sincerity.

The Tekka nodded, his features a harmonious blend of solemnity and gentleness. "Remember, every experience molds you," he intoned, his words resonating with wisdom. "Your journey is far from over, Liam. Embrace it." He stood next to Ding, placing a hand on his shoulder before giving me a final look. "I will see you after you pass."

"Wait!" I said, surprising myself. "Why...? Why did you put me in this exam?"

The Tekka smiled. "Your father wanted you to take part."

With those final words, he and Ding disappeared, leaving me solitary in the dorm room. I paused, allowing myself a moment to process the lingering emotions of the encounter. But the reality of the ongoing exam beckoned, my team undoubtedly awaiting my return. Inhaling deeply, I fortified my resolve, ready to step back into the present.

The hallways before me were bland and pale, stretching out for a dozen meters or so, leading into what seemed like an endless maze of identical turns and straights. Each corridor was a mirror image of the last, their monotony broken only by the gradually increasing silver numbers on the white wooden doors, dotting the walls at regular intervals.

As I dashed along, my boots thudded rhythmically against the hard, carpeted floor, the sound echoing around me. A few startled passersby quickly sidestepped out of my path, but none were familiar faces, and I had no intention of stopping for a conversation. My gaze flickered into each open doorway I passed, a fleeting hope to spot my group, but after minutes of this fruitless search, a sinking realization dawned: 'I have absolutely no idea where I am.' I had been running blindly through an unfamiliar building, hopelessly lost in my quest.

Glancing over my shoulder, I slowed, considering retracing my steps. But before I could decide, "Ouch!" My right shoulder crashed into someone, the impact spinning me to the ground. Scrambling to my feet, I realized whom I had bumped into – Leana, the blond-haired girl from Kai's group. She had been carrying a large stack of papers, which now lay scattered across the floor due to my clumsiness.

She laughed off the mishap and bent down to gather the papers. "Here, let me help," I offered, dropping to all fours and hastily scooping them into a disorganized pile before handing them back to her. Curiosity piqued, I glanced at the top sheet. "What are all of these for?" I inquired.

She regained her footing, clutching the recovered papers. "I'm not sure, actually," she confessed, looking at the papers with a puzzled expression. As she flicked through them, straightening each sheet, she continued, "They were given to me by the Eulis examiner back in the lunch hall." Her fingers moved methodically, aligning the edges. "Didn't get much explanation, just that they needed to go to the Minor examiner. Been wandering around a bit since I didn't get any directions," she explained with a light chuckle, revealing a flash of her bright smile.

Her hands paused as she recalled her encounter. "Met one of the students along the way. He was really helpful." She gestured vaguely, adding, "Said he passed last year's exam and was helping out as a first-year Eulis, or something along those lines…"

I nodded, though I wasn't familiar with the student assistance program she mentioned. There seemed to be a lot about Eulis I still didn't know.

As our smiles met, my mind briefly wandered, curious about how many other students might be involved in helping with the exams.

Leana's voice brought me back to the moment. "Anyway, he pointed me in the right direction. Quite friendly," she mused, her gaze drifting for a second before snapping back.

"Well, I better get these papers where they're supposed to go," she said with renewed focus.

She began to move away, but then stopped and turned slightly. "Oh, by the way," she added, "I saw your old group in the lunch hall. If you keep going down this hallway and follow the bends, you should find it easily."

After thanking her, I headed towards the lunch hall. Navigating through a small cluster of people at the entrance, I stepped inside.

The interior of the lunch hall was an assault on the senses. The floor was an eye-catching checkerboard of white and pink, starkly contrasting with the vivid yellow of the walls. The rhythmic clinking of kitchen utensils echoed from a small open doorway at the far end of the hall, opposite a long counter that stretched from one side of the room to the other. A queue of people waited in front of the counter, their anticipation palpable as they neared the front of the line for their meal.

Approaching the counter, the aroma of the food wafted towards me, a mix of scents that piqued my appetite despite the lackluster appearance of the dishes. The greasy meats and runny side dishes betrayed their hasty preparation, lacking the attention to detail one might hope for in a meal. Yet, if one sought visual vibrancy over gastronomic delight, this was the place. The dishes displayed a spectrum of colors rivaling the Crest of Nation, with its interplay of greens, blues, yellows, purples, and even more vivid hues.

The crowded room suggested that the food might be better than its appearance implied. I let my gaze wander, eavesdropping on snippets of conversation – some grumbling about past tests, others excitedly discussing family visits.

Spotting my group seated at a white rectangular table in the center of the room, I made my way over. Tyran and Naya were engaged in conversation with Lammat, who sat alone on the opposite side. I pulled out a spare chair and sat down across from Naya.

Lammat looked up, his expression shifting from surprise to a welcoming smile. "Oh hi, Liam, is everything okay?" he asked with his characteristic cheerfulness.

"Yeah, everything's fine," I responded, returning his smile. I tried to push aside the weight of the Tekka's words from my mind.

Lammat tilted his head, a hint of skepticism in his gaze. "Really?" He glanced at Tyran, then back to me. "We heard different."

My eyes flicked to Tyran, who quickly shook his head. "I haven't said anything, Liam. Just ignore him, he thinks he's being funny," Tyran remarked, his expression taking on a slightly darker edge. "But then again, how about filling me in on what I missed?"

I smiled back, opting for a bit of mystery. "Maybe some other time, Tyran. Besides, you're all bound to find out sooner or later."

"What's that supposed to mean?" Naya inquired, her curiosity piqued.

Tyran smiled. "Don't be so nosy," he teased, picking up a drink from the table and bringing it to his lips. "Just look at Liam's crest," he quipped quickly before taking a sip.

Reacting instinctively, I swung my foot under the table towards Tyran, but instead, there was an unexpected yelp. Naya toppled off her chair backward, clutching her leg. Tyran stared at me, his expression a mixture of confusion and surprise. I quickly got up and rushed around the table to Naya's side. Meanwhile, Lammat, along with a few others in the room who had witnessed the mishap, couldn't contain their laughter.

"Oh, I'm so sorry," I blurted out, extending a hand to help Naya to her feet.

She gave a slight laugh, despite the discomfort, and hopped on her unharmed leg. "Ow, bully!" She leaned on my shoulder for support, rubbing her injured shin.

Tyran stood up, his expression turning serious. "Okay, we've both finished here, so how about we head back over to our quarters?" He glanced down at Lammat. "You coming?"

Lammat, who was in the midst of devouring a large chunk of meat, looked up and shook his head. "No, I've still got some food to finish. But I'll be over in a few minutes, okay?"

"Alright, Liam, I'm yet to see you eat anything this exam, so pick something up and eat it while we walk back."

Acknowledging his response with a nod, I grabbed whatever looked interesting and we began to make our way toward our quarters, leaving the bustling lunch hall behind us.

As Naya settled onto her bed, my gaze drifted to the now silent fireplace across the room. Its crackling warmth had ceased, and the chairs it once heated lay empty. Approaching, I leaned against the chair where the Tekka had been seated, lost in thought about where they might have gone.

Tyran, seating himself on his bed, looked at me with a hint of curiosity. "So, Liam, are you going to share what the 'almighty' Tekka told you?" His gaze flickered to the chair behind me.

Settling down next to Naya, I responded, "I learned his name. You don't have to keep calling him the Tekka."

Surprise flickered in Tyran's eyes, and he exchanged a quick glance with Naya, who turned to me, her astonishment evident. "You know the Tekka's name?" she asked, her voice tinged with disbelief. "But, nobody's meant to know a Tekka's real name! It's a matter of security or... something. What is it?"

Before I could answer, Tyran interjected. "Liam, don't tell her." His gaze sharpened. "Is that all he told you? His name?"

"No, it was about something else..." I casually gestured toward my crest. "But if he asked you to leave, maybe I shouldn't tell you either," I said, pondering. "Though, I can't see what harm it would do if I did."

Throughout this conversation, Naya's eyes darted between Tyran and me. "What might cause problems?" she inquired, still massaging her injured leg. I glanced at the wound and was horrified to realize that my kick had scraped off a good amount of skin.

Concerned, I gently touched her arm. "Oh, Naya, are you sure you're okay?"

Naya laughed again, picking at the wound slightly, "Don't worry about it. I'm not bleeding. Just a bit bruised, is all."

Tyran let out an exasperated sigh. "Do we need to discuss this now?"

Turning back to Tyran, I shifted the conversation. "What can you tell me about Crossers, Tyran?"

He sat up, his frown returning. "Crossers? Not much is known about them. Zeipher is the most notorious Crosser… or was, since he's now frozen in the Glacier Kingdom."

My heart leaped at Tyran's mention of the word 'Kingdom.' A flurry of thoughts swirled through my mind, dominated by the echoing question, 'Could I truly be the Prince?'

Naya, her curiosity evidently piqued, turned towards Tyran with a tentative air. "Tyran, can I ask you something? It's okay if you'd rather not answer."

Tyran's expression shifted to one of guarded caution, but he motioned for her to go ahead.

She gathered her thoughts, her voice hesitant but firm. "You talked about Zeipher being frozen in time, like what Eulis described when he returned. Does that imply Zeipher might still be alive? And if someone were to remove the charm, would he come back… along with your father?"

A shadow crossed Tyran's face, his jaw setting firmly as he lowered his gaze to his intertwined fingers, then raised it back to meet hers. "I've also wondered that," he admitted, his voice laced with a blend of hope and skepticism. "I asked Eulis about the charm when I was a child. He was clear that not even the most powerful Guardians could break it." He let out a sigh tinged with a sense of irony and resignation. "It appears that paradoxically, only someone of Zeipher's caliber could..." He trailed off, leaving an unspoken understanding hanging in the air: Zeipher, alongside Meltek and Tyran's father, were indefinitely ensnared.

Naya's voice was soft, tinged with regret. "I... I'm sorry," she stammered, her hand reaching out to mine, seeking a comforting connection.

Tyran observed the gesture, his eyebrows arching slightly, then redirected his inquisitive gaze back to me. "Why this sudden interest in Crossers? Result of the...?" he gestured to the crest.

So he did know about me losing my memory due to its removal. I looked at Naya, but she was once again focused on her leg. Taking a moment, I replied, "It's just... curiosity. How do their powers compare to Guardians? Are Crossers inherently stronger?"

Tyran pondered for a moment, seemingly measuring his words. "Well, it's not straightforward," he started. "Take Zeipher, for example. His notoriety stems from his power before becoming a Crosser. Even as a Goud, he was able to stand up to a Guardian, I heard."

Leaning back, Tyran's gaze drifted off to the mountains framed in the window above Lammat's bed. "Crossers have a unique skill – they can emulate any spell or power they've directly witnessed." His eyes suddenly grew wider, a realization dawning on him. He turned back to me, his voice dropping to a more serious tone. "So, if a Crosser saw a Guardian use a cloning technique, for instance, they could replicate it exactly."

The tension in the room thickened, palpable, and electric, as Tyran's gaze bored into me, his suspicions mounting like a gathering storm. "What else can they do?" I asked, my voice a cautious whisper, as if afraid to awaken some hidden truth.

Tyran studied me, his eyes like piercing shards of ice.

"Depends on their encounters," he replied slowly, each word deliberate, hanging in the air like a loaded promise.

Meanwhile, Naya, distracted by a growing discomfort, rubbed her leg. "It's itching like crazy now!" she exclaimed, a grimace of discomfort etched on her face.

Suddenly, like a predator pouncing on its prey, Tyran sprung to his feet and closed the gap between us with startling agility. His eyes, intense and unblinking, locked onto mine. He reached out, his fingers brushing against my hair, murmuring to himself, "Not black…"

Naya's laughter, tinged with nervousness, cut through the tension. "Tyran, are you checking if Liam's a Crosser?"

His grin was wolfish, predatory. "Actually, yes."

In a heartbeat, Tyran's fist hurtled towards my face. Time seemed to slow as I felt the impact, a burst of pain exploding across my senses. I was sent spinning, my body crashing against the hard, unyielding corner of the fireplace.

"Tyran!" Naya's voice was one of shock and anger as she surged to her feet.

"That's why you have an Overseer!" he barked. "You have the copy ability, don't you? That explains everything! Like how you perfectly replicated that energy ball in the last exam." He lunged at me, his grip iron-tight on my collar, his fist connecting with brutal force against my mouth. "The Tekka reversed the Crosser transformation? Incredible!"

Naya's voice was sharp with fear. "He's not a Crosser, Tyran! You're acting insane!"

I writhed under Tyran's grasp, my mind racing. Tyran turned to Naya, his voice laced with a cold certainty. "You didn't see him in the forest, Naya! He did things no normal Minor could do. He replicated me, anticipated unseen attacks… and his speed…"

I mustered my strength against Tyran's unyielding hold. "I didn't mean to do any of that!"

Tyran's face was inches from mine, his breath hot with intensity. "I've always distrusted Crossers…"

"I'm not a Crosser, Tyran," I pleaded, turning to Naya, her face a portrait of terror. Facing Tyran again, I admitted, "But I was…"

Tyran's roar was triumphant. "There's the confession!" He pushed me back violently, then yanked me to my feet.

Naya's scream was piercing, desperate. "Tyran, he's bleeding! Enough!"

With a strength that seemed superhuman, Tyran hurled me across the room. I flew like a ragdoll, crashing into the bedpost with a sickening thud, knocking it clear out of the way before I collapsed to the floor in a heap. Scrambling to my feet, I stumbled towards Naya, only to see her step back, fear and confusion written all over her face.

As Tyran advanced, I raised my arms defensively, bracing for another blow. "Tyran… please! I didn't mean any harm." My voice was a desperate plea. "The Tekka told me I was a Crosser, but they removed my crest!" The words tumbled out in a rush, beyond caring about any consequences.

To my surprise, Tyran's arms extended, not to strike, but to gently pat my shoulders. "I know," he said, a mischievous glint in his eyes. "I just wanted to see if you could control yourself."

I stood there, dumbfounded, my expression one of bewildered shock. "What?" was all I managed to utter.

"I wanted to test your reaction," he explained, strolling back to his bed to sit down. Naya, caught in a dance of confusion, eventually settled on her bed, still processing the turn of events. Tyran lay back, his laughter filling the room. "That hit, Liam… it didn't really hurt you, did it?"

I approached him cautiously, still reeling from the unexpected ordeal. "Actually, yes it did. I think I'm bleeding."

He gave a small laugh with a hint of triumph. Sitting up, he reached under his bed, pulling out a small white medical kit. He flicked it open and casually tossed a bandage in my direction. "Clean up the blood," he instructed.

I stood frozen for a moment, my irritation at Tyran's

actions mingling with confusion. Eventually, I unwrapped the bandage and began to dab at my chin. The blood was minimal, but the fact that there was any at all was unsettling.

Tyran's smile seemed to grow even wider as he turned his attention to Naya. "See?"

Naya's eyes were fixed on my face, studying it intently. "There's no cut… he's healed already?" Her voice was filled with wonder and disbelief. She stood up, moving closer to get a better look. I instinctively pulled back, feeling like a specimen under observation. "This is just like what happened to his head the other day," she remarked, a note of realization in her voice. Tyran nodded in confirmation, and Naya's gaze shifted to the medical kit. "Hey! Why didn't you bring this out earlier for my leg?"

Tyran's grin broadened as he glanced at her leg.

Naya looked down, her expression transforming into one of shock. "It's healed!" she exclaimed. Both of us examined her leg, now devoid of any sign of injury. She turned back to me, her eyes wide with a mixture of awe and perplexity. "You healed me…" She began to step forward, then stopped abruptly. "You used to be a Crosser?"

I diverted my gaze from Naya, my voice tinged with uncertainty. "I don't know… that's just what the Tekka told me." Naya quietly sat down on her bed, her expression contemplative. "But I can't remember anything about being a Crosser. They said it was just for a few minutes before removing my crest. I'm sorry if this makes you uncomfortable, I didn't know how to bring it up."

Tyran's laughter rang out from his bed, breaking the tension. "I owe you an apology, Liam. The Tekka should realize he can't hide things from me." I glanced over at him, intrigued. "I first noticed something different about you back in the forest," he continued, a smile playing on his lips. "I've been trained to expect the unexpected, but beating someone like Kai? That was something else." His grin widened. "You went in with no plan and managed it by just standing there.

You created that copy, I'm sure of it. You must have seen that technique used somewhere before."

"You didn't have to attack him to prove it though!" said Naya.

Tyran ignored her, leaning forward, his tone serious. "Then there's your ability to heal wounds. Just a touch and they heal instantly." He paused, his gaze thoughtful. "You were a Crosser for only minutes, yet you've learned an incredible amount of magic in that short time." He raised an eyebrow. "Who would've thought we'd have friendly Crossers?"

The door opened abruptly, and Lammat entered with a buoyant energy. I quickly exchanged a glance with Tyran, silently conveying that this information was not for everyone. Tyran subtly acknowledged with a nod.

"Hello, everyone!" Lammat announced cheerfully, flopping onto his bed. "What's the hot topic today?"

Tyran looked over at him briefly before lying back down. Naya, wearing a gentle smile, turned to me. After a hesitant pause, she said "Liam, feel like taking a walk?"

Lammat sat up with a grin. "Seems like you two are hitting it off."

I shot Lammat a disapproving frown and turned back to Naya. "You sure?" She nodded, standing up and smoothing out her clothes. "Where are we going?" I asked, curiosity piqued as we headed towards the door.

She glanced at me, a mysterious smile on her lips. "It's a surprise. You'll see when we get there."

CHAPTER SEVENTEEN
Under the Starlit Sky

"Why aren't you more upset about what Tyran did?" Naya asked, her voice echoing slightly in the empty hallway as we ambled through the dimly lit corridors.

I pondered for a moment before responding with a subdued shrug. "He said it was just a test."

"But that doesn't justify him hitting you," she argued, her brow furrowed in disapproval.

I stole a glance at her, noticing her unwavering gaze was still fixed ahead. "For all I know, I was the one who created that copy of Tyran in the forest. And during the second exam... you saw what happened. I didn't mean to do any of it." I sighed, feeling the weight of uncertainty. "Honestly, I'm scared of what I might be capable of without realizing it."

Her expression softened as she finally met my gaze. "The fact that you didn't retaliate says a lot about your character, Liam."

I was puzzled. "What does that mean?" I asked.

"It means you're not what they label a 'Crosser'." She shook her head, her voice tinged with skepticism. "It's hard to believe they've found a way to reverse someone from being a Crosser."

Our conversation ebbed and flowed as we navigated the labyrinthine corridors of the building. Eventually, we reached a set of towering orange double doors. Naya paused, a hint of excitement twinkling in her eyes. With a gentle push against the metal bar, the doors swung open, revealing the expansive darkness of the night.

The outside world greeted us with a cool embrace, the night air crisp and refreshing. "It's quite dark," I commented, observing how the scant light from nearby lamps created pools of illumination in the surrounding gloom. Moths fluttered erratically around the lights, their wings casting fleeting shadows.

"The winter nights are drawing in," Naya remarked casually, her hand finding mine with an easy familiarity.

I hesitated momentarily. "But we were told to stay on the grounds."

With a light laugh, Naya reassured me, "We're not leaving the grounds, just the building. I found this spot when I was younger, and it's become my sanctuary." She gestured towards a gently sloping hill, its summit crowned by the silhouette of a lone tree, bathed in the soft glow of the moonlight.

Reluctantly, I allowed myself to be led by her, intrigued by the promise of this secret place she cherished. "My father worked here years ago, and I spent a lot of time exploring. This spot was my escape from my brothers, a place where I could just breathe and be myself." Her laughter, light and carefree, filled the night as we walked towards the hill, the grass whispering beneath our feet.

In a minute, we had reached the summit of the hill, where the tree stood like a sentinel against the starry sky. Naya settled herself against the tree's trunk and extended an arm, inviting me to join her. I lowered myself onto the cool, dry grass beside her, feeling the night's chill against my skin.

Turning my gaze away from the dim outline of the building, I looked upwards. The night sky was a canvas of darkness punctuated by twinkling stars, with wisps of blue clouds swirling gently overhead, dissolving into the void. "Wow, this is a nice place," I remarked, my voice carrying a note of wonder. I glanced at Naya. "You used to come here often?"

She nodded, her smile reflective. "Yeah, I loved it here. The stars always seem so much brighter and clearer. They light up the entire town like a fairy tale." Her voice quivered slightly, betraying a shiver.

Concerned, I leaned away to look at her. "Are you okay?"

Her teeth chattered as she nodded. "Just cold," she admitted, casting an amused look at my chainmail top. "That doesn't look very warm."

I smiled, feeling oddly detached from the cold. "I guess I just don't feel it much."

"Well, I do," she said, moving closer and resting her head on my shoulder. After a moment, she raised her head slightly. "Liam, do you really think you were a Crosser? It would explain a lot, but... is there any way to be sure?"

I wrapped an arm around her, offering warmth as she snuggled against my side. I had no answer to her question, and my silence seemed to communicate as much. She didn't press further.

"We're taught that Crossers are inherently evil... lacking restraint or mercy," she mused aloud.

I gave a soft shrug, my voice low. "I don't know what to say. I don't remember my past." I paused, my gaze dropping to meet hers. "Does that scare you? Are you afraid of what I might be?"

Naya's laughter was light, almost musical. "Afraid of you? That's impossible. There's something about you, Liam. Part of me says to stay away, wary that you might be just pretending to be this sweet, soft, slightly oblivious boy." Her grin widened, accompanied by another chuckle. "But I don't buy it. I've never been one to just go along with what everyone else thinks. You don't seem capable of hurting anyone. You're too... gentle," she said, exhaling a misty breath in the cold night air.

A question tugged at my mind. "Naya, why did you want to come out here?" I gently eased her away to look into her eyes. "You've been shivering since we sat down. If you're cold, we can go back inside."

She shook her head, her voice muffled against my side. "No, I'm fine. I just wanted to see if you were alright after what Tyran did. Maybe get away from him and Lammat for a bit." A soft laugh escaped her lips.

Remembering earlier events, I smiled. "I noticed they startled you a lot. You kept tumbling off the bed."

Her expression shifted to one of discomfort. "Yeah, sorry about that..." she began, hesitantly.

I looked at her, puzzled. "Why do you need to apologize? You didn't do anything wrong."

She sighed, sitting up straight. "No, I shouldn't have tried to kiss you."

Puzzlement clouded my face. "You tried to what?"

Her gaze bore into mine, disbelief and realization dawning. "You didn't realize? What did you think I was doing?"

My blank stare must have been telling. "What?"

Naya faltered, a blush creeping up her cheeks. "I know we've only just met, but..."

I laughed. "You know, I don't think anyone has ever tried to kiss me, let alone managed to."

She paused, her embarrassment turning to laughter. "You're kidding."

I pointed at my head. "I wasn't joking when I said I had lost my memory. Honestly, I doubt I've ever been kissed."

She let out a sigh. "When I tried before, it was to thank you for literally carrying me through the first exam. There's something about you..."

"Are you still thankful?" I asked, a hint of curiosity in my voice.

Naya's laughter was light, and she leaned her head against me once more. But this time, I gently nudged her away, leaning in closer to look into her eyes.

For a moment, she fell silent, the shivering ceasing. She hesitated, her eyes searching mine, squinting slightly as if trying to decipher a puzzle. Abruptly, she closed the distance between us, her lips meeting mine in a brief, surprising kiss.

As she pulled back, her smile was tinged with embarrassment. I blinked, slightly dazed, not quite sure how to react. Seeing my confusion, her eyes widened. "Oh, I'm sorry. I shouldn't have… Just forget it," she stammered.

"So that's what a kiss feels like?" I asked, still processing the new sensation. Naya nodded slowly, a soft smile playing on her lips. "Why do people do that?"

Her laughter mingled with a cough. "You're really something, Liam," she said, tapping my leg and sitting up a bit. "I was wondering, would you like to go to the dance with me after the third exam?"

"Are we not going with Lammat and Tyran?" I queried, still trying to understand.

Naya let out an amused sigh and placed her hand on mine. "Listen, Liam, I'm asking you on a date… just the two of us. As a couple."

I was puzzled. "Why me? Why not Tyran? You seemed to like him."

She chuckled. "It wasn't like that with Tyran. He's just… well-known, you know, because of his dad." She paused, her eyes glistening as they met mine. "But I like you."

"And that's why you kissed me?" I ventured.

"Yes, that's why," she confirmed.

Impulsively, I leaned in and kissed her again. She pulled back, a look of surprise on her face. I smiled, feeling a newfound confidence. "I like you too."

Lying in my bed, I found myself occasionally glancing over at Naya. Each time, I caught her quickly averting her gaze, a bashful smile gracing her features. The room was filled with a comfortable silence, punctuated only by the sound of Lammat's steady breathing and the occasional footsteps echoing in the hallway.

My eyes wandered to the window above Lammat's bed. The night sky was a deep shade of blue, adorned with twinkling stars. The silhouette of the tree atop the hill swayed gently in the night breeze, its form contrasted against the looming, dark outlines of the distant mountains.

A sense of contentment washed over me. For the first time in a long while, I felt genuinely happy. Surrounded by friends who cared for me, and who wanted my happiness as much as their own, I felt a profound sense of belonging. Sharing my thoughts and feelings with them bridged the gap of uncertainty and brought me closer to them.

I rolled over, pulling the covers a bit tighter around me, and closed my eyes. The rhythm of Lammat's breathing, unexpectedly soothing, was the last thing I was aware of before sleep enveloped me, carrying me away into a peaceful slumber.

CHAPTER EIGHTEEN
The Third Trial

The morning air in the dormitory was crisp, hinting at the approaching winter months. I awoke to the muted sound of activity around me, my mind immediately flooded with the realization of the day's significance: the third exam. I glanced around the room, noting Naya was already up and about, while Tyran's and Lammat's beds lay empty, the sheets neatly arranged.

I swung my legs over the side of the bed, feeling a bundle of excitement and nerves in my stomach. As I dressed, my movements were automatic, yet my mind was elsewhere, pondering the day ahead. Pulling on my clothes, I couldn't help but feel a sense of surrealness about everything.

Once ready, I approached the window, my thoughts drifting. The two distant mountains stood as silent guardians on the horizon. I squinted, trying to see if the palace was visible from this distance, but it remained elusive, shrouded in the morning mist.

Leaning closer, I exhaled slowly, my breath fogging up the glass. On impulse, I traced the outline of a palace on the misted window, a whimsical attempt to bring a piece of my lost past into the present.

Behind me, Naya's voice broke the quiet. "Feel like getting some breakfast?"

* * *

The morning at the lunch hall was filled with a casual ambiance, the kind that often precedes something significant. As we sat, our conversation meandered through trivial topics, from the dorm's less-than-comfortable beds to speculative musings about the impending exam. The only certainty we had was that it was once again set in the forest, a detail that seemed to loom large in our minds.

Lammat arrived a bit later, his presence immediately infusing the table with an added layer of cheerfulness. "Morning!" he greeted us, placing a loaded tray of food in front of him with a flourish.

Naya, with a hint of surprise, asked, "You haven't had breakfast yet?"

Lammat, grinning broadly, responded, "Of course I have! This is just round two!"

"We were trying to guess what today's exam might involve," I contributed, brushing away a stray crumb from the tabletop.

Lammat, now busy with something round and blue from his tray, looked up before popping it into his mouth. "Yeah? Any clues about where we're supposed to meet?"

Naya chimed in, "There were flyers posted. Looks like we're heading back into the forest."

His grin widened mischievously. "Don't worry, I'm sure you'll manage to stay awake this time," he joked, glancing at me with a playful nudge toward Naya, silently mouthing 'lazy'. I couldn't help but chuckle.

Naya, feigning indignation but clearly amused, retorted, "Hey, I passed, didn't I?"

Lammat leaned back, his expression turning contemplative. "You know, it's odd. So far, we haven't had to do anything... well, traditionally Lylackian."

His comment piqued my interest. "What do you mean?"

He elaborated, "Think about it. You could pass the first exam with stealth or sheer luck. The second was more about speaking up against wrongdoing." He shrugged, grabbing another morsel. "Not exactly the stuff of legends."

"So, you think they've toned down the exams this year?"

Lammat shook his head. "I remember stories of past exams being real challenges. They forged people like Meltek, Tylak, Eulis…"

"And Zeipher," I added, recalling the stories I'd heard.

"Exactly!" Lammat exclaimed, pointing at me in agreement. "Real powerhouses."

Naya, thoughtful, said, "Maybe they changed the exams because of what happened with Zeipher."

Lammat raised his eyebrows, tilting his head. "Why's that?"

Naya explained, "Well, he went berserk, right? Killed lots of people? Maybe they're trying to prevent another such incident."

Lammat shook his head, unconvinced. "I think it's more about strengthening the army. Saddul seems to be doing the same."

I looked up at him, "You think they're preparing for war?"

Lammat nodded solemnly, then his expression shifted to one of excitement. "Speaking of war, I heard about your little scuffle with Tyran last night." He playfully flicked a blue food item at me, hitting me squarely between the eyes. "How about a friendly match between us sometime?"

Naya burst out laughing. "I have a feeling Liam might be a bit more than you can handle, Lammat."

He flashed a cheeky grin. "He lost to Tyran, though, right?"

I laughed, "Yeah, you could say that."

Lammat's eyes sparkled with a hint of mischief as he leaned closer, his voice infused with playfulness and earnest suggestion. "You know, we've got a bit of time before the exam starts. What do you think about sneaking in a quick practice?"

Naya, her attention momentarily captured by the clock on the wall, weighed in. "Well, actually, we only have about thirty minutes before we need to be at the meeting point. I was planning to get there a little early, to maybe…"

"To catch a sneak peek of what the exam might involve?" Lammat interjected, a touch of understanding in his tone as he pushed his tray aside. "I see where you're coming from. Alright then, let's get going."

A grateful smile danced on Naya's lips. "Thanks, Lammat."

As we rose from the table, Lammat subtly edged closer to me, lowering his voice. "Listen, if today doesn't leave us any time for that one-on-one challenge, how about we pair up for the exam?" He gestured slightly towards Naya, adding with a sly grin, "Unless, of course, you've already been teamed up with someone else for the day."

I laughed, shaking my head. "No, no such plans yet."

Lammat's expression brightened. "Great! Let's team up then!"

Catching bits of our conversation, Naya looked back over her shoulder with a laugh. "What if the exam turns out to be solo today?"

With a playful scowl, Lammat retorted, "Then I guess I'll have to seek you out on the field of battle." He aimed a mock-serious glare at me.

Minutes later, as we ascended the staircase leading to the immense, dome-enclosed forest, a chuckle escaped me. The realization dawned that my last visit here was under less conscious circumstances.

"Hold on, we've been underground this whole time?" I

asked in disbelief.

Naya's laughter was sudden. "You've only just noticed?"

"But our rooms have windows," I countered, my confusion evident.

Lammat grinned, a hint of amusement in his voice. "Yeah, those aren't real. It's illusion magic. They show you whatever you want to see, really."

Naya sighed, a wistful tone in her voice. "I always see the city outside. What about you two?"

Lammat's smile widened. "I see a vast, empty field. Endless green grass."

I paused, feeling a touch bashful. "I saw that tree you showed me last night."

Naya's smile was gentle, yet quizzical. "Didn't you find it odd that you could see it from our room? That tree's in the garden way at the back of the facility."

I shrugged, feeling slightly lost. "Honestly, this place feels like a labyrinth to me. I have no idea how everyone navigates so effortlessly."

Naya's eyes twinkled with mirth. "It's sweet that you thought of going back there, though."

Lammat groaned playfully. "Oh, gods… You two were making out under that tree, weren't you?" Naya's laughter rang out as I stumbled over my words. Lammat rolled his eyes. "Yep, definitely a kiss."

Reaching the top of the staircase, the vast expanse of trees unfolded before us, and once again, I was enveloped by the glass ceiling. To my surprise, we weren't the first to arrive. Kai sat cross-legged, his gaze fixed on the forest, his attire still resembling intertwining vines. Beside him stood Leana, who turned slightly at our approach. Her smile was reserved as she met my gaze but remained silent, her eyes briefly flickering towards Kai with a subtle roll.

"Oh yeah," Naya remarked, a hint of deflation in her voice. "I forgot he passed the last exam."

"Thinking of settling some old scores?" Lammat asked, his

expression characteristically neutral.

Naya shook her head, a note of resignation in her voice. "Let's be real; I wouldn't stand a chance against him here, in this forest."

Kai stood, stretching slightly. "Glad to see you've learned something from our last encounter… Naya, right?" He turned to us with a smile that didn't quite reach his eyes. "Oh look, the whole gang's here."

"Oh look, it's plant boy!" quipped Lammat.

I offered a nod towards Leana. "Hi."

She returned the nod, her lips pressed in a tight line.

Kai stepped closer to Naya. "Look, I'm sorry for what happened before."

"It's alright," Naya replied, her voice carrying a note of indifference.

"Honestly, I thought you'd be nimble enough to dodge something so basic," he followed, his expression adopting a false look of concern.

Leana cringed at his words, her eyes closing briefly in discomfort.

Naya, taking a step towards Kai, her tone laced with a mix of sarcasm and challenge, said, "And here I was, thinking I was about to receive a genuine apology."

Kai laughed, his arrogance unabated. "Apologize for what, exactly? Remember, you were the one who attacked first."

Lammat, seizing the moment, jumped in with a question tinged with curiosity. "What about the rest of your team? They didn't make it this far?"

Kai's face lit up with a broad, almost triumphant smile. "No, they didn't pass. It's just the two of us," he said, turning towards Leana. "But I wouldn't be too concerned about our chances."

Leana managed a strained smile, though her eyes locked with mine, conveying a depth of unspoken words. I sensed an undercurrent of tension, something amiss in her gaze.

As Naya began to speak, "Whatever this exam has in store for us—"

"Forget it," I cut her off, gesturing away from Kai, near the gate that led into the forest. "Let's head over there."

Kai, with a dismissive mutter of "Whatever," turned his attention back to the forest, settling down on the ground once again.

Only a few minutes passed before the sound of footsteps signaled the arrival of more examinees. "Here they come," said Lammat, his gaze sharpening, and demeanor shifting to that of a seasoned observer, his eyes scanning the newcomers as they ascended the staircase.

The first to appear was a tall, lean figure with striking silver hair that cascaded down his back. "That's Eron," Lammat whispered, his eyes following the newcomer's graceful movements. "He's known for his agility and precision. Rumor has it he can scale any surface without making a sound."

Naya raised an eyebrow, clearly impressed. "And you know this… how?" she asked, but Lammat was already pointing back at the staircase.

Next came a duo, one with fiery red hair and a confident stride, the other more reserved, with a thoughtful expression and deep, dark eyes. "The redhead is Calia, and her blond quiet friend is Joren," Lammat continued. "Calia is all about raw power, while Joren is the brains. They're a formidable pair. Joren's known for outsmarting opponents in ways you can't even imagine."

I eyed Lammat but offered no comment. He pointed out each new arrival, sharing snippets of information as if he'd been meticulously cataloging their strengths and weaknesses throughout the exam. Every time I thought I had him figured out…

The fourth to emerge was a stocky individual with an easy smile and hands that never seemed to stop moving. "That's Rexus," said Lammat, a hint of caution in his voice. "Don't let him fool you. He's a master at crafting traps and illusions. People tend to underestimate him until it's too late."

Naya nodded, her eyes fixed on Rexus. "He looks harmless enough."

"Want to have a guess who put the trap together that took out Liam?"

My hand reached for the back of my head on its own. "Right," I said simply.

Finally, a figure who commanded immediate attention stepped onto the platform. Tall and imposing, with an air of undeniable authority, she had an intense gaze that seemed to miss nothing. "And she," Lammat said, his voice lower, "is Veyra. She's the one you need to watch out for. She's on par with Tyran in terms of strength and skill. Some say she's even better."

"Speaking of which..." said Naya, pointing at Tyran as he ascended, walking alongside the Goud examiner.

I exchanged a glance with Naya, both of us registering the significance of Lammat's warning.

Lammat leaned back against the fence, his eyes never leaving the new arrivals. "This exam is about to get a lot more interesting," he mused, a hint of excitement in his tone.

"You sure you don't want to team up with me instead, Liam?" asked Naya with a smile.

"Hey, I definitely got there first this time!" Lammat said with a chuckle. "Besides, something tells me we're all going to get the chance to unleash ourselves in this exam."

I nodded in agreement, feeling a surge of anticipation. "Let's see what they've got."

"Tyran!" Naya's voice cut through the murmur of the gathering, her hand waving energetically to catch his attention. With a nonchalance that seemed almost innate, Tyran approached us, hands comfortably buried in his pockets. Naya, undeterred by his aloof demeanor, plunged straight in. "If it's teams of two, do you fancy teaming up with me today?"

Tyran paused, his gaze briefly flitting over our group, before offering a non-committal shrug. "Sure, why not?"

Lammat chuckled. "See? He's absolutely thrilled, Naya!" His laughter was infectious, and I found myself joining in.

I turned to Tyran. "Any ideas what this exam might be about?"

His response was characteristically blunt, eyes scanning the forest ahead. "None I care to share," he said, his focus unwavering.

The moment was interrupted by the Goud examiner's commanding voice, calling all examinees to gather. We clustered together, forming a group. As I quickly scanned the faces, I counted eleven out of the original eighty who had started the first exam.

The Goud examiner waited for a hush to settle over us before beginning. "Congratulations to all of you for getting this far. I was hoping for a few more this year, but the Minor's exam seemed to cause more losses than expected."

"Losses?" I whispered to Lammat, a sense of unease creeping into my voice. "Did people die this year?" Lammat's response was a downcast look, heavy with unspoken confirmation, yet he remained silent.

The Goud examiner continued, undeterred by the undercurrent of tension. "Out of the eleven of you here, only six will pass." A ripple of protest fluttered through the group but was swiftly quelled as the examiner raised a hand for silence. "Also, unlike the previous two exams, this one may span several days." This time the announcement was met with silence, the air charged with unvoiced questions and apprehensions.

As the Goud examiner's announcement settled over us, he made his way to stand before the forest's gate, his presence commanding attention. "You'll need to form teams of three for this exam," he stated clearly. His words sent a jolt through my heart. My eyes darted between Tyran, Naya, and Lammat, each of us momentarily caught off guard. "One team will be two members," he added, "but that team will receive an additional couple of hours to plan for the exam." He scanned our faces, then gestured with his hands. "Well? Get to it."

Turning to the others, I felt the urgency of the moment. "So, what do we do now?"

Lammat, sticking to our previously discussed plan, stepped in closer. "I'm with you, Liam, no matter if you want a duo or trio."

Naya seemed momentarily hesitant. "Tyran, how about we be the team of two? Those extra hours could give us an edge…"

"No," replied Tyran flatly. "I don't need additional time."

Without another word, he turned and walked away, finally stopping in front of Kai and Leana. I stared after him, mouth agape, for what felt like minutes, only turning to find Naya and Lammat pulling the same expression.

"You're kidding me!" said Lammat, breaking the silence.

"What's he doing?" asked Naya.

"He's thinking Kai's stronger than us…" I muttered, a tinge of betrayal coloring my words.

"I mean," started Lammat, "I guess it makes sense… they're the only ones he's been able to get any sort of read on."

"Can I join your team?" asked Naya, still not looking away.

Our shared laughter lightened the mood, a momentary relief from the tension. Lammat, channeling Tyran's earlier nonchalance, responded, "Sure, why not?"

"We're absolutely thrilled!" I chimed in. Naya playfully swatted at me, her smile returning.

The Goud examiner's voice, filled with a sense of satisfaction, cut through the murmurs of the group, drawing our attention back to him. "That's what I like to see!" he exclaimed, appreciating the swift formation of our teams. "Nice and fast. It looks like we have our teams set." He then turned towards Calia and Joren, the duo among us. "You two can stay for the explanation, but you won't be participating until later today."

With a flurry of flicks of his wrists, the Goud conjured

eleven blue orbs that floated in the air before him. The orbs maneuvered themselves, aligning into groups that mirrored our newly formed teams, with one group consisting of just two.

"Hm, not bad control," muttered Lammat under his breath.

I immediately recognized it as a more advanced version of the Eulis' exam's magic. "Eleven at the same time?" I said, leaning toward Naya.

Naya nodded, her eyes fixed on the display. "Yeah, that's seriously impressive. He's maintaining complete control over each one."

The Goud examiner's voice brought our focus back to him as he announced, "These are your teams." He then reached into his pocket and pulled out a small purple crystal. With a casual motion, he threw it into the ground. The crystal rapidly expanded, embedding itself into the soil and standing taller than the Goud. "And this," he declared, "is your objective."

"What is that?" asked Lammat aloud to nobody in particular.

Naya, with a hint of surprise in her voice, answered, "Training crystals. You've never used one before?"

The Goud continued. "Each crystal is built to withstand a maximum of three strikes." To demonstrate, he casually threw a punch at the crystal, causing large cracks to spiderweb across its surface. "There's no limit to how hard you hit them." He then enveloped his fist with mana and delivered a powerful blow to the crystal. The cracks deepened, and fragments chipped away, yet the crystal remained mostly intact. "However, you can't just tap the crystals lightly," he said, demonstrating with a gentle knock that left the crystal unharmed. Then, with a swift, decisive punch, he shattered it, sending shards scattering.

I looked around to gauge everyone's reactions and my gaze briefly locked with Leana's. Her eyes held mine for a fleeting moment, revealing a depth of concern, before she looked away, her expression clouded with uncertainty.

"The heart of this exam," the Goud continued, "is to protect your crystal while attempting to destroy your opponents'."

His words sank in, and a wave of dread washed over me. I couldn't shake the feeling of guilt at my unease, aware of our team's apparent lack of combat experience.

"So, is this just a free-for-all battle royal?" asked Kai, raising his hand.

The Goud shook his head, dismissing the idea. "That wouldn't be fair to our duo," he said, his voice firm, signaling a more intricate challenge ahead. With a gesture, the floating orbs before us shifted, realigning to demonstrate his next point. Five of the orbs drifted to one side, and then two groups of three formed from the remaining six, mirroring our newly established teams, facing each other in a silent standoff.

"The first team to successfully shatter their opponent's crystal," he continued, his gaze sweeping over us, "will have the privilege of selecting a single member from the defeated team." As he spoke, one of the orbs seamlessly floated over to the opposing group, illustrating his point. The visual left us with an uneven scenario: a team of two and another now bolstered to four.

This visual demonstration, simple yet stark, sent a wave of tension through the group. The realization that our alliances could shift dramatically, depending on the outcomes of these clashes, added a layer of complexity and strategy that none of us had anticipated.

Naya's voice was barely above a whisper, yet it carried a weight of apprehension. "Oh no..." I reached for her hand, seeking to offer some semblance of comfort. Her grip was firm, her anxiety palpable.

"If you lose a match, are you out of the exam?" I asked, not fully understanding.

"No, you will only fail the exam if you are the only person left in your team. That's where our duo, Calia and Joren, come into play!" he announced, gesturing towards two orbs set apart from the rest. As he spoke, the four orbs representing the larger teams ascended, clearing space for the duo's orbs to join center stage.

"As before, the winning team will choose a member to join them from the losing team. But in a two-on-two situation," he continued, his voice lowering, "whoever isn't chosen..." The orb representing the selected individual shifted from one team to the other, symbolizing their potential transfer, before the lone orb abruptly vanished. "They will fail the exam immediately."

Gasps filled the air, one of them my own.

Calia's fiery hair seemed to bristle with indignation, "How is that fair? We get just one chance, while everyone else gets more?"

"While the rest of you head into battle without prior knowledge, our duo will be allowed to observe alongside the examiners," he explained, gesturing towards Calia and Joren. This promised them a strategic advantage, and a chance to study their potential opponents' tactics and weaknesses. Whichever team loses first will be going up against them next.

Tyran raised a question that seemed to linger in the air. "What about the other team of three? What happens to them?"

The examiner's response was swift and straightforward. "They won't have the same opportunity to observe the battles. However, they will be taken to a separate practice area equipped with a real crystal." He paused, allowing us to absorb the information. "There, they can strategize and coordinate, preparing themselves for the challenge ahead."

"But you said only six of us will move onto the next exam," said the boy Lammat named Rexus. "The numbers don't add up."

"Trust me, they will. The final match will be between two teams of five," replied the examiner. "The four not chosen from the losing team will be sent home."

Kai's question cut through the tension, his tone sharp with a hint of eagerness. "Who gets to decide who fights first?"

The examiner's response was laced with amusement, his laughter echoing slightly. "I'll leave that decision in your hands," he said. "The first team to issue a challenge, and have it accepted, will initiate the battles. Once accepted, the battle must take place within the hour. However, if the challenge isn't accepted within twenty-four hours, that team will fail the exam."

Without hesitation, Kai's demeanor shifted, his movements swift and decisive as he turned and faced me squarely. "In that case, I challenge your team," he declared, his eyes locked onto mine with unwavering determination.

A fleeting glance towards Tyran revealed the stark reality of our situation. The prospect of facing him in combat sent a myriad of emotions coursing through me. Was I truly ready to confront a former ally? I was still grappling with this quandary when suddenly, a voice broke the silence.

"We accept!" The words, clear and assertive, echoed around us. For a moment, I was taken aback, looking around to see who among us had responded with such readiness. The surprise was immediate as I realized that the voice was my own.

CHAPTER NINETEEN
Crystals of Conflict

Naya's reaction was swift and urgent. She yanked me back by the collar, spinning me around to face her. Her eyes were wide, her voice barely above a whisper but laced with concern. "What are you doing?" she hissed. "Didn't you hear me earlier? Going up against Kai is a bad idea."

Before I could respond, the examiner interjected, his tone light, almost playful. "I need a team majority to agree before the battle can begin," he announced, his arms crossed, a slight smirk playing on his lips.

"Sure, I'll agree!"

"Lammat!" Naya's voice rose in exasperation, her frustration evident.

The examiner clapped his hands together, seemingly pleased with the unfolding drama. "Alright, so we have our first two teams!" he declared. "Can our other trio remain here? You'll be set up shortly. The rest of you, follow me."

As we began to follow the Goud, he pushed open the gates and led us into the depths of the forest. Naya turned to us, her expression one of disbelief and concern. "What's wrong with you two?"

I was still trying to process my reaction. "I have no idea what happened," I admitted, the surprise still fresh. "The words just… came out."

Lammat grinned confidently. "We'll be fine," he reassured

us. His grin widened as he added, "Besides, wouldn't it be great to get some revenge on Kai for knocking you out, and on Tyran for abandoning us?"

His words, meant to be encouraging, hung in the air as we ventured further into the forest. The reality of our upcoming confrontation with Kai and Tyran, two of the most formidable opponents, loomed ahead.

As we followed the Goud examiner deeper into the forest, the dense canopy above us cast dappled shadows on our path. The air was filled with the scent of damp earth and the sound of distant bird calls. It was in this surreal setting that Calia and Joren approached us, their steps silent yet purposeful.

Calia, with her fiery red hair catching the sunlight filtering through the leaves, wore an easy, confident smile. I'm Calia, and this is Joren." She gestured to her companion, who, though silent, had an intense look in his eyes. It was as if he were analyzing us, taking in every detail from our posture to the subtleties of our expressions. "Looks like we'll be facing off next, then!"

Lammat let out a laugh. "Thanks for the vote of confidence!"

Calia's laughter, light and playful, eased the tension in the air for a moment. "I'm kidding, I'm kidding," she said, her eyes sparkling with amusement. "But really, Tyran and Kai? That's a tough first match." She shook her head, respect and concern evident in her expression. "Do me a favor, though. If you guys win, pick one of them for your team. I'd rather not face off against both in our match."

Lammat responded with a grin. "We'll keep that in mind. No promises, though."

As the conversation flowed, I found my gaze drifting to Leana, who walked a few steps ahead of us. Her blonde hair swayed in rhythm with her steps, catching glints of sunlight. Despite our occasional conversations, she remained an enigma, her true capabilities and strengths hidden behind a veil of quiet composure. Her presence on Tyran and Kai's team added another layer of unpredictability to the upcoming challenge.

Naya, still reeling from the recent developments, managed a polite but cautious response. "Nice to meet you, Calia, Joren." Her voice held a tinge of reluctance, betraying her wariness.

Calia's demeanor remained friendly, but there was a sharpness to her gaze, like that of a seasoned player gauging her opponents. "So, how are you feeling about the exam? It's quite a setup, isn't it?" Her tone was casual, but it was clear she was fishing for any insight that might give her an edge.

Before we could delve deeper into the conversation, the Goud examiner turned back to us, two crystals in hand. He presented one to each team with a flourish. "Here are your crystals. Remember, you need to choose where to position them. The only rule is they can't be placed closer than one hundred paces, nor greater than two hundred from your opponent's crystal." His instructions were clear, adding yet another strategic layer to the challenge ahead.

We each took a moment to examine the crystals, their surfaces shimmering with an inner light. The task of positioning them would require careful consideration, balancing defense and accessibility. As we pondered this new element of the exam, the forest around us seemed to close in, a reminder of the imminent battle and the necessity of a well-thought-out strategy.

Kai's nonchalance was evident as he toyed with the crystal, bouncing it on his palm before tossing it over his shoulder without a second thought. It landed in a nearby clearing, transforming into its larger form with a flourish. He sauntered over to lean against it, exuding a confidence that bordered on arrogance. "We'll be fine wherever, so why worry about it?" he declared, his gaze sweeping over us challengingly.

Naya reacted quickly. "Don't even think about it," she said firmly, snatching the crystal from Lammat's grasp before he could mimic Kai's carefree action.

"Aww…" Lammat muttered, his playful disappointment evident.

The examiner then turned to our team. "Take your time and place your crystal. Remember, it must be no closer than one hundred paces from here, but also no more than two hundred paces." He looked back to Kai's crystal and shrugged. "I was going to explain the rule that the challenged can see the challenger's crystal location, but not the other way around, but I guess that's no longer needed."

As we separated and ventured deeper into the dense forest, the task of finding the perfect location for our crystal sparked a flurry of strategic discussions among us. Lammat was the first to suggest, pointing towards a dense thicket. "How about there? It's well-covered, hard to spot."

I contemplated his suggestion, but something about it didn't sit right with me. "It's good for concealment," I mused, "but too dense. It might hinder our access when we need to defend it."

Naya nodded in agreement, her eyes scanning the surrounding terrain. "We need a balance of accessibility and defense. Somewhere we can react quickly if needed, but not too obvious for the others."

We continued to weave our way through the forest, each of us throwing ideas into the mix. I pointed to a small clearing near a brook. "What about near that water source? It's open, but we can use the sound of the water to mask our movements."

Lammat considered it, then shook his head. "As well as theirs. Besides, it's too exposed. We'd be in trouble if they approached from the cover of the trees."

Finally, Naya halted near a gently sloping hill with a cluster of boulders at the top. "Here," she said decisively. "We have the high ground, and these rocks provide natural cover. Plus, we can see anyone approaching from a distance."

Her choice made sense. The elevated position offered a strategic advantage, and the boulders could serve as both concealment and protection. We all nodded in agreement, and Naya carefully placed the crystal at the base of the largest boulder.

As the crystal transformed and grew, a bright beam of light emerged, tracing a path along the forest floor. Intrigued, I followed the beam with my gaze, noticing a similar light extending from Kai's crystal. The two beams met in the middle of the forest, and at their convergence, a large dome of red light erupted from the ground, encapsulating both our crystals and teams within its boundaries.

Moments later, Tyran's team, along with the Goud, Calia, and Joren, joined us in the center of the illuminated dome. The examiner's face bore a look of satisfaction as he surveyed the setup, the teams now enclosed in a space defined by the glowing barrier.

The examiner, with a gesture towards the line of light snaking across the forest floor, addressed us all. "As you may have noticed, hiding your crystal is futile."

The examiner cleared his throat, capturing our full attention as he prepared to detail the final rules of the exam. His tone was stern, underscoring the seriousness of his words. "First and foremost," he began, pausing for emphasis, "let me make this abundantly clear: killing is strictly forbidden in this exam. Any such act will result in immediate disqualification."

He scanned our faces, ensuring we understood the gravity of his statement, before continuing. "Injuries are a possibility in any combat scenario. Should you sustain an injury, I strongly advise you to exit the dome for medical treatment." His gaze lingered on each of us for a moment. "But remember, this is a crucial point – if you leave the dome of your own volition, there will be no re-entry. You will be out of the battle for good. I'm not risking additional injuries for no good reason."

Lammat, his brow furrowed in thought, raised a hand. "What if someone is forced out of the dome? Does the rule still apply?"

The examiner's nod was solemn. "Indeed, it does. The

barrier is designed for one-way entry only. However, if you're forced out, your participation is over until the reset."

"Reset?" I asked.

A hint of a smile then played on the examiner's lips. "You'll see," he said, his eyes twinkling with a mischievous glint, "there's one rule I've decided not to disclose. I think it'll add an extra layer of excitement to discover it amid battle."

"Weird..." said Lammat, casually.

The final instruction, however, was straightforward. "The battle begins the moment all teams have placed their hands on their crystals."

With that, he turned to Calia and Joren, inviting them to follow him out of the barrier. Their steps were measured, their expressions displaying anticipation and strategy as they exited the illuminated enclosure.

As the examiner and the duo exited the dome, I felt a surge of uncertainty mixed with determination. I took a few steps forward. "Tyran," I began, calling his attention to me. My voice was steady but filled with curiosity, "Why did you team up with Kai?"

He met my gaze, his eyes a well of unreadable thoughts. Then, without a word, he turned away, walking towards his crystal with Kai and Leana at his side. His silence left me with a sense of unresolved curiosity, but there was no time to dwell on it.

As we traced the line of light back to our crystal, our footsteps were measured, each of us lost in thought about the impending battle. Lammat broke the silence first, his voice tinged with a hint of frustration. "You know, with Kai here, he probably already has control over the entire forest." He shook his head, muttering, "Damned elementalists."

Naya nodded, her expression focused. "I've got a good handle on telekinesis and barrier magic. I should stay close to the crystal, and set up some defensive spells."

I weighed in, considering our strengths and weaknesses. "Maybe I should stay at the midway point," I suggested hesitantly, my concern about my combat skills surfacing. "And Lammat, you could be up front."

Lammat, however, was quick to shoot down the idea. "No, we can't play it safe. Our best shot is if we're aggressive. We need to prioritize attacking over defending. All that matters is landing three hits on their crystal first."

His words resonated with a sense of urgency, compelling us to adopt a more offensive strategy. We reached our crystal, standing before it with a newfound determination. Before we placed our hands on it, Naya shared a final thought, her tone laced with caution. "Be ready for an immediate attack, likely from Kai and Tyran together. They won't waste any time."

I nodded, my mind racing with possibilities. "If we get the chance, let's try to push them out of the arena."

With our strategy set, we each placed a hand on the crystal, bracing ourselves for the onset of the battle. For a moment, nothing seemed to happen, the forest around us eerily silent. Then, suddenly, the dome surrounding us turned a deep shade of blue, signaling the start of the battle.

Lammat and I immediately dashed off toward the opponent's crystal. Our strategy was clear - strike first, strike fast. The forest blurred past us as we sprinted through the underbrush, but what we saw upon nearing their crystal took us by surprise.

It was Kai who had stayed back as the defender. His hands were moving in a complex dance, manipulating vines and roots that wrapped around their crystal, creating a natural barrier. "Lammat, Kai's fortifying their crystal with—" I started, but my warning was cut short.

Suddenly, as if materializing from the very air itself, Tyran appeared. His emergence was like a force of nature – swift, powerful, and utterly surprising. The impact of his collision sent shockwaves through my body. He crashed into me with the full weight of his formidable training and unyielding determination. His grip on me was like iron, strong and inescapable.

For a fleeting moment, I was disoriented, struggling to comprehend the rapid shift in direction. Then, as Tyran's momentum forcefully propelled me with him, a chilling realization dawned on me. He wasn't just engaging in combat; he had a specific, calculated intention. His movements, precise and controlled, were driving me sideways, steadily and relentlessly.

The clarity of his plan struck me with a sense of terror. He was maneuvering me towards the edge of the dome, the transparent barrier that marked the boundary of our battlefield. This wasn't a fight; it was an attempt to remove me from the battle entirely.

I attempted to dig my heels into the forest floor, trying desperately to counteract his momentum. But Tyran's strength was overwhelming, his resolve unwavering. I could slow him, but not stop him. The edge of the dome loomed closer, the static buzz of the barrier growing louder in my ears. Panic surged within me as I realized the impending threat of being forced out of the dome – and out of the battle.

In a desperate bid for freedom, I twisted, turned, and pushed against Tyran's solid form. But his grip was unrelenting, his focus singular. We were inches away from the dome now, its energy field crackling with static energy.

Just as I felt the first tingle of the dome's barrier against my shoulder, a hand clamped down on Tyran's shoulder. He vanished from my field of vision as Lammat, displaying a strength I had never seen in him before, hurled Tyran backward, away from the dome's edge.

Gasping for breath, I stumbled, barely catching myself from falling. Lammat's voice reached me, a blend of reprimand and encouragement. "You're holding back, Liam! Come on, you're stronger than this!"

Regaining our composure, Lammat and I wasted no time. We bolted back towards Kai's crystal, which by now was nearly engulfed in a thick entanglement of vines. Kai had covered all but the smallest portion of the crystal – a mere tip peeking through the dense greenery.

With astonishing speed and precision, Lammat scooped me up, his muscles coiling like a spring. In one fluid, powerful motion, he hurled me directly toward the tiny exposed tip of the crystal. The velocity of his throw was such that I became a living projectile, cutting through the air toward our target.

As I soared towards the crystal, Lammat was already executing the next phase of his plan. His hands moved in a blur, conjuring an intense beam of energy that he directed straight into the heart of the vines. The beam, radiant and fierce, sliced through the foliage like a hot knife through butter.

The vines withered and burned under the onslaught of Lammat's energy beam, disintegrating in a matter of seconds. The path was clear for my approach, and as I neared the crystal, it began to glow with a bright light, reflecting and refracting Lammat's beam.

This display of Lammat's power was awe-inspiring. He managed to execute multiple actions simultaneously – launching me with pinpoint accuracy while strategically clearing a path for my attack.

As I braced for impact with the crystal, ready to deliver a blow, the world around me suddenly shifted. In a disorienting blur, I was teleported back to our crystal, flung through the air, and crashed into a nearby tree.

I dropped to the ground in a tangle of limbs. Regaining my footing, I looked around, still trying to process the abrupt turn of events. "What happened?" I groaned, my body aching from the collision.

Naya was panting, her back against a boulder beside our crystal, then sliding down. "You could have told me she was a fighter!" she exclaimed, the strain evident in her voice.

Lammat stood calmly, scanning the surroundings. "The dome's red again," he noted, a hint of amusement in his voice. "This must be the extra rule the examiner kept to himself." His chuckle was light, almost appreciative of the twist. "That's pretty funny."

Naya shot him a quizzical look, still catching her breath. "What? Did you manage to hit their crystal?"

"I nearly did," I replied, brushing off dirt and leaves. "But I got teleported back here just before making contact."

Lammat nodded, piecing things together. "It must have been my attack then. Damn, I thought we'd be able to land more than one hit." He mused, touching the crystal thoughtfully. "Clever. The crystals are connected, not only to each other but also to us."

I nodded, understanding. "The reset…"

"Like rounds in a fight?" Naya queried, slowly standing up.

"Exactly," Lammat confirmed. "Once one crystal receives damage, everyone is reset to their original positions." He glanced at me as I approached. "We probably need to all touch the crystal to restart the battle."

Kneeling in front of Naya, I asked with concern, "Leana made it here?"

Naya nodded, awe and frustration evident in her eyes. "By the gods, that girl can fight. If I hadn't put up barriers…" She paused, shaking her head. "My telekinesis did nothing against her."

"Is she fast?" Lammat inquired, his mind already strategizing.

"Not especially," Naya replied, massaging her arm. "She came from the trees. I tried pushing her away, but it was like hitting a wall." She winced as she flexed her fingers. "Blocked one punch, but my arm's taken a beating."

I reached out, gently touching her arm. She flinched initially, then relaxed, a look of surprise crossing her face. "Better?" I asked, hopeful.

A smile broke across Naya's expression as she stretched her arm, flexing her fingers with ease. "Any chance you can teach me that?" she joked, her spirits lifted.

I returned her smile, feeling a sense of pride and surprise. My ability to heal, both others and myself, was becoming more apparent and powerful.

Lammat interrupted our brief respite. "Come on, time for round two."

We gathered at the crystal, each placing a hand upon its surface. As the dome shifted back to blue, Lammat and I exchanged a determined nod. Without another word, we took off running once more.

As the second round commenced under the blue-lit dome, Lammat and I charged toward the center, our senses heightened and ready for confrontation. There, we were met by Tyran, Kai, and Leana, a trio poised and ready for battle.

"Leaving the crystal unguarded?" Lammat called out, eyeing them curiously.

Kai, with a sly grin, retorted, "Could say the same about you."

I lunged towards Kai, aiming a swift blow in his direction. However, my attack was abruptly intercepted as Tyran's hand latched onto my wrist. With a fluid motion, he twisted my arm, using my momentum to flip me over his back. I hit the ground with a thud, quickly rolling to regain my footing.

The battle then escalated into an intense exchange of blows and maneuvers. Tyran was a whirlwind of motion, his movements sharp and precise. He weaved around Lammat's attacks with a dancer's grace, always just out of reach, yet ever-threatening.

Vines whipped out of the ground, attempting to entangle our feet and disrupt our balance. I narrowly dodged a tendril that shot towards me, only to find myself facing Leana's calculated advance.

In a moment of imbalance, I stumbled, my foot caught in a loop of vine. Instantly, Leana's hand shot out, steadying me. Her touch was brief, but in her eyes, there was a flicker of unintended camaraderie. She quickly glanced towards Kai, concern etched on her face as if worried about having shown a moment of empathy towards the enemy.

It was this brief lapse that Lammat capitalized on. With a roar, he charged at Leana, catching her off guard and forcing her to shift her focus back to him. I took the opportunity to break free from the vine's grasp, jumping back into the fray.

The fight was a cacophony of clashing wills and skills, a testament to our resolve. Lammat's strength was like a force of nature, his attacks powerful and relentless. Tyran and Leana, a seamless unit, circled us with a predator's grace, their attacks coordinated and relentless. Leana's movements were fluid and precise, her strikes aimed with purpose. Tyran, meanwhile, darted in and out of reach, his well-timed parries and counterattacks keeping us on the defensive.

Kai, not content with just a supporting role, turned the forest itself against us. Vines, thick and thorny, erupted from the ground, entwining around our legs, trying to ensnare us. Their grip tightened with every second, making it increasingly difficult to move.

Amidst this, Kai called out to his teammates, "Go, hit their crystal!" Tyran and Leana didn't hesitate, breaking away from the melee and sprinting towards Naya.

Left to contend with Kai, Lammat and I faced a growing labyrinth of roots and vines. The vines constricted, binding our movements. I struggled against their embrace, but they were unyielding, tightening around me with every attempt to break free.

Lammat, however, was a force unto himself. His muscles bulged as he ripped through Kai's botanical bindings, his raw power evident in each torn vine. Kai, his face a mask of concentration, summoned more vines in response, but Lammat seemed to gain strength from the challenge, tearing through them with primal energy.

Just as Lammat broke through the last of the vines, reaching out to grab Kai, the world around us shifted. In a disorienting instant, we found ourselves teleported back to our crystal. As I regained my bearings, I saw the spiderweb of cracks covering its surface.

Naya, shaking her head in disbelief, voiced our predicament, "Leana came back... and she brought Tyran with her this time."

The situation was starkly clear. Despite our best efforts, the combined skills and strategy of Tyran and Leana, amplified by Kai's control over the elements, had outmaneuvered us.

"Sorry," I said softly, the weight of our situation settling in. "All three of them met us in the middle."

"All three?" Naya repeated, her surprise evident. "They left their crystal completely unguarded?"

"That they did," Lammat muttered, his voice laced with frustration and determination. "But don't worry, we can still win this."

I felt a surge of resolve. "And then we can get Tyran back," I said, offering them a reassuring smile.

Lammat looked at me quizzically. "You actually want him back?"

I paused, taken aback by the question. "What do you mean? He's our teammate."

"Liam, Tyran could have joined any team. He's pretty much famous here," Lammat pointed out, his tone matter-of-fact. "Why did he join Kai?"

I pondered for a moment. "Well, who would you choose?"

Naya chimed in, her voice thoughtful. "I'd choose that Leana girl."

"Yeah, me too," Lammat agreed, nodding. He shrugged, catching my eye. "Tyran's not a team player, is he? He's more likely to use you as bait than as an ally."

I shook my head, trying to refocus on the immediate challenge. "Well, that's beside the point now. They've adapted to me and Lammat just charging in. What should we do differently?"

Naya stepped forward, her expression determined. "Do you mind if I have a go at attacking?"

"Sure," I responded, feeling a shift in our strategy might

be what we needed. "I wouldn't mind trying my hand at defending the crystal, if that's alright."

Lammat chuckled, his confidence infectious. "Go for it! I trust both of you. Let's make this work." He then placed his palm against the crystal. "Don't worry, we've got this."

We gathered around the crystal, each placing a hand upon its surface. As we braced ourselves for the next round, the dome shifted colors, turning blue once again.

Alone at our crystal, I watched as Lammat and Naya vanished into the trees, their figures blending seamlessly with the dense forest. The stillness around me was unsettling, my senses stretched to their limits, awaiting any hint of movement or sound.

Unexpectedly, a voice shattered the silence. "Tyran has you completely read, you know."

Whirling around, I found Leana sitting casually atop our crystal. Reacting instinctively, I lunged at her, knocking her off balance and pinning her to the ground.

Leana let out a groan under my weight. "Ouch, that was a bit rough," she said with a hint of playfulness. "Not interested in talking then?"

I hesitated, realizing that she had plenty of time to hit the crystal. I slowly got off her, my mind racing with questions. "How did you get past me?" I asked, puzzled.

She sat up, brushing dirt off her shorts, a sly smile on her lips. "Let's just say I know my way around a forest. You really should pay better attention, not just straight in front of you." She playfully flicked my forehead, her teasing tone laced with a subtle warning.

Leana picked up a rock, twirling it between her fingers. "Why aren't you fighting?" I asked, still wary.

Her gaze met mine, the flirtatiousness fading into something more serious. "Because Tyran shouldn't be trusted. He always planned to join our team. Knew about the exam ahead of time, had it all figured out." She aimed a finger at me. "Told us everything we needed to know about your team."

"Why would he do that?" The question slipped out.

Leana shrugged, her eyes never leaving mine. "You should ask him." She sighed. "If I take any longer, I'll have to deal with Kai, so sorry about this." She suddenly launched the rock she'd been playing with straight at our crystal.

In a flash of motion, I dove, my hand outstretched. The rock was inches from the crystal when my fingers wrapped around it, halting its trajectory. A small victory, I thought, until I noticed the second rock.

It appeared from nowhere, a perfect throw from my blind spot. I barely had time to register it before it struck the crystal with a resounding crack that echoed through the forest.

Leana stood up, dusting herself off. "You really need to pay better attention, Liam," she said with a wink, just before vanishing.

As Lammat and Naya materialized beside me, their bodies tensed in combat stances, the air charged with frustration and determination. Naya's expression was one of disbelief, her voice tinged with regret. "No, we were so close!" she lamented, clearly ruing the missed opportunity.

"No, we weren't close at all." He muttered. He surveyed our crystal, now webbed with cracks. Kneeling, his eyes traced the path of light leading to the opposing team's crystal. "One more hit and we've lost this," he stated, his tone grave.

Naya turned to me, her brow furrowed in concern. "What happened here?" she asked.

Shaking my head, I recounted my encounter with Leana. "She's incredibly skilled. I didn't even hear her approach until she started talking," I admitted, still astounded by her stealth.

"She spoke to you?"

I nodded, recalling the conversation. "Yeah, but you're not going to like this." The revelation still hung heavily in my mind. "She said Tyran knew about this exam beforehand and planned everything. Him switching teams, sharing our skills... everything."

"Of course he did." Lammat sighed, a look of frustration

crossing his face. He extended his arm along the line of light towards the enemy's crystal, taking hold of the wrist with his other. "Think I can hit it from here?" he mused aloud.

Naya gasped. "You figured out how to use energy beams?"

I confirmed, "That's how we damaged their crystal last time."

Naya's astonishment grew. "That's an incredibly high-level ability!" Her gaze followed Lammat's arm. "But the distance... How far can you project a beam?"

Lammat clenched his hand into a fist and then slowly opened it, as if measuring the distance in his mind. "Honestly? About ten paces or so," he concluded, standing up. "But if we can get in closer..."

I chimed in, sensing a shift in our strategy. "All of us this time? As long as we can hit their crystal before they hit ours, we've still got a chance."

Naya confidently placed her hand on the crystal, her grin conveying both determination and a hint of mischief. "Don't worry about me lagging behind. I'm faster than I look," she said with a wink.

Lammat joined in, placing his hand next to hers. "If we lose here, then it's game over for team Lammat!" he declared, half-jokingly.

With a shared chuckle, I joined them, placing my hand on the crystal. "For team Lammat, then."

The dome shifted to blue, a visual cue for the beginning of the next round. With a united resolve, we dashed towards our opponents.

We reached the opponent's crystal without encountering any resistance. Lammat broke the silence, his voice tinged with urgency. "They might have had the same idea as us. They could be at our crystal already."

I didn't hesitate. Leaping forward, I aimed to strike their crystal, but Tyran materialized out of thin air once again, his foot arcing toward me in a swift kick. Time seemed to slow as

I moved to block, but Naya, with astonishing speed, jumped between us. Tyran's eyes shifted to her, a nonchalant tilt of his head, and then the kick connected. The sound of snapping bone was sickening, followed by Naya's agonized scream.

Her body curled around Tyran's leg before being flung away, disappearing into the underbrush. Fury overtook me, and I lunged at Tyran, a punch driven by raw anger. But before it could land, Leana appeared, her foot lightly prodding Tyran, effortlessly moving him out of the path of my attack.

Time resumed its normal pace, and my punch carried me forward, straight into one of Kai's roots. It pierced through my shoulder, twisting and anchoring itself into the ground, immobilizing me.

Lammat, who had been aiming an energy beam at the crystal, hesitated as our eyes met. Then, with a resolute expression, he turned and fired the beam at me instead. The vine was obliterated, freeing me from its grasp.

"Go after Tyran!" he shouted, charging up another beam and aiming at the crystal.

I propelled myself off the ground, soaring upwards towards the blue dome. Below, I spotted Tyran nearing our crystal. I descended rapidly, crashing down onto him just before he could strike. I pinned him to the ground, his face pressed into the dirt. "Why did you betray us?" I yelled. Tyran struggled, but I pressed harder. "You told them everything about us!"

"Not everything," Tyran muttered. In a sudden move, he twisted, snapping his own arm to break free. With his free hand, he pushed against my face, flinging me away.

I landed hard a few paces away, disoriented. Tyran stood up, his arm already healing. "So, all you have to do is make skin contact. Good to know."

I struggled to my feet, anger boiling inside me. "Why, Tyran? What did you have to gain from this?"

"You don't understand, Liam," he replied, his voice cold.

"I thought we were friends!" I shouted, my voice echoing

through the forest.

Tyran's laugh was harsh, void of warmth. "What gave you that idea?"

Driven by a blend of anger and desperation, I lunged at Tyran once more, my every muscle tensed for the attack. My fist sliced through the air, aimed with all the force I could manage.

With a swift, fluid motion that spoke of his superior combat training, he intercepted me. His hands grasped my arm, once again redirecting my momentum with a practiced ease. In one seamless movement, he twisted, using my force against me, and hurled me past him.

The world blurred as I spun uncontrollably before I crashed into our crystal. There was a deafening crack as the crystal fractured under the strain, the sound echoing ominously through the forest.

For a moment, time seemed to stand still. I floated amidst the remnants of the shattered crystal, its shards scattered around me like a mirror reflecting our defeat before time resumed and I crashed down to the dirt. The realization hit hard – we had lost. The plan, our efforts, our unity, all had come to naught in the face of Tyran's calculated betrayal and strategy.

I struggled to my feet, pain coursing through me, as the reality of our loss and the depth of Tyran's deception sank in. It was a bitter pill to swallow, the knowledge that we had been outplayed and outmaneuvered from the start.

As I struggled to keep my focus, Tyran's gaze lingered on me, unreadable and distant. The world around me faded in and out, my vision blurring with each passing moment. We were locked in a silent standoff, a wordless exchange that seemed to stretch on indefinitely.

Gradually, the others converged around us. Kai and Leana flanked Tyran, their expressions triumphant yet wary. Lammat, showing a rare seriousness, supported Naya as they made their way towards me.

"I'm sorry..." I managed to say, my voice barely above a

whisper, my gaze dropping to the ground.

Lammat smiled broadly. "You did great, Liam," he reassured me.

"If you didn't need to save me from the vine, if instead you hit the crystal..."

"Then you could have died," Lammat cut in, his tone grave. "That vine was insane. I wasn't sure how deep it had gone. It might've already punctured a lung." He gestured towards my chest.

Following his gaze, I saw the wound near my shoulder, the reality of the injury setting in only as I acknowledged it. "Ow," I grimaced, attempting to see the extent of the injury. "Did it go all the way through?"

Lammat winced. "Yeah, it did." His concern was evident. "You need to get that looked at immediately."

I shook my head, my eyes drifting back to Tyran. "We're not finished yet."

Naya, stepping closer, feigned a casual glance at my wound before whispering, "Why aren't you healing?"

I could only shrug in response. "Not sure. How are you doing?"

She glanced at her left arm, her expression hardening. "Tyran broke it," she said, her voice tinged with bitterness.

Gently, I took her hand, inspecting the injury. As I touched her, her eyes widened, a shiver running through her body, followed by a reassuring nod of acknowledgment.

Kai, breaking the tense atmosphere, clapped his hands together. "Good match, everyone!"

Naya, her patience wearing thin, turned to him. "Don't drag this out. Just make your choice."

Kai's smile didn't waver. "Oh, we've made our choice already."

Tyran, still looking at me, finally spoke. "Come on, Lammat," he said, his voice steady. "We're leaving."

CHAPTER TWENTY
The Siblings

Naya and I found ourselves reassigned to a new dorm room, markedly smaller than the one we had shared with Lammat and Tyran. The room had only two beds and a single window, its sparse furnishings a stark reminder of how close we had come to failing.

I lay on one of the beds, a deep sense of loss weighing heavily on me. The absence of Lammat and Tyran felt like a void, their departure leaving an unspoken tension in the air.

Naya, meanwhile, busied herself with attending to the wound on my shoulder. Her concern was evident in her gentle touch and focused expression. "You really should get someone to look at this," she urged, her voice laced with worry.

I winced as she prodded the wound, the pain more intense than I had expected. "No, I can't," I insisted, the memory of the medics' reactions still fresh in my mind. "Remember how confused they were when I healed before? If it happens again, they'll start asking questions. I don't want anyone looking too closely into what I can do."

Naya nodded in understanding but continued her careful examination. "It's strange that it hurts you so much," she mused, leaning in for a closer look. Last time you healed so quickly."

As she inspected the wound, a realization dawned on her. "Liam, the chainmail you were wearing, it looks like it's embedded in the wound. Maybe that's what's preventing it from healing?"

I winced as the pain intensified with the removal of my chainmail top. "Yeah, that hurt..." I admitted, trying to mask the discomfort.

Naya peered closely at the wound, her expression turning to one of concern. "Yeah, I can see them... inside you." She paused, looking at me earnestly. "I still think you should call a medic."

I considered her suggestion for a moment, then offered an alternative. "Or," I began, shaking my head, "you could use your telekinesis?"

Her eyes widened at the suggestion. "Liam, there's a hole right through you! I'm amazed you're not bleeding out!"

Despite the seriousness of the situation, I couldn't help but force a laugh, trying to lighten the mood. "Think of it as practice," I said, lying back down and looking up at her. "Please?"

Naya hesitated, weighing the risk. Her eyes flicked between the wound and my face, torn between concern and the desire to help. Finally, she took a deep breath, a look of determination settling over her.

"Okay," she said, her voice steady. "But you tell me if it hurts too much."

I nodded, bracing myself. As Naya concentrated, I could feel the subtle movement within the wound as she carefully manipulated her telekinesis to extract the chainmail links. It was an odd sensation, a mixture of sharp pain and relief as each piece was removed. My teeth gritted, trying to stop myself from moving or crying out.

I watched Naya's focused expression, her brow furrowed in concentration. The process was intricate and required her full attention. Despite the pain, I was in awe of her control and precision.

One by one, the links were extracted, and with each one removed, I could feel the wound beginning to heal. Naya worked meticulously, ensuring no further damage was caused.

After what seemed like an eternity, the last link was removed. I could feel the wound closing up, the pain subsiding. Naya let out a sigh of relief, her shoulders sagging as the tension left her body.

"You're okay," she said, more to herself than to me, a small smile of relief on her lips.

I sat up, testing my mobility, and found that I was indeed okay. The wound had closed, and there was no sign of the injury that had been there moments ago.

"Thank you," I said, genuinely grateful. "You probably just saved my life."

Naya's laugh was light and filled with a touch of disbelief. "I wouldn't go that far. It looks like your body was already healing, but the process halted when it encountered the chainmail links." She delicately lifted one of the tiny links on the tip of her finger, examining it closely. "I always thought armor like this was supposed to protect the wearer."

"Maybe it's ornamental?" I mused, recalling the decorative pieces I had seen at Ding's friend's inn. Picking up the chainmail top, a sense of nostalgia washed over me. "You know, this was my first gift."

Naya took the top from me, her eyes thoughtful. "You know what, it might take some time, but I think I can fix it." She extended her hand, intending to gather the scattered pieces with her telekinesis.

I started to protest, "No, you don't have to do that—" but stopped as I noticed Naya's expression falter. "Is everything okay?"

She lowered her arm, shaking her head slightly. "I guess I'm just exhausted." Placing the chainmail on the bedside table, she took my hand gently. "Time for us to talk about what happened?"

I nodded, the weight of the day's events heavy on my mind. "Time for us to talk…"

"Did you know Lammat was that powerful?" Naya asked, surprise in her voice.

"Honestly, I thought he was just messing around most of the time," I admitted.

"Me too!" she said with a laugh, but her mood quickly sobered. "When we lost... when they were choosing who would join their team... I was sure they would pick you."

I shook my head ruefully. "I was a mess out there. I barely knew what I was doing." I shrugged, still processing the tactics used during the battle. "Do you want to know how Leana hit our crystal that time? She threw a rock at it! A rock!"

Naya nodded, her expression somber. "She was incredible." There was a hint of respect in her voice. "Now their team has Tyran, Kai, her, and Lammat." She sighed deeply. "Do you think there's any chance we'll face them again?"

I squeezed her hand, feeling a resurgence of determination. "I know we will," I said firmly. "And we're going to get Lammat back."

The knock at the door was a welcome distraction from how heavy the room felt. I moved to open it, but Naya quickly threw my top to me. "Put it on - backwards!" I frowned, but did as she asked, and opened the door to find Calia and Joren standing there.

Calia wore an expression of concern and admiration. "Hey, just wanted to check in on you guys," she said. "Saw the battle – you two were pretty impressive against Kai. Not every day you see someone go head-to-head with an Elementalist."

I offered a half-smile, still feeling the sting of defeat. "Thanks. Didn't help us in the end though, did it?"

Calia leaned against the doorframe, a playful glint in her eye. "You know, when I said we might be facing you guys next, I was kidding, right?" I raised an eyebrow, prompting a chuckle from her. "Okay, mostly kidding," she conceded, her smile broadening.

Then, unexpectedly, Joren chimed in. His voice was soft but clear. "That jump at the end was something else, Liam. How did you manage to land right on top of Tyran like that?"

I paused, replaying the moment in my mind. "Honestly? I'm not really sure. It was just... in the moment, I guess. Probably more luck than anything."

Calia's laugh was light and genuine. "Well, let's hope that luck runs out soon, right? Because, no offense, but we're kind of hoping to win our next match." Her tone was teasing, but there was an underlying seriousness to her words. "Speaking of which, any idea how long till you're ready for the next fight? It's nearly midday, and the exam's at a standstill until then."

Joren, turning his attention to Naya, looked concerned. "Are you going to be able to fight with a broken arm?"

Naya shot me a quick, knowing glance and then turned back to Joren with a confident smile. "Oh, it's not broken. Just bruised a bit. See?" She demonstrated by moving her arm around, showing no sign of discomfort.

Joren looked puzzled, clearly recalling the battle's events. "But I'm sure I saw—"

Calia interrupted him with a laugh. "Joren, I told you, you're seeing things. She's tougher than she looks." She turned back, looking at both of us. "So? You nearly ready?"

"We'll be ready the moment Liam finds a new shirt."

Calia, eyeing my attire, remarked with a playful tone, "Look at that hole." She pointed at the small hole in the chainmail. "And not even a scratch on you, huh?"

Naya chimed in smoothly, "It's on back to front. We were just dressing it before you knocked. Thought we might be getting summoned, so he quickly threw something on."

Realizing why Naya had instructed me to wear my top backward—to conceal the now-healed wound—I joined in the lie. "Yeah, it's this side... ouch." Okay, you already know I'm not great at lying.

I caught Joren's eye, and for a moment, I thought I saw a flicker of doubt in his usually unreadable expression. It was hard to tell, but I had the sense he wasn't at all convinced.

"Give us half an hour, and we'll be ready," said Naya.

Calia grinned, "Great! So, should we do the whole

challenge thing?"

Naya laughed, "Let's just say it was a mutual challenge."

After a friendly goodbye, Calia and Joren left, and I leaned back against the door, a pang of guilt washing over me. "I feel bad for lying to them," I confessed, my voice low.

Naya nodded, understanding the sentiment. "It does feel bad, but tactically, it's the best choice for us right now."

"I know," I said, sighing. "But I can't shake the feeling that if we beat them, one of them will be failing the exam because of our actions."

Naya's response was pragmatic yet empathetic. She pulled a medical kit from under the bed and handed it to me. "Well, let's dress your wound so it looks like we're not liars. Take off your top again."

As I complied, removing my shirt to reveal unblemished skin, Naya began to carefully apply bandages, making it look as authentic as possible. The act of faking the injury felt strange, but it was a necessary part of our strategy. In this complex game of the exam, every advantage counted, even if it meant bluffing our way through.

True to our word, thirty minutes later, Naya and I made our way back to the forest, the cool air and rustling leaves greeting us as we approached the clearing. There, we found Calia and Joren already waiting, along with the examiner, who stood with a sense of purpose that matched the seriousness of the occasion. The forest, usually a place of tranquility, now felt charged with the anticipation of the upcoming battle.

The examiner, who had likely been waiting since our last exam concluded over an hour ago, greeted us with a nod of acknowledgment. "As this is a team of two battle, your crystals will only withstand two blows each," he explained, his voice carrying a weight that underscored the challenge ahead.

I swallowed heavily as he handed me a crystal, its surface shimmering subtly in the forest light. Calia received hers simultaneously. Without hesitation, she passed it to Joren, who caught it deftly and began to survey the surrounding area with a thoughtful gaze.

I couldn't help but notice the dynamic between them. Calia's immediate trust in Joren to choose the location for the crystal reaffirmed what Lammat had observed – Joren was the strategist, the thinker, while Calia was the fighter, the one ready to leap into action. Joren's eyes scanned the forest, assessing every tree, shadow, and potential hiding spot with meticulous attention to detail.

As we strolled through the forest, the conversation flowed easily among us, despite the competitive undercurrent. The dense canopy overhead filtered the sunlight into a dappled pattern on the forest floor, where ferns and small shrubs thrived in the cool, moist environment. The occasional rustle of small animals in the underbrush or the distant call of a bird served as a natural soundtrack to our walk.

Calia, with a cheerful demeanor, led the conversation. "I'm looking to be a Goud," she said, her eyes alight with ambition. "Always been fascinated by the role they play in maintaining order and justice."

"Wise girl," said the examiner, placing a hand on her shoulder.

Joren, meticulously scanning the terrain for the perfect spot to place their crystal, added in his calm, focused manner, "And I'm aiming to be a Eulis."

"Stupid boy," joked the Goud, giving Joren a playful push.

Calia laughed, "He loves his magic. Always been a bit quiet though." As we passed a large oak tree, its branches heavy with age, Calia turned back to us. "You know, Joren is actually my half-brother. He's a year younger than me." She paused for a moment, her tone becoming softer. "My mother passed away during my birth."

That revelation struck a chord with me. I found myself saying, "I lost my mother the same way." The words came out before I realized, a part of my history I hadn't intended to share.

The examiner glanced at me over his shoulder. Was that an expression of surprise or warning?

Naya gave me a look filled with compassion and a hint of surprise. I had never mentioned this to her before, and her expression made me wonder if I had revealed too much.

Calia seemed to sense the shift in mood and sought to lighten it. "Our dad's great, though. He met Jor's mother a few months later. They raised us both." She grinned. "We're really looking forward to seeing them at the upcoming dance."

At that, Joren suddenly increased his speed. He followed an elevated plateau, accessible only by a narrow path, creating a natural choke point. This position offered a panoramic view of the surrounding area, allowing them to spot approaching opponents early. He placed the crystal behind a large tree at the center of the plateau.

I shook my head, smiling in amazement. This tree provided both cover and protection, shielding the crystal from long-range attacks and forcing opponents into close-quarters combat.

"Wow, Joren," said Naya, scratching her head. "Don't feel like giving us a chance?"

"That's my brother for you!"

I thumbed the crystal in my hand, using Joren's vantage point to see if I could spot a decent place for our crystal. I turned to the two siblings. "The examiner said the challengers weren't allowed to see where the challenged placed their crystal, but we did say it was a mutual challenge, so…"

The Goud smiled, "That rule's in place for when we have more teams, so if you want to show them…"

"We do," I said. "It feels only fair."

Calia smiled, but Joren remained stone-faced.

As we started discussing our placement of the crystal,

Calia added a light-hearted suggestion to our competitive spirit. "Let's all try our hardest out there, but how about we make a pact? No breaking bones, okay? I'd hate for any of us to be wearing a cast at the dance."

I couldn't help but smile at her proposition. "Agreed," I said. "Let's keep it safe."

The forest around us was alive with the sounds of nature, a peaceful backdrop to the tension of the impending match.

"We could try the same spot as last time," Naya proposed. "It was a good location."

I nodded in agreement. Although we had lost, the previous spot had served us well, offering a balance of visibility and cover. We made our way through the forest, retracing our steps from the last round. The familiarity of the path was comforting amidst the uncertainty of what lay ahead.

As we reached our previously chosen location, I carefully placed our crystal on the ground, stepping back to let it grow... but nothing happened. There was no familiar burrowing into the earth, no sign that it was set.

The Goud, who had been watching us, let out a chuckle. "That's too far from your opponent's crystal," he informed us, amusement evident in his tone.

I turned wondering if Joren had somehow anticipated this, only to see him standing a couple dozen paces away in a large, open area devoid of any significant cover. The Goud pointed in his direction, still smiling. "There's your boundary."

Suddenly, the crystal I had just placed started to move on its own. It slid across the ground, as if being pulled by an invisible force, and came to a stop right at Joren's feet. As the crystal settled, it began its transformation, rapidly growing in size until it towered over all of us. Its surface shimmered in the light, casting prismatic patterns on the forest floor.

"What just happened?" I asked, confusion and surprise mixing in my voice.

The examiner's laughter subsided as he explained, "Each team only gets one chance to plant their crystal. If it's too far from your opponent's, it'll plant itself within the designated boundary."

Naya's voice was tinged with regret. "I should have been paying attention to the distances. Sorry, Liam."

I waved off her apology, my gaze fixed on Joren as he circled our crystal that now had no protection at all. His calm demeanor as he observed was intriguing. I couldn't help but wonder about the strategies flowing through his mind, and his ability to anticipate and outmaneuver. It was clear that Joren's tactical thinking was going to be a significant challenge in the upcoming battle.

CHAPTER TWENTY-ONE
Target Practice

The light emitted from the crystals began to interconnect, forming the familiar dome that would encapsulate our battlefield. The Goud, observing the final preparations, waved to us. "Good luck, everyone," he said before turning to exit the soon-to-be-sealed area.

I walked closer to our crystal, still processing Joren's tactic. "You planned that, didn't you?" I asked him, admiration and surprise in my voice.

Joren nodded, a serious look on his face. "Yes. It seemed you were more focused on the conversation than the positioning of the crystals."

Calia, overhearing the exchange, looked at Joren with wide eyes. "Wait, you used me to pull this off?"

Joren shrugged. "I found four other locations that would have been better suited for our crystal. The one I chose was the perfect distance to trigger this result."

I couldn't help but burst into laughter. "I feel like I should be annoyed, but I'm just impressed."

Joren, with a slight bow, replied, "It's not my desire to trick you, but it is my intention to win." He then turned and began to walk back to his crystal.

Calia, her cheeks flushed, turned to us. "I didn't know he was doing that, I promise!" she exclaimed.

Naya shook her head, her laughter joining mine. "It's

fine, we fell for it."

"I didn't even know the crystal would do that!" I admitted, still chuckling.

Naya sighed. "I did, and I still didn't think about it."

Calia, looking concerned, gestured towards our crystal. "But you're right out in the open!"

"Yes," Naya acknowledged with a resigned nod. "Yes, we are."

Calia gave us an apologetic wave before dashing off to join her brother. I laughed again, thoroughly enjoying the unexpected turn of events.

Naya, with a playful nudge, commented, "Well, even if we lose now, at least you found it funny."

"I like them," I said, folding my arms and looking up at our now-exposed crystal. "So, what are we going to do about this? We need a solid plan, but let's face it – we're not fighters, not like Tyran or Lammat."

Naya, her gaze fixed on the towering crystal, nodded in agreement. "Lammat said Calia was an excellent fighter. And Joren... well..." she pointed at the crystal.

I rubbed my chin thoughtfully. "What if one of us stays behind to guard the crystal? The other could try a sneak attack on theirs."

Naya shook her head, the idea clearly not sitting well with her. "But that leaves one of us to face both of them alone. And if we're honest, our strengths don't lie in solo combat."

I sighed, feeling the gravity of the situation. "You're right. Splitting up would just play into their hands."

A moment of silence passed between us before Naya's eyes lit up with a spark of determination. "Our best asset is our speed. What if we both attack together, as quickly as we can? We could approach from different angles, keep them guessing."

I nodded, considering the idea. "Sweep around the tree protecting their crystal, hit them hard and fast from both sides. It's risky, but it might just work."

Naya nodded, her expression resolute. "Our crystal can only take two hits, and it's completely out in the open. We don't have much of a choice but to reach theirs first."

I took a deep breath, feeling a surge of adrenaline at the thought of our daring plan. "Alright, let's do it. Together, and fast. It's our best shot."

We placed our hands on the crystal, a unified front ready to face our challenge. As we did, the dome shifted from red to blue, signifying the start of our critical battle.

We pivoted sharply and broke into a run. Each stride carried a mixture of determination and the adrenaline of the impending confrontation. We hadn't gotten far when a sudden, jarring noise echoed from behind us, halting us in our tracks.

I spun around, my heart pounding in my chest. The sight that met my eyes was almost unbelievable. The dome surrounding us shifted to red. Embedded in our crystal's side was a small, ordinary-looking rock, which slowly tilted before finally dropping to the forest floor with a dull tap.

"No way," Naya exclaimed in disbelief, her voice barely above a whisper.

"What just happened?" I asked, struggling to make sense of the scene.

Naya's gaze was intense. "He's using telekinesis to attack our crystal!" she realized aloud. "At this range?"

"Is that hard to do?" The very thought of someone manipulating an object from such a distance with such precision seemed almost inconceivable. But in my near-constant state of bewilderment, the line between the normal and the extraordinary had become so blurred that I struggled distinguish one from the other.

She shook her head, her expression a mixture of respect and frustration. "The skill required to do that... And this was his first attempt! How did he know how hard to push it?" Her voice trailed off, reflecting both her admiration for Joren's prowess and the daunting challenge it posed for us.

I stared at our already cracked crystal, a rush of thoughts

flooding my mind. Joren's telekinetic strike was a game-changer. It wasn't just the physical distance he had overcome; it was the precision, the control, and the tactical foresight. His first move in this battle had pushed us one step from defeat. Naya and I exchanged a look, a silent communication passing between us. We were back to the drawing board, our initial strategy now obsolete.

Naya moved closer to our crystal, her eyes scanning the forest canopy, searching for any glimpse of our opponents' crystal. After a moment, she shook her head, a look of resignation crossing her face. "We can't see their crystal from here. We have no choice but to separate," she concluded.

I ran a hand through my hair, feeling a sense of uncertainty. "So, zero strategy then. Everything we do now will be reactive." Doubt crept into my voice as I considered our situation. I was unsure of my abilities, unsure if I had the knowledge or skill to face what was ahead.

Naya turned to me, her eyes meeting mine. "I have to stay here and defend with my telekinesis," she stated, "but you'll have to go in alone."

The thought of going solo against Calia and Joren was daunting. I felt a knot of anxiety in my stomach, the weight of the responsibility heavy on my shoulders.

Suddenly, Naya stepped forward and took my hand, pulling me into a warm embrace. Before I could react, she gave me a reassuring kiss. "I have faith in you, Liam," she said softly, her voice filled with sincerity. "Just do your best. That's all I can ask for."

She pulled back slightly, a gentle smile on her face. "At this point, winning isn't the most important thing. I met you, and that means so much more." Her laughter, light and genuine, filled the air. "And hey, if we lose, we can always try again next year, right?"

Her words, her faith in me, it all helped to ease the doubts swirling in my mind. Naya's presence was a reminder of what we had gained from this experience, regardless of the outcome.

With a newfound resolve, I nodded. "Let's do this," I said, a determined glint in my eye as I placed my palm against the crystal.

With another kiss, Naya placed her hand on top of mine. "Go get them."

I dashed off into the forest, adrenaline coursing through my veins. The trees blurred past as I made my way toward Joren's crystal, my mind singularly focused on the task at hand.

As I neared, I spotted Calia standing guard, her stance relaxed yet alert. Without hesitation, I lunged forward, aiming a punch at her. But Calia, with remarkable agility, slid to the ground, effortlessly evading my attack. In one fluid motion, she pushed her hands against the floor, propelling herself upwards, her feet connecting squarely with my stomach.

The force sent me flying into the air, with Calia following close behind. We crashed down to the ground together, her weight pushing the air from my lungs. Before I could recover, Calia drew back her arm and aimed a powerful blow directly at the spot where the vine had pierced me in the previous fight.

As her fist connected, I felt only a dull thud. Was she holding back? Her expression turned to one of confusion at my lack of reaction. Belatedly, I remembered that I needed to maintain the illusion of injury. I grimaced and let out a strained groan, though my acting was unconvincing at best.

Calia paused, her brow furrowed as she tried to make sense of my reaction. With a quick maneuver, I rolled her off me, scrambling to regain my footing as she did the same. She moved gracefully, a few steps back, her eyes never leaving mine.

"What are you made of?" she asked, a hint of genuine curiosity in her voice. "A blow to an injury like that would have most grown men crying."

I grimaced, trying to maintain the performance. "Yeah, it, um... really hurt!" My words felt hollow, even to my own ears.

She continued to retreat, her gaze analytical. "I'm not

going to win a one-on-one with you, am I?" There was a note of resignation in her voice, mirroring the doubts that had been echoing in my mind.

Her words took me by surprise. The realization dawned on me that she was interpreting my lack of pain as an indication of extraordinary toughness. A smile involuntarily spread across my face, which she seemed to misinterpret as confidence. Calia took another cautious step back.

Seizing the moment, I challenged her. "Why don't we find out?" I advanced a step, my eyes locked on hers. But then I saw her gaze flicker momentarily toward our crystal. A surge of alarm shot through me. 'Don't do it,' I thought.

Calia spun on her heel and dashed toward our crystal. I had no time to waste. I also turned, my mind racing. We were closer to their crystal. There was still a chance. With every fiber of my being, I pushed myself towards their crystal, the distance closing with each stride.

I caught sight of it perched atop the plateau, partially concealed behind the tree. In a burst of adrenaline, I leaped up in a single bound, landing next to a startled Joren. Several rocks dropped from mid-air as he momentarily lost focus on his telekinesis, his confusion evident.

I moved to strike the crystal, but Joren quickly regained his composure. Wave after wave of telekinetic pushes slammed into me, each one a forceful attempt to throw me off balance. I tried to step forward, but the lack of grip on the ground nearly sent me tumbling. Instead, I planted my feet firmly, digging them into the dirt.

Reaching out to Joren proved futile; he was just out of my grasp. I dropped to one knee as the edge of the plateau loomed dangerously close. Time was running out, and I knew I had to act fast – the longer I delayed the more time I'd be giving Calia to shatter our crystal.

In a sudden reflex, I mirrored Lammat's stance in our previous battle. Gripping my right wrist with my left hand, I aimed my palm, channeling a surge of energy within me.

"No!" Joren exclaimed, his telekinetic force intensifying in a desperate attempt to stop me.

I released the energy beam just as I was thrown sideways off the edge of the plateau. The force of the beam caused me to spin in mid-air, and I landed heavily on the grass below.

Panting, I looked up to see Joren looking down at me. "You missed," he said.

I allowed myself a brief smile. "No, I didn't."

A loud crack caught Joren's attention. The tree started to splinter under its weight, dropping with a sudden lurch. My beam may have missed the crystal, but it hit the tree just right. It began to topple, falling directly towards the crystal. Joren jumped toward it using his telekinesis blast to push the tree away, but all he managed was to give it a spin. The tree was going to crush him.

Without a second thought, I sprang back up to the plateau. In one swift motion, I grabbed Joren by the collar and leaped backward. We landed together, a safe distance away, as the tree crashed down onto the crystal, cracking it before pivoting off the edge of the plateau.

I turned to Joren. "Why weren't you getting out of the way?" But before he could reply, his image ripped and I found myself stood back by Naya.

Naya immediately flung her arms around me, a mixture of relief and exhilaration in her expression. "Liam, you won't believe what just happened!" Her words tumbled out in a rush. "Calia got here, and I didn't know what to do. Joren's been throwing rocks at us this whole time..." She gestured towards the numerous stones scattered around our crystal. "But instead of just placing them down, I started hurling them at her!" Her excitement bubbled over with a delighted squeal. "One hit her right in the head, and she fell."

I frowned slightly.

"Yeah, I felt pretty bad about that," Naya admitted, her voice tinged with guilt. "But then when I hesitated, Calia just leaped at me! I barely managed to put up a barrier in time. She was pounding against it until she got teleported away."

I laughed, both at the scenario she described and her infectious enthusiasm. "That's amazing!"

"What happened on your end?"

I proceeded to explain how I managed to take down the tree protecting their crystal and how it ended up damaging the crystal as it fell.

Naya's eyes went wide, her mouth agape. "You can do energy beams now?"

I nodded. "Remember Tyran's words about Crossers having a copy ability?" Demonstrating the move, I let energy swirl and glow in my hand. "Seems I still have it."

"That must be how you did the energy ball in the second exam," she realized.

I lowered my arm. "We're on the brink of winning, Naya. This next round decides it all."

She nodded, her determination shining through. "Let's do the same thing again. You're quicker than Calia, and now we've got a way through their defenses."

Agreeing, I felt a surge of confidence. "Yeah, we've got this. Let's win."

We approached our crystal, each placing a hand on its surface, but nothing happened. Naya looked at me, slightly puzzled. "I guess they're not ready yet," she said.

I chuckled, a sudden realization hitting me. "Oh wow, how many times do you think we've made the other team wait? I hadn't even considered it!"

After a tense few minutes, the dome finally transitioned from red to blue, signaling the start of the round. I immediately sprinted toward their crystal, my heart pounding with anticipation. But only ten steps in, my instincts kicked in as I saw a rock hurtling towards me. I dodged swiftly, letting it hit the ground with a thud. Looking up, my eyes widened in disbelief – the sky was filled with a barrage of rocks raining down.

"I think I know why they were late!" Naya shouted, her telekinetic powers at full display as she caught the rocks mid-air. One rock, however, bounced off the ground and struck our crystal. My heart skipped a beat, but fortunately, it didn't crack.

"Do you want me to stay?" I yelled back, ready to change our plan if needed.

"No! I can do this!" Naya's voice was firm, filled with determination.

As I turned to continue my sprint, I was blindsided by a massive impact on the side of my head. For a moment, I thought it was another rock, but a flash of fiery red hair told me it was Calia. I dropped to my knees, the world spinning around me. Desperately, I reached out and managed to grab her ankle, pulling her closer.

"Get off me!" Calia shouted, delivering a sharp kick to my mouth. Pain exploded across my face, and I tasted blood. I felt my teeth loosen and spat them out along with a mouthful of blood.

"Liam! Are you alright? Hold on, I'll..." Naya's voice was laced with concern as she continued her struggle against the relentless rock shower.

"Don't stop!" I shouted back, gritting my teeth, refusing to let go of Calia's ankle. I knew I couldn't afford to lose focus now, not when victory was so close within our grasp.

Calia's sudden shift caught me off guard. She ceased her attempts to break free and instead leaped on top of me, her fists raining down on my face with a ferocity driven by desperation. "I have to win this, Liam! I need to win this with Jor!" Her voice was determined yet pleading.

In a swift move, I rolled onto my back, dragging her with me. With a burst of strength, I kicked her away from me before diving, rolling, and sliding between her and Naya. "I'm sorry, Calia," I gasped out, knowing full well the stakes of this match for both of us.

Her response was a raw, primal scream as she charged at me like a wild animal. She crouched and barreled into my waist. With a startling display of strength, she lifted me off the ground and ran, her resolve unyielding.

As the crystal whizzed past me, a chilling realization dawned – she was heading straight for the edge of the dome. Panic surged through me, and I began to frantically punch at her back and kick at her legs, trying anything to slow her down. But she was relentless. She knew my tactics, having seen Tyran try to push me out earlier. By lifting me off the ground, she had effectively neutralized my ability to slow her down.

As Calia and I neared the edge of the dome, her pace slowed ever so slightly for a final, decisive push. With a surge of strength, she hurled me forward, and I felt myself break through the dome's boundary. An eerie silence enveloped me as I crossed the barrier, the sounds of Calia's efforts replaced by those of the surrounding forest.

The sensation of passing through the dome was disorienting, a tingling engulfing me as I desperately tried to cling to the inside. But it was too late; I was already outside, suspended in a moment of uncertainty and defeat.

Calia's face, mere inches from mine, was a curious mixture of both triumph and shock. Her eyes, wide with realization, mirrored my disbelief. She frantically clawed at the air, her movements silent but urgent.

Then, in a moment that caught me off guard, I realized why she was so desperate. My left hand, which I hadn't even felt move, was gripping her arm — from the other side of the dome. We were connected, her on the inside and me on the outside, bound by the unanticipated consequences of her last move.

The barrier was unyielding. In a desperate attempt, I pushed against it, but I felt my left arm begin to slide out. I hastily corrected my action, trying to force my arm back in, but once it was out, it was impossible to push back in.

A sudden, sharp pain shot through my hand, causing me to shout out. Calia, in a state of wild panic, had turned and sunk her teeth into my flesh, my blood streaking down her chin. Her eyes, wide and frenzied, were no longer focused on me but on something distant, something desperate.

I glanced over at Naya, who was still in the midst of catching and deflecting the rocks. The onslaught had diminished, but I couldn't tell if she was aware of my predicament.

Another jolt of pain brought my attention back to Calia. She was now using all her strength to strike at my arm. Her expression was fraught with anguish as she looked at me, her lips silently forming the words, "Don't make me do this!" Tears were brimming in her eyes, reflecting the turmoil of her actions.

I stood there, frozen, as realization dawned on me. As long as I held onto her, there was still a chance – a chance for Naya to notice, a chance to turn the tide of the battle. But that hope was quickly overshadowed by a horrifying reality.

I screamed as my arm broke under the force of Calia's relentless blows. She wasn't just trying to make me release her; she was trying to sever my arm entirely. With each strike, her resolve seemed to grow, yet her eyes betrayed the agony of her decision.

As she raised her arm for one final, devastating attack, her eyes clenched shut in anguish, I made a split-second decision. In one swift, decisive motion, I pulled.

Calia's sobs filled the air, a raw sound of anguish and regret. She dropped to her knees, her emotions overflowing. I finally released my grip and lowered myself to her level, sitting in front of her on the forest floor.

"I'm so sorry, Liam!" she wailed, her voice choked with tears. "I'm so sorry." In a moment of raw emotion, she lunged forward, wrapping her arms around me in a tight embrace.

I couldn't help but laugh gently, trying to lighten the mood. "What are you sorry for?" I asked as I returned the embrace, trying to comfort her.

"Your arm!" she cried, pulling back to look at me, her

eyes filled with concern. "I said no broken bones!" She gingerly took hold of my arm, inspecting it with care. "How are you meant to fight now?"

I smiled reassuringly, noticing her pause as she turned my hand over, examining my arm. She looked up at me, her expression a mixture of confusion and disbelief. "Yeah," I said, tapping the bandages visible through the hole in my chainmail. "Turns out I'm a fast healer."

"I... didn't break your arm?" Her voice was a mixture of hope and uncertainty.

"Oh, no, you definitely did. You also knocked out my teeth!" I flashed a wide grin, showing off a fully healed mouth. "I've never felt them grow back before."

"By the gods," she whispered, her sobs subsiding into quiet, disbelieving breaths.

I gave her a playful punch on the shoulder. "You are a really good fighter, Calia." Taking her hands, I helped her to her feet.

Calia's head rested gently against my shoulder as we watched Naya through the barrier. "You need some training," she teased. "When I hit your chest and you barely flinched, I thought you were some battle-hardened warrior."

I chuckled. "What gave me away?" I asked, draping an arm over her shoulder in a friendly gesture.

She grinned, her eyes sparkling with mirth. "When you let a girl half your weight carry you out of the dome."

We both laughed, the tension of the battle melting away into a moment of shared humor. My gaze then shifted back to the ongoing struggle within the dome. "Who do you think will win?"

Calia inhaled deeply, watching intently. "Naya..." she murmured, nodding towards the dome. "She's stopped dropping the rocks."

Following her gaze, I noticed that Naya wasn't just catching the rocks anymore; she was also levitating the ones on the ground, aligning them at the same level. It was a display of concentration and control that was impressive to witness.

As we watched, Naya's movements became more fluid, her body language exuding confidence. She started hurling the stones back along the trajectory they had come from. "See? It's taking her a few tries to get the angle and strength right, but when she does…" Calia's voice trailed off as we saw Naya's form whip around, launching a volley of stones in a precise arc. Calia sighed, "Joren can't stop that many at once."

I turned to Calia, our eyes meeting. "I'm sorry," I said, placing my hand against the dome.

She smiled warmly, her eyes conveying understanding. "No, you're not." Her tone was light, devoid of any bitterness.

The dome disappeared, and my balance shifted. Calia linked her arm with mine as we began to walk forward. Naya let out a cheer of joy, spinning around, her face alight with triumph, but her expression softened as she saw us approaching together.

"Well fought, Calia," she said with genuine respect. Then she turned to me, and I could read the anticipation in her eyes. She knew what this moment meant, what was coming next.

We walked to the center of where the dome once stood, the remnants of our intense battle still visible in the scattered rocks and trampled grass. The air was thick with anticipation, a quiet tension that hung heavily over us.

Approaching from the opposite direction was Joren, his stride steady but a large bruise visible above his eye. As he neared, Calia broke away and ran to him, wrapping him in a tight hug that spoke volumes of their bond. After a moment, she released him and turned to face Naya and me, her expression a complex blend of relief and resignation.

"Don't draw this out," Calia said, her voice steady but tinged with sadness. "Just get it over with quickly."

Naya glanced at me, her eyes conveying a deep sadness. "This is your decision to make," she said softly. "They would both be incredible assets to our team."

I stood there, torn. The choice before me was agonizing

– choosing one meant leaving the other behind, a decision that felt impossibly heavy. Joren, with his strategic mind and quiet strength, or Calia, with her fierce determination and combat skills. Both had proven themselves more than worthy.

I took a deep breath, feeling the weight of their expectant gazes. My heart felt heavy as I made my choice, knowing the impact it would have. "Joren," I said, my voice cracking. The name hung in the air, a final decision that couldn't be taken back.

Joren's eyes widened slightly, surprise and sorrow flashing across his face. Calia's expression was one of stoic acceptance, but the disappointment was evident in the slight downturn of her lips.

Joren gave his sister's hand a tight squeeze before he released it and stepped forward to join us. As he did, I couldn't shake the feeling of loss that accompanied this victory. It was a moment filled with the knowledge of what, and who, we were leaving behind.

Calia gave us a small, brave smile, her eyes lingering on Joren for a moment before she turned to walk away, her red hair blazing in the sunlight.

CHAPTER TWENTY-TWO
A Silver Chain

As the Goud examiner led us through the maze-like corridors of the dormitory, the atmosphere was thick with the unspoken thoughts of our recent battle. We were now a team of three – Naya, Joren, and myself – each processing the day's events in our own way.

Upon reaching our new dorm room, Joren walked in without a word and promptly closed the door behind him. Naya and I exchanged a quick, puzzled glance. Joren's behavior was abrupt, perhaps a reflection of his complex feelings about the day's outcomes.

"He's either got a lot on his mind, or he's upset about Calia," I mused aloud, trying to gauge his sudden withdrawal.

"Could be both," Naya suggested quietly. She gave me a brief, understanding look before turning to enter the room, perhaps to give Joren some space or to offer a word of comfort.

I was about to follow when the examiner stopped me. "Liam, a moment, please."

Naya glanced back, then entered the room, leaving me alone with the examiner.

The examiner's gaze was contemplative as he addressed me. "How are you holding up? Have you had any contact with your Overseer today?"

I shook my head. "No, I haven't seen him. But if there's a

way to contact him, I'd be glad to hear it."

The examiner nodded slowly, and then his tone shifted, becoming more serious. "I've been observing your performance in the exam. You've demonstrated considerable skill and adaptability. However, I'm concerned about something else. It's come to my attention that Tyran knew about the exam details in advance and shared them with his team."

His words caught me off guard, "You know about that?"

He nodded. "If you get another chance to face him, well," the examiner's mouth quirked up slightly, "give him a punch in the mouth from me, will you?"

I let out a surprised chuckle, not entirely sure if he was serious or not. "I'll remember that," I replied with a grin.

The examiner wished me luck before departing. Upon entering the dorm room, the scene was quiet and contemplative. Joren stood by one of the windows, his gaze fixed intently on the view outside. Naya was seated on one of the beds, her posture relaxed but her eyes reflecting a sense of thoughtfulness. I walked over and sat beside her, joining in the silent observation of Joren.

"Has he said anything?" I whispered to Naya, not wanting to disturb the room's stillness.

"No, nothing," she replied softly. "He's just been staring out that window."

Curious, I spoke up. "What do you see when you look out of that window, Joren?"

His response was terse and unexpected. "Nothing."

I frowned, puzzled by his answer. "What do you mean, nothing?"

Joren continued to gaze out the window, his voice contemplative. "Pitch black. I understand that these windows are meant to show you what you want to see. It's strange, but I only see darkness."

His words prompted me to probe deeper. "You mean you don't want anything?"

Joren finally turned away from the window to face us.

There was a depth in his eyes, a look of introspection. "Of course I do," he said. "I want to pass the exam. I want to see my sister again. I want to meet my parents at the dance." He paused, his gaze shifting to me with a hint of curiosity. "I want to know how you can heal so quickly." I shared a glance with Naya. "But when I look at these windows… nothing."

I was taken aback by Joren's keen observation. "How did you…" I started to ask, but then corrected myself. Joren seemed the kind of person who noticed details others might miss. "How long have you known about my healing ability?"

"Since the first exam," Joren replied matter-of-factly. "I am right in assuming that you are the boy who fell for Rexus' trap?"

I nodded, still surprised by his deduction. "You've known for that long?"

He touched the back of his head, indicating the injury. "Subdural hematoma," he said "Nobody who suffers that kind of impact is walking around the next day. The only explanation is healing magic, yet I've never encountered anyone capable of performing one passively." His gaze shifted to Naya's arm. "Or able to share that ability with others."

Joren then brushed his hair aside and approached me. "Would you please heal my head wound?" His eyes flickered to Naya. "That was a remarkable number of rocks you sent my way."

"Thank… you," Naya responded what sounded like both pride and apology. "Sorry about your head."

"That's quite alright," Joren said, then turned back to me expectantly.

"Sure, I can heal you," I replied, feeling a bit nervous as I reached out and touched his arm. A moment later, his head wound visibly healed.

"Interesting," Joren observed, his tone one of genuine fascination. "You don't need to touch the injured part to heal it?"

I nodded. "No, the healing just sort of… happens."

"Can you teach me how to do it?" he asked, his voice

tinged with genuine interest.

The question caught me off guard, and a laugh escaped before I could stop it. "I don't even know how it works myself," I admitted. "It just happens on its own."

"Disappointing," Joren replied, his tone flat but not unkind.

There was a brief pause before Naya, looking thoughtful, broke the silence with her question. "Joren, you're not upset with us, right? About Calia failing the exam?"

Joren walked back to the window, his back to us as he spoke. "You mistake my mannerisms for sulking, perhaps? This is simply how I am. I experience emotions, but expressing them… that's not something I've mastered." He then lay down on one of the beds, staring up at the ceiling. "And it wasn't because of you that my sister failed. It was because of me."

Naya's brow furrowed in confusion. "What do you mean, 'because of you'?"

Joren's gaze shifted to me. "Liam was impressed by my strategy at the start of our match. He probably also realized that my first attack was a hit because I knew the distance between our crystals."

"200 paces…" I said, smiling in admiration of his astute observation.

"Exactly," Joren continued, a hint of satisfaction in his voice. "As long as I aimed toward the center of your crystal, I was likely to hit it. To be honest, I was quite impressed with myself on that one." He gave an uncharacteristic sigh. "That's why I was chosen."

"No," I said, shaking my head, but then hesitated as I realized he was correct. Although Calia was easier to talk to, and certainly friendlier, she lacked Joren's ability to strategize.

"Choosing me over Calia was a mistake," he stated with blunt precision. His words, clear and devoid of emotion, echoed with a sense of practicality. "All three of us here are adept at magic, but none excel in physical combat. Calia would have been the logical choice." His gaze then turned towards

Liam, maintaining a neutral expression. "Please, do not take offense. Your combat potential is evident, yet unrefined. Accepting Kai's challenge was a foolish decision."

Naya's smile broadened. "I have to agree with you on that one."

"Ah, then you, too, have noticed?" he inquired, a hint of curiosity in his tone.

"Noticed what?" I chimed in.

He turned slightly, addressing us both with a level of analytical clarity. "That the team which loses the first battle will, in all probability, find themselves engaged in every subsequent skirmish?"

Naya's smile faltered into a pause. "What?"

"I stand corrected..." Joren announced, straightening his posture. With a deft motion, he conjured eleven green orbs, each floating gracefully before him. Unlike the Goud's earlier demonstration, Joren's orbs were unique – they bore the faces of all the examinees, transforming from simple spheres into a gallery of portraits.

As Joren began to speak, the orbs shifted and moved, reflecting his words like mirrors to his thoughts.

"Kai challenged you, you fight him, but lose Lammat." The illusions shifted, and Lammat's image floated away from mine and Naya's. "This reduces your team to two. Next, you confront us, the sole duo. You succeed, and I join your ranks." Again, the faces shifted, and Calia's faded away. I looked at Naya with a hint of guilt, but she was staring in awe at the display in front of her. "Now, it's your turn to face the other trio. Having two bouts behind you, your chances of victory are heightened. You claim one of their members. Your team grows to four, leaving Kai's team, yet again, as your adversary."

Naya and I exchanged glances, our expressions a blend of astonishment and dawning comprehension.

"Wow, thanks, Liam!" Naya exclaimed, her hands cradling her head as a laugh escaped her lips. "I'm already feeling drained after just two rounds!"

Joren offered a suggestion, his tone even and deliberate. "Might I suggest that when the trio approaches us, we refrain from agreeing immediately?"

I nodded. "Yeah, that sounds like a plan. They're probably betting on us being exhausted. Best to face them after we've had some time to recover."

"Especially with Veyra on their team," he added, his gaze sharp.

"Veyra?" Naya echoed, a flicker of recognition in her eyes. "Oh, she's the one rumored to be as skilled as Tyran, isn't she?"

Joren's response was immediate, his voice devoid of emotion. "No, she is not on par with Tyran."

I let out a relieved chuckle. "Well, that's a bit of good news, at least."

"No," Joren corrected, his words cutting through the brief moment of levity. "She is significantly superior."

"Wonderful," I sighed, laying back with resignation and fatigue.

Joren loomed above, his figure casting a mechanical yet thoughtful presence. He peered down, eyeing the damage on my chainmail with a calculating gaze. "A break would give us time to mend your armor," he noted, scrutinizing the hole. "Are the bandages still necessary?"

I flushed, then lifted my chainmail off over my head and started to remove the clean bandages.

"Did you keep the fragments?"

Reaching into a pocket, I retrieved a small bag Naya had placed the links into and handed it to him. "Maybe I should learn telekinesis."

"I am surprised you have not mastered it yet. Considering your proficiency with beam projection," Joren commented, then, unexpectedly, his lips curved into a rare smile. "Perhaps you could teach me that technique later?"

Caught off guard, I stuttered, "I mean, I can try…"

He carefully emptied the bag's contents into his palm,

turning towards Naya. "Will you assist me in this task?" Without waiting for a response, he then instructed me, "Pass me your top."

I handing it over. As he accepted it, Joren suddenly paused, his voice softening. "Oh, I apologize," he said. "My earlier evaluation of your abilities was likely incorrect."

Puzzled, I asked, "What makes you say that?"

"You've done well getting this far with dampened mana. I can't even lift these links anymore." Joren glanced up, his gaze oscillating between Naya and me. "Were you unaware that you're wearing a dampener?" he inquired with a hint of surprise.

"A what?" I asked, my confusion apparent.

"You do realize that this isn't armor, yes?"

I turned to Naya, seeking clarification. "Isn't this armor?"

She grasped the armor, examining the links now resting in Joren's hand with a newfound perspective. "So that's it!" she exclaimed, a light of realization in her eyes. "Liam, when I tried to repair this earlier, I figured I failed because I was exhausted."

"Right...?"

"But even now, I can't lift them! They won't budge! Liam, this is a dampener!"

"Okay, you keep saying that word, but I don't know what it means."

As she tossed the chainmail back to Joren, who scrutinized it with a mechanic's precision, she explained, "A dampener is an enchanted item designed to suppress the user's magical abilities. They're typically used in recreational competitions to level the playing field."

Joren nodded in agreement. "If Liam has been performing at this level while encumbered by a dampener, his true capabilities remain unseen."

"So, you're telling me this isn't armor?"

"Did it offer you any protection?" asked Joren.

"No..."

"Then it is not armor."

I touched the spot near my shoulder when Kai's vine struck. My mind raced with the implications. Ding had given me this 'gift' the morning after we met. I had worn it faithfully every day, thinking it was a protective armor. Was he intentionally trying to weaken me?

Naya, with a determined gaze, took the chainmail from Joren and handed it to me. Then, with a graceful motion, she opened her hand, forming an illusory orb in the air before her. It shimmered with a subtle glow, unmistakably similar to the orb showcased in the second exam.

"Everyone, try this," she urged, her voice laced with curiosity.

One by one, orbs materialized in front of us. Joren's being the largest, then mine, and finally Naya's, each pulsating with its own unique energy.

"Liam, could you stop your orb now?" Naya asked, her gaze fixed on me.

I let my orb fade away, watching it disappear into nothingness.

Naya's focus intensified as she took the chainmail back from me. The moment it left my hands, her orb vanished completely. She looked surprised, then passed the armor to Joren. When he touched it, his once impressive orb diminished, shrinking to the size of a fist.

Naya's voice was tinged with nervousness as she turned back to me. "Try the spell again, Liam, but this time without touching the armor."

I focused, reopening my hand. The room was instantly bathed in a brilliant green light, so intense that the orb itself was indiscernible, its radiance reaching every corner.

"By the gods..." Naya gasped, her hand flying to her mouth in shock.

"Fascinating," Joren murmured, his voice tinged with a rare hint of wonder.

I closed my hand, snuffing out the spell and the

overwhelming light, leaving us in a stunned silence. The revelation was clear – the chainmail had been a shackle on my true potential, and without its weight, my magical capacity was evidently far greater than any of us had anticipated.

"Can you fix the armor, please, Joren?" I asked quietly, my gaze fixed on the ground.

"Liam, you don't need to wear it!" Naya interjected, her hand gripping my arm with concern.

"Please, Joren?"

"Without it, you're so much more powerful," Naya persisted.

"Without it, I'm more dangerous!" My voice rose unexpectedly, cutting through the air. Naya recoiled slightly, a look of surprise and perhaps fear flickering across her face. This was the first time I had ever raised my voice at her. I looked up, meeting her eyes. "I was given this for a reason. Clearly, my power needs to be… dampened."

Joren, who had been quietly observing the exchange, finally spoke up. "Whoever gave this to you, I do not believe they intended to permanently limit you."

"How can you be sure?" I countered, my frustration evident. "Back in our fight, what if I had unleashed that beam without wearing my chainmail – my dampener? What then?"

He shook his head, a thoughtful expression on his face. "I cannot say for certain, but it might be worth testing." A small, rare smile appeared on his lips. "My point is, if the intention was a permanent restriction, it wouldn't have been given to you in the form of something you can easily remove." His words were spoken with a logical calmness.

Naya's eyes widened in realization. "That's right! It could have been something permanent like an earring, or even an implant…"

Joren added, his voice steady, "Or ingested, at least for a day."

Naya hesitated, noticing my puzzled expression. "The dampening charm doesn't work on just any material. It's most effective on metal, not fabrics or stones."

"Even the smallest piece," he observed. I turned my attention to Joren, who held a single link between his fingers, his orb once again reduced to the size of a fist in his other hand. "Potent," he concluded succinctly.

Naya then addressed the issue at hand. "Liam, the links are too tiny to handle with our fingers alone. We'd need specialized equipment or telekinesis. But we can't touch the armor and use telekinesis simultaneously."

Joren interjected with a thoughtful murmur. "Two people could manage it, though…" He demonstrated by levitating the link in front of him. "One person holds it, while the other performs the repairs."

I looked at them, a glimmer of hope sparking within me. "Can we do that? Can you two work together to fix it?"

"Yes, but I won't." As I started to object, he raised a hand, effectively silencing me. "Provide a logical justification, and I may reconsider. I do not acknowledge reasons rooted in sentiment or recklessness."

"Joren, I need my powers under control."

"Then learn to control them yourself, and use this when needed." He tossed me the chainmail. "It doesn't need to be repaired for it to work. Leave the links with me, and I will practice putting them back together." He waved a dismissive hand as he moved back to his bed and lay down, tossing a handful of links into the air and catching them effortlessly with his telekinesis. "If you want to put it back on, do so."

Naya took hold of my hand. "I'll go with whatever you decide, but you know my opinion."

I lifted the chainmail, turning it over in my hands, contemplating the damage. My gaze shifted to Naya. "Do you think… maybe I should see what I'm capable of before I put it back on?"

In one fluid motion, Joren scooped up the links from the air, placed them into the bag, and pocketed it while rising to his feet. "Yes."

CHAPTER TWENTY-THREE
The Training Dome

Naya and Joren were my guides through the maze-like corridors of the facility, their footsteps tapping rhythmically against the cold stone floors. Without warning, Naya stopped and turned to face us. "I'll catch up with you in the training room," she said, her voice echoing slightly in the vast hallway. With a determined nod, she disappeared down a branching corridor, leaving Joren and me to continue our journey alone.

We descended a set of stone stairs, delving further into the bowels of the building. Finally, Joren pushed open a heavy door, revealing the crystal exam training room.

To say it was large is an understatement. Vast may be closer to what I mean. A perfect cylinder spanning a hundred paces across, it soared upwards, crowned by a vaulted dome that seemed to stretch endlessly overhead. In its center stood a solitary, tall crystal, its multifaceted surface alive with shimmering refractions from the artificial lighting.

Joren scanned the room with a critical eye. "Practicing outside would be ideal to avoid damage, but we can't risk anything reaching the city."

The gravity of his words hit me. "I hadn't even considered that!" I exclaimed, a bit startled by the thought.

"How far can you extend your beam currently?" Joren inquired, his tone indicating this was more than just idle curiosity.

I shook my head, feeling a surge of uncertainty. "I don't know. The first time I used it was during our fight."

Joren looked at me with a mixture of disbelief and intrigue. "Your first attempt was successful? That's hard to believe."

I remembered the chaos of that moment. "I didn't see its full extent. I was too preoccupied with not falling off the edge."

"And I missed its impact," Joren added, "as I was focused on ensuring your fall." He nodded decisively. "Then that is our starting point."

He led me to one wall of the dome and positioned me to face the crystal. "Keep your dampener on for now. Aim just beside the crystal."

I crouched down, bracing my right foot against the wall. "Okay, here goes nothing."

Joren's analytical nature was evident as he crouched down beside me, adopting my stance with precision. "Would you mind explaining your technique?" he inquired, his eyes keenly observing my posture.

I hesitated, trying to put into words something that had come instinctively. "Well, it's not exactly clear-cut. I sort of… channel energy from one hand to the other, passing it through the wrist. Then, I concentrate it in my hand, allowing it to build up there."

Joren's brows furrowed in concentration as he attempted to replicate my method. "That's quite complex," he mused. "You have to guide the energy flow within your body?" He shook his hand, flexing his fingers in a way that suggested he was feeling something unfamiliar. "With telekinesis, the process is more external. You release the energy and manipulate it around the object. It's mainly about condensing the energy, making it tangible."

He continued to experiment for a few moments, yet his hand never started to glow. Finally, he stood up, a look of resolve on his face. "I'll need to practice this technique of internal energy direction. For now, let's focus on your capabilities. Let's see how far you can extend your beam." With that, he jogged back towards the door, signaling for me to begin.

I felt the familiar surge of energy building within me. With a deep breath, I released it, feeling the force of the beam push me against the wall as it erupted from my hand. I watched as the beam traveled across the room and dissipated.

"How far was that?" I called out, trying to gauge the distance.

Joren jogged back to my side, his expression a mix of surprise and respect. "About twenty paces," he announced. "Nearly halfway to the crystal."

"Twenty?" I echoed. "Lammat can only project up to five paces!"

Joren nodded thoughtfully. "Perhaps this is your unique talent, then."

I frowned slightly, unsure. "What do you mean?"

As Joren continued to emulate my technique, flexing and gripping his wrist in an attempt to understand the process, he elaborated. "Each of us has a specific talent, an area where we naturally excel. Once identified, it's crucial to hone that skill to its fullest potential. Some are gifted with multiple talents. For me, it's telekinesis." He paused, reaching into his pocket and pulling out the bag of chainmail links. With a swift motion, he tossed it towards me. "Catch!"

Catching the bag, I couldn't help but look perplexed at Joren's reaction.

"I speak to you about telekinesis, and you use your hands to catch?" His gaze bore into me with incredulity. "Well, I suppose you're just starting out." He nodded toward the bag. "Try releasing mana from your body and wrap it around the bag."

Focusing on the bag, I visualized it rising into the air. To my amazement, it did exactly that.

"Oh..." Joren sounded impressed. "We hadn't quite

reached the lifting stage, but that's impressive."

Experimenting, I twirled the bag in the air, visualizing my mana forming a bowl, and the links poured out into it. "Wow, so you just think what you want it to do, and it happens?"

Joren watched intently, a curious glint in his eyes. "Not exactly, at least not for me." He moved closer to the floating bag, scrutinizing it as if trying to decipher my mana. The links rose, spun in the air, and then settled back down. "You're not holding the links? You created a telekinetic surface?"

"Was that wrong?" I asked, unsure.

"No, it's just that..." He paused, scratching his head. "I'm not accustomed to surprises," he admitted, his voice flat. "Normally, I manipulate each item individually. Your method seems more akin to barrier magic."

"Could we use this to lift a person?" I queried, intrigued by the potential.

Joren's expression transformed into a wide grin. "Let's find out!"

My excitement mirrored Joren's as I watched the links cascade back into the bag. He deftly caught it mid-air as I released my telekinetic grip, tucking it away safely in his pocket. "Do you want to give it a try first?" I asked, my grin as wide as his.

"With your regenerative abilities, I'm far more at ease," he responded, his gaze sweeping over me, assessing the best approach for this unique endeavor.

His comment made me pause, a hint of apprehension creeping in. "What was that?" I asked, my excitement mingling with a touch of nervousness.

Joren seemed to sense my concern and quickly reassured me. "I've always been curious about lifting a person, but never had the opportunity to try it safely." He noticed my worried look and shook his head, smiling. "Don't worry, I'm not planning to break any bones."

There was something infectious about Joren's enthusiasm. In these moments of excitement, his usually stoic, mechanical demeanor melted away, revealing a more human side.

He began explaining his technique. "When I lift inanimate objects like the links or rocks, I encase them in a sphere of mana and compress it. Since they're solid, there's a limit to how much I can compress."

"That makes sense," I nodded, following his logic.

"For something like fabric, I use a looser compression. I maintain a gentle grip, stopping as soon as I feel any give in the material." He gestured towards me, his finger circling in the air. "With you, I suspect the approach will be somewhere in between."

"Hold on a second," I said, holding up my hands. "You're going to wrap me up in mana, then compress it?"

"Of course!"

"So you might not break a leg, but there's a chance you'll crush me?"

"Yes, exactly!" he replied, eyes sparkling with enthusiasm. "Let's begin!"

"No!" I said quickly stepping to the side, as though dodging an attack. "I don't want to be crushed!"

"Liam," he said with a sigh. "I am highly skilled at telekinesis. The likelihood of an accident is, let's say, fifty percent?"

"Fifty?!"

"Okay, forty."

I gave him an annoyed look.

"Forty-five?" He sighed. "Listen, you'll be fine. You have your healing ability. And I'll stop immediately if anything seems off. Besides, the more I practice, the better I'll become."

Taking a deep breath to steady my nerves, I exhaled slowly, trying to find a semblance of calm. "Please, Joren, let's not make this a decision I'll regret." With a tentative step forward, I prepared myself, consciously relaxing my muscles, ready for whatever bizarre sensation was to come.

"Okay... here we go..." Joren announced.

I was decidedly not ready for whatever bizarre sensation

was to come. It started with a gentle, yet firm pressure encasing my body, steadily increasing in intensity. But soon shifted to an awkward feeling of pressure under my armpits and around my groin. "Not happy with that feeling, Joren."

He looked at me, a bit puzzled. "Where did you expect to be lifted from?" Joren retorted. "Lean back, and I'll catch you. It might be easier."

Taking a deep breath for courage, I let myself fall back, expecting Joren's telekinesis to catch me. Instead, I hit the floor with a thud. "You said you'd catch me!" I complained, half-laughing despite the shock.

"I'm sorry, your weight was more than I anticipated. But don't worry, I still have you," Joren reassured, his face again concentrating. Gradually, I felt myself lifting off the ground.

I couldn't contain my excitement, grinning widely as the room seemed to drift around me. "You're doing it!" I shouted, throwing my arms in the air. But then, a tiny release, and I suddenly spiraled backward, crashing to the floor with a heavier thud.

Joren peered down at me, his expression unreadable. "You moved," he stated simply.

Rubbing my back, I replied with a groan, "Yeah, sorry about that." I pushed myself up to my feet. "What happened?"

"When you moved your arms, you disrupted the mana structure. It's like popping a bubble," he explained.

"Do you want to try again?" I asked, still feeling the thrill of the brief flight.

Joren shook his head. "No, your movement showed the limitations of my approach. If I can't predict where the object will be, I can't lift it effectively." He shrugged with a hint of resignation. "Would you like to try lifting me?"

Nervously, I faced Joren, my mind racing with the possibilities and risks. "I'm worried I might crush you," I admitted, my voice tinged with genuine concern.

Joren offered a reassuring smile. "Your method is different, Liam. You don't encase objects in mana; you just lift them. It's safer."

Taking a deep breath, I focused on creating a telekinetic structure beneath Joren's feet. However, as I concentrated, I quickly realized that as long as he stood firmly on the ground, my approach wouldn't work.

Shifting tactics, I visualized two loops of mana forming under Joren's armpits. With a gentle upward pull, I felt a thrill of success as Joren was lifted slightly off the ground. Encouraged, I then attempted to manipulate the force under his feet.

To my delight, Joren began to move, swinging around in the air with an exhilarated expression. His excitement was infectious, but his movements made me nervous. Acting quickly, I wrapped him in a blanket of mana, hoping to stabilize his position.

The effect was immediate. Joren froze in place, suspended in mid-air, grinning from ear to ear. A sense of glee washed over me as I carefully rotated him, marveling at the control I had. "How does it feel?" I asked, grinning as I slowly lowered him closer to the ground.

But Joren didn't respond. His eyes were fixed, unblinking. Realizing something was wrong, I hastily lowered him to the floor and released the mana.

Joren gasped for air the moment he was free, his chest heaving. "I couldn't breathe!" he exclaimed, shock and relief in his voice.

I knelt beside him, guilt washing over me. "I'm so sorry, Joren. I didn't realize..."

He waved off my apology, still catching his breath. "It's alright. We learned something important." Despite the scare, there was a hint of excitement in his voice. "What did you do?"

"I wrapped you with my mana."

"Wrapped me?" he frowned. "As in encased me?"

"I didn't encase you in a compressed ball of mana," I said with a slight shrug. "I just sort of... enveloped you."

He seemed puzzled, his eyes flickering between my

hand and my face. "I don't quite understand…"

"Let me just show you." I focused, visualizing my mana as a vibrant green, and slowly began to wrap it around Joren's legs.

His reaction was immediate. His eyes widened in astonishment, his arms lifted in a mixture of surprise and curiosity. He seemed torn between asking me to stop and wanting to learn from the experience. As I gently lifted him into the air, his legs buoyed by my mana, he burst into a wild, uninhibited laugh. "Incredible, Liam!" he exclaimed. "Move me closer to you!"

As I drew him nearer, Joren extended his hand. I reached out to shake it, but he batted my hand away. "No, I'm trying it on you!"

"Go ahead," I said, standing still with a smile.

I felt the sensation of lifting off the ground, but just as quickly, there was a disruption, and I found myself back on the floor.

Joren laughed, frustration and amusement in his tone. "I'm getting closer, but my mana isn't dense enough yet." His gaze met mine, a look of admiration and wonder. "You truly are unique, Liam."

The door swung open and Naya stepped into the room. Her eyes immediately locked onto the sight of Joren, suspended in mid-air, surrounded by a shimmering green aura.

"Is that… telekinesis?" she asked, her voice a mixture of astonishment and curiosity. Her gaze shifted to the mana. "Why is it green though?"

Joren, still floating, nodded with a grin. "Indeed, but there's more to it," he said. "Liam's using an illusion to make his telekinesis visible. It's quite ingenious, actually."

I shrugged, feeling a bit sheepish under her gaze. "I didn't think much of it. It just felt natural to use a visible form of mana if I was showing someone how to do it."

Joren's expression was one of undisguised amazement. "What Liam's done here isn't common," he explained to Naya.

"He's seamlessly combined telekinesis, barrier, and illusion magic into one. It's quite extraordinary."

Naya's eyes widened, her astonishment evident. "That's incredible, Liam. Hardly anyone can do that, especially not at our age."

Joren, his feet still off the ground, chimed in, "I've yet to meet an adult who can control three spells at once like this!"

Feeling the weight of their praise, I carefully lowered Joren back to the ground, letting the green mana dissipate as he touched down. Both Naya and Joren gasped loudly, their expressions each one of shock.

"What happened? What did I do?" I said, hands up in the air.

Naya bounded towards me, her voice carrying concern. "Why didn't you absorb the mana?" Her brows knit together in perplexity.

Simultaneously, Joren echoed her sentiment, his tone laced with incredulity. "You didn't absorb your mana!" The word 'mana' resonated between them, a chorus of confusion.

Caught in a whirlwind of their synchronized questioning, I glanced between them, a fog of incomprehension clouding my understanding.

Naya, stepping closer, the distance between us shrinking, questioned with a gentle yet earnest tone, "Is that what you've been doing this entire time, Liam?" Her eyes searched mine, seeking answers in their depths.

"Have I done something wrong?" My voice was a whisper, a mere breath in the vastness of our conversation.

Joren, too, closed the gap, his gaze flickering towards Naya. His voice carried a hint of alarm, "Is he trying to kill himself or something?"

In a gesture of concern, Naya captured both my hands, her grip firm yet comforting. She raised them towards her chin, her eyes imploring. "Liam, this is important. We don't have infinite mana. It takes time, weeks, months to recover expended mana." Her words fell like raindrops, each one imbued with urgency.

Joren, his expression softening, added, "Surely you know this," his eyes returning to me, a canvas of concern.

Naya continued, her voice unwavering, "Every bit of mana is important. Each thread you release is still tethered to you. You don't just cut those lines when you're done with them, you pull them back in." Her gaze locked onto mine, forging a connection, and ensuring my comprehension.

Feeling a weight settle in my chest, I admitted, "I'm sorry, I didn't realize..."

Joren, his demeanor shifting to a more analytical stance, inquired, "Have you felt ill? Or dizzy after doing a spell?"

"No, not that I recall," I responded, my voice steady.

"Okay, Liam, that's good," Naya replied, her tone shifting to one of soothing calmness. "Do the orb spell again." She released my hands, stepping back, granting me the space to manifest my magic.

With a sense of newfound understanding, I opened my hand, conjuring the orb of light. My eyes sought Naya's for affirmation, ensuring each movement adhered to her guidance.

"Good," she approved with an encouraging nod. "Now, pull it back, nice and slowly so we can see it."

I concentrated, feeling the strands of mana that tethered the orb to me. With deliberate care, I reeled them back. The orb, responding to my will, began to disassemble, its luminescent particles retracting into my palm like celestial fireflies seeking refuge.

Joren's exclamation broke the spellbinding moment. "I knew it!" He thrust his arms skyward in a dramatic display, then pointed an accusatory finger at me. "I saw him release the orb back in the dormitory. I thought I must have imagined it, but no." He paused, a look of realization dawning upon him. "That means he did the same with the orb he held after he took off the dampener! How can he still be standing after throwing away that much mana?"

Naya's gaze, like a beacon, drew me back from Joren's

incredulity. "Listen to me, okay? You need to pull in your mana after every single use."

"I understand, I'm sorry." My words were heavy with a concoction of concern and baffled guilt. "What about energy beams, though? Am I meant to retract them?"

Joren sighed, a sound that spoke of resignation and experience. "That's one of the reasons I never focused on learning the skill. An energy ball, beam, or anything that you essentially throw... you don't get that energy back." He paused, his eyes locking onto mine, ensuring his message was clear. "That's why you're only meant to do a few in a single fight. After that, it'll take you a few days to recover."

"But what about when you were throwing those rocks?"

"That's different," Joren responded. "As the rock is launched, we gather the mana behind it, almost to a point. The rock is accelerated and pushed. After it is in motion, we reabsorb the mana again."

Naya, her expression laced with concern, asked, "You really don't feel dizzy? At all?"

"No, not at all!" I affirmed, perplexed by their astonishment.

Joren, his curiosity piqued, inquired, "How do you not know this? Are you not Lylackian?"

"Joren, that's enough," Naya interjected firmly, her voice a protective shield as she positioned herself between us. Her demeanor softened as she faced Joren, her words faltering like a stream over stones. "The circumstances are... Liam recently..." She grappled with the right way to express the complex situation.

Without hesitation, I filled the silence with my truth. "I lost my memory."

Naya's gaze pivoted back to me, her eyes wide with understanding and empathy. She reached out, enveloping my hands in hers.

Joren, absorbing this revelation, nodded, a semblance of understanding dawning on his face. "That makes sense." He shrugged off the weight of the previous tension. "Very well. What shall we do next? Want to train with us, Naya?"

Naya, standing steadfast by my side, turned to Joren, her expression one of surprised relief. "That's it? No more questions?"

Joren's response was matter-of-fact, his mechanical personality resurfacing like a well-oiled machine. "Liam can't remember. Likely had his crest removed. None of my business. Still an impressive person. Fast learner. Will not make the same mistake again."

I observed Joren, noting the rigid return of his analytical demeanor. "Are you alright, Joren?"

His reply came with a firm nod and a rare, genuine smile aimed at me. "Of course! I learned a new ability today, as did you." His tone carried a note of satisfaction. "Today has been a good day."

Naya's voice slowed, her words threading through the air with a hint of poignancy. "The day your sister failed the exam?"

Joren's reply was layered with an unexpected optimism. "Had she not, I wouldn't have teamed up with you."

Glancing downwards, I noticed a bundle of white cloth lying abandoned on the floor. Puzzled, I pointed and asked, "What's that?"

"Oh," Naya approached the bundle and deftly picked it up. With a few smooth motions, she unraveled it, revealing a pristine white long-sleeved top. "This is to replace your chainmail," she explained, her voice laced with a touch of practicality.

Gratefully, I accepted the garment from her. "Oh, thank you! Where did you get this from?"

She replied, "There's a tailor near the canteen. I thought you'd rather not be topless during the rest of the exam." Her gaze then shifted, a hint of curiosity in her eyes. "Did you manage to see how powerful you are without the dampener?"

"No," I admitted, my mind wandering back to our recent

activities. "We got distracted practicing telekinesis and energy beams." As I spoke, I began to replace my chainmail with the white top.

Joren's keen eyes glinted, and he nodded. "Ah, yes. New crest. Theory confirmed. Frustrated I hadn't noticed before. Will pay better attention next time," he mused aloud, his analytical mind piecing together the clues.

Donning the top, I turned to Joren. "Are you sure you're alright? Your speech pattern..."

Joren nodded, seemingly aware of his altered state. He took a deep, steadying breath, an effort to regain his usual composure. "I'm sorry... I tend to get like this when I'm extremely shocked. Will try to do better." He closed his eyes briefly, chastising himself for the lapse. Upon reopening them, he offered me a smile. "Sorry."

Holding the chainmail top in my hands, I contemplated its future use. "Should I just put this over the top?" I asked, uncertain of the proper course of action.

Naya, with a slight edge of reprimand in her voice, reminded me, "Well, you were meant to come here to see what happens if you cast a spell while you're not wearing it."

"Yeah, sorry about that..." I replied, a tinge of apology coloring my words.

As I pondered the fate of the chainmail, a thought emerged. "If we're not going to fix it, is there a way to turn it into something else?"

Naya, considering the possibilities, suggested, "How about a gauntlet?"

Joren, however, was quick to counter. "Too fragile," he stated flatly. He took the chainmail from me and knelt on the floor. From his pocket, he produced a small knife and the bag of broken links. With deliberate motions, he began to twist the knife, skillfully breaking the links.

"Hey, now..." I started, my instinct to preserve the chainmail surfacing.

But Naya, placing a calming hand on my chest, reassured

me, "Just leave him to it, Liam. I'm sure he knows what he's doing." Trusting her judgment, I allowed myself to relax.

"How about you try out the orb spell again?" she suggested. "I want to see how big it is without the chainmail."

Guiding me towards the crystal at the center of the room, she prepared me for another attempt at the spell, her presence a steady anchor in the sea of our ongoing magical exploration.

In the vastness of the domed room, a sense of tranquility washed over me. This was my moment to truly gauge the magnitude of my illusion spell, unbound by the constraints of walls. Opening my hand, I unleashed the spell. A massive green sphere of energy erupted, filling the room with its luminescent presence.

Naya, taken aback by the sheer size of the orb, stepped backward repeatedly, her gaze fixed upwards, attempting to discern its summit. Eventually, she found herself against the wall.

"Liam... It has to be more than fifty paces across." She slowly returned to my side, her eyes still locked on the awe-inspiring orb, her voice barely more than a whisper. "Imagine if this was an energy ball..." she muttered, lost in thought.

Curious, I asked, "What's the difference?"

"They're similar, but there's a crucial difference. The illusion orb, like this one, is made of loose mana. It's expansive, less controlled. An energy ball, on the other hand, is mana that's massively condensed."

I turned to her, intrigued. "So, make it smaller?"

"Yes," she continued, her eyes reflecting the orb's glow. "The size is indicative of the strength. The tighter you can compress it, the more force it holds. Think of it as a coiled spring – the more compact it is, the more potent the release."

With Naya's guidance echoing in my mind, I focused on the orb. "Like absorbing it, but not letting it enter my body?" I asked, seeking confirmation.

"Exactly," she affirmed. "Imagine drawing it in, condensing it, but keeping it external."

I nodded, channeling my intent into the spell. The orb responded to my will, the green energy beginning to condense. I felt the mana pulsate, growing denser with each passing moment.

Naya watched intently as the orb shrank. "That's it, Liam. Keep going."

It continued to shrink, the green energy condensing under my will, until it transformed into a large ball, about the size of a child.

Naya's sudden burst of laughter, light and unguarded, filled the room. "Liam, this filled up half the room only a few seconds ago!"

"Do I keep going?" I asked, my focus still locked on the energy ball.

Her smile vanished, replaced by a look of astonishment. "You think you can?"

"I only stopped because I wasn't sure how small to make it."

"Liam... how small do you think you could make it?" Naya's asked slowly.

With a casual shrug, I compressed it further. A split second later, it was the size of an eyeball. "I doubt it would be very useful this size," I remarked casually.

Suddenly, Naya stumbled forward, bumping against my chest. "Be careful!" she exclaimed, her gaze fixed on the orb, her eyes wide with a mixture of awe and apprehension.

"Sorry. So what am I meant to do with it now?" I inquired, unsure of the next step.

Naya took an unsteady step back, her voice tinged with worry. "Liam, I think this was a mistake."

Puzzled, I asked, "What have I done wrong this time?"

"That is far too much energy. Liam, you need to absorb it, don't break the connection with it, no matter what."

Her words sent a chill down my spine. Slowly, methodically, I began to unravel the orb, reabsorbing the energy. But as I did, my body grew heavy, and I stumbled, my connection to the orb wavering.

"Liam! Stay with…" Naya's voice trailed off as darkness crept into the edges of my vision. Pain erupted in my head, my chest tightened, and my limbs burned with an agonizing intensity. I glimpsed Joren, his face etched with a cold calculating look, rushing towards us. I tried to scream, but my voice was a silent cry of despair.

My gaze returned to the orb, the realization dawning on me - I still hadn't absorbed it. I was out of mana! I was dying! I felt a sharp pain in my knees and realized I had fallen to them. I forced every fiber of my being to focus on the orb and continued to absorb it, strand by strand. My body rippled, screamed, and started to tear itself apart! I needed to absorb the mana now! I reached out, grabbed it, and my world went black.

CHAPTER TWENTY-FOUR
The Finger

Engulfed in a dark abyss, I floated aimlessly, a solitary soul adrift in an endless void. A voice, distant and echoey, repeated incessantly, "I'm so sorry, Liam." The words reverberated through the emptiness, each utterance a haunting refrain.

Time lost its meaning in that void, until slowly, light began to pierce my vision, piece by piece, and the silhouette of someone formed in front of me. I blinked, as the darkness began to recede and the image of Naya, her face framed against the domed ceiling appeared. It took a moment for me to realize I was lying on her lap, looking up into her tear-streaked face.

As my eyes met hers, her expression transformed into a smile of profound relief. "Oh, thank the gods!" she exclaimed, her voice choked with emotion. Gently, she stroked my hair, her touch soothing.

A sudden flash of pain coursed through my head, prompting me to raise a hand to my throbbing temple.

"Seems new hand just as good as old hand," I heard Joren's voice, tinged with curiosity and disbelief.

I glanced down to see Joren, his gaze fixed intently on the floor. "My head is killing me," I groaned.

Naya's hand continued its comforting motion. "I'm sorry, Liam. I shouldn't have asked you to try out the spell. I shouldn't have mentioned energy balls. You must have used up all of your mana."

"Lucky you didn't die," Joren added, his eyes still avoiding mine.

"What are you doing?" I inquired, curious despite my pain.

"Dropping mana down hole. Trying to find bottom. Unsuccessful," he replied, his focus unwavering.

With Naya's assistance, I managed to sit up. "What hole?"

Joren rose to a kneeling position, and that's when I noticed a small hole in the floor.

"When you passed out, you dropped the energy ball," Naya explained, her voice still laced with worry.

"Not before grabbing it idiotically," Joren commented bluntly, his expression serious. "You destroyed your hand. Everything but your little finger." He held up a bloodied piece of flesh, showing an unmistakable fingernail.

I gasped and quickly looked at my hands. To my relief, they were intact.

"Watching it grow back was fascinating," Joren observed. "However, leaving evidence like this around will likely generate unwanted questions." Without a second thought, he dropped the finger down the hole and briskly rubbed his hands together. "Shall we get something to eat?"

Pausing for a moment, I turned to Naya. "Did Joren just drop my finger down a hole?"

"A deep hole," Joren added nonchalantly. "Don't worry, nobody will find that."

Naya rolled her eyes at Joren's comment, then let out a short, sob-coated laugh. "He's weird, Liam." She turned her attention back to me, her expression shifting to one of concern. "Would you like to try to stand?"

With her help, I slowly got to my feet, feeling the weight of my body as if for the first time. "Everything aches," I admitted, my voice shaky. "Everything feels stiff."

"It's likely because of the mana loss," Naya said, her support unwavering.

"Has it happened to you before?" I asked, curious about her own experiences.

Naya shook her head. "It's drilled into us at a pretty early age never to cut mana unless necessary."

"Right, of course..." I murmured, feeling somewhat isolated from their world of magical norms.

Joren, ever practical, repeated his earlier suggestion. "Is that a no on getting something to eat?"

I managed a weak laugh but shook my head. "You can go ahead. I think I should lie down."

Naya began to guide me towards the door, her arm a steady presence. "You really should eat something first. It's the fastest way to get your mana back."

The door abruptly swung open with an air of uninvited intrusion, interrupting the stillness of the room. Veyra entered first, her height almost matching mine, moving with a silent, lethal grace. Her short blonde hair framed a face that was a study in stoicism, her eyes sharply assessing the scene before her, silently appraising and categorically dismissing in the same breath.

Rexus, puffing out his chest with a brutish confidence, followed closely behind. He approached me with a wide, mocking grin. "There you are!" he exclaimed. Before I could react, he clamped a heavy hand on my shoulder, giving me a rough, jostling hug that was more of a shake. "We've been searching for you three. Thought you might want to push on with the exam," he said, his voice laden with a taunting undertone. He leaned in closer. "Heard you found one of my traps in the forest! You know it was meant for your feet, not your head!" He gave a loud laugh.

Eron silently lingered near the doorway, his intense gaze scrutinizing the room. Each time my attention drifted away from him and then back, I noticed something peculiar. Eron had shifted positions - not drastically, but just a few paces. It was enough movement that I became aware of my lack of awareness. It was as though with each glance away, he seemed to silently, almost imperceptibly, move, like a shadow subtly altering its form with the shifting light.

Veyra's voice, cold and precise, cut through the air. "He looks rough," she remarked, nodding towards Liam. "Is he going to be able to fight?" She looked around the room, "What have you been doing in here?"

Naya, standing her ground, replied firmly, "You'll find out tomorrow, I'm sure."

"Tomorrow?" asked Rexus with a whine. "You not doing another match today?"

"We've had our share of fights today," replied Naya.

"So what's wrong with him?" asked Veyra.

"He's fine," answered Naya, moving me past the three and toward the door.

"He doesn't look fine," said Rexus. "Guess my trap hit him harder than I thought." He gestured to the training room. "If you won't be fighting us today, how about a bit of practice?"

"We're not interested in a show-and-tell," I said, surprising myself with how sharp my words were, cutting through any pretense of camaraderie the group might have been feigning.

Veyra nodded, her eyes on mine. "Then we will speak to you in the morning at the forest." There was a pause, a brief moment where the tension in the room became almost tangible. Then, one by one, the trio turned to approach the crystal. As we walked away, I cast a glance over my shoulder. Veyra's steely eyes were fixed on me, her gaze intense and unwavering, as if she was etching every detail into her memory. The moment lingered, a silent exchange laden with unspoken challenges and calculations, before the door closed behind us, cutting off the connection.

As we walked away from the encounter, Naya let out a gasp, as though she'd been holding her breath. "Gods, did you see her?!" she exclaimed. "That girl is terrifying! I've never met someone and felt like I was constantly on the verge of being attacked, yet she just stood there!"

"I didn't get that impression," I responded, still mulling over the intense interaction we just had.

"I genuinely believe I may be in love," said Joren, looking perplexed.

We turned to him in surprise. "What?" Naya blurted out.

Joren's eyes had a distant, admiring look. "She was perfection. Her movements, precise, with not a wasted step. Her gaze, those eyes… She probably already knows everything we're going to do in tomorrow's battle. I had to bite my tongue to avoid agreeing to battle her today!"

"Is that why you were so silent?" I asked, a chuckle escaping my lips.

Joren, lost in his thoughts, didn't seem to hear me. He turned around and started walking backward, a contemplative expression on his face. "Do you think they would mind me watching them practice?"

Naya quickly spun him back around, a hint of urgency in her actions. "Yes, they would mind, and you'd probably spill all our secrets just to impress her. Come on!"

His shoulders slumped in resignation. "We are definitely going to lose to them tomorrow."

In the sparsely filled lunch hall, Naya, Joren, and I found solace at a secluded table. The usual cacophony of voices was absent, amplifying the sound of my every bite into an echoing reminder of my physical discomfort. Each chew of my sandwich was a laborious task, my body protesting in achy defiance.

Trying to inject some levity, Naya elbowed Joren lightly. "So, Joren, still caught up in thoughts of Veyra?"

Joren, momentarily distracted from his food, shot back with a wry grin. "Speaking of romance, what's going on between you two?"

I blushed, but Naya laughed. "I don't know, what are we, Liam?"

I shook my head. "I'm just eating my sandwich."

Our banter was interrupted when an extra tray clattered onto the table, and Lammat dropped down into a spare seat next to Joren.

"Lammat!" Naya gave a joyful laugh and leaned across the table, wrapping her arms around him.

I smiled, placing down my sandwich. "How's the new Team Lammat treating you?"

Lammat made a face. "Kai thinks he knows everything. And Tyran? They're like two peas in an arrogant pod. The only thing keeping me sane is Leana."

"Yeah, Leana's alright," I agreed with a nod.

Lammat turned to Joren, "Hey! I'm Lammat. You're Joren, right? My replacement?"

Joren looked at him, then looked away. "Yes."

Lammat paused, sharing a glance between me and Naya. "Great!"

As we chatted, exchanging stories, Lammat suddenly fixed his gaze on me. "Liam, you alright there? You're looking a bit worse for wear."

Before I could answer, Naya jumped in, her voice hushed. "He's recovering. Used up all his mana today, went a bit overboard with a spell. I've never seen someone with mana exhaustion before."

Lammat frowned, his concern evident. "That's not mana exhaustion. If it was, he'd be on death's door." He looked to Naya. "If it was, you'd take him to a medic, rather than a lunch hall, right?" his tone taking on an almost parental reprimand. An unusual change from his usual joviality.

I attempted a reassuring smile. "Well, you should've seen me a while back. I was practically a ghost."

Unconvinced, Lammat reached across the table, placing his hand gently on my neck, and guiding my face towards him. His eyes bore into mine, serious and intent. "You need to recover, Liam. I'm counting on you. It's your job to win me back, yes?"

My forced smile slipped away, and I nodded firmly. With those parting words, Lammat stood, leaving his almost untouched meal behind. He strode away, his silhouette gradually merging with the dim light of the hall.

"I like him," Joren remarked, as he slid Lammat's tray towards himself.

Naya chuckled. "Why, because he gave you food?"

Joren shook his head, pausing as he picked up a forkful. "No, it's because he genuinely cares." He took a bite, contemplating. "You can tell he really misses you."

Naya's gaze shifted to me, her expression thoughtful. "You think we can win him back?"

I nodded, taking another bite of my sandwich, my determination unwavering. "I know we will."

In a matter of seconds, Joren had almost cleared Lammat's tray, stuffing as much as he could into his mouth. His expression unreadable, he suddenly stood up. "Where's the tailor's, Naya?" he asked through a full mouth.

Naya looked puzzled. "Just down that corridor, but why?"

Without a word, Joren turned and strode off, leaving us in a silence filled with questions. Naya watched him leave, then turned to me with a small laugh. "He's so strange," she said, amusement lacing her words. "But, in his own way, he's kind of… wonderful."

Back in our room, Naya and I lay on our respective beds, our gazes fixed on the bland ceiling above. The quiet hum of the evening wrapped around us, a stark contrast to the day's earlier tumult.

Breaking the silence, Naya turned her head towards me. "How are you feeling now that you've eaten?"

I flexed my fingers, surprised at the relative ease of the movement. "Actually, much better," I admitted, a note of relief in my voice. The food had worked wonders, restoring a sense of balance to my body.

"Just... don't practice any more magic until morning, okay?" Naya's voice held a tinge of concern.

I nodded in agreement, even though she couldn't see it. "I won't," I assured her.

After a moment, I asked a question that had been lingering in my mind. "What do you think it's like for Lammat, having to be with Kai and Tyran?" she looked over at me frowning, "I know I asked him during our meal, but really, how well do you think he's coping?"

Naya sighed, her voice carrying across the quiet room. "Well, their personalities might clash, but I bet their fighting styles complement each other." She paused, then added, "Remember, Lammat is a fantastic fighter. He's got a few years of training and development on us."

I chuckled softly. "I keep forgetting he's older."

Naya's response came with a hint of a laugh. "Maybe it's because of his childish behavior."

I reflected on an earlier encounter. "During the first match, there was this moment when Tyran almost forced me out of the dome. If it weren't for Lammat stepping in, I don't think I could have stopped him." I paused, the memory vivid in my mind.

"You never mentioned this before..." said Naya.

"The way Lammat intervened... it was effortless," I added, a note of admiration in my voice. "Honestly, there's a good chance that Lammat is physically stronger than Tyran. The ease with which he handled the situation... it was something else."

I lay there, staring at the ceiling, pondering the strength and skill Lammat possessed. It was a humbling reminder of the various levels of prowess within the exam, and how much I still had to learn.

The door to our room swung open, and Joren strode in with a purposeful gait. Without a word, he approached me and said, "Hold out your non-dominant arm."

Obliging, I extended my left arm. Joren crouched down, revealing the remains of my chainmail. He carefully unraveled a strip from it and held it up.

Taking my arm, he draped the strip over my hand, wrapping it around my wrist. There was a soft snapping sound as the links tugged themselves together, forming a secure fit.

"How does that feel?" Joren asked, looking up at me with a hint of expectation.

I turned the new accessory over, examining it. Joren had transformed the sleeve of the chainmail into an armlet. Attached to the clasp were three small metal circles. Curious, I tugged at one of them. It resisted at first, but with a bit more force, it popped free. I inspected it closely before letting it snap back into place against the chainmail.

"Magnets?" I inquired, looking up at Joren.

"Yes, strong magnets," he nodded, a hint of pride in his voice. "I asked the tailor for his strongest ones." He quickly unclasped the armlet and showed me the other side where another trio of magnets were embedded. With a deft movement, he spun it around his wrist, the ends snapping together. "This should be easier to equip and remove than your chainmail." He hooked a finger under it and gave it a firm tug, removing it with ease, then handed it back to me.

I mimicked Joren's motion, finding that I could don the armlet and remove it with relative ease. "Thank you, Joren! This is wonderful!" My eyes then drifted to the remnants of my damaged chainmail top. "What do we do with this?"

Joren scooped up the chainmail, laying it out in front of him. "Only one sleeve has been shortened. I can still repair the hole if you wish. The spare links and those from the other sleeve should balance it out."

"But we don't need it anymore," Naya interjected from her bed.

Joren began working on the other sleeve with his knife. "Then I shall use it as practice," he said, focusing intently on the chainmail, his hands skillfully manipulating the links.

Naya, intrigued, sat up to watch Joren's meticulous work on the chainmail. Her curiosity piqued, she asked, "Hey, I've been meaning to ask. Have you been teamed up with Calia since the beginning?"

Joren didn't look up from his task. "No," he replied. "She started with that Rexus guy, trying out for Gouds. I was with some other Eulis'."

"Are they still in the exam?" Naya probed further.

"I am the only one from the original team who passed," Joren stated matter-of-factly, his focus unwavering from the chainmail.

"Even in the second exam?" I chimed in. "I thought you were meant to fail if your partner failed."

"A lie," Joren said with a nonchalant shrug. "Evidently, I tried to save his life, but he didn't reciprocate."

I sighed, feeling a pang of guilt. "For my illusion, Kai, Leana, and Lammat all died. I only started moving when the examiner turned to attack Tyran." I offered a small smile to lighten the mood.

Joren looked up, a flicker of recognition in his eyes. "Yes, I remember you crashing into Tyran's desk." He paused, setting down his knife. "It's a dream illusion spell. The desks and chairs were likely coated in the spell, so when the Eulis triggered it..." He clapped his hands together, before shrugging and returning to his work. "Very clever spell."

"You died," Naya said, turning to me.

Feigning offense, I retorted, "You didn't rescue me?"

She laughed. "In my defense, in my illusion, you told me not to worry, as you were an expert at that spell."

I nodded in agreement. "Yeah, Lammat said the same to me."

Our conversation meandered through various topics for the next few hours, filling the room with a comfortable camaraderie. Eventually, we decided to call it a night. I lay back down, the stress of the upcoming battle lingering at the back of my mind. However, exhaustion took over, and the next thing I knew, it was morning.

CHAPTER TWENTY-FIVE
A Team Of Tricksters

Naya, Joren and I ascended the staircase to the surface in contemplative silence, the only sound being our footsteps echoing off the stone steps. Each of us was lost in thought, mentally bracing for the confrontation that lay ahead.

The further we climbed, the more the ambiance began to change. A faint light filtered down from above, hinting at the world that awaited us. As we neared the top of the staircase, anticipation hung heavily in my chest.

Emerging from the underground, the early morning mist enveloped the air, lending a surreal quality to the landscape. The towering trees, shrouded in fog, seemed to whisper with every rustle of their leaves. Veyra and Eron, along with the Examiner, stood at the gate, awaiting our arrival, their postures a blend of ease and readiness.

Naya, upon seeing them, whispered to Joren and me, "You think they've been waiting long?"

Joren glanced at our opponents and shrugged. "We're here now. That's what matters."

I nodded in agreement, my attention shifting to Veyra and Eron. Veyra's confident stance and keen gaze contrasted with Eron's quieter but no less intense presence. The Examiner greeted us with a professional nod.

Notably absent from their group was Rexus. His usual brash energy was replaced by the stillness of the morning.

Naya, perhaps in an attempt to assert our presence, addressed Veyra. "Hope you're ready for a real challenge today," she said, a playful yet competitive glint in her eyes.

Veyra's response was as direct as her posture. "I'm always ready." Eron, standing silently beside her, gave a slight nod, his expression unreadable but clearly in agreement.

While we waited for Rexus, I turned to the Goud, who stood observing us with a neutral expression. "Do you ever sleep, or do you just wait here for us to show up?" I asked, half-joking.

He smiled faintly. "The life of an Examiner doesn't afford much rest during the exams."

Our conversation was cut short by the sound of footsteps. Rexus, with his characteristic lack of urgency, sauntered up the path, yawning loudly and stretching his arms leisurely.

"Glad you could join us," Naya remarked dryly as Rexus finally reached us.

Unperturbed, Rexus just smirked and joined Veyra and Eron.

The Examiner then presented each team with a crystal. "These have been charmed to withstand three strikes," he explained, pushing open the gates.

As we took our crystal, the weight of the decision on where to place it lay heavily on our shoulders. The forest around us felt like a silent witness, its shadows and light playing across the path, as if hinting at the numerous possibilities and outcomes of the day's battle. We turned expectantly towards Veyra's team. Their response, however, was an array of blank expressions.

"Where do you plan to place your crystal?" I asked.

Veyra, her expression unchanging, replied coolly, "We won't be sharing that information. But feel free to place yours."

Naya, her brows furrowed, chimed in, "The team that issues the challenge is supposed to place their crystal first, right?"

Veyra nodded, an air of certainty about her. "That's

correct. But we didn't issue the challenge."

I countered, recalling the previous night's interaction, "But you did, in the training room last night."

Veyra's response was quick. "At which point? When Rexus inquired about continuing the exam, or when I questioned if you could even fight?" Her nod towards me punctuated her statement.

Naya, slightly taken aback, stammered, "I was sure you issued the challenge."

It was Joren who clarified, with a hint of resignation in his voice, "Actually, Naya, it was you. Just moments ago when you asked if they were ready for a real challenge."

Naya began to protest, but the Examiner interjected, his voice carrying the weight of authority. "I would also consider that a challenge, Naya."

Rexus, who had been quietly observing the exchange, suddenly raised his hand in a mocking gesture, inviting us to lead the way. "After you," he said, his tone dripping with derision.

Joren approached me and reached for the crystal I was holding. "Mind if I place it today?" he asked, his tone casual yet determined.

Surprised but intrigued, I handed it over without hesitation. "Sure, go ahead."

With the crystal in hand, Joren began to walk through the forest, his steps measured and purposeful. As he moved, he discreetly slipped the crystal into his pocket. In its place, he pulled out a knife, expertly twirling it around his fingers in a display of dexterity.

After a few moments, he turned to the Examiner. "Are weapons permitted in the exam?" Joren asked, the knife still dancing between his fingers.

The Examiner nodded affirmatively. "Examinees are allowed to bring anything from outside, as well as use any items available within the complex."

"Thank you," Joren said, acknowledging the confirmation

with a nod.

He then turned to Veyra, continuing to walk but with his gaze fixed on her. "If I manage to beat you one-on-one, will you be my date at the dance in a few days?" he asked, his tone surprisingly earnest.

Veyra, for the first time, seemed visibly taken aback, almost stumbling in her step. "A date?" she echoed, her composure momentarily faltering.

Joren nodded, his expression serious. "I'm not trying to trick you. I'm just confident I can beat you. You strike me as someone who only respects those who can compete at your level."

Veyra glanced briefly at her teammates, then gave a mocking smile. "You think you can beat me one-on-one?"

"Certainly," Joren replied with unwavering confidence.

Veyra laughed, attempting to mask her intrigue. "That's not going to happen."

"Then take the bet," Joren challenged.

She considered for a moment. "Alright, say I take the bet. What do I get if you can't beat me?"

"Whatever you want," Joren said dismissively, the knife still in motion. "I'm not going to lose, so feel free to choose whatever."

"Talk about having a death wish," muttered Rexus.

Veyra, after a moment's contemplation, nodded her agreement to Joren's challenge. There was a hint of curiosity in her eyes, a rare crack in her usual stoic demeanor. "Alright, I accept your bet," she stated, her voice carrying challenge and intrigue.

His smile was faint but evident as he carefully stowed the knife away, his fingers deftly manipulating the object before it disappeared from sight. In its place, he retrieved the crystal, holding it up briefly for all to see.

Then, with a sudden movement, Joren hurled the crystal through the air with considerable force. It arced gracefully before landing with a thud that seemed to echo through the forest. Watching it quickly grow into its larger form, a sense of dread washed over me. The crystal had landed in the exact spot where Naya and I had ours in the previous battle against Joren – out in the open, vulnerable and exposed.

I instinctively opened my mouth to protest, but a glance at Naya halted my words. Her eyes met mine, conveying a silent message of caution.

Joren, seemingly pleased with his choice, turned back to face Veyra, his demeanor nonchalant, almost carefree.

Rexus, who had been observing the exchange couldn't hold back his reaction. "That's where you're placing your crystal?" he asked, his voice booming with laughter, finding the audacity of the move either foolish or bold.

Veyra, on the other hand, remained silent. However, judging by her expression, it was clear she hadn't expected this turn of events.

Joren, unfazed by the reactions, kept his smile. "Apparently, we are allowed to see where you plant your crystal if you invite us, but don't worry about that. We'll see you soon." His words were light, but they carried an undercurrent of confidence and a hint of a plan.

Veyra took a few contemplative steps back, her fingers idly rolling the crystal, her gaze distant as if pondering a deeper strategy. Then, with a swift turn, she walked away, her team falling into step behind her.

As soon as they were out of earshot, I spun around. "What are you doing? Why are you putting us out in the open?"

Naya, mirroring my concern, said pointedly, "Joren, if you're thinking of betraying us…"

Joren met our gazes, his expression thoughtful. "You think that if I make us lose, they'll choose me to join them?" He paused, allowing the question to hang in the air, but neither of us responded. "You both managed surprisingly well in this area last time. It seemed like a disadvantage, but you turned it into an advantage. One that we will also improve." He glanced back, ensuring Veyra's team had disappeared into the forest.

"You have a plan?" I asked, a flicker of hope igniting.

"Many." Abruptly, Joren turned back, extending his hands towards the crystal. The ground began to tremble, the soil churning and separating under his command. "Naya, assist," he instructed. Catching my eye, he said, "Lower it. Gently."

Naya, though initially confused, raised her hands towards the ground. "What am I doing?"

"Use your mana to tug at the ground. Pull it to pieces. When those pieces lift, cast them aside and grab the soil beneath," Joren guided her.

I couldn't help but smile, realizing Joren's intent. "You're turning the soil into sand?"

"Not sand, just loose soil. We don't have long. Hurry."

As Naya and Joren worked in tandem to transform the terrain, I carefully enveloped the crystal in my mana. Ensuring not to damage it, I wrapped it in an extra layer of energy and gently lowered it, pausing at any sign of resistance. Where possible, I lent a helping hand with my telekinesis, assisting in loosening and digging through the soil.

"Sorry, Joren," Naya apologized, her movements frantic as she churned the ground.

"It's understandable, do not worry," Joren reassured her, his focus unwavering. "We're going up against a trapper and a sneak. Both can't work as well in an open space. Veyra is the only unknown element, but if she is a fighter, then it's best we see her coming."

As I watched Joren's mind work, I couldn't help but be impressed by his tactical acumen. His ability to analyze and adapt to the situation was remarkable.

After a couple of minutes, the crystal was fully submerged, leaving only a patch of loose soil to mark its location.

As I began to carefully unwrap and reabsorb the mana from the crystal, a sudden wave of nausea overwhelmed me. The world tilted, and I found myself dropping to one knee, the unexpected motion causing me to instinctively sever the mana connection.

Naya was at my side in an instant, concern etched on her face. "You haven't regained enough mana since last night," she said, her voice laced with worry.

"I'm fine," I managed to say, though my voice betrayed my condition. I forced myself to stand, but dizziness washed over me, blurring my vision momentarily. "I'm sorry, I cut the mana again."

"Liam…"

As I focused on regaining my composure, a faint light crept out from the ground, snaking its way toward the forest. The other team had successfully planted their crystal.

Joren, taking charge with a decisive tone, said, "Liam, you should refrain from using any more magic. You'll be an upfront fighter instead." He glanced at Naya. "You stay back for now in defense. I will lead the attack with Liam in support. I need him to see their crystal."

We all nodded in agreement, understanding the need to adapt our strategy to the circumstances. Placing our hands on the crystal, we readied ourselves to begin the match.

However, the match didn't start. Minutes ticked by, stretching into an uneasy wait, our anticipation turning to confusion.

Breaking the silence, I voiced my concern. "Are they allowed to wait this long before starting the fight?"

Naya pondered aloud, "There was never any time limit given."

Joren, his gaze scanning the surroundings, added, "I see. They're likely using this time to set up traps." He looked at me. "Use this time to rest and get your strength back."

An hour passed in this state of uneasy vigilance before the dome around us finally shifted to a deep blue, signaling the start of the match. The delay, intentional or not, had given our opponents ample time to prepare, and us plenty to worry about.

Joren started to move through the forest, and I followed

close behind. My muscles were tight and uncomfortable, protesting every step I took. The residual effects of my overexertion were more evident now, as I struggled to keep pace with Joren.

As we advanced through the dense foliage of the forest, the rustle of leaves and the occasional snap of a twig underfoot accompanied our cautious steps. The dappled sunlight filtering through the canopy above cast shifting patterns on the ground, adding to the tense atmosphere.

Suddenly, the quiet of the forest was broken by the presence of Veyra and Eron, emerging from between the trees like specters. Veyra's posture was tense, ready for action, while Eron moved with a quiet, deadly grace.

Joren, his eyes narrowing as he assessed the situation, posed a question to me with a hint of irony in his voice. "I don't suppose you can handle them both?" His words, though rhetorical, hung in the air, underscoring the gravity of the challenge we faced.

As I squared off against Veyra, I gathered the remnants of my strength and lunged forward, aiming a swift kick at her. My muscles, tight and uncooperative from overexertion, screamed in protest. But the desire to prove my worth, especially in my weakened state, pushed me beyond the pain. Veyra, with the poise of a seasoned warrior, effortlessly evaded. It was a single, perfect step. The minimal movement required, a perfect calculation of distance that allowed her to avoid my strike effortlessly.

Not to be deterred, I quickly followed up with a punch, pouring every ounce of my will into the movement. But Veyra, as if dancing to a rhythm only she could hear, pivoted gracefully out of harm's way. My fist whistled through the air, grazing her so lightly I could barely feel it.

She touched her cheek where my fist had almost landed, a look of mild surprise on her face. "Most people can't even get that close," she said, her voice betraying a hint of respect.

Frozen in the moment, I stared at her, ready to continue

our duel, but she simply smiled and crossed her arms. "Your father would be proud of you, Prince Lexis."

The words hit me like a tidal wave. "What did you just call me?" I stammered, feeling my legs buckle slightly under the weight of her revelation.

Veyra's laugh was soft, almost apologetic. "I'm sorry for your loss, but I think he'd be proud of the person you've become." Her eyes softened. "Your mother, too. It's a shame you never had the chance to meet her."

"You… knew her?" My voice was barely a whisper, my mind racing with questions.

"No, but my parents spoke of her often. She was a remarkable queen."

Before I could digest this new information, Joren's voice rang out. "Liam!" I turned to find him with one arm slung around Eron's shoulder, the other pointing excitedly at his companion. "We share a birthday!" His voice was filled with an uncharacteristic glee.

Veyra interjected, her proximity startling me as I turned back to face her. "Your birthday is coming up soon." She was now unsettlingly close, her hands gently grasping mine. She leaned in, her lips barely brushing against mine. "Happy early birthday, my prince."

"Liam!" Joren's shout jerked me away. I pulled back from Veyra, turning to see him beaming. "Eron's agreed to be my date for the dance!"

I frowned, turning back to Veyra, ready to reject her unwanted advance, but eager to hear how she knew about my past, but I suddenly felt a sharp impact on my shoulder. Whirling back around, I found myself face-to-face with Eron. His movements were a blur, his fingertips striking with pinpoint accuracy. He delivered a series of rapid strikes, three down one arm, then mirrored the action on my other. As I instinctively moved to step back, Eron's final jab hit my thigh, throwing off my balance and sending me tumbling backward onto the forest floor.

Joren, quick to react, unleashed a telekinetic blast aimed at Eron's side. Eron, however, seemed to anticipate the attack. With a spin, he dropped low to the ground, evading the blast. Then, in a fluid series of movements, he rose, delivering a barrage of jabs to Joren. Each hit landed with surgical precision, rendering Joren's limbs limp and unresponsive. The final, decisive jab to Joren's forehead sent him crashing to the ground, his body going limp like a puppet with its strings cut.

In a desperate attempt to turn the tide, I forced myself back to my feet and charged at Eron. His eyes widened momentarily in surprise at my approach, but he quickly regained his composure and leaped backward, out of my reach. Hindered by my still-recovering body, I was unable to close the distance between us. I stood there, next to Joren's limp body, feeling both helpless and frustrated.

"Are you alright?" I asked Joren, concern lacing my voice.

His response was weak, barely audible. "I don't think so."

I looked up, ready to reengage, but found Eron had disappeared. A sense of urgency gripped me as I realized I had also lost sight of Veyra. Frustration mounted within me – how could I have let her slip away unnoticed?

I shifted my stance, my eyes darting around the forest, seeking any hint of their whereabouts. The realization that Veyra was nowhere to be seen gnawed at me, a tactical oversight I couldn't afford.

In that moment of distraction, Eron reemerged like a phantom, his rapid strikes landing across my body. He twisted, span, and side-stepped, circling my slow form. The blows were more of an annoyance than genuinely painful, yet they served to heighten my irritation as their speed increased. I was frustrated, not just with Eron's relentless assault, but with myself for losing track of Veyra.

In a burst of exasperation, I shouted and swung out instinctively. My fist connected with Eron's face with a solid thud, the force of the impact sending him reeling and tumbling to the ground.

As Eron crumpled, the sudden shift back to our starting point caught me off guard. We were teleported back to the crystal, with Joren lying motionless beside us. I stood there, the adrenaline still coursing through my veins.

Naya, her face etched with frustration and concern, paced back and forth. "I can't handle Veyra," she admitted, her voice tense. "I tried everything – barriers, rocks, telekinetic pushes. I even tried grabbing her at one point. But she just flowed past everything like water in a river." She paused, emphasizing her next words. "If you two combined can't stop her, I certainly can't."

"What did she do when she realized there was no crystal?" I asked.

Naya gestured towards a spot on the ground. "She just buried her fist to get it instead." Following her point, I saw the tip of our crystal barely visible, a large crack marring its surface.

Suddenly, Naya's attention snapped to Joren's motionless form. She rushed to his side. "Joren! What happened?"

His words were slurred, his face pressed against the forest floor. "Eron is an energy blocker," he managed to say. Naya carefully turned him over, and his eyes found mine. "Any chance you can heal this?"

I placed my hand on Joren. To my relief, he began to stir, his fingers flexing slowly. "We will add that to your abilities then," he said, sitting up with effort. "Can't be energy blocked."

Puzzled, I asked, "What do you mean?"

Joren took a moment to collect his thoughts before explaining. "Energy blocking is a rare ability, difficult to master to that level. It involves injecting minuscule amounts of mana into another person's energy flow. It's like introducing a foreign element into a stream, disrupting the natural current. The blocker can target specific areas, rendering them temporarily useless."

"But it didn't work on me?" I asked, perplexed.

"Evidently," Joren replied, his tone carrying a hint of both surprise and curiosity. "Why did you freeze up in the fight?"

"What? I didn't freeze up," I protested.

Joren raised an eyebrow. "Standing perfectly still in the middle of a fight? I'd call that freezing up. What else would you call it?"

I shook my head, raising my hands defensively. "You mean when Veyra started talking to me? What was I supposed to do, hit her mid-sentence?"

"Talked to you?" Joren's interest was piqued.

"That why you attacked Eron?" I questioned, gesturing toward Joren, recalling the strange turn of events. "Immediately after you agreed to go to the dance with him?"

Naya interjected. "You made a date in the middle of a fight?"

I looked back at Joren, who now wore a knowing grin. "Ah, I see… very clever," he said with a nod, clapping his hands toward me in an exaggerated manner. "Even more impressed with her now. But how did she do it? Did you actually hit her? I didn't see any contact."

"What are you—"

"She got you with a dream spell."

"A dream spell?" My mind raced back to the conversation from last night. "She made me see things?"

"And hear things, apparently," Joren added, still smiling. "I asked Eron to the dance?"

I glanced back along the light streaking across the ground. "So… how much of that was real?"

"You were fighting Veyra, then you just stopped," Joren explained. "I called out to you a couple of times as she ran away, but you only started moving again when Eron attacked you."

The realization that I had been completely under the spell's influence was unsettling. "But it was so seamless, so lifelike," I remarked.

Naya nodded sympathetically. "Most dreams feel real while you're in them. The more interesting they are, the deeper the dream." She suddenly laughed. "I can't believe you dreamed up Joren asking Eron to the dance!" She doubled over.

"But how did she make me think all that?" I asked, my thoughts returning to her words about my parents, and my supposed lineage as a prince.

"She cast the spell, but the content was all from your subconscious," Joren surmised, tapping his finger against his lips thoughtfully. "It tells us she's not as skilled with the spell as she could be. Otherwise, she'd have made it less confusing and more manipulative."

Naya stood back up, still smiling from the revelation. "So she could have had it just convince Liam he was running over to the crystal to score a point?"

Joren nodded, his mind already racing with implications. "Yes, but that could have woken him up from the excitement. If it were me, I'd have simply had the examiner appear and create a delay of some sort." He smiled, a glint of strategic thought in his eyes. "This is good news. We can use this."

"What is?" I asked, my mind still spinning from the realization that my encounter with Veyra had been an illusion.

"This means she hasn't told her team about her spell," Joren said.

Naya looked puzzled. "What makes you say that?"

Joren explained, "After Liam was under the spell, Eron saw the chance for a free, unguarded attack and took it, while I was right in front of him."

"So?" Naya prodded for more clarity.

I chimed in, understanding dawning. "So, I was already out of the match at that point. Eron should have turned his attention to Joren."

"Exactly," Joren affirmed.

Naya considered this. "Maybe he wanted to energy block both of you?"

Joren shrugged. "But why? Energy blocks only last about

twenty minutes at the most from even the most skilled users. If he were that good, which I doubt he is, we would have just waited it out between rounds."

I added, "Joren was his best option, but I was his easiest. He chose the easiest." A realization hit me. "They aren't working as a team."

Joren nodded, satisfied with our analysis. "Alright, now we need to figure out how she cast it on you. Did you touch her at all?"

"Only lightly. My knuckle grazed her cheek…" I recalled the moment, the subtlety of the contact.

"That's all it needs," Joren said. "Remember when I said the Eulis coated the table and chairs during the exam? Guess what Veyra coated."

"Her skin?" Naya guessed, her eyes widening. Joren nodded. "So if we touch her, we'll be put to sleep?"

I stepped forward, a new determination in my voice. "Alright then, how do we take her out?"

CHAPTER TWENTY-SIX
Dreams

As the dome's light shifted to a vibrant blue, the signal was clear. I burst forward, my heart pounding with adrenaline. The forest blurred past me as I ran toward the center of the arena, where I once again encountered Veyra. She stood there, a picture of focused calm, her eyes locking onto mine.

We faced each other in a tense standoff. Veyra moved first, trying to dodge around me with her characteristic agility. This time I was ready. Matching her speed, I grabbed the fabric of her clothing, using the momentum to spin her back to face me. She was fast, undeniably so, but in that moment, I managed to make contact.

Veyra, seizing the moment, moved swiftly to grab my hand. But anticipating her move, I quickly released my grip, causing her to stumble slightly in her momentum. She quickly recovered, using the opportunity to try to escape. However, I was one step ahead. I sprang forward, cutting off her path, my body moving almost on instinct.

I wasn't trying to fight her in the traditional sense; my objective was simply to prevent her escape. Each movement was calculated, not to strike, but to contain and control the space between us. Veyra, realizing my intent, shifted her tactics. She darted left and right, looking for an opening, but I matched her every move.

Our dance was one of strategy and speed. Veyra's

attempts to break free were met with my determined efforts to keep her in place. It was a battle of wits as much as agility. I could see the frustration building in her eyes with each failed attempt to slip past me. She was used to opponents trying to overpower her, but my approach was different – I knew she was better than me, but I wasn't trying to win.

The forest around us seemed to blur into a backdrop, all my focus narrowed down to Veyra's movements and my counter-moves. This was not just a physical confrontation; it was a mental one, a test of endurance and tactical thinking. I was determined not to let her spell or her speed give her the upper hand. This was a new kind of battle, one where the first to falter could lose everything.

Suddenly her stance shifted. She squared up, launching a series of calculated attacks. Each strike was a test of my reflexes. I focused intently, parrying her blows while ensuring her skin never made contact with mine. "So you figured it out," she remarked, a grin spreading across her face even as her attacks continued relentlessly.

"All I have to do is avoid touching your skin," I replied, deflecting another strike with my arm.

Her grin widened. "Well then, you're going to have to do better than that!" With those words, her assault intensified, her fists and feet becoming a blur. I bobbed and weaved, dodging and blocking, but her speed was overwhelming. One well-placed strike slipped through, connecting with my face.

Instantly, the forest was gone. I stood before a man in a long white robe, his white hair framing a kind face with piercing blue eyes. "You're doing well, Son," he said, his voice filled with warmth and pride.

The moment of peace was shattered by a searing pain in my leg. Reality snapped back into focus, and Veyra stood before me, her expression one of shock and awe. "You're kidding..." she gasped.

Without a second thought, I pulled Joren's knife from my leg and launched myself at her. We clashed again, our moves a whirlwind of action and reaction. Amid our exchange, her skin brushed against mine again, and the world shifted once more.

I found myself beside a man with dark hair and a beard, his gaze fixed on a distant horizon. "They'll come for us, one day," he said solemnly.

Pain jolted me back to the present. Veyra stared at me, disbelief etched on her face. "You're intentionally stabbing yourself?"

As I engaged with Veyra, the battle became a surreal experience, my consciousness flickering between two worlds. With every touch from her, I was plunged into vivid, dreamlike scenarios, only to be yanked back to the harsh reality of our fight by the sharp pain I inflicted on myself.

One moment, I was in the midst of our duel, parrying and dodging her strikes. The next, I found myself as a young boy, playfully dueling with wooden swords against royal guards in the sunlit courtyards of a grand palace.

I lowered the knife again.

Veyra's elbow connected sharply with my temple, and I reached out in a daze, managing to grasp her belt. She grabbed my wrist and the sound of orchestral music filled the air. I found myself in a dance, the steps coming to me as naturally as breathing.

Another jolt of pain brought me back.

I pulled Veyra closer, aiming for a head-butt, but my forehead collided with her shoulder uselessly as she adeptly twisted away.

Our battle continued, a relentless exchange of blows. Each touch from Veyra plunged me into a fleeting dream, before returning to the here and now. The illusions were brief but intense, each a stark contrast to the grim reality of our duel. But each time, I fought my way back, refusing to succumb to the spell's seductive pull.

The forest shifted to nothing but a mixed hue of greens and browns as we danced our deadly dance. It was more than a clash of skills; it was a battle of endurance, will, and my mind's ability to discern reality from illusion. I was determined not to let her spell dominate me.

Veyra's sudden move caught me completely off guard. She grabbed the blade of the knife, her expression one of fierce determination. Startled by her boldness, I hesitated, not wanting to cause her any further injury by sliding the knife out of her grip. She took advantage of my momentary pause, deftly twisting my grip and pulling the knife away from me.

In a swift, calculated motion, she reached out towards me. Reacting instinctively, I leaped back, creating a gap between us. But Veyra anticipated my move. With a rapid step, she maneuvered past me and delivered a precise stamp to the side of my knee.

There was a sickening pop, and I crumpled to the forest floor, a sharp pain shooting through my leg. I clutched at my knee, the intensity of the pain overwhelming. I waited for the familiar sensation of healing, but it didn't come. Veyra stood above me, now holding the knife, blood dripping from her hand, her expression questioning and respectful.

"Why didn't you use this on me?" she asked, her tone curious. "You must have known my grabbing it was a last resort. You could have easily pulled it free."

Grimacing from the pain, I managed to reply, "That could have caused long-lasting damage. I didn't want to do that to you."

Veyra nodded, a hint of understanding in her eyes. "Same here. That's why I dislocated your knee rather than break it. Pop it back in, rest it, and you'll be good as new in a few days."

"Sorry, I'll need him to be ready a little sooner than that."

At Veyra's startled turn, Joren came into view, a picture of focused determination. He was kneeling, his left hand gripping his right arm tightly, his right hand clenched into a fist. It was the unmistakable posture of someone preparing to launch an energy beam.

"Joren, don't!" I shouted, fearing the implications of such

a close-range attack.

Veyra stumbled backward, alarm written all over her face. The threat of being hit by an energy beam at almost point-blank range was a stark and immediate danger.

Joren opened his hand, but instead of an energy beam, he released a telekinetic blast. The force of the blast was amplified by a handful of soil, which flew directly into Veyra's face.

She instinctively covered her eyes, spitting and wiping away the dirt, trying to regain her vision. When she looked back at Joren, he was slowly lifting into the air, hovering ominously above her. "I look forward to dancing with you," he said, his voice calm.

With that, he unleashed another blast, this time using both hands. The force knocked Veyra off her feet, sending her crashing to the ground.

Dazed, Veyra lay on the forest floor as Joren landed softly in front of her. He stood over her for a moment, an imposing figure, before extending his hand towards her.

Veyra looked up, a hint of confusion flashing across her face before it settled into a smirk. She reached out, taking his hand.

"No, wait!" My warning came out as a desperate shout, but it was too late.

As their hands made contact, Veyra laughed, standing up on her own. "And there I thought you had it figured out," she said, a soft chuckle escaping her lips. Suddenly, her smirk fell away, and she gave a look of utter surprise.

"We did," Joren replied calmly. In a blur of motion, his arms moved through the air, his fingers targeting Veyra's joints with precision. She attempted a wild, frantic punch, but Joren caught it effortlessly, his fingers spreading out and rolling up her arm, rendering it limp and unresponsive. He then delivered two final hits to her hips, and she swayed, losing her balance. Joren caught her as she began to topple, gently lowering her to the ground.

"Good work, Liam." Joren approached me with deliberate care, his eyes scrutinizing as he examined my knee. His hands, skilled and precise, gripped and turned it quickly. A pop resonated, signaling everything was back in place, and I stood, testing the renewed strength in my leg. My gaze drifted to Veyra, her expression a vivid display of shock at my movement. "Looks like we've finally found a limitation of yours," Joren noted.

"What, that I can't heal dislocations?" I responded, a hint of amusement in my tone.

"How is this possible?" Veyra's voice was tinged with confusion and disbelief. "What did you do to me?"

Joren, with a hint of slyness in his smile, crouched beside her. "Multiple things, one of them you're really not going to like." He reached into his pocket, revealing a small bag. "We have dampeners. Liam here needs it to prevent himself from turning into a god," he explained, glancing at her with an awkward air, "And now I'm afraid you have one, too."

"What?"

"That moment I shot dirt into your face? I was also carrying one of these." He opened the bag, unveiling a minuscule link, and displaying it for her inspection. "After Liam here used up all the mana you'd coated your skin with, we needed a more permanent solution to prevent you from casting it again," he said with a casual shrug. "At least until you pass it, that is."

"Pass... it...?"

"Yeah, sorry, but I kind of... steered it down your gullet."

"You what!?"

"Yeah, I'm still tethered to it, so I know it worked. I wanted to ensure it didn't enter your lungs." He clapped his hands together, a gesture of completion. "And now we're untethered. Perfect!"

"You decided not to tell me the whole plan, I see," I commented.

"What, with the energy beam? I've seen how terrible an

actor you are, Liam. I wanted her to open her mouth, and the best way to do that was through surprise. Your panic enhanced the effect."

"And the flying?"

Joren stepped closer, his posture relaxed yet confident. "It looked really impressive, right?"

I laughed, the absurdity and thrill of the moment mingling. "But I thought you said your method only works when you know exactly where something is."

Joren's smile broadened, a spark of cunning in his eyes. "I did. It just so happens I happen to know where I am all the time." He turned, pointing deeper into the forest. "Alright then, off you go. I'll keep an eye on her. My energy blocks only last six and a half minutes, so that gives you five to hit their crystal. I'll carry her back to Naya to let her know the news."

Following the guiding light through the forest, I arrived at a small clearing where the crystal was, guarded by an unconscious Eron, his long silver hair covering his face. It was a strangely peaceful sight amid the intensity of the exam.

As I cautiously stepped forward, the ground beneath me suddenly shifted. Without warning, a trap sprung from the forest floor, a complex network of ropes, vines, and wooden bars unfolding like the limbs of a spider. It ensnared me mid-step, lifting me off the ground and tethering me between two large trees. I was caught like a fly in a spider's web, ropes and vines wrapping tightly around my limbs, rendering me immobile.

Rexus emerged from the shadows, a smirk of triumph on his face. "Wondered if anyone would ever make it this far," he said, relishing the sight of my entrapment.

I struggled against the bindings, but each movement only tightened the trap's grip. Rexus, watching my futile attempts, chuckled darkly and pointed to a vine that extended from the trap. My eyes followed it to a small deer caught in a secondary trap. The vine from my trap was intricately connected to the one ensnaring the deer, ensuring that any movement I made would tighten its hold on the animal.

Rexus's voice carried a tone of sadistic pleasure. "The more you struggle, the more our little friend here suffers."

The realization of the situation struck me hard. I stopped all movement, not wanting to risk harming the deer. Rexus stood up, his smirk growing wider. "Good choice. So how about we wait here for a little while? I'm sure Veyra will be done with your crystal shortly."

Lying suspended and restrained, I was overwhelmed by a sense of helplessness. The deer's frightened eyes seemed to meet mine, as though silently pleading for safety. I realized that I was not just physically trapped by Rexus's cunning design, but also morally bound by the desire to protect an innocent life.

Nodding toward the unconscious Eron, I asked Rexus, "What happened to him?"

Rexus approached me, his eyes cold and unyielding. He seemed to relish the control he had in this moment, a predator savoring his power over the prey. His gaze turned back to Eron, lying motionless against the crystal. "What do I care?" he said with a shrug, his voice devoid of empathy. "The freak never said a word. After the exam started, he just turned up like this. I figured one of you took him out." His eyes narrowed as he assessed me. "I reckon it was you."

Confused, I asked, "How did the round start if he's unconscious?"

Rexus sneered. "Took his hand and slapped it on the crystal, didn't I? Useless as he was, just taking up space. Veyra didn't like it, but she caved when I pointed out we were leading the match." Looking in the direction of our crystal, he mused aloud, "Speaking of which, what's taking her so long?"

"She's been dealt with," I responded, trying to keep my

voice steady despite the situation.

Rexus stepped closer, his face twisting into a cruel smile. "Liar," he hissed and delivered a vicious punch straight to my face. The impact caused the trap to tighten its grip, ropes, and vines constricting painfully. A distressed noise from the deer made my heart sink. I remained still, suppressing any reaction that could further endanger the animal.

Turning his attention back to me, Rexus's expression darkened. "Since you took out one of my team, seems only fair I return the favor." He unleashed a barrage of blows, each one more savage than the last. The trap responded in kind, tightening with every movement I made, the deer's cries of pain becoming more agonized.

Then, with a particularly brutal hit, the deer fell silent. It continued to move weakly, the trap now visibly strangling it. Panic and desperation surged through me. I needed to act, and quickly.

Rexus continued his merciless beating, his fists raining down on me. Each hit was a clear message of his enjoyment in causing pain, his eyes alight with a disturbing glee. I had to endure, knowing that any attempt to defend myself could spell the end for the deer.

Time was slipping away, each second dragging out like an eternity. The situation was dire – I was trapped, unable to defend myself, and an innocent life hung in the balance. At this moment, Rexus wasn't just an opponent in an exam; he was a true embodiment of cruelty and malice. I needed to find a way out of this trap – a solution that could save both the deer and myself from Rexus's twisted game.

There was a sudden flash of purple. Naya rushed past me, barreling into Rexus. She moved with purpose, her mana materializing into blades that she used to deftly slice through the rope constricting the deer's neck. As the rope fell away, I felt a sudden shift, and I dropped sideways to the forest floor, now supported by only one tree.

My heart pounded in my chest as I watched the deer,

lying motionless for a few tense seconds. The suspense was almost unbearable, but then, miraculously, the deer unsteadily rose to its feet and darted off into the forest. The sight of it running to safety brought a momentary sense of relief amidst the chaos.

With the deer free, I began to struggle against my bindings, but as I moved, the rope around my neck tightened, constricting my breath. Panic set in as I fought for air, my vision starting to blur.

Naya was a whirlwind of action, her mana blades flashing as she alternated between battling Rexus and cutting through the ropes binding me.

Despite her efforts, the lack of oxygen was rapidly taking its toll. My struggles grew weaker, and the world around me started to fade into darkness. The last thing I saw was Naya fighting fiercely against Rexus before everything slipped into blackness.

I gasped back to consciousness, Naya's hands unwrapping the rope from my neck, untangling me from the trap. "What happened to Rexus?" I managed to croak out, still disoriented.

"He's out cold," she replied, her voice heavy with exhaustion.

Our moment of relief was abruptly shattered. A bloodied Rexus suddenly appeared behind Naya, wielding a wooden spike. In a split second, he plunged it into her neck. Reacting instinctively, I reached out, grabbing Rexus's hand and gently twisting it. To my surprise, I felt bone snap under my grip. I quickly removed the spike from Naya's neck and touched her face, healing the wound.

I faced Rexus, my expression calm, but inside, a storm of anger was brewing, a tempest of emotions I had never felt before. As I locked eyes with him, I felt an inexplicable pull, a sensation as if the very fabric of reality was bending and warping around us. In an instant, the forest, the traps, and the chaos of the exam seemed to dissolve away, replaced by an endless expanse of pure white.

In this surreal landscape, it was just Rexus and me. The world around us seemed to pause, waiting, watching our every move. It was a domain where our conflict was the sole focus.

"What the…" he said, looking around. "What did you…?"

I approached Rexus, each step measured and deliberate. The anger within me, usually so well-contained, now flowed freely, a river of rage unleashed. I struck him, my blows fueled by a cold, detached fury. Each hit was precise and calculated to inflict maximum damage. I could hear the sickening crunch of bones breaking under the force of my assault.

Rexus tried to defend himself, his movements desperate and erratic, but he was no match for the intensity of my onslaught. My fingers turned into instruments of retribution, scratching and tearing at him, leaving deep, ragged marks. The surreal nature of this white void seemed to amplify my every action, each strike resonating with an almost chilling clarity.

Time seemed to stretch on indefinitely in this strange place. What might have been minutes or hours, I couldn't tell. All I knew was the singular focus of my actions, the need to make Rexus pay for what he had done. Eventually, he lay on the floor, a bleeding, broken form, a testament to the fury I had unleashed.

As suddenly as it had begun, reality snapped back. I found myself standing before Naya, who was rubbing her healed neck. "Thanks for that," she said, her voice reflecting shock and gratitude. "I think he was trying to kill me."

We turned to look at Rexus. He stood motionless, his arms hanging relaxed at his side despite one of them being grotesquely mangled at the hand. In the aftermath of the surreal and violent encounter, a heavy silence fell over the clearing, broken only by the distant sounds of the forest.

Naya pushed Rexus forcefully. "The examiner said no killing!" she snapped.

Rexus, seemingly devoid of any will to resist, didn't try to catch himself. He simply toppled over, collapsing to the forest floor in a heap.

Naya scoffed, "Whatever," and walked past his prone form. With a determined stride, she reached the crystal and delivered a solid punch to it.

A second later, we found ourselves teleported back to our crystal. The sudden shift in environment was disorienting, but it was a relief to be back.

"Took you long enough," Joren remarked, a hint of amusement in his voice. "My conversation with Veyra started to get awkward. I had to apologize each time I reapplied the blocking."

"I didn't know you could do that," I said, genuinely impressed by his skill.

Joren chuckled. "I used to do it to Calia all the time for fun." Naya and I exchanged unimpressed glances. Joren hurriedly added, "She let me! She wanted to learn how to stop it but never managed." He shrugged. "I'm not really a fighter, so I haven't needed to use it in a long time."

Naya laughed, a light-hearted jab in her tone. "Well, I'm sure you were a perfect gentleman, while you disabled the girl you've asked to the dance."

I couldn't help but join in the laughter, the tension from the ordeal beginning to fade away.

"So, what happened to you?" Joren asked, turning his attention back to the events that had unfolded.

Naya's expression darkened slightly. "Eron's unconscious, as is that freak, Rexus," she said, her voice tinged with disdain. "I hope he gets thrown out."

We stood around the crystal, each of us with our hands lightly resting against its surface. The crystal's energy hummed beneath our fingertips, providing a gentle, almost soothing sensation that formed a sharp contrast with the recent turmoil.

"Hey, look…" said Naya, nodding.

We followed her gaze to see Veyra approaching us, accompanied by the examiner, who carried an unconscious Eron in one hand and a catatonic Rexus in the other.

"What's going on?" Naya inquired, her eyes on the two motionless figures.

Veyra shrugged, a look of resignation on her face. "I give up," she declared. "My team's out of action, and there's no way I can beat you in my current state."

Joren responded with a smile. "Practical."

"But we still have two hits each," I pointed out, unsure of the implications.

"Doesn't matter," the examiner interjected. "With her team out of action, she has the right to forfeit." He then lifted Rexus, presenting him to us, his expression still blank. "I don't do magic," the Goud examiner admitted, "So if one of you can undo whatever spell you cast on this one, I'd appreciate it. Rather not use a Eulis if I can avoid it."

"Spell?" Naya echoed, her tone one of confusion. "I just hit him."

A flicker of concern crossed my mind, and I crouched down to look into Rexus's eyes. That familiar pull surged within me, and suddenly, I found myself in a world of pure white, crouched before a mangled form. I reached out and touched the quivering body, feeling the pull once more.

In an instant, we were back in the forest. I leaped back as Rexus let out a blood-curdling scream. He scrambled to his feet, still screaming, until his gaze met mine. His expression remained unchanged, but the screaming ceased abruptly. After a few tense moments, he took a few steps back before turning and running out of the dome, still silent.

"Well, that's going to be fun," the examiner remarked dryly, hoisting Eron onto his shoulder and preparing to follow Rexus. "Enjoy your new team," he said to Veyra, his voice laced with a hint of irony, before walking away.

CHAPTER TWENTY-SEVEN
Unveiled Potentials

In our new four-person dorm room, reminiscent of the one I originally shared with Tyran and Lammat, we settled into an atmosphere of tension and curiosity. Veyra, now part of our team, was seated on her bed, her concentration intense as she attempted to cast a mana orb. However, her efforts were futile; she couldn't generate anything.

Naya, observing Veyra's struggle, sat down next to her. With a sympathetic expression, she revealed a dampener link that Joren had given her. Mimicking Veyra's actions, Naya too tried the spell, but just like Veyra, she failed to produce an orb.

"I'm sorry we had to resort to such trickery," Naya apologized softly, her tone genuine.

Veyra shrugged, a hint of resignation in her voice. "I understand. My team was entirely Gouds, and yours had only one," she said, pointing at me.

Joren, who was lounging on his bed, chuckled. "Liam isn't a Goud."

Veyra looked confused. "But he didn't do any magic during the fight."

Naya jumped in. "Remember how Liam looked back in the training room? He was suffering from mana exhaustion. He wasn't allowed to risk using magic, so he had to resort to physical combat only."

"Yeah, when he fought Calia, she said Liam was more of

a nuisance than a challenge," Joren added with a smirk.

Veyra shook her head, her gaze shifting to me. "He was more than just a nuisance when I fought him," she said, her tone tinged with respect. "I've spent my entire life mastering the water form of combat, focusing on evasion. By the end of our fight, his skill felt like it rivaled mine. Coating my skin with the sleep charm was just a secondary defense; no one was ever supposed to land a blow."

"His ability rivaled yours?" said Naya, looking at me knowingly.

Veyra's eyes met mine. "Where did you learn the water form?"

Before I could respond, Naya interjected, "So what made you surrender in the end, Veyra?"

Veyra sighed, a contemplative look crossing her face. "It wasn't just about winning or losing. It was about recognizing when to fight and when to step back. My team was out, and I was compromised. Continuing would have only caused more harm than good."

As Veyra finished speaking, the room descended into a thoughtful silence. Her words lingered in the air, prompting a moment of introspection. I found myself reflecting on the tumultuous events of the exam, my mind turning over her reasoning. It dawned on me that perhaps the true aim of the exam was far more intricate than I had initially thought.

The challenges we faced weren't just a measure of our combat skills or magical prowess; they seemed to delve deeper, probing into our character, judgment, and adaptability. It wasn't just about how well we fought or how cleverly we used our abilities, but also about how we made decisions under pressure, how we handled unexpected alliances, and how we adapted to scenarios that defied our expectations.

As I pondered this, I looked around at my new team - at Naya, Joren, and Veyra. Each of us had been brought together by the whims of the exam, yet now we sat together, united by shared experiences and new understandings.

"How are you feeling now, Liam?" Naya asked, leaning slightly past Veyra to get a clearer view of me.

I nodded in response, a mixture of relief and hesitance in my voice. "Yeah, I'm perfectly fine now. But I'm still not sure about using magic again," I admitted, the thought of revisiting that pain causing a ripple of concern within me.

Joren, his focus elsewhere, casually floated his knife near the ceiling. "Hopefully, you'll feel able before our encounter with Tyran."

Naya, her concern abruptly shifting to a realization, slumped onto Veyra's bed. "Oh gods," she muttered. "I'd forgotten they're next." She exhaled a loud, weary sigh. "It feels like it's been ages since we lost Lammat to them, not just yesterday."

"Oh, by the way," started Veyra, her short blond hair swaying with each turn of her head as she glanced between Naya and me. "What did you two do to Rexus? When I got sent back to our crystal, his blocker still had me immobile," she explained, a hint of irritation in her tone as she gestured toward Joren, who didn't react, his gaze fixed on his knife. "I tried asking for help, but he just lay there, staring into the sky."

"I fought him," Naya clarified, her voice carrying a sense of determination. She materialized the mana blades she had used earlier, demonstrating their form. "These can slice through objects like rope but are designed to inflict only superficial wounds on flesh. They can't do... whatever happened to him."

I spoke up, "I think... it was me." My eyes met Naya's, searching for some understanding.

Naya's expression turned to one of curiosity. "What did you do?" she asked. "He seemed genuinely frightened after he came to."

My response faltered, "I..."

Joren interrupted, his voice cutting through my hesitation. "He doesn't know," he stated matter-of-factly. The knife he had been levitating dropped, the point landing deftly on his finger and spinning rapidly with precision. His dexterity looked impressive for a moment, until he lowered his hand, and the knife remained in place, still spinning. He sat up, facing me with a speculative gaze. "I have a theory. Indulge me," he said, a thoughtful smile crossing his face. "Hold out your hand, and generate a spark between each finger. After that, turn it into a fist, and shift the spark to in front of your knuckles."

"A mana gauntlet?" Veyra said, her voice laced with intrigue.

"Well that's easy," started Naya, lifting her hand.

"Stop!" Joren shouted, startling everyone with his uncharacteristic loudness. "I want Liam to try."

I extended my hand nervously, as Joren instructed. I flicked my fingers, flexed them, trying every motion I could think of to spark the magic, but nothing happened. No matter what I did, the spell just wouldn't manifest. It was like reaching for something just beyond my grasp, frustrating and bewildering.

"But that's a basic spell," Veyra started, her voice laced with disbelief. "How can you not..."

Joren, seemingly oblivious to Veyra's words, cut in. "Naya, now you do it."

Naya, with a confidence I envied, spread out her fingers. Lines of sparking energy danced between them, and as she clenched her fist, a gauntlet of shimmering mana materialized around her hand. The spell was both elegant and powerful, a testament to her skill.

"Good," Joren nodded. "Now, maintain that and add the blades as you did earlier."

Naya's face contorted with concentration. The air around us seemed to pulse with her effort. But as she attempted to combine the spells, the gauntlet flickered and vanished. She let out a short laugh, tinged with frustration. "I can't do it," she admitted, her smile wry.

Joren turned back to me, his gaze was piercing, yet encouraging. "Liam... try again," he urged.

With a deep breath, I held out my hand once more. To

my astonishment, before I even fully grasped what I was doing, an elaborate, sturdy gauntlet materialized, almost like a second skin over my hand.

"What the..." Veyra began, her voice trailing off in shock.

Without missing a beat, Joren instructed, "Add the blade."

Obediently, a blade emerged from the gauntlet, resembling Naya's but with an appearance of being sharper, and more refined. Its ethereal edge gleamed with an intimidating focus.

Veyra's mouth hung agape, her eyes darting between my hand and Joren, anticipating his next directive.

Joren's voice was calm, yet laden with expectation. "Show us your orb, Liam."

I flipped my hand, opening my palm. There, hovering in the air, was my orb, as large and vibrant as it always was, undiminished.

"Three?" Veyra exclaimed, rising to her feet and stepping back as if needing physical distance to comprehend the scene. "He can do three spells at the same time?"

Joren's grin broadened. "Liam... catch."

In a swift motion, he snapped the floating knife from the air and hurled it towards me at a frightening speed. Instinctively, I raised my gauntleted hand, shutting my eyes tight, bracing for the impact. But the pain never came. Cautiously, I opened my eyes and saw the knife, suspended midair, held securely in the center of my orb. With a mere thought, I maneuvered the knife back across the room to Joren.

"F...f...four?" Veyra stuttered, her awe rendering her almost speechless as she collapsed onto a bedside table, her eyes wide with disbelief.

Joren plucked the knife from the air, his expression one of triumph. "Now, Liam," he said, his voice heavy with implication, his eyes intently fixed on me. "Cut the mana."

Naya gasped and leaped to her feet, turning towards me, her voice filled with alarm. "No!"

Without a second thought, I severed the connection to

the mana. In an instant, the gauntlet, blade, and orb dissipated, vanishing into a wisp of smoke that slowly drifted away, leaving nothing but a lingering sense of power that had been, just moments ago, at my command.

"He didn't absorb it?" Veyra found her voice, still perched on her table, her tone a mix of surprise and horror.

"Liam!" Naya exclaimed. She instantly rounded on Joren with a protective fierceness. "What do you think you're doing? He's only just managed to get his…"

Joren, however, wore a smile of understanding. "Liam, how do you feel?" he asked, his eyes fixed on me.

I paused, examining my hand, and turning it over. "Fine… I feel fine," I replied, a sense of wonder in my voice. My gaze lifted to meet Joren's. "There's no pain." Swiftly, I reformed the gauntlet, materializing a blade, then severed it before reforming it again, all without a hint of discomfort. "It's not hurting."

"What is going on?" Veyra interjected, her voice filled with confusion as she stepped closer.

"Liam, hold on," Joren said. He gestured toward the gauntlet. "Absorb it."

I absorbed the mana from the gauntlet. As I did, a sharp pain exploded in my hand, radiating up my arm, shoulder, chest, and into my head. I couldn't help but cry out, my hand instinctively going to my temple. Naya was at my side in an instant, embracing me, yet her comfort couldn't dull the sharp sting of pain. Almost reflexively, I summoned the gauntlet again and then cut it loose.

The pain vanished.

I exchanged a shaky nod with Naya, drawing a deep, steadying breath.

Her eyes, wide and filled with worry, turned to Joren. "What does this mean?"

Joren's response was measured, laden with significance. "It means we've been the ones causing his pain all this time."

Veyra, cautiously stepped around the room, positioning

herself between me and the door, as though ready to make a run for it. "Did he copy Naya's gauntlet spell?"

"Indeed," Joren confirmed.

Veyra's thoughts raced aloud. "So what? Is he a Crosser? Only Crossers can copy spells," she mused, her speech quickening with each revelation. "Did he also copy my technique? Is that how he learned water form? But his hair's not black! Guardian? No… not white…" She halted, taking an unconscious step toward me, her gaze fixed in an expression of awe and bewilderment. "What is he?"

Joren's voice, tinged with emotion, broke the tension. "I told you, during our fight," he said, tears glistening in his eyes. "Liam's a god."

CHAPTER TWENTY-EIGHT
Illusions of the Mind

"I'm not a god," I retorted, glaring at Joren with frustration.

Joren, undeterred, spread his hands wide as the Crest of Nations symbol materialized, floating and rotating in the air. "Well, you're certainly not a Minor! Not a Goud, Eulis, Crosser, or Guardian," he stated emphatically. "You're all of them, and yet none of them." His voice lowered to a whisper, filled with awe. "You're something new."

"Just stop telling people I'm a god!" I snapped, the label grating on me.

Joren chuckled, rising to his feet with a flourish. "Liam, you can regenerate! You can heal others! If not a god, then what are you?" he challenged.

"Joren…"

Veyra interjected with surprise, "He can regenerate?"

Joren nodded. "Yes, when I threw the knife, I wanted to demonstrate that. But he caught it instead."

I blinked in disbelief. "Wait, what? You tried to stab me?"

With a nonchalant wave, Joren replied, "I was curious about how many spells you could handle simultaneously."

I rose to my feet. "Joren! Do not stab me just to test a theory!" As I stood, I stumbled slightly, looking down to find Veyra crouching at my knee, her fingers probing gently.

"So, that's how you moved so quickly after I dislocated it…?" she murmured, more to herself.

I let out a long groan and gently shook off her hands, moving back to my bed to lie down. I turned to Naya, seeking some semblance of sanity. "Any chance you can stop these two?"

Naya glanced at Veyra, her expression thoughtful. "We're still… figuring things out," she admitted.

Veyra, her mind racing with new information, turned to Joren. "Wait… during our fight, you mentioned he has a dampener." My frustration peaked, and with a groan, I raised my left hand, pulling down the sleeve to reveal the circlet to her. "You mean to say he can perform all those spells even while dampened?"

"You should see what he can do without it," Joren said, a mischievous grin spreading across his face.

"Is that what you want?!" I snapped, my frustration boiling over. In a swift motion, I stood up, unfastened the circlet, and tossed it to Joren. I turned to Veyra, expecting her to retreat, but instead, she stood her ground. Her expression showed concern, but there was a determined glint in her eyes. She wanted to see this. "Fine, then! Let's go to the training hall!" I declared, turning towards the door.

The moment I took a step, the world around me twisted and blurred. My eyes widened in shock, and I spun around. Joren had dropped to the floor, while Naya and Veyra simply stood there, staring in disbelief. The familiar surroundings of the dormitory had been replaced by the white, domed ceiling of the training room.

A heavy silence enveloped us for a moment, each of us absorbing the startling reality of what had just occurred. The air was thick with astonishment and disbelief.

Then, breaking the silence, Joren's laughter boomed through the room, rich and unrestrained. "I knew it!" he exclaimed, his voice echoing off the walls. He pointed at me, still sitting on the floor, a look of wild triumph on his face. "This! This is why I wanted Liam to see their crystal in the last match!" He proclaimed, his laughter undiminished. "I knew you could teleport! But to bring others along without a touch? Remarkable!" In a burst of energy, he leaped to his feet and scooped me up in a whirlwind of an embrace.

"He can do that?" asked Veyra, pointing at me, but looking at Joren. "How did he move more than one person?"

Naya stepped closer, her hand finding its way to my chest, grounding me. "Are you okay? Remember, stay calm," she urged softly.

I nodded, still reeling from the unexpected teleport. "I… I didn't mean to do that," I confessed, my voice tinged with shock.

Naya frowned at Joren as she pushed him away from me. "Did you plan this?"

"What? No!" Joren's smile faltered, and he turned to me with a hint of concern. "Wait… Are you actually angry with me?"

I glanced at him, trying to find the right words. "No, not angry, I'm just…"

Joren straightened up, his demeanor shifting to one of apology. "Sorry. It wasn't my intention."

I waved off his concern. "Don't worry about it."

He shook his head, regret and reflection in his expression. "My excitement got the better of me. As mentioned previously, I find you…" He paused, looking me directly in the eyes, his face a mask of seriousness. "… unique."

Veyra, still watching us with a cautious eye, chimed in. "Is that the first time this has happened?"

Naya nodded, then turned to Joren. "Maybe we should put the dampener back on."

"No," I interjected, softly shaking my head. "We came here to do this yesterday, before I collapsed."

Naya reached out to halt my advance. "We still don't fully understand what triggered that, Liam."

"Actually, we do," said Joren. "Liam doesn't just regenerate his body, but his mana as well." He crouched down, examining the hole left by my energy ball from the previous day. "Once he casts a spell, the mana within him is already replenished. Making him reabsorb the mana overloaded him."

Veyra took a step closer, her gaze fixed on me. "He can regenerate his body, as well as his mana?" She hesitated, a noticeable swallow betraying her nervousness. "May I... see?"

I paused for a moment, looking around the training room. It showed significant signs of use compared to yesterday. The walls were damaged in areas, leaving small piles of debris scattered around on the now uneven floor. My eyes returned to Veyra and I exhaled a resigned sigh. Lifting my finger, I formed one of Naya's mana blades at its tip. Then, holding out the palm of my other hand, I carefully drew a line across it with the blade. "Just so you are aware, I still feel pain," I said, bluntly. Blood began to pool slowly in my hand, but the cut seemed to vanish the moment the blade moved across my skin.

"It's healing faster than before..." Naya observed, peering over my shoulder.

I extinguished the blade and turned to Veyra. She reached into her pocket, producing a small, clean cloth, and gently wiped the blood from my hand. Her eyes locked with mine, a mixture of wonder and disbelief in her gaze. "Are you sure you're not a god?"

I shot her a glare. "Veyra..."

"Sorry, sorry..." she chuckled softly, handing the cloth to me and stepping away. "I've never seen anyone regenerate before. I mean, I've heard stories, but... He's right, you are unique." She paused for a second, then bit down hard on the flesh of her thumb.

"Veyra!" I admonished.

"They said you could heal others." She held the thumb toward me, a small bead of blood building up.

I felt a surge of annoyance. "I am not a jester, here for your amusement!" She remained silent, simply holding my gaze with a steadfast look. I sighed, gently poking her in the forehead. "Next time you hurt yourself on purpose, I will let you bleed."

She nodded, her expression serious, still extending her thumb toward me.

"Uhh, it's already healed," said Naya, offering a weak smile.

Veyra glanced at Naya, then back down at her thumb. She cautiously placed it in her mouth, her eyes growing wide in disbelief. She looked up at me again before removing her thumb to examine the healed skin. Her other hand slowly rose to the spot where I had touched her forehead, her eyes meeting mine, a look of wonder and realization dawning on her face.

Joren cleared his throat, drawing our attention. His usual jovial demeanor had shifted back to his more mechanical, analytical persona. "Perhaps we should all train. I learned how to float because of Liam yesterday; maybe he can help us all learn something new." He nodded thoughtfully. "It's not often one has an ally capable of learning all spells."

Naya looked taken aback. "He taught you how to float?"

Joren demonstrated by slowly lifting off the ground. "Not quickly, and a strong wind would knock me over," he admitted, glancing at Veyra, "but it is impressive."

Veyra laughed, finally tearing her eyes from mine. "Are you kidding? That's one of the reasons I gave up! I thought you could fly!"

Joren nodded in agreement. "Not kidding. I am still a beginner."

"Well, damn," Veyra muttered, placing her hands on her hips, almost scolding herself. "I wonder if I could have landed at least one more hit on your crystal..."

Joren gestured towards the crystal in the center of the room. "Why not try now?"

She shook her head dismissively. "No point. With this dampener in me, I can't do much. I use my mana to accelerate my movements by strengthening my muscles." Demonstrating, she crouched and leaped, but without any notable height. She laughed it off. "See? Nothing."

Naya turned to Joren, her face adopting a cringe. "How long does food stay in the stomach?"

"Approximately one to two hours before moving to the small bowel," he answered promptly.

"I don't suppose you…" Naya started to ask, but Veyra cut her off.

"It's the first thing I tried after my body started functioning again. Didn't work," she stated flatly, her gaze returning to Joren with a hint of annoyance. "However, it was extremely unpleasant."

I paused, a thought slowly forming in my mind. "I have an idea…"

"If you're thinking of ripping it out of me, then healing me, you have another thing coming!" Veyra exclaimed, a hint of panic in her voice.

"More like… using telekinesis to remove it…" I made a gentle plucking motion with my hand.

"Through my mouth?!" she said loudly, her eyes widening as she took a step back.

"Not a terrible idea," Joren mused, looking at me with a thoughtful expression. "If anything were to go wrong, who better to help?"

"No! No way! Not happening!" Veyra protested.

Naya stepped forward, her hands resting reassuringly on Veyra's arms. "You tried to get it out on your own, and that didn't work. Honestly, we have no idea how long it could stay in you." She offered a sympathetic smile. "It's not a pleasant thought, but it is a sensible option. Especially with Tyran's team on the horizon."

Veyra hesitated, then spun around to face Joren, jabbing a finger into his chest. "This is your fault! If anything goes wrong, I'll make sure he does the same to you!"

Naya moved close to me, her voice low. "Are you certain you can do this?"

I nodded confidently. "It's strange, but without the dampener, everything feels more intuitive. I don't even need to consciously direct the mana; it just… knows.”

Meanwhile, Veyra seemed to be a bundle of nerves, bouncing on her feet and shaking her hands. “Okay, so how do we do this? Do I just open my mouth? Should I lie down?” As I took a step towards her, she jumped back. “Should I be unconscious for this? Can someone knock me out?”

I chuckled. “What happened to the confident girl we met here yesterday?”

“Yesterday’s me hadn’t met today’s you!” she retorted, waving a finger at me but still bouncing anxiously. Then, a light of realization sparked in her eyes. “My spell! You saw my sleep spell! Use it on me!”

Joren interjected, shaking his head. “You’d already covered your skin with it. Liam needs to witness the spell being cast before he can learn it. That’s how he picked up Naya’s blades today and my telekinesis yesterday.”

“Yesterday?!” Veyra exclaimed in disbelief.

I stepped forward again, gently taking hold of her shoulders. “I have a spell that will put you to sleep,” I assured her in the calmest voice I could muster.

Startled by my advance, she flinched slightly but then ceased her nervous bouncing. Taking a deep breath, she nodded. “I trust you,” she said, her voice barely above a whisper, offering a small, tentative smile.

I locked eyes with Veyra and gently pulled. She yelped in surprise as the familiar training room dissolved into an endless expanse of white. Spinning around, she blurted out, “You teleported me again? Where…” Her eyes flicked to mine. “Did you already do it? Did it go wrong? Am I dead?”

I couldn’t help but smile. “This is a world within my mind,” I explained. “This is the spell I used on Rexus.”

“You used that spell on me?” she exclaimed, rushing forward to grab my arms. “Rexus… he went… crazy…”

“Yes, he did,” I confirmed, my voice steady. “He tortured a wild deer, strangled me, then stabbed Naya in the neck.” As the gravity of my words settled in, Veyra’s grip loosened. “I brought him here, and we fought. I won." A vision of Rexus's broken body briefly materialized on the floor as a stark reminder.

Veyra gasped, stepping closer to the apparition. "Is that… him… now?"

I shook my head. "I held him here for a while, then released him when the Examiner asked." Looking into her eyes, I added, "He tried to kill Naya… I couldn't let him get away with that."

Her expression hardened, a reflection of my own resolve. "I'd have done the same."

Rexus's image faded. "As far as I understand it, this world is of my own making. Here, I allow you to shape it." I chuckled. "As you see, it's still quite empty. I haven't had the chance to… fill it."

"You mean I can…?" Veyra's voice was a hushed murmur, tinged with a sense of wonder. As the words left her lips, the stark white void around us began to shift and morph. Slowly, colors bled into existence, painting a vivid landscape where once there was none. The transformation was mesmerizing: a rustic log cabin emerged, nestled beside a tranquil, shimmering lake. The scene was bathed in the golden hues of a setting sun, casting long, peaceful shadows across the landscape.

Veyra, her eyes wide with disbelief, knelt. She ran her fingers through the grass, her expression a blend of joy and amazement. As she looked out over the lake, the surface of the water rippled gently, reflecting the dusky sky and the first twinkling stars of the evening.

Slowly, she reached out into the air, and as if responding to her thoughts, a glass materialized in her hand. She examined it, turning it over, watching the light play off its surface. Hesitantly, she brought it to her lips and took a cautious sip. "Everything… feels so real," she whispered.

I nodded. "Someone I know created this spell to give people a second chance to live a life they couldn't otherwise." Watching her face light up with wonder, I added, "In his world, he was the only one who could change things, but here, you can create anything you can imagine."

Veyra paused, her gaze lingering on the cabin. "Anything?" she whispered.

"Anything."

Then, as if summoned by her deepest wish, the cabin door creaked open. A woman with long blond hair flowing down to her hips, clad in a blue dress, emerged. She extended her arms towards Veyra, her voice gentle, "Hi, Ra-Ra."

In an instant, Veyra closed the distance between them, wrapping the woman in a tight embrace. They sank to the ground together, Veyra's tears flowing freely, a mixture of joy and relief marking this reunion. "Mother!"

Giving Veyra and her mother a brief moment, I slowly made my way over to them, placing a gentle hand on Veyra's shoulder. "I'm going to leave to remove your dampener now," I said softly. As she looked up at me, her eyes were filled with tears. "Just be aware..." I paused, ensuring she understood, "Time here moves differently, like in a normal dream. I've tried to make it as regular as possible, but... I can't be certain how long I'll be gone."

Veyra nodded slowly. "I... I'll be alright..."

I crouched down to meet her gaze. "You have to remember, none of this is real." My eyes shifted briefly to her mother. "She isn't real." Veyra's response was a shaky nod, an acknowledgment of the painful truth. "I'll be back as soon as I can, and then I'll take you with me," I reassured her.

Her nod was more resolute this time, her breath steadying. "Yes, we have an exam to pass."

With that, I transitioned back to the real world. The training hall materialized around me, and I saw Veyra standing motionless. I gently leaned her backward, easing her down to the floor. "Open her mouth," I instructed Naya, who quickly complied. As Veyra's lips parted, I shifted my focus, directing my mana down her throat. "Something is blocking me," I said, glancing at Joren.

"That would be the lower esophageal sphincter," said Joren, leaning in close.

"So I understood the word 'lower'," I replied, with a glare.

"It seals off the stomach, so your food and drink doesn't just come straight back out when you're upside down," said Naya, causing me to look at her. "Like when you're doing a handstand?" She met my blank expression. "Just be careful with it."

"Okay, so what do I do?"

"Just gently apply more pressure until you push past it, then hold it open with your mana while you search around," answered Joren, his expression one of pure fascination.

I closed my eyes once again. Though I saw only darkness, my senses painted a vivid picture. The resistance eased, like a door quietly unlocking. Carefully, I maintained a steady stream of mana, holding the pathway open. Soon, I located the link, ensnaring it with a slender tendril of mana. With utmost care, I withdrew it, feeling its form slide up and out.

I carefully extracted the dampener from Veyra's mouth, the silver glistening as it floated before me. With the task complete, I shifted my consciousness.

As I reentered the mindscape, I found Veyra and her mother seated together on a quaint wooden bench overlooking the lake, their figures silhouetted against the radiant backdrop of the setting sun. The sky was ablaze with a breathtaking array of colors, from fiery oranges to deep, soothing purples, reflecting off the lake's surface in a dance of light and shadow.

Approaching them slowly, I felt a sense of intrusion into this tender, private moment. "How long was I gone?" I asked softly, my voice barely more than a whisper in the serene quiet of the evening.

Veyra turned towards me, her face aglow with the gentle light of the sunset. A soft, contented smile graced her lips. "About an hour," she responded, her voice imbued with a sense of peace.

A twinge of unease tugged at my gut, the implication of her distorted sense of time weighing on me. It brought a stark realization of what Rexus might have experienced, but I pushed the thought away. I forced a lightness into my voice. "It's been less than a minute."

She turned, giving her mother a lingering embrace before standing and approaching me. Slowly, the image of her mother and the warm, inviting cabin behind her began to fade, like mist dissipating under the morning sun, leaving us enveloped in the pure, tranquil white of the mindscape.

I was struck by Veyra's strength, her ability to let go of this beautifully crafted illusion. It made me wonder if I could have done the same, had I been in her shoes, faced with a loved one I had lost.

"Less than a minute, huh?" Veyra echoed, a hint of wistfulness in her tone.

I nodded, acknowledging the bittersweet nature of our shared experience. She stepped forward and wrapped me in a tight embrace, her arms conveying both her gratitude and a sense of closure. After a brief pause, she planted a gentle kiss on my cheek, whispering a heartfelt "Thank you." She then stepped back, her eyes meeting mine with a profound intensity. "This was the most beautiful thing I could have ever asked for. But please... if I ever ask you to bring me back here for this..." Her voice faltered, tears brimming in her eyes. "Don't."

I nodded solemnly, fully comprehending the depth and significance of her request. The air around us was thick with a poignant mixture of emotions – a blend of happiness and sorrow. For Veyra, this was not just a simple farewell; it was a definitive final goodbye.

CHAPTER TWENTY-NINE
The Ripple of Strength

Veyra sat up slowly, her eyes fixed on the silver link floating in front of me. "There it is," she said, a smile playing on her lips. Her eyes began to water slightly, and Naya, concerned, leaned in closer. "You alright?"

Veyra wiped her eyes dry, chuckling lightly. "Just my throat tickling," she said, her gaze flickering towards me. I couldn't help but return her smile with one of my own.

"Alright, want to see if you're back to normal?" I asked, taking hold of her wrist to help her to her feet.

With a newfound energy, Veyra leaped into the air, soaring surprisingly high before landing gracefully. She then burst into a sprint, her movements fluid and swift. She weaved and dodged around the room with remarkable agility, her every move a testament to her regained strength. Finally, she came to a halt and faced us with a triumphant grin. "Looks like I'm back!"

Joren, with a casual flick of his hand, telekinetically grasped the link from me and tossed it down the hole.

"Just dropping it on top of my severed finger, hey?" I joked.

"Ensuring a second Liam does not grow," he replied dryly.

I stared at him, stunned. "You're joking, right?"

His smile broadened, a clear sign he was beginning to

relax again. He looked around the room, scooping up a chunk of loose concrete. "Tyran's team trains harder than ours does."

"No kidding," Veyra walked around, running her hand across a damaged patch on the wall. "We used it twice yesterday, and left it in pristine condition."

"What should we do?" said Naya. "Should we try us all against Veyra, to see if she could have scored another point?"

"Or," Veyra countered quickly, her eyes sparkling with a challenge, "We could try all of us against Liam. You know, see if we'd stand a chance against him without a dampener?" The suggestion hung in the air, charged with excitement and curiosity.

All eyes turned to me, expectant. I nodded and shrugged. "Sure, I mean, if you want."

Joren quickly laid out the rules. "The goal is to prevent Liam from reaching the crystal. Liam, start with your back to the wall."

I walked over to the wall, my back against it, watching as the others huddled together, quickly devising a strategy. I gave them ample time, knowing they'd want to form a solid plan. When they finally broke apart, they encircled the crystal, Veyra at the center.

"Begin," Veyra announced.

In an instant, the world seemed to ripple around me. When it settled, I found myself standing behind them, on the other side of the crystal. Without hesitation, I reached out and touched it. "Does this count as a point?" I asked, half-joking.

The three spun around. "Oh, come on," Veyra groaned. "It's not fair if you teleport."

Joren pondered, "Is it okay if he does it during the next match?"

"Fine, fine…" I conceded, returning to the wall.

"You know, you become a lot more arrogant without your dampener," Naya remarked with a smile, though it didn't quite reach her eyes.

"Sorry," I replied, feeling a hint of guilt. "How hard do

you want me to try?"

Joren was practical. "It's likely you can just teleport while wearing your dampener, so it's not a good way to test your abilities."

Veyra suggested, "Try it without using any mana. I want to see how you compare to earlier."

"No mana, got it, but none of you hold anything back," I said, bouncing on my feet before crouching into a ready stance. "Let's begin."

Veyra didn't waste a moment, charging at me with a series of rapid, powerful strikes. Each punch and kick she delivered was aimed with precision, forcing me back against the wall. I ducked and dodged, using only my innate speed. Her eyes were alight with determination, reading my movements, adjusting her attacks. I countered with a feint, leading her to believe I was retreating, only to sidestep at the last second, narrowly avoiding a spinning kick that whistled past my ear.

Joren, observing from a distance, chose his moment to strike with telekinesis. Suddenly, I felt an invisible force attempting to lift me off the ground. Anticipating this, I grounded myself, leaning into the force and using it to catapult myself forward, turning his power to my advantage. I rolled on the ground, evading another wave of Joren's telekinetic push that was aimed at where I had just been.

Naya, seeing an opening, joined in. She was the most versatile of the trio, her tactics constantly changing. She started with barrier magic, creating shimmering walls of energy around the crystal. I approached, feigning an attack, then retreated, drawing her out. As she pursued, she switched to telekinesis, sending a barrage of small objects my way. I weaved through them, stepping closer toward her, feeling the rush of air as they whizzed by.

As I advanced, blades shimmered around her hands. I knew I couldn't block them without mana; I had to rely on evasion. My mind flashed back to Veyra's water form, and I danced around her strikes, each move calculated, each step deliberate. Our dance was a perilous one, a game of razor-sharp edges and swift movements.

The battle escalated, the dome reverberating with our exertions. Veyra re-engaged, her attacks now more fierce, fuelled by the knowledge that I was holding my ground. Joren, not to be outdone, intensified his telekinetic efforts, loose concrete and bursts of force coming at me from all directions.

I was constantly on the move, a target that refused to be caught. I used my surroundings, the open space of the dome, to my advantage, constantly changing directions, never predictable.

The tide turned when they attempted a coordinated attack. Veyra and Naya came at me from opposite sides, Joren ready to catch me if I slipped through. It was a well-planned trap, but in their coordination, there was a brief moment of predictability.

I feinted towards Veyra, drawing Joren's focus, then spun, narrowly missing Naya's blade and heading straight for the crystal. Joren's telekinetic grasp reached out, but I dove forward in a roll, slipping under his power and reaching out to touch the crystal.

We stood there, panting, a mutual respect in our eyes. It was an intense, adrenaline-fueled battle that had pushed each of us.

Naya dropped to the floor, absorbing her mana-blades. "That... was... intense..." she said through heavy breaths.

"You've got to tell me who trained you," said Veyra, stretching out her limbs, as though preparing for another round. "You mirrored my water form against Naya. It's impressive, yet somewhat unsettling, how swiftly you absorb and apply new techniques."

"And none of you were holding back?" I asked.

Joren quickly dashed towards me, delivering several energy-blocking jabs to my limbs. He paused when I didn't react, then simply shrugged. "Figured that wouldn't have worked on you. So yeah, I wasn't holding back."

Veyra sighed. "Right, of course. Immune to energy blocking. No wonder Eron came back unconscious." She laughed. "Shame. He seemed nice."

"I didn't mean to knock him out," I said. "I just... landed a clean hit."

"I'm sure he's fine," said Veyra. "I checked if he was breathing at the same time I checked Rexus." She gave a small laugh. "Would have been nice of you to heal him though, rather than letting him get carried away."

"Best not to share our abilities outside of the group," said Joren.

"Tyran already knows," muttered Naya. "So he's probably already told the rest of his team."

Joren nodded. "Best that everyone but Eron knows," he said, smiling.

I laughed. "Oh, come on, don't make me feel bad. What was I meant to do, just reach out and heal him right in front of the examiner?" I shook my head. "Anyway," I said turning to Veyra, "Do you mind if we try a one-on-one? Not getting to the crystal, just testing your ability to dodge."

"Mind?" she replied, her eyes gleaming. She jumped to the middle of the room. "I was about you ask you!"

"He just beat us one on three, what will we learn from this?" said Naya.

Veyra simply planted a thumb against her chest, looking at Naya as though it was the most obvious thing in the world. "I'm training to be a Goud. I'll only get better if I fight people better than me."

"I was hoping we could practice me going up against your water form," I said.

"Even better!" Veyra replied, but quickly paused. "Will you be using your dampener?" I shook my head. "Perfect!"

"Just don't use that dream magic this time. I'd rather not have to constantly stab myself this time."

Veyra laughed. "Don't worry, I haven't cast that. You

know, I thought you were crazy at the time! Thought you were destroying your leg just to try to beat me. Who's insane idea was — it was his, wasn't it?" She aimed a thumb at Joren.

"It worked, didn't it?" he said, pushing some loose debris down the hole.

I smiled. "Okay, you ready?"

"Ready."

I made the first move, lunging towards Veyra with a calculated grab, aiming to swiftly conclude the match. But Veyra, embodying the essence of her water form, danced away effortlessly. I truly understood why her style was called 'water form.' Her movements were fluid, smooth, and continuous, making it incredibly difficult to predict where she would be next. She glided around the training hall with a grace and fluidity that was mesmerizing, turning each dodge into an art form.

As the fight progressed, I noticed a change in Veyra's tactics. With no goal of reaching the crystal, her movements became more unpredictable, and her dodges were more spontaneous. She twisted and turned with an uncanny sense of where I would strike next, always a step ahead of me.

I increased my pace, throwing a series of feints and jabs, attempting to corner her and anticipate her evasive maneuvers. But she responded with an elegant grace, her body swaying and bending away from my every attempt to capture her. The training hall resonated with the sounds of our exertion – my heavy breaths and determined grunts contrasted with her light, controlled steps. It was a dance of attack and evasion, a physical conversation where each of us pushed and probed the other's skills.

With each close call, each near-grab, I noticed Veyra's smirk widen, her eyes sparkling with the thrill of the challenge. She seemed to relish the test of her dodging skills, and it only fueled my determination more.

The match evolved into an intense display of endurance and skill. My attempts to catch her grew more inventive, but so did her escapes. There was a moment when I almost had her, my arms closing in, but she ducked and rolled away at the last second, popping up behind me with a triumphant laugh.

I began to adapt to her rhythm, gradually anticipating her fluid movements. I was getting closer each time, a brush against her sleeve here, a fleeting touch of her skin there. Veyra's style was all about flow and adaptation, and I found myself learning, in real time, how to disrupt that flow.

The turning point came unexpectedly. Veyra executed a particularly intricate dodge, and in that split second, her foot caught slightly on the uneven floor of the training hall – a minor imperfection that had gone unnoticed until now. It caused a momentary lapse in her flawless evasion, and I seized the opportunity, reaching out and finally managing to secure a grip on her arm.

As I gently restrained her, Veyra let out a small laugh, admiration and surprise in her eyes. "Guess the training hall isn't as perfect as the water," she remarked playfully. "In my typical training environment, the floor is flat, no room for stumbles."

I released her, stepping back with a smile. "Your water form is incredible, Veyra. It's like trying to catch flowing water in your hands."

She flicked a hand through her hair, still smiling. "Well, you did a pretty good job at it. I'll need to practice more. The forest is probably even more unpredictable."

Naya, stepping away from the wall, turned her attention to Veyra. "Mind if I try against you?" she asked, a spark of eagerness in her voice. "I'm getting a little tired of always guarding the crystal with magic."

Veyra, momentarily taken aback, chuckled softly. "I forgot you didn't choose Eulis or Goud at the start," she remarked with a newfound respect. "Of course, let's see what you've got."

As the girls prepared to spar, I joined Joren, settling beside him to observe the match.

At Veyra's nod, Naya launched into action. She moved quickly, her approach more physical than her usual magical engagements. Veyra responded with her characteristic fluidity, each dodge a graceful dance.

As they circled each other, Naya attempted a series of swift jabs, but Veyra moved like liquid, each evasion seamlessly leading into the next. It was clear that Veyra was not just evading; she was also observing, learning Naya's patterns.

I leaned closer to Joren. "Do you think there are any other skills you could teach me?"

Joren, his attention momentarily shifting from the match, lifted a small rock before him, nodding thoughtfully. "My focus has been on refining telekinesis," he began, his voice reflecting his deep concentration on the subject. "I haven't yet perfected this, so am not willing to lean into too much else, yet." The rock in front of him vibrated subtly in the air.

"What's the goal here?" I inquired, intrigued by the trembling stone.

"This," Joren gestured at the rock, "is a test of precision over power. I'm attempting to split this rock in half using telekinesis alone. It's a step towards understanding the subtler aspects of force application. The end goal is to learn controlled destruction – to crush objects."

Inspired, I levitated a nearby rock, mirroring his action. As I concentrated, the rock began to quiver. "This is trickier than it looks," I admitted. "Feels like it would be easier to just crush it."

Joren nodded, finally glancing my way. "Simpler, perhaps, but not as instructive. The act of crushing is brute force, straightforward destruction. But to split something cleanly requires understanding its structure, identifying the right points of stress. It's about finesse, not just strength."

I focused on the rock, trying to apply what he said. "So it's more about skill than raw power?"

"Exactly," Joren said, his rock now vibrating more

intensely. "Consider this: crushing a rock skips several stages of its breakdown. You miss the opportunity to create something useful in between, like gravel or stone chips, jumping straight to dust. It's akin to learning – taking shortcuts might get you to an end quickly, but you lose out on the depth of understanding that comes from a gradual process."

As we watched Veyra and Naya's match, Joren nodded towards Veyra, using her as an example to explain a concept. "See how Veyra moves? It's not just physical. She's channeling mana directly into her muscles. It's why her movements are so fluid and rapid."

I observed Veyra closely, noticing the seamless way she flowed from one position to the next. "So, it's not just reflexes?"

Joren shook his head. "It's more than that. Her maneuvers aren't merely responses from her brain. She's manipulating mana directly within her muscles, allowing her to move faster than normal. And she's mastered it to the point where she uses only the necessary amount of mana for each movement. It's precise control."

I watched in awe as Veyra dodged another of Naya's strikes. "Sounds like she's got an edge there."

"Indeed," Joren said. "But it's a dangerous technique. Overextending the mana could lead to muscle tears. It requires a high level of control."

"Could she learn to use energy beams, then?" I asked, recalling our earlier discussions about the technique.

Joren pointed towards Veyra. "Exactly what I was leading towards. Because of her mana control, she would certainly be more capable at it than I am. Her proficiency in flowing mana through her body suggests that she could already form the energy in her palm, ready to be released."

"We should teach her how to do it!"

Joren, however, shook his head. "Her mana reserve is likely quite low, given how constantly she absorbs it. Firing an energy beam would expend a significant portion she couldn't get back. In this exam setting, that's not advised. We can't afford such a loss."

Watching Veyra's effortless evasion, I nodded in understanding.

"In combat, especially in a team setting like ours, it's crucial to balance individual strengths with the collective strategy. Veyra's current technique offers more sustained utility than a single, high-cost attack would. Besides," he faced me and grinned. "We have you."

As the battle between Naya and Veyra raged on, a crackling tension electrified the air of the training hall. Naya, her energy seemingly boundless, began to form mana blades, their ethereal edges glinting menacingly. Veyra's eyes widened in genuine surprise at their sudden appearance in the fight, but she didn't falter.

"I assumed you were already manipulating your muscles with mana. Like that time you jumped and landed on Tyran," Joren continued.

I shrugged. "Maybe I was. More often than not, I do things without realizing."

"Then I recommend you practice."

Naya's movements became more aggressive, the blades slicing through the air, each strike coming perilously close to Veyra. Despite this new threat, Veyra maintained her composure, her water form movements allowing her to fluidly evade every attack.

The climax of their battle came when Naya executed a double-handed cross slice, a move both daring and desperate. Veyra, in response, performed an acrobatic backflip, narrowly avoiding the blades. A small tuft of her hair, however, wasn't so lucky and floated gently to the ground, severed by the close call.

Exhausted, Naya collapsed to the floor, gasping for air. She picked up the tuft of hair, holding it up with a tired but triumphant grin. "I'm counting this as a win," she joked, then added with a hint of concern, "Sorry, Veyra. I'm not sure Liam can regenerate hair."

Veyra laughed, running her hand through her hair. "That's a sign I need to have a cut anyway. It's why I keep it short."

"Yeah, I can see why."

Both fighters stood, exchanging compliments and smiles. "That was close with the blades," Veyra admitted. "Didn't expect that. You nearly had me there."

Naya, still catching her breath, replied, "I was saving them for a surprise. But you still dodged." She turned to Joren. "Alright, you're up!"

"No point, already beaten her," he stated, his voice carrying a hint of finality.

Veyra's mouth fell open in disbelief. "That didn't count! We agreed to a one-on-one! You attacked me during my fight with Liam!"

"I attacked after he was already down with a dislocated knee. That fight was over," Joren countered calmly.

Unfazed, Veyra stretched her arms. "Alright, so let's go again!"

Joren, however, remained unshaken. "You would win this time."

"Come on, let's have a true one-on-one fight. You still want to go to the dance with me, right?" She flashed a cheeky smile.

Joren shrugged. "I never really expected you to go through with that." I noticed a fleeting look of disappointment cross Veyra's face, quickly masked. "My saying that was part of the plan. You likely knew nothing about me, so my coming across as confident against the strongest fighter in the exam would have put you on edge. People on edges are easier to push over."

Naya, who had stepped closer, looked at Joren with an expression of admiration and intrigue. "Gods, your brain is impressive..."

He smiled modestly. "Still think Calia would have been a better choice for you."

Veyra, not to be deterred, turned her attention to me.

"Alright, how about you, Liam? Want to go again? Maybe try a real fight this time, instead of just me dodging? I'd like to work on my offense."

I stood up, ready for the challenge. "First one to get touched loses?" I proposed.

She nodded, a determined gleam in her eye. "Alright, sounds good."

The fight initiated abruptly with Veyra springing into action before I was fully prepared. Reacting instinctively, I dodged to the side just as her fist connected with the wall, shattering it. In that brief moment, I noticed she had surrounded her fist with a mana gauntlet, which she quickly reabsorbed.

Using the momentum from my dodge, I kicked off the broken wall, putting some distance between us. As I raised my hands in a defensive posture, I called out, "Wait, what are the rules?"

Veyra didn't pause in her attack as she answered, "No mana attacks for you, including telekinetic attacks, but feel free to use non-offensive magic."

The fight escalated, and I found myself heavily relying on water form, my movements flowing more fluidly than before. As the bout continued, I started experimenting with channeling mana directly into my muscles, much like Veyra, granting me sudden surges of speed.

I teleported behind Veyra. To my surprise, she managed to react, dodging just in time. It was evident she was adapting quickly to my tactics. She took a brief moment to regroup, then faced me with a determined look. "You're getting faster, Liam. Stop holding back, this is training! Push yourself!"

Accepting her challenge, I teleported again, but she anticipated and dodged. "Stop using tricks! Show me your real speed," she demanded.

With a grin, I focused my mana into my legs, then unleashed it against the floor. The ground cracked under the sheer force, propelling me sideways through the air. Mid-air, I spun my body with telekinesis, landing against the wall with such impact that it cratered under me. Then, in a fluid motion, I propelled myself from the wall, hurtling back toward Veyra and stopping abruptly right in front of her face, both of us locked in a moment of surprise and exhilaration.

In the brief pause that followed, a rush of air and debris shot past us, pelting the opposite wall. Naya and Joren, caught off-guard, were quickly shrouded in a cloud of dust and small rocks.

Veyra's gaze, filled with shock and disbelief, wasn't on me but rather fixated on the destruction behind me. I turned to see the extent of the damage – an entire section of the dome's wall had been torn open, revealing a cave-like opening that led to layers of rock and soil. Amid the debris, I noticed the exposed framework of the wall – steel rods that had once reinforced the concrete now lay bare, twisted, and broken.

I turned back to Veyra, noting Naya dropping a barrier that had protected her and Joren from the debris. "Was that telekinesis?" Naya asked, her voice one of confusion.

"No," Joren muttered. "That was a vacuum."

"My eyes couldn't follow him…" Veyra blinked slowly, then cautiously checked herself over. "He moved so fast that the air rushed in to fill the space, bringing all that debris with it…" Her voice trailed off.

I looked at the damage, a sense of realization washing over me. "I didn't mean for that to happen," I admitted, understanding the sheer force of what I had unintentionally unleashed.

Joren nodded, his analytical mind processing the event. "That's twice you've done that, now."

"Twice?" I repeated.

"When you scaled down your energy ball, you compressed it so quickly Naya was pulled toward you."

"That's what that was?" said Naya.

Joren approached cautiously, placing a gentle hand on Veyra's shoulder and guiding her a few steps back from me. "Using your mana, Liam, how fast can you move?" he asked, a curious but cautious tone in his voice.

I raised one arm, beginning to move it slowly from side to side. Gradually, I increased the speed, channeling more mana into my muscles. As the velocity intensified, a strange sensation began to ripple through my arm. I could feel the bone straining under the stress, a sharp pain followed by a crack and immediate healing. I stopped, alarmed by the sensation.

Joren observed closely, his expression serious. "Use your mana to not only control your muscles but also reinforce your bones."

Accepting Joren's advice, I closed my eyes for a moment, concentrating deeply. I visualized the mana flowing not just into the muscles of my arm but also weaving into my bones, reinforcing them like the steel rods within concrete behind me. It was a complex balance, channeling the mana to two different tasks simultaneously.

As I opened my eyes, a newfound confidence surged through me. The mana was flowing as I had visualized – a dual stream of energy, one part enhancing motion, the other reinforcing structure. My arm felt steadier, stronger, yet no less agile. I cautiously resumed the movement. At first, my arm moved at a manageable speed, a blur of motion. Gradually, I increased the pace, the mana flowing more freely now, guided by my focused intent.

As the speed intensified, a remarkable transformation occurred. My arm's movement transcended the normal limits of human perception, the rapid back-and-forth motion creating the illusion of duality – as though I had two arms moving in perfect synchrony.

Veyra instinctively stepped back as the air around us stirred into a breeze, caused by the sheer speed of my movement. Joren raised his hand, signaling for me to stop. I slowly ceased, feeling the air settle around us.

Veyra, her eyes wide, glanced between my arm and the damaged wall behind me. "If he hadn't stopped, he would have killed me…" she murmured.

Joren reached into his pocket and pulled out my dampener. "For now, I think you should keep this on."

CHAPTER THIRTY
The Unseen Hand

Hours later, we found ourselves back in the lunch hall, a stark contrast to the intense training session we had just endured. I sat there, idly playing with the circlet now wrapped around my wrist. After experiencing a greater extent of my abilities, wearing the dampener felt like walking with weights strapped to my legs. Despite the restriction, I was confident that my newfound understanding of mana manipulation made me a formidable asset to the team.

We had only been seated in the lunch hall for about half an hour when Kai and Leana entered the room. Kai walked in with his usual air of confidence, while Leana followed quietly, her eyes often downcast.

As they approached our table, Kai wasted no time launching into his usual taunts. "I hope you'll be a better match for us now, after all that training," he said, his smirk evident. His gaze then shifted to Veyra. "How did you manage to lose to a team like this? Expected better from you."

Veyra didn't respond verbally; instead, she picked up her sandwich, taking a deliberate bite, her expression unchanging.

"How are you doing, Leana?" I asked, trying to steer the conversation away from Kai's taunts. "Thanks for looking after Lammat for us."

Leana smiled, then opened her mouth to respond but caught Kai's eye. The unspoken message between them was clear, and she closed her mouth, opting for silence. Kai, seizing the opportunity, interjected, "Are you two friends now? Do you know each other?"

Leana's reply was cautious. "No, we don't know each other."

Kai's smirk widened as he prodded further, his words dripping with sarcasm. "Developed a soft spot for him, have you? Or just want him as a pet?" His eyes narrowed slightly as he continued. "Is that why you wanted him to join us instead of Lammat after the last battle?"

The atmosphere grew tense, the air thick with unspoken conflict. It was at this moment that Lammat appeared, draping his arm casually over Kai's shoulder. Kai tensed, as if to shrug off the contact, but then hesitated, leaving Lammat's arm in place. I wondered for a moment if I sensed a flicker of fear in Kai, but then dismissed it, considering that he might be trying to project a false sense of unity.

"Hey, team!" said Lammat, purposefully directing his words at our group rather than Kai and Leana. "Now that it's four against four again, we should get this over with." He locked eyes with me, a hint of nostalgia in his expression. "Missed my old team, you know?" He placed a hand to the side of his mouth, conspiratorially, but spoke loud enough for the room to hear, "Our current dorm smells like rotten wood and manure."

Kai visibly stiffened at Lammat's remark but maintained his silence. After a moment, he spoke up, his voice tinged with resignation and disdain. "Let's just get this over with," he said flatly. "I don't care if we win or lose. If we lose, we'll finally be rid of Lammat. If we win, Leana gets a new plaything, and maybe she'll stop moping around."

At his words, Lammat's demeanor shifted subtly. He squeezed Kai's shoulder, a seemingly friendly gesture that caused Kai to visibly jump, yelp, and step back. The vines that normally adorned and formed part of Kai's clothing unfurled slightly, extending outwards towards Lammat in a defensive display.

Lammat, however, remained calm, his movements slow and deliberate as he turned to face Kai. There was a brief, tense standoff between them.

Kai, breaking the tension first, lowered his eyes. The vines around his body tightened, weaving back into their usual form as clothing, a clear sign of de-escalation.

Lammat then turned his attention back to our table, his usual cheerful demeanor returning as if nothing had happened. "So, let's count that as a challenge, shall we? I'll second it. Shall we begin?"

As I looked around at my teammates, I realized that all eyes were on me. At that moment, I felt a surprising blend of pride and responsibility. It dawned on me that my team, this group of individuals I had come to respect and rely on, were looking to me for leadership. It was a role I hadn't anticipated assuming, but in their expectant gazes, I found a newfound confidence.

I stood up, feeling the weight of the moment. Extending my hand towards Lammat, I smiled. "Ready to come back?"

Within the dense forest, the atmosphere was thick with anticipation as we prepared. As the challengers, they had to place their crystal first. Unlike the casual, over-the-shoulder approach Kai had adopted in our first match, this time he handed the crystal to Lammat with an awkwardness that seemed uncharacteristic of him. Lammat, with a laugh, passed it to Tyran.

Tyran, holding the crystal, glanced at each member of my team, his gaze assessing and calculating. When his eyes met mine, they lingered, a silent exchange hanging in the air. Just as I was about to break the tension with a wave, he turned and walked deeper into the forest.

My heart raced with the gravity of the match ahead. In our last encounter, we had lost three to one, and it was clear that they hadn't been overly concerned with defending their crystal. This time, the stakes felt even higher.

As we trailed behind Kai's team at a measured distance, the forest around us seemed to hold its breath in anticipation of the upcoming battle. Naya, walking beside the examiner, broke the silence with a question. "Will it be four hits on each crystal this time?"

The examiner shook his head in response. "The two-hit rule was only for the two-on-two match. This will be a standard three-hit match." His words added another layer of tension to the air.

Deeper into the forest, Tyran, with a sense of purpose, began to scout for the perfect spot to place their crystal. He eventually chose a location nestled between two sturdy, large trees. The area was heavily surrounded by a dense network of roots, intertwining and sprawling across the forest floor. Observing his choice, I couldn't help but speculate on the strategic advantage it could provide for Kai.

Once their crystal was securely formed, it was our turn. As we turned to find a suitable location for our crystal, I caught Lammat's eye and offered him a smile. My sight then shifted to Tyran. His expression was unreadable, but I knew behind those eyes lay a mind adept at strategy and manipulation. It was a reminder to stay vigilant and prepared for whatever he might have planned.

Leaving their team behind, our walk to select our crystal's location was a balance of vocal strategy, discussion, and introspective silence. Each step we took was weighed with the importance of our decision. Joren occasionally pointed out potential spots, assessing their defensive merits, while Naya mused over the best way to utilize her barrier magic. Veyra remained quiet, her eyes scanning the forest.

The walk through the dense forest seemed to stretch on, the silence around us punctuated only by the sounds of nature and our soft footsteps. Joren led the way, the crystal hovering before him like a guiding compass, his eyes constantly scanning the surroundings. We trusted his judgment implicitly, our confidence in his strategic mind evident as we followed his lead.

Eventually, Joren came to a halt. "This place should be most suitable," he declared, his voice carrying a sense of finality. "Very few obstacles in between, so it should be a straight run." We nodded in agreement. With a nod of his own, Joren released the crystal. It gently landed on the ground, then began to grow in size.

As the connecting light stretched toward Tyran's crystal, Joren positioned himself with his back against ours, leaning casually against it as if to claim it as his territory.

I approached, placing my hand on its surface to signal my readiness. "Joren, any chance you can do that stone trick right at the start like you did against us?"

"Last time was easier," Joren responded thoughtfully. "Because you placed your crystal out of range, I knew its exact distance when it shifted into position. I am not certain of the exact distance this time."

As he spoke, the dome around us formed, its red hue casting a tint over the sky.

"Does that mean you can't do it?" I asked, a tinge of disappointment in my voice.

Joren levitated a small rock before him. "Of course, it doesn't," he replied confidently, slapping his hand onto our crystal. His action was a silent affirmation of his readiness and capability.

Veyra, with a smile of determination, placed her hand next to Joren's. "We have our plans. We can do this," she affirmed, her confidence infectious.

Naya stepped forward, placing her hand beside mine on the crystal. "Let's go," she said, her voice steady and resolute.

The moment the dome shifted from red to blue, Joren let loose with the rock. We all held our breath, watching it arc upwards gracefully before it disappeared into the foliage of the dense forest canopy.

I looked up at the dome, a smile of anticipation on my face. But then, realization dawned on me – it was taking too long. The dome hadn't shifted back to red, indicating a hit.

"Did you miss?" Veyra asked, a hint of concern in her voice.

"Curious, I—"

The snapping of branches echoed through the forest, and we gasped in unison as a boulder, half my size, mirrored the trajectory of Joren's small rock. It soared through the air with an intimidating presence.

"By the gods..." Naya whispered in disbelief.

"Kai can throw rocks?" I asked, my voice laced with shock.

Without hesitation, Naya stepped forward, conjuring a barrier in the boulder's path. At the same time, Veyra leaped to the side and then, with remarkable speed, sprinted and launched herself into the air to meet the boulder side-on. For a fraction of a second, she seemed to cling to it before pushing off with all her strength. Her effort slightly altered the boulder's course, but a collision with our crystal still seemed imminent.

Reacting, I threw up a secondary barrier behind Naya's, reinforcing it just in time. Both barriers shattered upon impact with the boulder, but they had done just enough. The boulder missed our crystal by the barest margin before crashing to the ground and rolling out of the dome.

"That was far too close," Naya said, her eyes tracking the boulder as it came to a stop. Suddenly, her eyes widened. "Oh no..."

Following her gaze, I saw Veyra casually walk over and sit down atop the boulder. Her effort had pushed her out of the dome. Although her lips were moving, no sound reached us from outside the boundary.

Joren, catching her attempt at communication, pointed to his ears and shook his head.

Veyra rolled her eyes in understanding and then gestured towards me with a clear "You're up" motion.

Joren turned to me, his expression resolute. "Be quick," he said, a sense of urgency in his voice.

I nodded in understanding. In an instant, the world around me shifted, the scenery blurring into streaks of color before solidifying again. I found myself standing right in front of Tyran's crystal.

"Liam!" The shout pierced through the silence. It was Lammat's voice, tinged with surprise. "Did you throw that?"

I glanced over my shoulder to see a grinning Lammat standing beside Kai, who was staring at me, his eyes wide with disbelief. I noticed a small rock, Joren's projectile, slipping from Kai's grasp as he reflexively threw his arms toward me. Vines erupted from the ground, snaking rapidly in my direction. Without hesitation, I spun around and delivered a forceful punch to the crystal. The impact reverberated up my arm as I felt the familiar sensation of being pulled back to our crystal.

Back at our base, Naya let out a cheer, vibrant and filled with relief. "Nice! Good timing, Liam. Tyran and Leana were almost on us."

Veyra re-entered the dome, now tinted red again, and gave me a playful punch on the shoulder. Her eyes sparkled with confidence. "Excellent! We've got this match in the bag." She firmly placed her hand back on our crystal, ready for the next phase. We all quickly followed suit, our hands collectively signaling our readiness.

As the dome transitioned back to blue, Veyra, Naya, and I sprang into action, leaving Joren as our steadfast defender. We hadn't gone far when Tyran and Leana appeared, closing in with determined strides. "You take Leana," Veyra directed towards Naya.

"Got it," she replied, her focus narrowing.

Veyra turned to me, her expression serious. "That leaves Kai and Lammat for you, Liam."

"Understood," I responded, bracing myself for what was to come. With a thought, I teleported, reappearing near their crystal.

I smiled wryly, taking in the sight of the vines Kai had conjured around their crystal, forming a living barrier. I lunged forward, aiming for a gap in the green defense, but my movement was abruptly halted mid-air. Twisting around, I found myself face-to-face with Lammat, his hand gripping my arm with surprising strength. He lifted me effortlessly, a playful yet disapproving look on his face. "Oh, come on, Liam!" he chided, shaking his head. "That's boring! You can't just keep repeating the same trick."

I struggled against his hold, trying to break free. "I thought you wanted me to win you back?" I challenged.

His grin didn't waver. "I do! But you have to earn it. Not with cheap tricks, but by proving your skills as a fighter." His eyes shone with genuine belief in me. "I know you can do this, Liam."

Before I could respond, he swung me with unexpected force. The sensation of the dome's boundary tingled as I crossed it, a vivid reminder of the rules of the match. I landed outside the dome with a thud, slightly disoriented but unharmed. As I stood up, brushing dirt off my clothes, I looked back at Lammat, offering him a smile despite my disappointment.

He remained standing just inside the dome, frowning curiously at me. His arm, up to his elbow, was protruding through the barrier. His fingers wiggled back and forth as he struggled to pull it back in. I stepped closer, grinning at the unexpected turn of events. Pointing at his arm, I shook my head in mock disapproval. Though he couldn't hear my laughter, his expression showed he realized his mistake. He had inadvertently trapped himself, effectively taking him out of the round alongside me.

Lammat's expression shifted to a smile, a silent acknowledgment of the situation. His arm, previously struggling for freedom, went limp in resignation. I offered a sympathetic shrug but then gasped in surprise.

Slowly, ever so slowly, Lammat's arm began to retract back through the dome. I watched, eyes wide, as his elbow freed itself. Lammat's slow but steady progress meant he would soon rejoin the battle, tipping the scales back to a four-on-three. My team was at risk of being outnumbered again.

Reacting fast, I grabbed Lammat's hand and started to pull, planting my foot against the dome. He tilted his head, but his speed didn't slow.

Panicked, I attempted to teleport back inside the dome, but my efforts were in vain – the spell failed, repelled by the barrier. Without hesitation, I channeled mana into my legs, propelling myself up and onto the dome. I scrambled forward, maintaining my balance as I ran, scanning the area below. Naya and Leana were engaged in a fierce battle, with Naya seemingly gaining the upper hand, driving Leana back towards their crystal.

Further ahead, I noticed a tree shattering at its base – a clear sign of Tyran and Veyra's intense confrontation. The forest around them was bearing the brunt of their power, echoing the ferocity of their duel.

As I continued my run atop the dome, I finally caught sight of Joren, steadfastly guarding our crystal. He looked up, instantly spotting me waving at him frantically. Without a moment's hesitation, he leaped into action, matching my position above him.

As I ran, I nearly lost my footing, skidding on the dome's surface. Struggling to maintain control, I managed to correct my trajectory and kept moving, tracking Joren's movements below, guiding him to where Veyra and Tyran were fighting. Joren, with incredible agility, dove into the fray, catching Tyran off-guard with a series of rapid jabs, and bringing him to the ground.

Veyra, seizing the opportunity, darted off to aid Naya, leaving Joren to continue his focused assault on Tyran with a few more mana blockers. After confirming Tyran was incapacitated, Joren swiftly turned his attention to the remaining adversaries.

Meanwhile, Leana, now outnumbered, darted back and forth in a state of apparent panic. The situation had rapidly turned into a three-on-one confrontation. Joren, with his strategic precision, slid forward and delivered two rapid jabs to the back of Leana's thighs, causing her to collapse to the ground. Rolling over to sit up, Leana watched resignedly as Joren, Naya, and Veyra sprinted towards her team's crystal. She flopped onto her back, seemingly accepting the turn of events. Noticing me atop the dome, her expression momentarily brightened into a smile. She raised a hand in a friendly wave, which I returned before quickly following after my team.

As I ran along the dome, I caught sight of the intense motion below. Kai was holding his own against all three of my teammates, his vines whipping furiously through the air. Joren was almost entirely entangled, struggling against the constricting vines. Naya, fiercely determined, cut through the approaching vines, but they pushed her back. Veyra, in her element, circled the crystal, gracefully evading the vines with her water form, clearly focused on their target.

Amid the chaos, Lammat, who had remained stationary since his arm was trapped, was now almost free. I slid down the side of the dome and twisted mid-air, catching Lammat's hand in both of mine and pulling it to my chest. Surprised, his eyes snapped from his hand to meet mine, a smile slowly spreading across his face as he stopped struggling against the dome's barrier.

Veyra made contact with the crystal.

"Two down, one to go!" Naya exclaimed as we all reemerged around our crystal, her eyes shining with the thrill of the moment. She was practically bouncing on her toes, her usual calm demeanor replaced by a contagious energy.

Joren couldn't hide a grin that stretched across his face. "I have to admit, I didn't expect us to take the lead this quickly," he said, his voice filled with pride.

Veyra nodded. "We've got them on the defense now. Just one more hit and we'll be done."

I nodded, feeling a surge of confidence. "We're so close now. Let's stay focused and finish this strong." The prospect of winning and bringing Lammat back to our side was a powerful motivator.

As we gathered around our crystal, there was a sense of excitement in the air. Everyone was ready to place their hands on the crystal, signaling our readiness for the next round, except for Joren. He sat calmly on the ground, his focus on the stones he was levitating in front of him. Veyra glanced down at him. "You going to join us?" she asked.

Joren didn't look up from his stones. "Six minutes and twenty-eight seconds," he said matter-of-factly.

"What?" Veyra responded, slightly puzzled.

"That's how long my mana blocks last," Joren explained, lying back on the ground and tossing the stones up into the air before catching them again. "I got Tyran and Leana with them, so they won't be ready to fight for a while." With this realization, we all lowered our hands from the crystal, understanding belatedly dawning on us. "How did you end up outside the dome, Liam?"

I recounted the chain of events - how Lammat countered my teleport, his unexpected strength, how he threw me out of the dome, and his subsequent struggle with his hand trapped in the barrier. As I spoke, Joren's stones stopped their aerial dance, his gaze locking onto me, intrigued by the narrative.

Veyra laughed after hearing the story. "Wow, I want this guy on our team!"

Naya chimed in. "It's strange, he never stood out in the previous exams. I heard Kai was able to beat him pretty easily."

"He seems to learn pretty fast," I added. "When I first teleported, he seemed surprised, but didn't move to stop me. At first, I thought he might let us win, but now I think I just caught him off-guard."

"I had a lot of fun fighting Tyran," said Veyra. "He moves a lot like you, Liam, so our practice paid off. His style resembled fire form, but with an emphasis on dodging as well."

Naya, curious, asked, "How does fire form differ?"

"In fire form, there are no dodges at all. You're meant to head straight toward your opponent, using only attacks and blocks. If you can't block it, you allow it," Veyra explained, gesturing with her hand. "You see what he did to the forest? That wasn't me, that was all him. The guy is strong."

As our discussion wound down, Joren stood up and walked over to the crystal, placing his hand on it. "It's nearly time," he said, a note of determination in his voice.

We all followed suit, placing our hands on the crystal once more. "One last time," Veyra said, her voice filled with resolve.

The dome shifted to blue, and we all set off again, leaving Joren to defend our crystal.

Tyran's team had revised their strategy, and now it was Tyran, Leana, and Lammat who met us head-on in the middle of the dome.

I hesitated, unsure about engaging Lammat. But he left me no choice, launching into an attack with a speed that belied his earlier playful demeanor. Veyra clashed with Tyran in a flurry of aggressive moves, while Naya and Leana exchanged rapid strikes and parries.

Lammat's fighting style was a stark contrast to his usual laid-back attitude. He moved with effortless grace, his attacks seemingly casual yet frighteningly fast. I shifted into water form, fluidly dodging his strikes.

As Lammat and I circled each other, he spoke, his voice calm amidst the chaos. "You've improved a lot these past few days, Liam." His words were encouraging, yet I remained focused on his every move, aware of his deceptive speed.

The proximity of our three fights made the battlefield chaotic. In a sudden shift, Lammat broke from our engagement and swiftly delivered an energy block to Naya's shoulder. Her arm dropped, rendered useless, her mana blade vanishing into thin air. Before I could even think to assist her, Lammat was back, engaging me with renewed vigor.

With Naya now weakened, Leana swiftly gained the upper hand. Her movements were sharp and precise, culminating in a powerful strike that sent Naya crashing to the ground, unconscious.

Leana quickly turned her attention to Veyra, assisting Tyran. Together, they proved too much for Veyra's defensive tactics. Despite her best efforts, she was soon overwhelmed and pinned to the ground, struggling futilely.

I tried to intervene, but Lammat intercepted me. His movements were a blur, effortlessly dodging my counterattacks and then swiftly immobilizing Veyra with precise energy blocks to her limbs. Standing over her, he declared, "That's me done for this round," and folded his arms, stepping back from the fight.

With Veyra and Naya out, Tyran and Leana focused their assault on me. Tyran's attacks kept me on the defensive, while Leana's swift strikes forced me to constantly shift my focus. The combination of their onslaught was disorienting. Each hit I took from them was a jarring reminder of the situation's gravity.

I was caught in a whirlwind of evasion and counterattacks, desperately trying to find an opening or a moment to regroup. My mind raced for a strategy, a way to turn the tide against the odds. The fight was intense, and every second counted. I needed to find a way to outmaneuver them, to use my skills to their fullest if I had any hope of turning this dire situation around.

As Tyran and Leana continued their relentless assault, I felt myself being inexorably pushed back towards our crystal. With each step backward, my situation grew more desperate. The combined might of Tyran's ferocity and Leana's agility was overwhelming, and I struggled to find an opening to counterattack.

Just as I was nearing the brink of defeat, Joren came into view, rushing to my aid. He dived towards Tyran, aiming to immobilize him with his energy-blocking jabs. But Tyran was ready; he shielded himself with his arm and countered with a powerful blow to Joren's stomach. The impact lifted Joren off his feet and sent him crashing to the ground, leaving him gasping for air.

Tyran then turned to me, grabbing my hand with his functioning right arm. As he nodded, his left arm, previously limp, began to move again. "Thought so," he muttered, before quickly re-engaging. In the corner of my eye, my attention was briefly caught by Leana's swift movement. She dashed towards our crystal, and with a regretful glance in my direction, struck it decisively.

In an instant, Naya and Veyra reappeared beside the crystal, and I quickly knelt to heal Joren. "Sorry, Liam," he wheezed out, still struggling to recover.

"Not your fault," I said, walking over to Naya and Veyra, and reaching out to both of them.

Veyra sat, punching the ground, as Naya groaned, coming back to her senses. "What happened?" Naya asked, confusion lacing her voice.

"Leana knocked you out," I informed her, keeping my tone even despite the setback.

Naya expressed her annoyance with a frustrated huff.

"Lammat was asking questions about you, Liam," Veyra said, her gaze holding mine. "He wants to know what's holding you back."

"What does that mean?" I asked.

"He seems to think you should be able to beat him in a one-on-one," Veyra explained as she stood up. "He seemed... disappointed, somehow. Says you're meant to save him."

I mulled over her words. Lammat's perception of my abilities and his apparent disappointment gave me pause. Determined, I placed my hand on the crystal again. "We're so close," I said to the team. "Just one more hit on their crystal.

Joren, can you send a barrage of rocks at their crystal while the rest of us rush in?"

Joren nodded and we all placed our hands on the crystal, ready to re-engage. As soon as the dome shifted to blue, Joren immediately got to work, launching every stone he could find toward their crystal.

Our feet pounded the forest floor, closing the distance to the center where our adversaries awaited. Lammat, with a newfound focus, engaged Veyra in a duel. His movements were a blur, each attack strategically aimed to test her defenses.

Meanwhile, Tyran turned his attention to me. His eyes were cold, his expression calculated as he moved with a predator's grace. I braced myself for the confrontation, trying to anticipate his strikes. But Tyran's speed was on another level. His fists were like pistons, striking with mechanical precision and overwhelming force. I dodged and weaved, trying to create an opening, but his agility left no room for counterattack.

Each of Tyran's punches felt like a hammer blow, driving me back step by step. I was on the defensive, barely managing to stay upright under his assault. The forest around us became a blur as I was forced back, desperately trying to regain my footing.

A particularly heavy blow from Tyran sent me crashing into a tree. The impact reverberated through my body, and as I started to slump to the ground, Tyran continued his offensive, his fists a storm.

An arm shot out with sudden ferocity, halting Tyran's punch in mid-air. Both Tyran and I looked up in stunned silence to see a dark-haired man now standing between us. His presence was commanding, exuding the aura of a seasoned warrior. Dressed in a black felt jacket that did little to conceal his imposing physique, he surveyed the scene with a steely gaze. In a swift, powerful motion, he upended Tyran, sending him crashing to the ground with a thud that resonated through the quiet of the forest. Tyran, lying prone and visibly shaken, looked up at the man towering over him. A look of recognition washed over his face. In a hushed tone, filled with disbelief, Tyran uttered a single word, "Dad?"

CHAPTER THIRTY-ONE
Fury Unleashed

As I steadied myself against the tree, the sight of Tyran's father standing before us filled me with a sense of foreboding. Tyran, still on the ground, stared up at his father, his expression one of pain and confusion.

"Why?" Tyran's voice broke the tense silence, a single word loaded with years of unspoken questions and emotions. I looked to the man for an answer, but he remained silent, an unreadable statue. Tyran's eyes then shifted to me, and in them, I saw a storm of hurt and accusation. "Why would you do this to me?" he asked, his voice raw.

Before I could grasp the full weight of his words, Tyran exploded into action. He lunged at me with a ferocity that was both terrifying and awe-inspiring. His fist connected with such force that the tree behind me splintered and shattered, sending wooden shrapnel into the air. I felt the bones in my body fracture and then knit back together in an instant.

As I tried to locate Tyran again, another devastating blow landed, catapulting me through the air. Mid-flight, Tyran's grip on my foot arrested my momentum. He spun me around and released his grip, flinging me out of the dome with inhuman strength.

I tumbled across the ground outside the dome, my body a whirlwind of pain and confusion. I scrambled to my feet, frustration boiling over at being ejected at such a pivotal moment. As I regained my bearings, I saw Tyran leap through the dome's barrier, his pursuit relentless and unyielding, no longer caring about the exam.

Tyran was a blur of motion, a tempest of unbridled fury. I raised my arms in defense, but where I had found Tyran fast before, now he was a force of nature. Each of his strikes was a thunderclap, swift and ruthless. I managed to dodge a blow, using the brief respite to try and reach my circlet, seeking to unleash my full potential. But before I could touch it, Tyran's next hit sent me hurtling through the forest.

Trees crashed down around me as I streaked through the woods, a human projectile of Tyran's wrath. I managed a nimble dodge, creating a moment's gap between us. Seizing the opportunity, I sprinted along the forest's edge, barely keeping ahead of Tyran's assault.

Then came the rain of explosions. I spun around to see Tyran unleashing a barrage of energy balls, each one a deadly comet streaking through the air towards me. In desperation, I leaped onto a tree, climbing higher, branch to branch, in a frantic attempt to evade the onslaught.

Suddenly, Tyran's next strike connected, launching us both skyward. We burst through the glass dome above the forest, shattering a section into a thousand sparkling fragments. Suspended in mid-air above D'wan Ma'hal, the cityscape sprawled beneath us, a breathtaking backdrop. As we hung there, suspended in the void, I saw the extent of Tyran's self-inflicted devastation. His arms and legs, bent and twisted at unnatural angles, were being moved solely by his sheer will and mana manipulation.

We began to plummet back towards the earth, but even in this descent, Tyran's assault did not cease. His fists were relentless, each blow a hammer of wrath and pain. Blood streamed from his mouth, a stark contrast against his pale, furious face.

In a fleeting moment of clarity amidst the chaos, I reached out to heal him, my hand extending towards his battered body. The instant my skin made contact with his, a ripple in the air enveloped us, and I found myself teleported back to the crystal inside the dome. I crashed onto the floor, my body aching from the ordeal.

Naya's gasp was sharp as she dropped next to me, her eyes wide with concern. My body was wracked with pain, the sensation of my bones knitting back together was both excruciating and surreal. I looked down to see a hole in my lower leg slowly closing up, likely a result of one of Tyran's energy balls.

"What happened to you?" Naya asked, hovering anxiously, her hands moving uncertainly as if she wanted to help but didn't know where to start.

The healing process was intense, but finally, my body stilled as the repairs were completed. Sitting up, I caught Veyra and Joren's shocked expressions. Their eyes were fixed on me, a mixture of awe and disbelief in their gaze.

Joren glanced over to Veyra and muttered, "God."

I groaned as I stood up, feeling the last of the pain ebb away. "If I were a god, we would have won already," I replied, trying to lighten the mood despite the gravity of the situation.

Naya stepped in front of me, her eyes brimming with tears. "Liam, who did this to you? What happened?"

"Tyran's dad is here, in the dome," I explained, the words sounding almost unbelievable even to my ears.

"What?" she exclaimed, her confusion evident.

"Tyran got angry when he saw him, forced me out of the dome, then followed me out to continue the fight."

"He followed you out of the dome?" Veyra interjected, her brow furrowed in concern.

"His body… it was worse than mine. Even broken, he continued fighting me," I said, recalling the harrowing intensity of Tyran's actions.

Joren closed his eyes, exhaling deeply. "Foolish," he said, his tone laced with frustration. "I told you it was dangerous to push yourself too much with mana. Now you've seen the result."

"I should go check on him before the round," I said.

As I started to walk towards their crystal, Naya reached out, grabbing my arm, and pulling me to face her. "By the sounds of it, you're the last person he wants to see, Liam," she said earnestly. Her eyes searched mine, conveying concern and caution. "Well... second to last..."

"What do you mean?" I asked.

"Tyran's father is dead," Naya replied, firmly.

I shook my head in disbelief. "I saw him."

"You created a copy of him, just like you did with Tyran during the first exam," Naya explained, her eyes locking onto mine. "You probably saw a drawing of him or something."

"But, I didn't..." I protested, the pieces not fitting together in my mind.

"Liam, you did," Naya sighed, her frustration barely contained. "Both Tyran and Lammat said you did, and we've seen over and over again that you don't know what you're doing!"

A heavy silence descended upon us. "Naya—" I began, but she swiftly pulled me into an embrace, cutting off my words.

"It's not your fault, Liam, but eventually you're going to have to admit that you're wrong," she said, her voice muffled against my shoulder. She then pushed me back, holding my gaze with an intensity that was both caring and stern. "Liam, you're incredible. You're remarkable. You're unbelievably powerful... But you're dangerous."

"Naya—" Veyra attempted to interject, but Naya cut her off sharply.

"No, he needs to hear this! Liam, you teleported an entire room of people to a completely different room without meaning to. Gods, you heal yourself and others without even knowing how! What makes you think you aren't capable of making a copy of a person?"

Joren stepped forward, placing himself between Naya and me. He gently placed his hands on my arms, giving me a reassuring smile. "Try it now," he urged softly.

"What?" I was taken aback by his request.

"Make a copy of Tyran's father." As he spoke, a strange ripple of energy surged through me. I turned to find a figure standing next to me, the spitting image of the man I had seen earlier, observing us with a curious gaze.

"I... I didn't..." My voice trailed off, disbelief and realization dawning on me.

"You didn't mean to," Naya finished for me. She shook her head, her expression softening. "I know it's not your fault, but you need to be more careful, Liam."

"I know I wouldn't be happy if someone summoned a copy of my mother without my permission," said Veyra, not quite meeting my eyes.

"It's not actually Tyran's father," Joren said, a note of intrigue in his voice. "That's just a duplicate of Liam, blended with an illusion spell." He moved closer, his eyes analyzing the figure with keen interest. The duplicate extended a hand, cautioning Joren to keep his distance. "Incredible. The attention to detail is astounding."

"Joren," Veyra interjected, her tone edged with frustration. "That's not helpful."

"Alright," Joren conceded. He turned to the illusion, continuing to examine it. "Liam, how would you feel if someone made a duplicate of your family member without asking you? Magic isn't something to be taken lightly, it requires—"

Before he could finish, my form wavered again, and there stood a man in white robes, his hair as white as snow. He turned towards me, and those piercing blue eyes — I recognized them from the dream Veyra had shown me. Abruptly, the duplicate of Tyran's father knelt, forming a cross over his chest.

My body rippled once more, and another figure

appeared, also kneeling before the white-robed man.

The man in white gave a soft chuckle. "How many times must I tell you not to do that, little Brother?"

The man beside Tyran's father didn't rise, his gaze fixed on the ground. "I'll stop when you stop calling me little," he replied, a smile playing on his lips.

"Stand up, Meltek," the man in white said, his laughter light. "You're making Liam uncomfortable."

"Meltek..." Naya murmured, stepping back slowly.

Meltek rose, moving forward to ruffle my hair. "Will you ever stop growing, little Lexis?" he teased with a laugh.

"Prince Lex—" I instinctively started to correct Meltek, the words slipping out before I could stop them.

I looked over at Naya and the others, only to find them staring in shock. Joren had fallen to his knees. "He's not a god... he's royalty."

"Are these your friends, Liam?" the man in white asked, stepping forward and extending a hand.

I shattered the illusions, scattering the mana. My breathing quickened, my mind spinning. I reached for the crystal and placed my hand on it.

"Liam—" Naya began.

"We need to win this match," I said, my voice sounding distant, as if it didn't belong to me.

"Prince Lexis died," Veyra muttered to herself.

"Apparently... not..." Joren added.

I met Naya's eyes and took a deep breath. "I will tell you everything, okay?" I said, forcing a smile. "After we win Lammat back."

"Liam—" Naya began, her voice laced with concern.

"Please," I interjected, offering a nod of understanding. "Let's talk after the match."

Naya reached out and clasped my hand, then laid her fingers upon the crystal. Her touch was gentle, yet resolute.

"We don't have a strategy," Veyra pointed out, her hand joining Naya's on the crystal, her expression serious.

"I believe all of us rushing might be the best option," Joren suggested, his hand also finding the crystal. "Together, we can do it."

I nodded in agreement, watching the dome turn a calming shade of blue. As we re-entered the forest, a torrent of thoughts swirled in my mind. What would our conversation entail after the exam? How could I possibly explain what I didn't know? The man in white – my father. Tyran's father, Meltek – figures shrouded in familiarity. How will my friends view me now?

My thoughts were abruptly shattered as Tyran, Lammat, Kai, and Leana emerged from the forest's embrace.

"They have the same idea as us?" Naya mused, an edge of suspicion in his voice.

Veyra shook her head slowly. "No, something's different. They're not assuming any tactical formation... they're here to parley." Our pace decelerated to a cautious walk as we neared them. I sought Tyran's gaze, but he pointedly avoided mine.

"We figured we'd handle this the old-fashioned way," Lammat declared, his tone casual yet firm, a half-smile playing on his lips. "Each of us picks one opponent. Once a fight concludes, the victor steps back and awaits the outcome of the others. No interference, and no rush for the crystal until all duels are resolved. The team with the most victories claims the prize."

"And if it's a draw?" Veyra inquired.

"The contest resets," Lammat replied with a nonchalant shrug.

"I choose Veyra," Tyran announced, still evading my gaze.

"Then my opponent shall be Leana," Joren stated decisively.

Lammat's laughter broke the tension. "Seems it's you and me again, Liam." He extended his hand toward me. "Do we have an agreement?" I stepped forward, my eyes locked on his, wariness etched into my every move. As my hand neared his, he swiftly grasped my wrist instead.

"What are you doing?" I demanded, my voice dropping to a whisper, confusion, and suspicion mingling in my tone. "Do you want us to win you back or not?"

His smile was enigmatic, yet there was a softness in his eyes. "As I've said, you must prove your worth." His hand moved to my sleeve, pulling it back to reveal the chainmail dampener. "I've been curious about this," he noted, eyeing it closely. "What is it?"

"It dampens my powers when it touches my skin," I explained briefly.

A flicker of understanding crossed Lammat's face. "That explains quite a bit," he muttered, examining the magnetic clasp and releasing it. He held it before him, examining it closely. Seizing the moment of his distraction, I thrust forward, my fist connecting solidly with his jaw.

His head snapped back, but his feet remained unmoved. Slowly, he turned back to face me. "I said not to hold back," he reprimanded. Before I could react, a crushing blow to my abdomen sent me staggering, breathless, and fighting nausea. "I guess we don't have an agreement, then."

The air around us erupted into chaos as both teams engaged in their respective battles.

Lammat started walking towards my crystal, his focus unwavering. Fueled by desperation, I teleported before him, gasping and unsteady. "Stop," I managed to utter.

"When you anticipate an impact, create a barrier at that precise point. The larger the barrier, the less harm you'll endure," he instructed, then launched another attack. I raised my hands defensively, but they were ineffective, and his fist connected with the side of my head. The world spun as I hit the ground, his advice echoing in my mind. "You relied on your hands, not a barrier," he noted, stepping over me.

I tried to grab his clothing, to halt him, but he brushed my hand away with ease, continuing his relentless advance towards my crystal.

My eyes swept the area, frantically searching for his team, for my team. Then, mustering all my strength, I teleported to his crystal. From behind, Lammat's voice pierced the tumult. How had he caught up to me so quickly?

"I asked you not to rely on tricks!" he said. "Fight, Liam! I know you have the strength!" His words ignited a spark within me, and I charged towards the crystal, only to be intercepted by him, my momentum diverted sideways. My body slammed against a tree, but I used the impact to pivot, pushing Lammat aside, ensuring the tree didn't stop his momentum. "That's it! Better!" he called out, his figure swiftly disappearing from view.

As quickly as he vanished, however, he reappeared, landing another blow to my ribs. Our fight quickly escalated, each strike and parry more intense than the last. We were two forces colliding, our battle a tempest that swept from one end of the dome to the other.

Lammat's attacks were rapid, each one a test of my limits. I felt the air rush past me as I narrowly dodged a powerful kick, responding with a rapid series of punches. Lammat parried them effortlessly, his expression a mask of focus. Our fight was a whirlwind of energy and skill that left no room for error.

Suddenly, Lammat broke away, dashing towards my crystal with lightning speed. Adrenaline surged through me as I leaped after him, intercepting his path and blocking his advance. Our eyes met, a silent acknowledgment of the high stakes of this duel. Lammat smiled wryly and engaged again, his strikes coming faster, pushing me back.

Then, like a tempest unleashed, Veyra burst into the fray, her form a blur of motion. Casting aside her usual dance of avoidance, her every move was an aggressive onslaught aimed at Lammat. The ferocity of her attacks was a stark contrast to her graceful dodges, as she wove a non-stop assault.

Lammat, caught off guard by the sudden addition, found his rhythm disrupted. His wry smile faltered, replaced by a scowl of concentration as he parried and countered with dwindling efficiency. The fluidity of his movements began to stiffen under the pressure of Veyra's unabating assault.

As I parried another of Lammat's strikes, my gaze flickered to the side, catching a glimpse of Tyran embroiled in his own battle. Surrounded by both Joren and Naya, he moved with a desperation that bordered on recklessness. Nearby, Kai lay prone, his labored breathing a testament to the battle's toll, while Leana offered a silent vigil, her hands gently cradling his head.

Refocusing on the duel at hand, I stepped in beside Veyra, our attacks synchronizing into a storm of blows. Lammat, now besieged on two fronts, his expression a mask of frustration, was gradually losing ground. Though he was a formidable opponent alone, the combined might of Veyra and I began to erode his defenses, our coordinated strikes a testament to our training. Each exchange, each feint and parry, brought us closer to turning the tide, our unity in battle slowly wearing him down.

Veyra, with a burst of speed, closed in on Lammat, her fists moving in a rapid, rhythmic pattern, a dance of agility and force. Each strike was a testament to her skill, a blur of motion aimed at finding any gap in Lammat's defenses. Lammat, unyielding and strategic, matched her pace. He moved with a calculated grace, his responses not just defensive but tactically offensive, turning Veyra's speed against her.

In a moment that seemed suspended in time, he pivoted, channeling his energy into a counterstrike that caught Veyra squarely in the midsection. The impact was thunderous, lifting Veyra off her feet and sending her crashing to the ground, gasping for air.

In that same breath, Lammat found himself abruptly toppled. His feet were swept from under him by an unseen force. It was only after he fell that I realized Joren had intervened, his attention momentarily diverted from his battle with Tyran to aid us.

Tyran, ever observant, capitalized on the split-second Joren's focus wavered. He delivered a swift, punishing blow that caught Joren off-guard, sending him reeling through the air, unconscious before his body even hit the ground.

Reacting almost on instinct, I capitalized on Joren's unexpected intervention, not willing to let his sacrifice go to waste. With Lammat momentarily disoriented from being knocked down, I gathered my energy swiftly, the telekinetic force building within me like a coiled spring. Without a moment's hesitation, I released the energy in a focused burst towards Lammat.

The blast struck him with unrelenting fury just as he regained his footing, the impact far more potent than I had anticipated. Lammat's arms flailed for balance, but the force was overwhelming. It sent him cartwheeling backward, a blur of motion against the backdrop of the forest. Trees and underbrush became mere smudges of green as he tumbled through them, each collision marking his hasty retreat from the battlefield.

I wasted no time dwelling on the success of the maneuver. I pivoted on my heel and, with all the speed I could muster, leaped towards Tyran. The urgency of the moment propelled me forward, my focus narrowing to the impending confrontation with Tyran, who was already turning to face the new threat I posed.

With a swift vertical motion, he sent a slicing energy blade my way. Reacting on instinct, I dodged, feeling the blade narrowly miss, grazing my fingertips. The sting was brief, my body's regenerative abilities quickly repairing the damage.

Charging towards Tyran with renewed determination, I aimed a powerful punch in his direction. He reacted just in time, conjuring a shimmering barrier. But my momentum was too great; my fist crashed through the barrier, propelling Tyran backward and out of the dome.

In that brief interlude, my gaze swept across the dome, checking on Naya, Joren, and Veyra. It was then I caught sight of Lammat, his figure once again cutting through the fray, dashing towards us with a steady drive. The air around him seemed to warp and ripple, distorting with the intensity of his magic.

As my attention shifted to Veyra, the world around us seemed to dip into a surreal slow motion. I watched, captivated yet anxious, as her arm rose in response to Lammat's charge, her movements heavy and deliberate as if she were pushing through an invisible resistance. The air itself seemed to thicken, capturing this moment in a slow dance. Lammat's approach contrasted sharply with the dreamlike quality that had overtaken Veyra's defense, her blow descending towards him in a graceful, languid arc that seemed almost detached from the urgency of their confrontation.

Droplets of sweat from Veyra's brow floated beside her like tiny, glistening pearls, suspended in the thickened air. The scene unfolded with an otherworldly beauty, each movement of her muscles, each ripple of her clothing, drawn out in an exquisite, dreamlike vision. Time itself appeared ensnared in a viscous grip, slowing her every motion to a mere fraction of its usual speed, turning the battlefield into a canvas of elongated seconds and stretched reality.

This revelation sent a jolt through my system, heightening my awareness to a razor-sharp edge. I turned my focus back to Lammat, and it was then that I felt an extraordinary lightness in my being. Gravity had seemingly loosened its grip on me. My feet barely touched the ground as I moved, each leap and twist carrying me farther, higher, with an almost impossible agility. I felt unbound, free from the laws that governed movement and space.

In that moment, propelled by the newfound lightness, I acted. With a burst of speed that seemed to bend the very air around me, I leaped forward, intercepting Lammat's path with my own body. The collision was inevitable, yet I felt ready, my heightened senses allowing me to meet his attack with a precision that turned his momentum against him. Our encounter was a clash of velocities, his charge met with my interceptive strike, a meeting of forces that sent ripples through the air.

In this altered state, my reflexes were honed to perfection, my body responding with a fluidity that bordered on the preternatural. I could perceive the trajectory of Lammat's attacks before they were fully unleashed, allowing me to weave around them with the grace of a leaf caught in a gentle breeze. Each pivot, each roll and dive, carried me through the air like a specter, untethered from the mundane restrictions of the physical world.

Lammat, likely sensing the shift in momentum, redoubled his efforts, weaving in and out of our engagement with the agility of a seasoned warrior, making quick, strategic advances toward my crystal. Each of his attempts was a calculated strike, designed to catch me off guard and claim victory. Yet, with every lunge he made, I was there to meet him, our clashes escalating across the breadth of the arena, a dazzling display of our prowess and determination.

As the battle raged on, the energy between us crackling with intensity, I subtly began to guide our conflict, maneuvering us closer to Lammat's crystal. It was a delicate dance, each step and pivot calculated to slowly but surely draw him away from his objective and towards vulnerability. The air around us hummed with the energy of our exchanges, the ground beneath our feet bearing the scars of our combat.

Seizing a moment, I tapped into the deep well of energy within me, feeling it surge through my veins with a pulsating rhythm. With what felt like a practiced motion, I leaped high into the air. My hand clasped my wrist tightly, channeling a torrent of power into my palm, transforming it into a beacon aimed directly at Lammat's crystal.

But Lammat matched my audacity with his own. In a display of sheer agility that bordered on the impossible, he positioned himself beside me, his presence casting a shadow over my intentions. His hands, swift and sure, clasped around my arms, lifting them just as the energy beam erupted from my palm. The beam, a brilliant column of raw power, shot upwards, tearing through the air and illuminating the arena with its fierce glow.

Undaunted by Lammat's interference, I concentrated on the beam, my resolve unyielding. The power within me felt endless, a boundless sea of mana at my disposal. Gritting my teeth, I began the arduous task of lowering my arms, each inch gained a testament to my will against Lammat's strength. The beam, once astray, slowly arced downwards, a force driven by my determination as we gently landed on the ground.

Lammat strained against me, his power formidable, but the steady descent of the beam was inexorable. It inched closer to his crystal, a looming threat that promised victory for me and defeat for him. The energy that poured forth from my palm was a vivid declaration of my resolve, a stream of light that sought to claim the match in a brilliant, decisive stroke.

"Stop, Liam!" he screamed. I pushed harder, forcing mana into my muscles, demanding they overpower him. I felt my arms begin to break. Lammat closed his eyes, turning his head away as the beam continued to lower. "Liam!" he shouted.

With a sudden, swift motion, Lammat rolled around me, delivering a sharp kick to the back of my legs. A wave of icy shock coursed through my body, and I crumpled to the ground, the energy beam dissipating from my grasp. In a move reminiscent of our first match, but with far greater force, Lammat hurled me through the air. I collided with the ground, feeling the unyielding grip of gravity reclaim its hold over me. Struggling to rise, my body refused to obey, paralyzed by the sheer impact.

A shadow loomed over me, and I shifted my gaze upward to find Lammat crouching beside me. He grasped my collar, dragging me across the floor, and propped me against a tree. My crystal stood in our direct line of sight.

"You've destroyed the glass dome," Lammat stated flatly, pressing a finger into my neck. A sudden rush of sensation returned to my head, allowing me to move it once again. I looked up, seeing the sky through patches where the glass surrounding the forest had been. "That was reckless, Liam," he said, turning away, his tone devoid of its usual warmth.

"You've energy-blocked me?" I asked, my voice a mixture of disbelief and realization.

"You fail to grasp the result of your actions," he said, his laugh devoid of its typical joy, replaced instead by a tinge of sadness. "Look at the damage you did." Following his gesture, I saw remnants of the dome's framed glass. "Your beam was initially aimed downwards. Had I not redirected it, imagine the destruction to the exam halls below."

A heavy "Oh…" escaped my lips.

"One must always be mindful of their surroundings," he sighed, shaking his head before striding towards my crystal. His movements carried a weight of disappointment and resolve.

"No, stop!" My voice was desperate, but my body remained unresponsive, my internal pleas for movement going unanswered.

"I needed you to defeat me, Liam," Lammat spoke, his back to me as he continued forward.

"Please," I implored, "just let me win you back."

Lammat paused, his shoulders tensing. "You have remarkable strength for someone your age, but against a trained adult, you're still just average. Your potential is vast, yet your current abilities fall short of overcoming me."

"But Lammat, if you do this—" I began, my voice laced with urgency.

"You'll no longer be with your friends, I know," he interjected, reaching my crystal and turning to face me. "I fear they're holding you back." With those words, he swung his arm, shattering the crystal. I felt a surge of emotions — despair, frustration, an urge to lash out — but my limp body could only offer a silent, helpless gaze as the red dome faded around us.

Lammat's figure loomed into view, his expression unreadable as he approached. He stopped briefly, surveying me with a look that seemed to penetrate the very core of my being. Then, without a word, he crouched down beside me.

His hands, those same hands that had just been instruments of battle, now gently slid under me, lifting me with unexpected tenderness.

As he raised me from the ground, the forest began to slowly pass by, creating a surreal backdrop to the numbness enveloping my senses.

"I'm fine, remove my block, and I can walk," I murmured, my voice barely above a whisper, feeling the sluggish weight of my thoughts.

Lammat continued onward, his gaze fixed on the path ahead. "Trust me, I'm doing you a favor by not giving you a choice here," he responded, his voice carrying a note of weary resignation, yet devoid of any intention to heed my request.

"What do you mean?" I asked.

Lammat sighed. "You're going to have to say goodbye, Liam."

Cradled in Lammat's arms, I was acutely aware of the contrast between his firm hold and the gentleness with which he handled me. It was a strange juxtaposition, reflecting the complex layers of our relationship — adversary and mentor, opponent and protector.

"Liam!" Naya's voice pierced the quiet, laced with concern and urgency.

"He's fine, just energy-blocked," Lammat replied calmly, setting me down gently on the forest floor.

Naya hastily positioned me upright, her hands trembling slightly. "Then... that means—"

"It means your team has lost, I'm afraid," the Examiner's voice resonated through the clearing, tinged with a note of solemnity. I turned to see him surveying the forest and the remains of the domed ceiling above us. He inhaled deeply, his exhale long and fraught with resignation. "The power of you youngsters is escalating since the integration of magic," he observed. Turning back to us, his expression grew more serious. "Due to the extensive destruction, the final match will be suspended. The victorious team will instead select two members from the defeated team."

"Liam," Lammat stated, his voice firm, though he avoided my gaze.

The Examiner nodded in acknowledgment. "And your second choice?"

Lammat's response was indifferent. "I don't care." He then turned his back to the unfolding scene. As he walked, he removed a loose silver band from his wrist and let it fall. The band, my dampener, landed on the forest floor with a soft, almost inaudible clink.

I found my voice, weak but determined. "What will happen to those not chosen?"

"The two who remain will unfortunately fail the exam," the Examiner answered, his tone carrying a hint of regret.

My gaze drifted across my teammates - Veyra, Joren, and finally settling on Naya. A heavy weight settled in my chest, and a dryness caught in my throat.

Tyran approached us, his gaze methodical yet lingering on Naya, still holding me upright, with a hint of something unreadable. "Let's go, Veyra," he said at last, turning to follow after Lammat.

The Examiner then scooped me up, his grip firm yet not unkind. Naya's arms dropped down to the floor, unresisting. "Wait!" I protested, trying to look back at my friends.

"Sorry, lad," he said softly, "but it's best this way." With that, he carried me away from the scene, each step taking me further from my team, from the forest, and from a chapter of my life that had closed as abruptly as it had begun.

CHAPTER THIRTY-TWO
Defeated

For the next hour, I lay motionless on my bed in our new six-person dorm room, the weight of defeat pressing heavily on my chest. Kai, Leana, and Tyran, the victors of today's events, lay on their respective beds. There was a tangible silence between us, punctuated only by the occasional rustle of fabric or a muted sigh. Their victory, in stark contrast to my failure, created an unspoken barrier, a divide that was felt more than seen. Lammat, the catalyst of this shift in our dynamics, hadn't returned to the dorm, his absence adding to the heavy atmosphere.

Veyra sat at the foot of my bed. Occasionally, she tried to offer comfort, her words attempting to pierce the thick veil of my disappointment. "There was nothing you could have done differently," she would say, her voice gentle yet persistent. But her attempts to console me were met with brief, non-committal responses. The reality of my failure, the weight of not having been able to bring Lammat back to our side, sat heavily with me, and I wasn't in the mood for conversation.

Kai, Leana, and Tyran's victory felt like a personal affront, a reminder of where I had fallen short. The room was filled with the tension of unspoken thoughts and feelings, a mix of triumph and loss coexisting uncomfortably in the same space.

I wasn't even aware of when the energy block had lifted,

so deep was my introspection. It was only when I finally decided to roll over, seeking a physical escape from my thoughts, that I realized I could move again. The return of my mobility seemed inconsequential in the face of my internal turmoil, a small shift in a landscape overshadowed by defeat and the daunting uncertainty of what lay ahead.

I touched my wrist, searching for the familiar feel of the dampener Joren had made for me, only to be met with bare skin. The realization dawned on me – Lammat had been wearing it during our battle. Even with him being limited, at my best, I still didn't stand a chance.

The room was a cauldron of mixed emotions and unspoken tensions. Veyra broke the silence with a question directed at Tyran. "Why did you choose me to move on to the next round?" she asked.

Tyran, who had been lying on his bed staring at the ceiling, turned to face her. "You were the best of the three," he said matter-of-factly.

Veyra's response was quick, a hint of defensiveness in her voice. "You'd be a fool to dismiss Naya and Joren."

Tyran sat up, his gaze direct. "I didn't dismiss them. This exam is about finding the best of the best. Naya is an average fighter and magic user. Joren, a below-average fighter but above-average with magic. You, however, are an excellent fighter and an average magic user. With more practice in magic, you could become an incredible Goud."

Veyra shifted uncomfortably. "My mana reserves are small. I don't consider myself special in magic."

"But when you use magic, you put everything into your gauntlet and shields," Tyran corrected her. "If you maintained them for more than a second, your body would adapt, increasing your reserve."

The room fell into a contemplative silence before Veyra asked, "What's next for us?"

Kai, who had been quiet, spoke up with a laugh. "The ridiculous dance is in a couple of days. Can you believe they give such short notice?"

Veyra nodded, recalling, "All former examinees are allowed to attend."

Kai's laughter continued. "Not everyone, considering at least a third were killed or injured in the first exam." Leana, sitting quietly until now, bowed her head, looking visibly upset.

Veyra frowned. "Are you actually laughing about so many students dying?"

Kai shrugged. "It's surprising Lylackia still allows deaths during exams. Eulis changed everything after the King was killed, but kept that?" Veyra glanced at me, but I remained expressionless, lost in my thoughts.

Tyran added, "While it's not against the rules to kill, it's not the intended goal. Accidents happen. The strong survive. Killing should be defensive - a last resort."

Kai's laughter cut through the tense atmosphere, sharp and devoid of empathy. "Tyran should speak for himself," he said with a sneer. "As far as I'm concerned, the weak do nothing but drain resources. Everyone had those pouches; they could have surrendered at any point. The only things that stopped them were either their own stupidity or their egos."

Veyra paused, her eyes narrowing slightly. "Sounds like you're speaking from experience," she remarked, her voice edged with accusation.

"So what of it?" Kai retorted, his demeanor unapologetic.

Veyra's posture shifted. She turned to face Kai directly, her words sharp and clear. "Did you intentionally kill anyone during the exam?"

"Intentionally?" Kai mused, as if pondering the question. "No, I just assumed they'd be able to defend themselves. I was genuinely surprised at how weak they were."

Veyra stood up, her voice rising slightly. "So you admit it?" Kai responded with nothing more than a mocking shrug.

I glanced at Leana, who averted her eyes, her discomfort plain. "A girl with dark hair wearing a blue headband. Kitel.

Did you fight her?" Veyra pressed on.

Kai laughed dismissively. "What, you think I'm going to ask their names or care what they were wearing?"

As Veyra took a step forward, Leana suddenly leaped off the bed, positioning herself next to Kai. At that moment, the vines that had been tightly coiled around Kai's body began to loosen, a silent but unmistakable sign of potential conflict.

"Stop it, both of you. What's done is done," Tyran interjected, his voice firm.

Veyra, however, took another step forward, her resolve unshaken. "Done? Oh, believe me, I haven't even started."

"And you're not going to," Lammat's voice commanded attention as he entered the room. His gaze swept over everyone, his expression stern and unyielding, only softening slightly when his eyes met mine. "I don't know what's going on here, but we need to save our fights for when we're training or taking an exam, not in the room we're meant to sleep in."

"Forget that. No way I'm sharing a room with a killer," Veyra shot back.

"Killer?" Lammat repeated, turning his attention to Kai.

Kai's laugh was derisive. "The new girl's upset because I may have killed her friend."

"Her name was Kitel!"

"I don't care!"

"Kai!" Lammat's voice thundered through the room. "That's enough!"

Kai's demeanor momentarily softened, but he quickly rose to his feet, confronting Lammat. "You want to know what I've had enough of?" He jabbed a finger into Lammat's chest. "You, and your —"

His words were abruptly cut short as Lammat's hand shot up, gripping Kai's finger. In an instant, the vines that had been loosely wrapped around Kai tightened around Lammat's hand and arm.

Lammat's gaze didn't waver from Kai's, his voice steady and commanding. "You're going to want to let go of me, right...

now…"

Kai's facade of toughness wavered, a flicker of fear betraying his attempts to appear unshaken. "You need to stop pushing me around! You don't know who you're dealing with," he blustered, trying to mask his apprehension.

"We both know that's not the case," Lammat countered calmly, his eyes scrutinizing Kai. "You're a reject. A half-blood. Discarded by the elementals. Nobody cares about you, not even your bodyguard here." His nod towards Leana was dismissive, yet pointed.

"Lammat," Leana interjected softly, her voice laced with a plea. "Please, let him go."

Lammat's grin was sardonic, his tone mocking. "Maybe he's trying to impress Liam and Veyra. Maybe he just wants to be noticed a bit more, who knows?" He feigned thoughtfulness, looking at the ceiling before fixing his gaze back on Kai. "Perhaps losing a few fingers will get you noticed. That ought to get people talking about you."

"Lammat," Kai said, his voice now tinged with genuine nervousness.

"I'll make it simple," Lammat continued, his voice taking on a menacing edge. "I'm going to count down from ten. Not in seconds, but in the number of fingers you'll have left if you don't release me." He cleared his throat for effect. "Ten—"

Instantly, Kai's vines retracted, his posture shifting to one of surrender. "Okay, I'm sorry, I'm sorry," he stammered.

Lammat released his grip from Kai's finger, then gave him a final, patronizing pat on the cheek. "Next time I start from nine," he warned, his tone firm yet nonchalant. Turning towards me, his expression shifted to a weak smile, a stark contrast to the stern demeanor he had just displayed. "Can I have a word?" he asked, his voice now softer, more inviting.

Veyra exchanged a glance with me, and I nodded in agreement. "Can Veyra come too?"

Lammat hesitated, then nodded in assent. We followed him out of the room, leaving the tense atmosphere behind. He closed the door and immediately opened the one opposite, leading us into another six-person room. This one, however, was empty.

We had only taken a few steps into the room before Lammat turned to me. "Liam, I'm sorry. I know you were close to Naya. I didn't mean to…"

I raised my hands, signaling him to stop. "It's okay, Lammat. Do you know how she's doing?"

"I don't, I'm afraid. I looked for her, but I think she's already been escorted out."

My eyes lowered. "I didn't get to say goodbye."

"That's my fault, I'm sorry," he said, his voice heavy with regret. "I put too much pressure on you, and it wasn't fair."

Veyra, seemingly out of nowhere, interjected with a question. "How old are you, Lammat?"

"Erm, twenty?" he answered, taken aback by the abrupt query.

"And you've never taken the exam before now?" Veyra probed, sitting down on one of the beds, her eyes still fixed on Lammat. "You made everyone in that dome look like amateurs. The two of you at the end were nothing but blurs to me."

"I'd never decided on a faction," Lammat admitted with a nonchalant shrug. "I've always been drawn to physical combat but fascinated by magic too. The only faction that sits in the middle are the Minors."

I couldn't help but ask, "Then why didn't you fight like that during our first match against Tyran?"

Lammat sighed, a hint of sadness in his eyes. "You're all practically kids compared to me. Remember how easily I threw Tyran when I pulled him away from you?" The memory of Tyran disappearing from my sight was still vivid. "After that, I realized I needed to hold back. I don't want to injure anyone."

"But you didn't hold back against me," I pointed out.

"That's because you, Liam, are different. You have this instinct that the others lack," Lammat explained, placing his hands on my shoulders. "Your approach to magic is so natural, so effortless. It's part of you in a way that I haven't seen in anyone else here, me included."

Veyra nodded in agreement. "Yeah, I've thought the same, if I'm honest."

Lammat continued, his tone growing more serious. "You have a potential that's beyond rare, Liam. I know it might sound exaggerated, but you have the power to change things on a grand scale."

"What are you talking about?"

Lammat smiled, before poking me in the forehead. "How much of your memory did you lose?"

"Uhh…" my mind raced, trying to remember how much I told Lammat about myself.

He laughed. "It's hard to hide an ignorance of the world. You come across as too intelligent to also be so utterly clueless."

"My earliest memory is from a few days ago, just before the exam," I said, glancing over to Veyra.

She frowned, glanced down at my wrist, then met my eyes. "Why did they remove your crest?"

"Smart girl," said Lammat through a laugh. "Didn't even need to see it."

"I don't want to talk about it," I said, looking down at my hands.

Lammat's expression grew grave. "Lylackia is under threat from Saddul. They've developed weapons, technology that can cause untold devastation."

Veyra scoffed. "That sounds like a conspiracy theory."

"I've seen proof," Lammat countered. "An area of desert, larger than D'wan Ma'hal, turned to glass in an instant. It's real, and they're just looking for an excuse to use it against us."

"Where did you see this?" I pressed, intrigued yet skeptical.

"My father was in intelligence. He showed me a photograph – it's like a picture, but it captures reality as it is."

I struggled to grasp the concept but pushed that aside.

"And what does this have to do with me?"

"You're only sixteen, Liam," Lammat said earnestly. "Look at the difference between us. Imagine your power when you reach my age."

Veyra interjected, "But you still haven't answered his question."

Lammat exhaled deeply, his gaze fixed on me. "Your abilities, if honed and developed, could rival or even surpass any technological horrors they think up."

I shook my head in frustration and disbelief. "How can you possibly think I should bear such a huge responsibility?"

Veyra looked at me intently, her gaze sharp. "Shouldn't you?" she countered softly, prompting a moment of reflection.

"I see..." said Lammat, his gaze lingering on Veyra, before responding with a weary shake of his head. "It's not just on you, Liam, but on those like you as well. When I was your age, magic was hardly what it is today. We amused ourselves with simple tricks, like making lights dance in the air or levitating objects a few feet off the ground."

Veyra's smile held a touch of nostalgia as she chimed in, "You're starting to sound like my father. 'In our time, we didn't have mana to enhance our strength. Everything we achieved as Gouds, we achieved on our own.'" Her expression softened as she turned to Lammat, a hint of jest in her tone. "So, what you're suggesting is we use Liam as a sort of deterrent? 'Cross us, and we unleash Liam'?"

"Why not?" Lammat pressed, his gaze piercing. "Have either of you come across someone with abilities like his? Veyra, you've trained with him. You know what he's capable of."

Veyra shrugged, her casual demeanor masking the gravity of her words. "Liam's the first I've seen who can heal. That alone—"

Lammat's attention abruptly shifted to me, his brow furrowed not in surprise, but disapproval. "She's seen you heal?"

I tried to interject, "Yeah, sorry I didn't tell you about that
—"

"I'm not concerned about that!" Lammat interrupted, his voice rising in frustration. "I've known you'd activated your healing abilities since you recovered from that head injury. That's not the issue here."

Confused, I looked from Veyra back to Lammat, seeking clarity. "Then what's the problem?"

Lammat's frustration was clear as he paced. "Healing is a bloodline magic, Liam. It's a closely guarded secret, not something to be flaunted or shared lightly. And yet, here you are, revealing it to everyone." He paused, running his hands through his hair in exasperation. "Didn't anyone explain the significance of this to you? The need for secrecy?"

I was at a loss. "Who are you talking about?"

With a gesture of desperation, Lammat exclaimed, "The one who removed your crest! Eulis! Your Overseer! The Tekka! Didn't they tell you anything about the importance of keeping your abilities hidden?" His words hung in the air, heavy with the weight of unspoken rules and hidden truths about my powers and heritage.

I opened my mouth to reply but stopped myself. "How did you know Eulis took my crest away?" I asked, my curiosity ignited.

"Because he was the only one who knew the spell six years back," Lammat answered, massaging his eyes with his hands. He glanced up, his expression shifting to one of perplexity at my astonished gaze. "Healing magic is exclusive to the royal lineage, your *highness*." His tone carried an extra weight as he stressed the final word.

"Wait, you're aware he's the Prince?" Veyra interjected, disbelief coloring her tone.

"Of course, I'm aware," he chuckled lightly. "I'm probably among the scant few still living who knew Liam in his youth. Who else do you think my father served?" he sighed softly, a note of nostalgia in his voice. "Well, technically, he was under Zeipher's employ, but... well, you know..."

"You knew me?" I questioned, my heart pounding.

He offered a smile. "Yes, I did. You were quite the handful as a youngster, yet even then, there was no denying your competence at combat."

"You saw me fight?"

"Saw you? I fought you! I was your sparring partner! Your father arranged for us to practice together nearly every day!"

"Every day?"

"Pretty much." He gave me a fond smile. "Not for too long, maybe half a year, maybe less."

"So, when did you realize I was the same person?"

Lammat shot me a glance, his eyes dancing with a blend of humor and reminiscence. "The very second you introduced yourself during the first exam," he began, a lighthearted tone underpinning his words. "See, the Prince's true name was top secret, only to be revealed when he took the throne. My family and I used to live in the palace, tucked away in the lower levels. It was a different world down there."

He leaned forward, the corners of his mouth turning up in amusement. "Then one day, I got called up to the training hall, and there you were. You just sauntered over, all casual, and said, 'I'm Liam. Want to spar?' I almost couldn't believe it. Here was the Prince tossing his name around like it's nothing."

"Yeah, he was always Prince Lexis to me, growing up." Veyra, curious, tilted her head. "So, what did you do when you found out?"

With a shrug and a playful smirk, Lammat replied, "I played dumb, didn't I? Acted like I didn't hear the name. You were just a nine-year-old kid, and I was the wise old age of thirteen. During our spars, I just never used your name. It was like that first intro never happened. And you never brought it up again, so neither did I." He grinned. "It felt like he'd shared a secret with me, so I kept it to myself, and just stuck to the sparring."

"Is that how you knew I could heal?" I probed further.

"Are you asking if I ever injured you? Aside from a few minor bruises, no, not really. However, during our last session, I accidentally caused your lip to split open," he recalled, pointing to the center of his own lower lip. "Blood was everywhere. You were panicking, I was panicking, but then your father appeared, calmed you down, examined your lip, and then led you from the room." He smiled at the memory. "As you were leaving, you turned back to look at me, waved, and smiled. That's when I saw it."

"The King healed his lip?" said Veyra, her voice steady but filled with a sense of wonder.

"The King healed his lip," Lammat repeated softly, his voice carrying a weight of memories. "I told my father what I had seen. Healing magic, something everyone thought impossible. At first, he told me I must have imagined it, that I was seeing things, but I insisted that I knew what I had seen." His voice softened. "That was the only time in my entire life that he beat me. I promised that I wouldn't talk about it ever again, but he didn't stop. I still remember the tears in his eyes." Lammat's eyes began to water, reflecting a deep, unresolved pain. "I woke up to find him sobbing over me."

"Lammat…" I said, quietly, my voice filled with empathy for his pain.

"Later that night, he told me everything. Maybe as a way to apologize, maybe to stop me from trying to investigate or talk to other people about it." He laughed, though it was devoid of humor, more a release of pent-up emotions. "You see, if anyone ever found out about the bloodline magic, they were to be immediately executed. Technically, my father was meant to inform Zeipher, and I would have been killed."

"But… why?" I asked.

"Crossers…" muttered Veyra, her voice a soft echo in the room.

Lammat grinned at her, his expression momentarily lightening. "Head of the class, again! People keep comparing you to Tyran, but you really are so much smarter than he is," he said, his tone one of genuine admiration.

"Sorry, what do you mean by Crossers?" I asked, feeling a bit lost in their exchange.

Lammat smiled patiently at me, ready to share knowledge that felt both forbidden and essential. "If a Crosser were to ever see a member of the royal bloodline heal, then they would immediately have that ability. They could then pass that on to any other Crosser they came across. Eventually, you'd end up with an army of indestructible, all-powerful beings that might as well be gods."

Veyra glanced at me, her look conveying understanding and a hint of fear. "Yeah, I get that..."

"You know what?" Lammat suddenly perked up, clapping his hands together as a smile found its way back to his face. "We've still got a few days before the dance. Why not explore the library?"

Veyra's jaw dropped slightly. "There's a library here?"

"Yep, this place is like a treasure trove," Lammat beamed. "Ever stumbled upon the gravity or weight rooms?"

Veyra jumped. "I've only been to the crystal room! I had no clue they have gravity rooms here!"

"Wait, why would I go to a library?" I asked.

With a grin, Lammat replied, "Figured it would be the best place to read up on the stuff that's missing from that brain of yours. Everything from Saddul, to the royal family, to Crossers. I'm surprised you didn't see it, it's right next to the canteen." He extended his hand towards me. "Let's head over. I'll swing by for Veyra after I drop you off."

"Why not bring her along now?" I questioned.

Lammat chuckled. "Thought you'd mastered teleportation by now. You'll find plenty about it in the library. Teleportation's tricky; you can only envelop someone you're touching. It's a challenge to transport more than one." Reaching out again, he gestured for me to join him. "Are you ready?"

Veyra offered an encouraging smile. "Go on, Liam. Show him."

I met her smile, then turned to face Lammat's puzzled look, folding my arms. "Are *you* ready?"

In an instant, the surroundings blurred and shifted, and we were in the canteen. Lammat, his hand still outstretched, let it fall to his side as he took in the new setting. "By the gods," he breathed. "How did you do that?"

Before I could speak, Veyra interjected with a light laugh. "He doesn't know. Seems like he's just innately gifted when it comes to magic."

Lammat's eyes were wide as he faced me again. "You didn't even touch us. You managed to encase us in mana from afar and teleport us here." His words weren't a question, but a firm statement. He stepped closer, his hands on my shoulders, searching my eyes for answers. "And you're not even fatigued. How deep is your mana pool?"

"Deep!" emphasized Veyra.

"Joren suggested it might be, well, limitless," I admitted, feeling a twinge of vulnerability.

"He doesn't even reclaim his mana," Veyra added.

I managed a faint smile. "Trying to reclaim it… it's excruciating. Feels like I'm on the verge of death."

The joviality drained from Lammat's face, replaced by a look of profound concern. Before I knew what was happening, he enveloped me in a tight hug. "Oh gods, Liam. I had no idea. Forgive me." His hand rested reassuringly on the back of my head. "I just thought it healed you. I didn't know. That's why… Oh, gods."

Gently extricating myself, I sought clarity. "Lammat, what's the matter?"

His gaze met mine, filled with a stark realization. "Liam, absorbing mana should only be painful if… if you're a Crosser."

Veyra's laugh carried a note of unease. "He can't be a Crosser. His hair's blond!" She looked to me for confirmation. "Right?" I met her eyes, then glanced down at the floor. "Oh gods…" she whispered.

"Removing your crest, that's what turned you back from

being a Crosser?" Lammat's question cut through the lingering silence, his tone a blend of skepticism and awe.

I found myself nodding, a slow, deliberate motion, my gaze anchored to the floor as I wrestled with the admission. "Yeah… but it took my memories," I confessed, the words heavy with the weight of loss and revelation.

Lammat absorbed this with a thoughtful pause, his eyes reflecting the depth of the revelation. Eventually, he settled into one of the numerous vacant seats scattered around the canteen, a space that felt too large for just the three of us. "It's incredible, really, that they've managed to devise a cure for Crossers," he mused aloud, his gaze drifting upward to catch Veyra's. "You wouldn't know where Eulis might be, would you?"

Turning to Veyra, I saw her divert her gaze, a hint of discomfort or perhaps sadness flickering across her face. "No, sorry. Last I heard, he went on a mission, and never returned," she responded, her voice tinged with a note of resignation.

"That's the same story I've heard," Lammat echoed, a hint of somberness in his voice as he turned back toward me. The atmosphere seemed to shift as he delved into the topic at hand. "Crossers don't have an endless well of mana. They just have a lot of it. Their mana isn't stored in their aether heart—"

"Their what?" I asked, interrupting him.

"Aether heart," he repeated, his enthusiasm for the subject matter evident despite the somber context. "It's essentially the organ that generates mana, commonly referred to as the mana core, or simply 'core'. Some even call it a mana sack." He briefly shook his head, as if to clear it from the tangential thoughts, and refocused. "But Crossers, they're an anomaly; their mana isn't confined to just one organ. Instead, it's stored throughout their entire being—every organ, muscle, and vein serves as a vessel. Picture an aether heart, but on the scale of an entire person, and you begin to grasp the root of their immense power."

"I didn't know Crossers had that kind of ability," Veyra

chimed in, her voice laced with newfound understanding and intrigue.

With a decisive gesture, Lammat stood up, his hand rapping against the table as if to signal a transition from discussion to action. "Well, let's not just talk about it. There must be a book or two that can explain all this in more detail than I can." His statement was an implicit invitation, and with a sense of purpose, he led the way out of the canteen.

We followed him, our footsteps echoing in the quiet. Taking the first door on our right as we exited, the transition from the canteen's familiar confines to the library's vast and hushed expanse was almost immediate.

As we stepped forward, the library unfolded before us like a grand hall of wisdom, transcending the very essence of a mere room. Vaulted ceilings stretched overhead, not unlike the branches of an ancient, hallowed tree, with frescoes that danced with images of arcane rituals and mythical beasts engaged in silent battles across the expanse.

Light poured through large, arched windows, casting a warm, golden hue across the expanse, illuminating the countless rows of towering shelves. These wooden sentinels, rich in hue and ornately carved, held the weight of centuries— tomes, scrolls, and manuscripts, each a bearer of forgotten tales and arcane secrets.

The library's heart hosted a grand globe, a meticulously crafted orb depicting realms both known and mystical, encircled by study tables that bore witness to countless hours of scholarly pursuit. Among the shelves, artifacts of a bygone era stood encased in glass, their silent stories as captivating as the texts that surrounded them.

Here and there, secluded nooks and grand tables offered sanctuary to those who sought the embrace of knowledge, their lamps casting a soft, inviting glow. At the center, a spiral staircase wound its way downwards, hinting at the vast collections that lay beyond, each floor a new chapter in the endless pursuit of understanding.

Pausing amidst this temple of knowledge, Lammat turned to us with a gesture that seemed to encompass the entirety of the library's majesty. With a wide grin and a sparkle in his eyes, he announced, "Welcome to the library."

CHAPTER THIRTY-THREE
The Library

In the days that followed our exploration of the library, I found myself deeply engrossed in the myriad of books it housed. The library became a sanctuary for my thoughts and a bridge to the memories I had lost. Veyra, Lammat, and I chose to distance ourselves from the rest of our group, seeking solace in an adjacent dormitory. This offered us a quiet retreat, a place to unwind and gather our thoughts amidst the ongoing tension with Kai.

The library quickly became a key to unlocking the past I couldn't remember. One of the most captivating reads detailed Lylackia's history as a warrior culture. Despite their martial prowess, Lylackians engaged in conflict solely for defense, embodying a principle of strength used only to protect. This resonated deeply, painting a picture of a people who valued peace over conquest. The same texts spoke of Lylackia's preference for simplicity, a society that eschewed the lure of scientific advancements for a life deemed already fulfilling. This philosophy of contentment with what one has, of finding richness in the simplicity of life, struck a chord, offering a glimpse into the soul of Lylackia.

Veyra's inclination for action soon became apparent. The library's stillness, while a haven for me, was a cage for her restless spirit that yearned for training, for the thrill of combat that words on a page could not satisfy. When Tyran approached her on our second day, proposing training in the gravity room, she seized the opportunity with an eagerness that was both admirable and infectious. The two of them promised a spectacle of skill and power that I, too, was keen to witness. Though I managed to pull myself away from my studies just once, the clash between Veyra and Tyran was nothing short of mesmerizing. Their prowess and intensity in battle was a vivid reminder of the world beyond the library's quietude. Yet, as captivated as I was by their duel, a nagging sense persisted within me, a feeling that there were more crucial matters at hand, secrets within the pages that I was yet to uncover.

As I continued to explore the library's vast collection, I stumbled upon a biography that immediately caught my eye: "King Lexis: The Unruly Prince." The book promised insights into the life of my father, a man whose legacy I was only beginning to understand.

The biography painted a vivid picture of a kind and compassionate ruler. One chapter, in particular, resonated with me deeply. It recounted a tale from my father's youth when he, as Prince, decided to participate in the training exam, much like the one I had found myself in.

He anonymously entered the competition, blending seamlessly with the other hopefuls. It wasn't until the final exam that his true identity was unveiled, and upon this revelation, a shift occurred among the participants. The other examinees, out of respect or perhaps fear of offending royal sensibilities, refused to engage with him in combat.

Faced with their reluctance, my father made a decision that spoke volumes of his character. Fearing his presence might unduly influence the outcome or rob the other entrants of their fair chance, he chose to forfeit, stepping down from the competition. What followed was a moment of profound humility; he joined the spectators, sitting among the commoners as if he were one of them, not above but alongside. This gesture seemed to ignite a renewed vigor in the examinees, who, inspired by his act, performed with even greater determination. That year, the narrative noted, was marked by an extraordinary outcome as all twenty-three participants rose to the rank of Goud.

Reading about this episode in my father's life, I couldn't help but smile, feeling an invisible thread of connection weaving through time, linking his path with mine. It was heartening to know that, in some ways, I was retracing his steps, possibly even within the same walls of this grand library where he might have once sought solace or inspiration, perhaps even sitting at the very same table he once did in this vast library.

My journey through the pages of his life continued, leading me to another chapter that shed light on a more personal aspect of his story—the beginning of his courtship with a woman named Kitara, who would later become Queen, my mother. The revelation of her name struck a chord within me, a piece of my identity falling into place. I found myself fixated on her name, tracing the letters with my fingers as if to commit them to memory.

The next page revealed a delicate drawing that captured a tender moment: two teenagers dancing amidst a crowd of indistinct figures. The caption below read, "The Prince and Kitara dancing after the exam." Time seemed to stand still as I lost myself in the artwork, imagining the scene, the emotions, and the blossoming love between my parents.

Lammat, noticing my prolonged silence, wandered over to see what had captured my attention so completely. His eyes widened slightly as he took in the scene depicted on the page. Without a moment's hesitation, he gently tore the page from the book and handed it to me. Despite the solitude of our corner in the library, I instinctively glanced around, half-expecting to find disapproving eyes on us. Though I knew the act of removing the page was wrong, the significance of the gesture outweighed any sense of guilt. I carefully pocketed the drawing, offering Lammat a grateful smile that conveyed a depth of appreciation beyond words.

While immersed in the texts of the library, I delved further into the history of Eulis's transformative impact on

Lylackia. I was struck by the narrative of how he meticulously introduced magic, especially to a society steeped in tradition and warrior values. Eulis didn't just advocate for the use of magic; he embodied the very essence of change, demonstrating through simple, yet profound teachings, how magic could seamlessly integrate into and enhance Lylackian life. His initial lessons focused on the practical applications of magic in agriculture, medicine, and defense. He gradually shifted the collective mindset, illustrating that magic could indeed coexist with our values of simplicity and strength.

As Eulis's teachings took root and Lylackia began to flourish under this new magical paradigm, he sensed that his mission was reaching a point of fulfillment. Haunted by the shadow of his perceived failure to protect the King, Eulis saw the successful integration of magic into Lylackian society as a form of atonement. Yet, feeling unworthy of forgiveness or redemption, he chose self-exile, disappearing from public life at the zenith of his influence.

Or so the author of this text thought. I wondered how many others were aware of Eulis's dual life as the Tekka. How did nobody recognize him? Had he used an illusion to change his face? Was this knowledge confined to a select few, or had whispers of his true identity begun to permeate the echelons of our society? The thought lingered as I pored over the texts, each page offering not just insights into our past but also into the intricate web of secrets that bound the present and future of Lylackia.

The transition from my secluded study sessions to the shared moments in the new dormitory was subtle yet significant. Tyran's unexpected inclusion in our quiet refuge one night bridged the gap we had cautiously maintained. His presence, while initially surprising, did not disrupt the harmony we had found. Instead, it added a new layer to our dynamic, blending the boundaries between focused study and the interpersonal connections that were slowly weaving themselves back together.

In the dormitory, laughter and stories flowed freely

among Lammat, Tyran, Veyra, and me, creating a sense of normalcy amidst our unique journey. Yet, as I joined in the camaraderie, a sense of sadness tugged at me. Naya, a key part of my life, was missing from these final exam preparations. I had eagerly anticipated seeing her again at the dance, the excitement of our reunion repeatedly playing in my mind. Now, with Veyra unwittingly blending into the dynamic Naya once occupied, I couldn't help but feel a twinge of loss and guilt. The joy of our current gatherings was shadowed by the absence of Naya, a silent thread of sorrow woven through our shared moments.

The afternoon before the dance, Lammat and I were seated at a sturdy oak table in the library, surrounded by a small mountain of books we had gathered in our quest for knowledge. The air was thick with the musty scent of old paper and dust as we delved deeper into Lylackia's history and secrets.

Amid our research, Lammat picked up another tome from the pile, flipping through its pages with practiced ease. The rhythm of his perusal was familiar by now, a silent dance of search and discovery we had both become accustomed to. However, this time, something changed. His fingers slowed, then stopped altogether, hovering over a particular page as a shadow of hesitation flickered across his features.

For a long moment, Lammat remained still, the book open in his hands, his gaze fixed on the words before him. It was clear he was grappling with something, an internal debate that felt like it broke through the quiet of the library. Eventually, with a resigned exhale, he seemed to come to a decision. Carefully, almost reluctantly, he turned the book around to face me, pushing it gently across the table with a look that mingled reluctance with a sense of necessity.

I eyed him with curiosity, noting the change in his

demeanor. "What's this about?" I asked, my voice low in the hushed atmosphere of the library.

Lammat's reply was tinged with a cautious tone. "It's a section about Crossers," he said, his eyes briefly meeting mine before dropping away. "Specifically, it suggests how one might become a Crosser."

The seriousness of his expression and the weight of the topic at hand prompted a careful approach. I reached out, my movements measured, and pulled the book closer.

Autopsy Report of a Crosser Subject:
Initial Observations and Surgical Procedures

Subject Identification: *The individual in question, henceforth referred to as Subject A, was formerly known as Feldspar, a blacksmith by trade residing in Eldwyn's District.*

Incident Report: *Subject A was apprehended on the 23rd of May, at approximately 02:14 hours, following a disturbance of screaming reported at his residence. Hudders dispatched to the scene discovered Subject A in an altered state, identifiable as a Crosser due to his previously blond hair now being pitch black, standing over the deceased body of his spouse. Notably, Subject A exhibited no resistance to capture and appeared devoid of any visible emotional response.*

Initial Examination:

03:30 hours: Subject A was securely restrained and subjected to a preliminary medical examination. An attempt to extract a blood sample resulted in the emission of a dense, black vapor from the puncture site, presumed to be a highly concentrated form of mana.

Observation: *Conventional methods of sedation, including the administration of high-dosage tranquilizers, proved ineffective.*

* * *

Surgical Procedure:

04:45 hours: Given the unresponsiveness to pharmacological interventions, a decision was made to proceed with exploratory surgery under restrained conditions, with Subject A remaining conscious.

04:50 hours: Initial incision made in the dermal layer elicited vocal responses indicative of pain from Subject A, yet no blood was observed. Instead, a black vapor, similar in composition to the earlier mana emission, emanated from the incision site.

05:10 hours: Surgical removal of the distal phalanx of the left digit resulted in the immediate disintegration of the severed appendage, transforming into the same black vapor upon detachment.

05:15 hours: A repeat procedure on an adjacent digit confirmed the initial observation; the detached tissue underwent rapid disintegration, suggesting a self-destructive property of Crosser physiology upon separation from the main body.

05:25 hours: Administration of an oral suppression device to mitigate auditory distractions.

05:30 hours: An extensive dissection of the upper limb was conducted, culminating in the removal of the entire hand. The dismembered appendage vanished in a manner consistent with previous observations, reinforcing the hypothesis of mana-induced disintegration post-severance.

Exploratory Thoracotomy:

06:00 hours: An incision was made into the thoracic cavity, revealing internal anatomy consistent with human physiology, yet devoid of any blood. Subject A remained responsive throughout the procedure.

06:20 hours: The Aether Heart, significantly enlarged—approximately twice the size of that observed in a Goud practitioner—was located and surgically excised.

06:22 hours: Upon removal of the Aether Heart, both it

and Subject A's entire corporeal form instantaneously transformed into black vapor, concluding the procedure and the subject's existence.

Conclusion*: The surgical exploration of Subject A has provided invaluable insights into Crosser physiology, notably the manifestation of mana as a physical and integral component of their anatomy. The critical observation that the removal of the Aether Heart results in the immediate disintegration of the Crosser posits a potential method for neutralizing such threats. Although relatively harmless for non-Crossers, it is surprising to see this result. However, the irreversible loss of the subject and the termination of further research avenues must be acknowledged as a significant oversight in the experimental design. Future investigations should prioritize non-lethal methodologies to allow for extended observation and study.*

As I absorbed the chilling details of the surgical procedures performed on the Crosser while he was still alive, a wave of disgust washed over me. I couldn't help but look up at Lammat, my eyes wide with disbelief. "They were operating on him while he was alive? While he was conscious?" I asked, the words barely escaping my lips.

Lammat, his expression unreadable, didn't utter a single word. Instead, he silently pointed to the next page, urging me to continue reading.

Journal Entry: Interview with Subject A

Today's interview with Subject A, conducted prior to the surgical exploration, was aimed at understanding the events leading to his wife's death and his subsequent transformation. Subject A's demeanor was notably detached, displaying neither remorse nor sadness as he recounted the circumstances.

Subject A described his wife's long battle with mana sickness, marked by intense daily pain, which he likened to 'being pierced by needles throughout her body'. According to his account, her suffering was such that it led her to repeatedly implore him to end her life as a means of escape from the relentless agony.

For years, he resisted her pleas, adhering to a hope for her recovery or relief. However, on the night in question, he described a moment of capitulation to her persistent requests. In an act that he portrayed as a response to her suffering rather than an expression of emotion, he used his hammer to end her life.

The screams reported by neighbors, he clarified, were his own, emanating from his grief in the aftermath of the act. Notably, Subject A emphasized that his transformation into a Crosser occurred post facto, not as a precursor to the act. This detail challenges the commonly held perceptions about Crossers and the sequence of events that lead to such a transformation.

Subject A's lack of emotional response during the interview was consistent with observed Crosser characteristics, including diminished emotional capacity and inhibitions. This encounter underscores the need for a deeper investigation into the psychological and physiological changes accompanying the transformation into a Crosser, particularly in the context of traumatic or emotionally charged events.

I looked up from the journal entry, the weight of its contents settling heavily within me. Across the table, Lammat met my eyes. "What does that mean?" I found myself asking, breaking the silence that enveloped us.

There was a momentary pause, as if he was carefully choosing his words amidst the quiet hum of the library. "It suggests," he began, his voice low and reflective, "that Crossers aren't the inherently evil entities we've been conditioned to see them as." He tapped lightly on the journal in front of me, a gesture that seemed to emphasize his point. "This account implies they could be born from an act of love."

"Love?" The question slipped out, tinged with skepticism. The concept felt incongruous, almost alien in the context of the dark transformation we were discussing.

"Yes, love," Lammat reiterated, leaning back slightly in his chair, which let out a soft creak under his weight. He glanced around the library, as if ensuring our conversation remained private amidst the ancient tomes that surrounded us. "There's a common misconception that Crossers are born purely from the act of killing. But if that were true, battlefields would be overrun with Crossers. This account," he nodded toward the journal, "paints a different picture. It's the overwhelming guilt towards someone you deeply care about, coupled with a lack of mana control, that triggers the transformation. It's akin to a defense mechanism; the body shuts off all emotions to protect itself from the unbearable weight of that guilt."

"Guilt? Love and guilt cause a transformation?"

He paused, picking up a pencil and rolling it between his fingers, lost in thought for a moment. "Eulis might have known about this," Lammat continued, his voice gaining a speculative edge. "His emphasis on mana control for Lylackians wasn't just about enhancing our abilities. It was a preventive strategy against the emergence of new Crossers. By mastering our mana, we shield ourselves from the emotional extremes that could lead to such a drastic transformation. And it appears to have been effective; it's been three years since the last Crosser was reported."

As I grappled with the unsettling details revealed in the journal, a question gnawed at the edges of my mind, momentarily distracting me from the horror of the experiments described. "Who could have performed such in-depth research? Could Eulis have written this?" The thought was a flicker of hope, a desperate attempt to associate the clinical observations with a figure I respected, rather than an unknown entity.

Without a word, I flipped the journal over, searching for any clue to the author's identity. My heart skipped a beat as I saw the name 'Zeipher' embossed on the front cover. In a reflexive motion, driven by revulsion and shock, I dropped the book as if it were aflame, my hands retracting instinctively. My eyes snapped up to meet Lammat's, betrayal and disbelief in my gaze. "You gave me something to read written by the man who killed my father?" The question emerged more as an incredulous whisper.

Lammat exhaled a heavy sigh, his expression one of resignation. "Don't act like that, Liam," he implored, his tone weary yet firm. "If I'd told you upfront that Zeipher had penned it, your curiosity would've been piqued regardless. The need to understand, to know more, would have drawn you to Zeipher's words regardless of the personal enmity. I chose to let the findings speak for themselves, without the shadow of his name clouding your judgment."

His rationale, though difficult to accept, sparked a reluctant nod from me. The tension that had built up began to ebb, replaced by a reluctant acknowledgment of the complex situation we were navigating. The revelation that Zeipher, a figure so entwined with my personal anguish, could provide insights into the nature of Crossers was a challenging concept to reconcile. Yet, as I sat back, allowing the implications to sink in, I realized the value of the knowledge we had uncovered transcended personal grievances. It was a sobering reminder that understanding often comes from the most unexpected sources, and wisdom can be found even in the writings of those we least admire.

"Do you think that's what happened to me? That I killed someone the night I transformed?"

Lammat held my gaze, his expression thoughtful yet uncertain. "I don't know," he admitted, his voice carrying a hint of helplessness. "It's possible you were simply in shock, that the sudden surge of memories overwhelmed you. There's also a chance you were aware of Zeipher's theories about Crossers and tried to block those memories to prevent a transformation. The Hudder that connected with your mind might have removed those mental barriers without realizing it."

His words offered little comfort but sparked a flurry of thoughts. I leaned back in my chair, the weight of our discussion pressing down on me. "Maybe we should have been focusing on how to regain my memories instead," I mused aloud.

Lammat closed the book in front of him with a soft thud, breaking the heavy atmosphere. "How about we go check out the gravity room?" he suggested, a hint of enthusiasm creeping into his tone.

I remembered my brief glimpse of it. "I saw Tyran and Veyra in it, but I didn't understand what was special about the room. They just seemed to move around a bit less."

Lammat's grin widened, the familiar spark of adventure lighting up his eyes. "Oh, you've got to try this," he insisted, the excitement in his voice infectious.

CHAPTER THIRTY-FOUR
A New Form

As we walked through the examination halls, the familiar yet expansive corridors of the school stretched out before us. It was strange to think of these halls, which I had come to associate with the rigors of the exam, as part of a functioning school.

"I keep forgetting this place is actually a school," I mused aloud. The realization sparked a new curiosity in me. "Where are all the classrooms, though? I've been here a week and it feels like I'm still discovering new places."

Lammat gave a nod. "There's a lot more to this place than meets the eye. The classrooms and training areas are spread out, each designed for different disciplines and levels of training."

The conversation naturally shifted as we continued our walk. "Why don't we just teleport to the gravity room?"

Lammat laughed, taking the question in stride. "Teleportation is a bit of a mana drain. It's not something you'd want to use for just getting around, especially in a place like this where everything's within walking distance. Plus, it's usually reserved for emergencies or, you know, showing off."

"Why is it a mana drain? How does it work?"

"When people move around, they leave behind a trail of mana." He answered, casually. "It's invisible to most, but it's there. The stronger your mana, the longer your trail sticks around before it fades."

"Invisible to most? Can anyone actually see these mana trails?"

"Some can," Lammat replied. "Hudders have a sense for mana but can't visually see it. They can feel someone's strength just by being close. But seeing mana, that's a rare gift."

Realizing we had digressed, Lammat steered the conversation back to teleportation. "The thing about teleportation is, it connects two points within your mana trail. It's like creating a doorway that links where you are to any place you've left your mana in the last few days."

I raised an eyebrow, intrigued. "It lasts that long?"

"For most, it's just a day or two. I've managed about a week," Lammat said with a hint of pride.

Curious, I prodded further. "What happens if you try to teleport to a place where your mana trail has disappeared?"

"You get ripped in half and die horribly." My heart leaped at the thought, but his immediate laughter reassured me. "I'm just messing with you, Liam. If there's no mana trail, the teleportation simply doesn't work. No harm done."

I chuckled awkwardly at Lammat's jest, giving him a playful nudge on the shoulder. "So why does it drain mana then?" I asked, still trying to wrap my head around the nuances of teleportation.

Lammat shifted to a more explanatory tone. "Teleporting isn't free; it consumes a substantial amount of mana, particularly for longer distances. The mana you use gets left behind, creating a trail. It's irrecoverable in that sense, but the silver lining is that it establishes a path that allows for easier teleportation in the future to those same locations. Plus, the more mana you've spent in a particular area, the less you need to use to teleport back there. So if you've lingered in a room for a while and then traveled to another city, returning to that room would consume less mana than teleporting to the room next door, which you haven't been in as much."

This information made me ponder my own abilities.

"Would I run into that issue, though?" I questioned, thinking about my seemingly infinite mana reserves. "If my mana keeps regenerating, I shouldn't ever really run out, right?"

Lammat looked at me, his expression thoughtful. "I'm not entirely sure," he admitted. "In theory, you shouldn't have a problem given your unique situation. But there's a possibility, however remote, that if you teleported over vast distances without pause, you might deplete your reserves faster than they can regenerate. It's all about how quickly your mana comes back."

I thought back to the areas I'd visited, wondering if I still had mana on the boat that dropped me off at D'wan Ma'Hal's port, before quickly deciding I had no interest in finding that out.

"Having a lot of mana isn't always an advantage," he said, his voice echoing slightly in the hallway. "In combat, it can sometimes be crucial to mask your true power from an opponent."

Intrigued, I asked, "But how do you hide something like that?"

Lammat paused, considering his response. "It takes a lot of effort. What I do is calm my body, and focus on minimizing any unnecessary release of mana. Instead of letting it dissipate into the air, I visualize wrapping it tightly around myself. If there's an excess, I'll swirl it close to my body, but always keep it contained."

I shook my head, slightly overwhelmed by the concept. "That sounds incredibly difficult."

"It is, at first," Lammat admitted with a nod. "But I've been practicing it for years. Now, it's almost like breathing to me—no conscious thought required." He glanced at me, a speculative look in his eye. "If you could see mana, I could show you how to do it. Considering you retained the Crosser's knack for copying abilities, it would be quite beneficial for you."

The idea piqued my interest. "So, if I met someone who

could see mana, I could potentially copy that ability?"

Lammat's response was encouraging. "You probably could, yes. And finding someone with that ability should be a priority. It would expand the range of skills you could mimic, especially since not all abilities involve visible manifestations of mana, like energy beams."

"Do you know anyone with that ability?" I asked.

"Sadly not. But if I meet one, I'll be sure to let you know," he replied, smiling at me. "Anyway, hiding your mana can be a double-edged sword. Take teleportation as an example. I have fewer places to teleport to because I leave less of it behind. I can only teleport to places I've spent a long time in."

At that, we reached the gravity room's entrance, Lammat confidently pushed open the heavy double doors, pausing our discussion. The gravity room still held an air of mystery and intrigue for me. As we entered, I took note of the room's unusual layout—a large square chamber with a raised metal platform dominating the center. The platform was surrounded by thick glass walls that stretched from the floor to the ceiling, creating a barrier that separated the central area from the rest of the room.

In the heart of this setup, on the platform itself, sat a large silver orb, about half my height. Its smooth, metallic surface caught the light in a way that made it seem almost otherworldly. The last time I was here, I had watched through the glass as Tyran and Veyra closely examined this orb before squaring off in a hand-to-hand duel. Their combat, intense and focused, had been a sight to behold, but I hadn't stayed long, my curiosity about the library's secrets pulling me away.

Now, standing at the threshold of the gravity room once again, I couldn't help but feel a surge of curiosity. There was something about this room, with its imposing glass walls and the mysterious orb, that sparked a sense of eagerness within me. I wanted to understand what had made Veyra so excited to train here, to grasp the full potential of what this room offered.

Lammat led me through an arch in the glass wall, where, near the entrance, a smaller silver sphere perched on a raised pedestal caught my eye. We advanced toward the main sphere at the platform's heart, its silver exterior gleaming in the light. Lammat gestured toward its smooth surface, advising, "Put your hand here, but don't move it just yet."

"What's this room meant to do?"

With a chuckle, Lammat responded, "Why do you think they call it a gravity room?" He then leaned closer, his voice taking on the tone of a teacher explaining something to an especially slow student. "This sphere controls the room's gravity. Slide your hand to the right, and the gravity increases. Move it to the left, and the gravity decreases until it's back to normal levels. If at any point you need to reset the gravity instantly, just drag your hand up or down."

Encouraged by his instructions, I tentatively began to move my hand to the right across the metallic surface. However, Lammat quickly intervened, swiping his hand downward on the sphere to reset it, and then asked, "Got anything in your pockets?"

Puzzled, I checked and found Ding's note and the cherished drawing of my parents dancing. "You might want to leave those outside the glass," Lammat advised, hinting at the potential risk to these items. I complied, placing them carefully beside the door before returning to the sphere.

With a renewed focus, I slowly dragged my hand to the right on its surface once more. Initially, nothing seemed to change, but then I noticed the room's lighting transitioning from white to a calming shade of blue. I paused, looking up inquisitively.

"Feeling the change already?" Lammat asked, observing my reaction.

"Just the lights," I replied, still uncertain about the gravity's alteration.

"Keep going," Lammat encouraged with a nod, a hint of excitement in his voice.

As I continued swiping, a question surfaced. "How high can the gravity be increased?"

"No idea," he answered. "Back in the day, the gravity room had a column instead of a sphere. It came with gauges that showed exactly how much the gravity was being increased. People used to push themselves, trying to outdo each other's records. It became a bit of a competitive sport," he explained, a hint of amusement in his voice. "But that led to its own set of problems—broken bones, serious injuries, and in some unfortunate cases, fatalities."

I paused in my action, absorbing his words.

"Yeah," Lammat continued, "they realized the competitive aspect was doing more harm than good. So, they switched to this sphere model. The beauty of it is in its simplicity and safety. If the gravity gets too intense and forces your arm down, it'll just slide down on the sphere, instantly resetting the room to normal gravity. Prevents people from going overboard and hurting themselves."

While he spoke, I continued swiping my hand from left to right. "Are you sure it's doing anything? Can you feel it yet?"

"Don't worry about me," he said, walking over to the glass wall opposite and leaning against it. "I did this with Tyran a few days ago, and he needed to stop long before I needed to. Feel free to speed up."

Growing more curious about the effects of the gravity room, I began to swipe my hand more briskly across the sphere, eager to experience the change. After a few more swipes, I felt my first noticeable difference; my clothes began to weigh down on me.

"I can feel my clothes getting heavier," I mentioned to Lammat, trying to gauge if this was a normal part of the process.

Lammat burst out laughing. "I was wondering when you'd notice that. You might want to extend your mana a bit and weave it into and around your clothing. Otherwise, you might end up giving me more of a show than you intended."

Taking his advice, I concentrated on feeling the fabric against my skin, channeling my mana into my clothing. Almost immediately, they felt lighter, less burdened by the increasing gravity. Encouraged, I resumed swiping my hand across the sphere, pushing the gravity even further.

Curious about the level of gravity we had reached, I asked, "How strong do you think the gravity is now?"

Lammat extended his hand, releasing a small stream of green mana which plummeted to the floor with surprising speed. "Hard to say exactly, but I'd guess we're around three times normal gravity by now," he estimated.

Feeling emboldened, I continued to increase the gravity until a discomfort began to settle in my legs and back. "I'm starting to feel it now," I admitted, the strain becoming more pronounced.

"Try walking around a bit, see how that feels."

Moving felt like wading through thick mud, each step exaggerated and laborious. Lammat, watching my struggle, advised, "You can stop here, or push it a bit more. It's most effective when moving becomes a real struggle."

As he spoke, Lammat effortlessly pushed off the wall and strode towards me with surprising ease, unaffected by the gravity that was challenging me.

Amazement mixed with a hint of frustration as I observed Lammat's casual demeanor under the heightened gravity. Despite having my dampener removed and feeling stronger than ever, Lammat's ease in these conditions highlighted a gap in our capabilities. Just how much stronger was he than me? The question lingered as I focused on adjusting to the room's demanding environment.

As I continued to swipe my hand across the sphere, gradually increasing the gravity within the room, Lammat shared a thought-provoking hypothesis. "You know, this room might be uniquely beneficial to you, Liam, more than anyone else on the planet," he mused, his gaze fixed on me as I struggled against the growing pressure. "Muscle growth and toning come from recovery after damage. Given your rapid healing, you could significantly expedite this process. With naturally stronger, larger muscles, you'd be capable of channeling even more mana to enhance your strength."

I paused to glance down at my arms. They were toned, sure, but far from what I'd consider muscular. The idea of using this room to not only adapt to higher gravity but also to enhance my physical strength was intriguing.

With a few more determined swipes, the weight of the increased gravity began to press down on me with an intensity that made every movement a battle. Taking a few labored steps back, I struggled to keep upright, feeling as though an immense weight was pushing me down. "I think... this is as much as I can handle," I gasped out to Lammat, fearing any further and I'd be flattened to the floor.

Lammat approached, now visibly feeling the gravity's toll on his own body. Standing before me, he extended a hand. "Hit it," he instructed simply.

I threw a punch, but Lammat tilted his head slightly, unimpressed. "Without using mana to boost your strength," he clarified.

With a groan of frustration, I attempted another punch, this time without the aid of mana. My arm moved sluggishly through the heavy air, barely making contact with Lammat's wrist.

"And there's our first goal," Lammat declared, a hint of satisfaction in his voice.

For the next hour, we repeated the process relentlessly until I managed to land a punch with some semblance of force behind it. Lammat's smile widened. "Alright, looks like you're getting the hang of this gravity. Now, let's work on blocking."

Without warning, he delivered a slow slap to my face. "Hey!" I protested, caught off guard, yet laughing at the absurdity. "I wasn't ready! It's still so hard to move."

"You're improving faster than you realize," Lammat reassured me, a twinkle in his eye. "Just try to block it, I won't go full force."

As we continued, my movements grew more adept, the oppressive weight of the gravity room becoming less and less a factor in my mind. Eventually, Lammat had us circling the sphere, practicing our strikes and blocks while navigating the intensified gravity, always keeping the sphere within reach to quickly reset the room if needed. The training was grueling but effective, each repetition making me stronger, more resilient, and surprisingly, more agile in the face of such overwhelming force.

Our concentration was abruptly broken by the sound of the doors swinging open. Veyra sauntered in, the crisp sound of her biting into an apple echoing off the walls, with Tyran closely trailing behind her. "Here you two are," she announced with a playful lilt in her voice, her eyes scanning the room before settling on Lammat and me.

"We looked for you in the library," she continued with a smile. "Didn't expect you to finally tear yourself away from your books." Her gaze lingered on the sphere at the center of the room, her expression one of admiration.

Feeling the residual effects of the heightened gravity, I took cautious, wobbly steps toward them, managing a weary grin. "This room is pretty spectacular," I confessed, my voice betraying my fatigue.

Veyra's smile widened, dwarfing mine. "I love it! I can feel myself getting stronger each time I use it." Her enthusiasm was infectious. "If I were you, Liam, I'd practice water form in here."

"Why's that?"

"The difference in speed when you turn off the gravity is incredible!" She paused for emphasis, her eyes sparkling with the thrill of the challenge. "Have you taken a break yet? Tried moving with the gravity off?"

I shook my head, realizing I hadn't yet experienced the contrast.

"How long have you been training in here?" asked Tyran.

Lammat answered with a glance at an unseen clock. "Nearly two hours?" he estimated, his voice carrying a note of satisfaction at our endurance.

"And how intense have you made the gravity?"

Lammat's response was lighthearted, yet challenging. "Why don't you step in and find out for yourself?"

Tyran grinned. Turning to Veyra, he extended his hand, signaling for the apple she was still holding. Initially taken aback, Veyra quickly understood his intention, took a final, defiant bite, and then handed him the remains of the apple with a roll of her eyes and a smile.

Tyran hurled the apple through the glass archway into the gravity-affected zone. The moment it crossed the threshold, the apple's trajectory plummeted dramatically, hitting the floor with a wet splat, the fruit disintegrating into a mess of paste and juice on impact.

"Ouch," Veyra quipped, her tone a blend of jest and admiration. "They're putting us to shame."

Lammat gave me a sideways look. "Let's take a break," his voice carrying both concern and a sense of accomplishment for the progress we'd made.

As Lammat reached out towards the sphere, intending to reset the gravity, Tyran's urgent voice halted him in his tracks. "Wait!" The room fell silent, all eyes turning towards him as Lammat's hand paused mid-air. Tyran's intense gaze met mine, a challenge evident in his expression. "Don't you want to see how much you can handle?" he asked, his question loaded with unspoken excitement.

Lammat, now with his hand withdrawn from the sphere, gave me a look that mixed caution with curiosity. "Pushing your limits here can be risky. Idiots have come in alone to test themselves, which I wouldn't recommend. But with all of us here, and with the ability to control the sphere from the outside, we could intervene if necessary."

Veyra, unable to contain her amusement, chimed in. "This is one of those moments Naya would've called you out on, saying it's a bad idea. But honestly, I'm intrigued to see how far you can go, too."

With a resigned chuckle, Lammat stepped out of the gravity's field, his body visibly relaxing as he passed through the glass archway. "We'll manage the gravity from here," he assured, his voice tinged with a playful note. "Just try to keep your feet on the ground and your face away from it."

The decision seemed to have been made for me, but the truth was I was eager to discover my limitations. The thought of my regenerative ability made the prospect less daunting. Memories of Joren, and how he had dropped my severed finger down a hole, flickered through my mind, bringing an odd sense of nostalgia and courage.

"I'll do it," I declared, feeling a surge of determination.

Tyran, with a nod of readiness from me, approached the sphere. "Ready?" he asked, his tone serious yet expectant.

"Ready," I confirmed, my feet planted firmly, my body tensed for the impending shift in gravity.

With a deliberate motion, Tyran ran his hand in a sweeping motion across the sphere, and the effect was immediate. The gravity intensified so rapidly that it forced me into a crouch, eliciting a shout of surprise from my lips.

"Tyran!" Veyra's voice was one of rebuke. "Ease into it, will you?"

Lammat's laughter echoed from the other side of the glass. "It's fine. Hey, Liam! You can start using mana in your muscles again! Training's done, this is just for fun!"

"You're kidding me..." said Veyra, her words quieting as I slowly began to stand up straighter as the mana surged through my bones and muscles, reinforcing my body, overcoming the oppressive force that sought to keep me down.

"Nice job! Keep it going!" Lammat's encouragement echoed through the gravity room, his voice a beacon of motivation amidst the intensifying pressure.

Veyra turned to Lammat. "You've been training without using mana?"

"No point in training with mana. How's that supposed to strengthen your muscles?"

Encouraged by Lammat's shout, I glanced at Tyran, who was still in control of the sphere. With a nod from me, he swept his hand across the surface once, twice, then a third time for good measure. The gravity intensified with each pass, and I felt my arms drop heavily to my sides. The sensation was unlike anything I'd experienced before—my muscles straining, fibers tearing and then knitting back together in a continuous cycle of damage and regeneration.

The pressure became so overwhelming that I couldn't keep my head raised. Unseen by me, Tyran executed another swipe across the sphere. My knees buckled under the invisible weight, and I found myself collapsing to the floor, arms outstretched to break my fall. It was as if I were shouldering the weight of an entire building.

Determined, I channeled more mana through my body, commanding my limbs to withstand the relentless force. Gradually, I managed to move into a kneeling position, despite the agony I felt as the bones in my ankle fractured and healed repeatedly. As I lifted my head, the muscles in my neck contorted, torn apart by the gravity only to be mended instantaneously by my regenerative abilities.

Through the glass, I caught a glimpse of Lammat shielding his eyes, unable to witness my struggle, before he abruptly slammed a hand against the glass, a clear sign of his distress. Turning to Tyran, I found his gaze locked on mine, his expression one of curiosity, but with a touch of concern. After a silent exchange, he hesitantly moved his hand further to the right, increasing the gravity once more.

Summoning every bit of strength, I pushed off from my knees, rising to my feet with a defiant shout. Just as the gravity seemed insurmountable, something within me shifted, a sudden release that dramatically lessened the pressure. Confused, I looked to Tyran, expecting to find him easing the gravity, but his hand was still in place, his surprise mirroring my own.

Veyra, struggling to reach Lammat without taking her eyes off me, finally grabbed his shoulder. He turned back to look at me, and to my astonishment, laughter burst from him.

Perplexed by their reactions, I glanced down, noticing for the first time the blue energy seeping from my skin, pooling on the metal floor beneath me. It flowed like a smoky, liquid cascade. Even as I lifted my hand, the blue smoke trailed down my arm, a mesmerizing display of power I had never witnessed.

"Uhh, what's happening?" I asked, my voice laced with awe and confusion.

"You just transformed into a Goud," Lammat declared, as he banged on the glass in celebration.

"A natural Goud," Tyran added, his smile genuine and approving.

CHAPTER THIRTY-FIVE
Unveiling of Blue

Taking a step towards the glass archway, I was immediately struck by the ease with which I could move. Each movement was fluid, almost effortless, as if I had shed an invisible weight that had been holding me back. My gaze shifted to Tyran. "Did you lower the gravity?"

Tyran shook his head, a look of awe on his face. "You unlocked the Goud seal," he said, his voice filled with respect and disbelief.

Puzzled, I pressed for clarification. "Sorry, but I don't know what that means."

Veyra couldn't help but laugh. "You spent all that time in the library and didn't look up transformations?"

"I only looked up information about Crosser transformations. They're meant to emit black energy. But this is blue!"

Lammat's grin widened, his eyes twinkling with a mixture of pride and mirth. "Well, I guess you're not a Crosser anymore." He motioned for me to come out of the gravity-affected area. "Come on out of there. Tyran, you might as well turn it off."

With a swift downward swipe on the sphere, Tyran deactivated the gravity alteration. The sudden shift caught me off guard, and I stumbled, my steps uncoordinated and exaggerated. As I tumbled out of the doorway, Tyran was quick to catch me, steadying me with a firm grip.

"How does it feel?" he inquired, his gaze scrutinizing my every move.

"I feel like I've forgotten how to walk!" I exclaimed, bewildered by the strange sensation of lightness I felt in my limbs.

"You'd probably feel this way even if you hadn't transformed," said Lammat. "You got used to moving in high gravity, so now, normal gravity feels off. You're exerting more force than necessary."

Tyran and Veyra chimed in, trying to help me acclimate. "Everything feels too easy, right?" Tyran asked.

"Like you're floating?" Veyra added, her grin wide.

Frustrated by my clumsy attempts to regain balance, I pleaded, "Yeah, how do I stop it?"

Lammat's laughter filled the room, a sound that somehow made the situation less daunting. "Liam, teleport us to the forest, will you?" he suggested.

The process felt smoother than before, the mana flowing more freely around me. In an instant, the gravity room vanished, replaced by the lush greenery and fresh air of the forest. No ripple, no warping, just one moment there, and now here.

Tyran turned to Veyra. "I believe you now."

Veyra's laughter filled the forest clearing.

Looking up, I couldn't help but notice the large slash across the glass dome above us, a stark reminder of the energy beam I had unleashed during my intense fight against Lammat. The sight brought back a flood of memories.

My attention was drawn back to my hand as I observed the blue energy now gracefully swirling around my fingers before floating up into the air. "Right," I mused aloud, the realization dawning on me. "The gravity isn't pulling it down anymore."

Veyra's voice broke through my contemplation. "Gotta say, you look pretty good with blue hair," she teased, giving my shoulder a friendly squeeze.

Shocked, I turned to her. "My hair is blue?"

Laughter erupted from both Lammat and Veyra, while Tyran allowed himself a small, amused smile. "The downside of transforming naturally, I'm afraid," Lammat explained, his voice tinged with humor.

Panic set in. "But the dance is tomorrow!" I exclaimed, the thought of attending with such a drastic change in appearance sending a wave of anxiety through me.

Veyra rolled her eyes. "The boy manages to pass the exam without even finishing it, but he's more worried about how he looks?" She landed a playful punch on my shoulder, shaking her head in disbelief. "People don't do this anymore!" she added, gesturing towards me with a wide sweep of her hand.

"People don't transform?" I asked, still trying to wrap my head around the concept.

"Not naturally," Tyran clarified. "At the end of the exam, those who pass have their seals unlocked magically. Eulis figured out how to do it years ago."

Veyra chimed in, her voice softening slightly. "I've never known anyone around our age who has transformed naturally."

"What's the difference?"

Tyran seemed contemplative for a moment before responding. "Well, natural Gouds tend to possess a greater inherent strength compared to their unnatural counterparts. It's as if the transformation taps into something more primal, more essential within them. And then there's the visual aspect— natural transformations tend to be more... vivid. Unnatural Gouds don't usually experience such stark changes in appearance, like the brightness of the hair color."

Lammat quickly interjected with a proposition. "Come on, let's recreate that final round. You and Veyra against me and Tyran."

Veyra's eyes lit up. "Sounds good to me!" she exclaimed. "What are the rules?"

Without any preamble, Tyran's arm whipped forward, launching an energy ball straight at my face with startling speed. Reflexively, I batted it aside with such ease that it felt like swatting a fly, the action so effortless it surprised even me. It bounced off my hand, before exploding somewhere behind me.

"Right, so no rules," Veyra concluded, a smirk forming on her lips. She then turned to Lammat with a playful plea. "At least go a bit easy on me, will you?" Without waiting for a response, she launched herself in his direction.

Simultaneously, Tyran set his sights back on me, his approach rapid and determined. Yet, as he advanced, I found myself retreating not out of necessity, but to gauge his tactics. In a surprising maneuver, Tyran generated energy balls in each hand, then transformed them into small beams, propelling himself forward with increased momentum. Despite his sudden burst of speed, I was unphased. When his punch came, I blocked it effortlessly, my movements fluid and confident.

His assault continued with a high kick aimed at my head, but with a simple tilt of my head, I dodged with ease. Seizing the opportunity, I caught his leg, using his momentum to throw him back. The sound of shattering glass filled the air as his momentum abruptly slowed, leaving him twenty paces away.

"What was that?" I asked.

"I'm learning, too, Liam," he answered.

Observing the blue energy wisps curling away from my skin, I couldn't shake the feeling that I wasn't being pushed to my limits as I had been in our previous encounter.

Turning to face Tyran, I hesitated before voicing my thoughts. "Do you mind if I go up against Lammat?"

Tyran, taken aback by my request, could only muster a puzzled, "What?"

Feeling somewhat awkward, I continued, "I hate to sound rude, but this isn't challenging me enough." I struggled to find the right words, aware of the delicate balance between expressing my need for a greater challenge and not diminishing Tyran's efforts.

Tyran's response to my request was a contemplative silence, his eyes locked on mine as he weighed the challenge I had unwittingly posed. After a moment, his features softened into a smile. "Alright," he conceded, "if you can get by this next attack without taking any damage, Lammat's all yours."

With a slight lean back, Tyran's arms became a blur, a flurry of motion as he conjured dozens, perhaps hundreds, of small energy balls. They surged towards me like a swarm, their intense white light nearly overwhelming, a torrent of power aimed directly at my position.

In that instant, the teachings of Joren crystallized in my mind, a clear path forward emerging amidst the chaos. Extending my mana outward, I ensnared each of the incoming energy balls within an orb of my creation, effortlessly diverting their trajectory and holding them suspended in the air beside me.

I began to advance towards Tyran. Through the intermittent flashes of light, I could see the resolve etched on his face, a testament to his determination. Yet, beneath that resolve, I sensed the onset of exhaustion, the toll of his barrage evident in his stance.

"Tyran," I began, my tone infused with genuine concern, "you're going to deplete your mana at this rate." He ceased his attacks, his arms falling limply to his sides as he met my gaze, a hint of resignation in his eyes. "Don't be reckless," I urged.

His confusion was evident as he voiced his bewilderment. "I don't get it," he admitted. "A week ago, you were no match for me."

I nodded, acknowledging the truth in his words. "I know." Around me, Tyran's halted attacks hung suspended, a captivating display of energy and control that encircled me like an intricate shield.

With a gesture of goodwill, I consolidated the captured energy into a single, large orb before transforming my mana into a receptacle to safely lower it to the ground. "Reclaim your energy," I offered, stepping past him with a nod of respect.

His question was laced disbelief. "How? How did you become so powerful?"

Pausing, I pondered how best to articulate the transformation I had undergone, the journey that had led me to this moment of revelation. The words escaped me almost without thought, a simple declaration of my newfound identity. "I'm Prince Lexis," I stated, a sense of clarity and purpose imbuing my voice. With that, I continued forward, leaving Tyran to contemplate the enormity of the revelation.

I navigated through the dense underbrush of the forest. The foliage seemed to part reluctantly before me, revealing the duo in a somewhat comical scene as I pushed my way through a final group of bushes.

"What are you doing?" I called out, curiosity and concern in my voice as I quickly jogged over to them. Lammat was sat perched atop a visibly flustered and squirming Veyra.

"Liam, get him off me, will you?" Veyra's voice was a blend of annoyance and embarrassment, her cheeks tinged with a slight flush.

Lammat looked up, a wide grin spreading across his face. "She wanted to practice her water form evasion," he explained, his amusement evident. "Told me to try and restrain her. So I did."

With a chuckle, Lammat gracefully stood, extending a hand to help Veyra back to her feet. Brushing herself off, Veyra inquired, "What happened to Tyran?" Her tone was casual, but the question was laced with genuine curiosity.

I scratched behind my head, feeling a twinge of guilt at the memory. "I hate to say it, but with this Goud transformation... Tyran wasn't a challenge anymore. So I told him I didn't want to fight him."

Veyra winced sympathetically. "Ouch, bet he didn't take that well. I mean, I get it, but still... ouch."

Lammat interjected with a thoughtful expression. "That's part of the seal breaking, I'm afraid. It can mess with your mind. Gouds are known for their arrogance, but you shouldn't let that control you. There's still plenty you can learn from Tyran."

I glanced back, half-expecting to see Tyran following, but he hadn't ventured deeper into the forest after me. "I didn't mean to be rude," I murmured, the regret clear in my voice.

"I'll go look for him," Veyra offered, a determined glint in her eye. "Let you two test Liam's limits before it wears off." Without another word, she dashed off toward the entrance, her figure quickly swallowed by the dense foliage.

"Wears off?" I echoed, puzzled.

Lammat laughed. "You won't have blue hair forever," he clarified, a twinkle of mischief in his eyes. "It only appears when you use a significant amount of mana, enough to make it visible. So, we'd better figure out just how much stronger you are now while it's still on the surface."

Lammat cast a thoughtful glance upwards, as if piecing together a puzzle from our shared experiences. "You remember at the end of the second exam, when the examiners left, Eulis teleported, and the Goud...?" He trailed off, his gaze fixed on me, inviting me to recall the event.

"He just ran, right?" I offered, remembering the sudden departure of the Goud, a blur of motion.

"Exactly," Lammat confirmed with a nod. "Try running as fast as you can now. Just a quick start and stop, to begin with."

Taking a deep breath, I mentally prepared myself, recalling the sensation of enhanced strength and agility that now coursed through me. With a burst of energy, I propelled myself forward. The forest around me became a blur, the trees and underbrush merging into a whirl of greens and browns as I accelerated at a breathtaking pace.

The realization that I needed to stop hit me almost as an afterthought, and I attempted to plant my feet firmly on the forest floor to halt my momentum. However, the speed at which I was moving rendered my usual methods of stopping ineffective. My feet tangled, and I found myself tumbling forward uncontrollably, the ground and sky swapping places in my vision until I crashed into the wire fence that marked the forest's boundary.

Dazed, I lay on my back, the familiar sight of the damaged glass dome overhead coming into focus.

Lammat's face soon appeared above me, a look of amusement in his expression. "Fast, hey?" he quipped, offering a hand to help me up.

"What went wrong?" I asked, still trying to catch my breath and make sense of the unexpected crash.

"Friction isn't much use at those speeds," Lammat explained, his tone shifting to that of a teacher imparting a crucial lesson. "You're going to have to learn a whole new way of moving." Demonstrating his point, Lammat strode towards the nearest tree. With an effortless grace, he placed one foot on the trunk and proceeded to walk vertically up it as if defying gravity itself.

My mouth fell open in astonishment. "Well, that's new."

Lammat chuckled. "No, it isn't," he countered. "Remember what you did to keep your clothes on in the gravity room? It's the same principle. Just apply it to your feet instead." With that, he blurred towards me in a swift motion, leaving a significant dent in the tree's trunk, a testament to the technique's effectiveness and the control it required.

Standing back up, I focused intently, channeling mana into my feet. Curiosity piqued, I lifted one foot, examining its underside only to find it caked with grass, leaves, and soil.

Lammat, observing my examination, offered a piece of advice. "Yeah, it's harder on surfaces that aren't solid. For areas like this, you need to extend your mana a bit deeper into the ground."

"Makes sense…" I murmured, absorbing the nuance of this new technique.

Encouraged by my understanding, Lammat urged, "Great! Do it again, then."

I didn't hesitate. With a burst of energy, I propelled

myself forward, the forest once again blurring past me. This time, however, I was prepared. As the need to halt my sprint approached, I extended my mana further than before, anchoring it deep into the earth beneath me. For added stability, I enveloped my shoulders in telekinetic mana, using it to push myself down and backward, aiding in my deceleration.

The result was astonishing—I stopped almost instantly, the abrupt halt sending a small flurry of leaves swirling around me. The sound of clapping broke the silence, and I turned to find Lammat, a broad smile on his face, offering his applause. "Good job! Do it again," he encouraged, his enthusiasm infectious.

What followed was a thrilling series of sprints around the interior perimeter of the forest. Lammat and I, fueled by a competitive spirit and a desire to master this new method of movement, raced each other through the dense foliage. Each sprint was a blend of speed and control, a delicate dance of pushing our limits while maintaining the precision required to navigate the unpredictable terrain.

With each lap, I felt more attuned to the flow of mana, learning to adjust its depth and intensity based on the ground beneath me. The forest floor, with its patchwork of solid earth, tangled roots, and scattered debris, presented a challenging but exhilarating obstacle course. Lammat proved to be an adept and nimble competitor, his movements a combination of grace and power, each step leaving a faint imprint on the earth, a sign of his careful mana manipulation.

As we continued, the boundary between competition and camaraderie blurred. Each successful sprint, each sharp turn and sudden stop, became a shared victory. The air was filled with the sounds of our exertion—rapid footfalls, heavy breathing, and the occasional laughter as one of us executed a particularly impressive maneuver.

The forest, with its towering trees and dappled sunlight, transformed into our arena, witnessing the rapid evolution of my abilities. With Lammat's guidance and the spirit of friendly competition driving us, I delved deeper into the potential of my Goud transformation, each moment a step closer to mastering the extraordinary capabilities that lay within.

CHAPTER THIRTY-SIX
Friendship

A sliver of early morning sunlight breached the tranquility of my sleeping quarters, its gentle warmth teasing the edge of my consciousness. Despite the inviting glow, I rolled away, seeking refuge under the comforting weight of my blanket. The day's responsibilities could wait; the soft embrace of my bedding promised a few more moments of blissful reprieve.

The sound of stirring in the room eventually pierced my cocoon of warmth. Curiosity nudging me awake, I peeked over my blanket fortress to find Veyra in the midst of her morning ritual. She was on her feet, engaging in the timeless dance of lazily slipping into her shoes, punctuated by a languid stretch and a cavernous yawn. Our eyes met, and I offered her a sleepy smile from beneath my shield of fabric.

"Oh, good morning," she greeted, her voice flavored with the remnants of slumber. She shook off the last vestiges of drowsiness, her posture straightening as she acknowledged the start of a new day. "It looks like we're the last up. I heard Lammat stirring, but Tyran was already gone by then." She settled at the edge of her bed, her gaze drifting towards me again. "I see your hair's gone back to normal, finally."

Instinctively, my hand rose to sift through my hair, a tactile confirmation of its return to familiarity. "Oh, thank goodness," I exhaled, a weight lifting.

"You looking forward to tonight?" Veyra's inquiry pulled

me from my thoughts, a gentle nudge towards the impending evening's festivities.

The mention of the dance sparked a delayed recognition, my mind momentarily adrift in the sea of recent events. "Oh yes, the… dance, tonight. Yes, I suppose I am." Amidst the anticipation, thoughts of Naya surfaced, an undercurrent of longing in the wake of excitement. "Are you looking forward to your dance with Joren?"

A playful roll of her eyes betrayed Veyra's attempt to feign indifference, a smile tugging at the corners of her mouth despite her efforts. "He didn't beat me."

"You know he beat you," I teased, drawing a genuine laugh from her. "Do we wear these clothes, or do we have to get others?"

"Don't worry about that. The Eulis can tailor our clothes to whatever we fancy. You should go see them with Tyran and Lammat when you can. It seems fashion isn't exactly a priority for you boys," she jested, her good-natured ribbing further lightening the mood.

Curiosity piqued, I ventured, "Do you know what you'll be wearing?"

The shift in Veyra's demeanor was subtle but noticeable; her confident smile gave way to a hint of vulnerability. "No, I… You don't happen to know Joren's favorite color, do you?"

Her query, innocent as it was, coaxed a laugh from me. "No, sorry. Grey, perhaps?"

"Grey?" Her laughter mingled with mine before she sighed, her gaze wandering to the illusionary window. "I guess you'll see what I wear tonight," she promised, a hint of mystery in her voice. Turning back to me, she added, "…I think I'm going to sort it out now, so if you want, you can go find the boys and get your outfits sorted as well." With a final smile, she exited the room, leaving me alone with the morning light and a day filled with promise.

I remained in bed for a while longer, clinging to the hope of drifting back into sleep. The weariness hung over me;

my eyelids were heavy, almost promising that sleep was just a moment away. I hadn't noticed Lammat or Tyran getting up, but the opportunity to drift back into dreams was rapidly diminishing with each passing moment. The sound of footsteps and muted conversations outside my room kept pulling me back to wakefulness. Even covering my head with a pillow didn't help block out the noise.

Resigned to the inevitability of the waking day, I pushed the blanket aside and sat up, feeling the weight of sleep still clinging to me. My limbs felt unusually heavy, a stark contrast to the lightness I'd experienced during the previous day's transformation and training. It was as if my body was reminding me of its need for rest, even as my mind urged me forward. Stepping out into the corridor and wondering where I might find Tyran and Lammat, I headed towards the canteen. But just as I started, they appeared around a corner ahead of me.

"Hey, you two," I greeted them as I approached. "We have the dance later, and we're supposed to pick out some clothes. Veyra thought it'd be good if we went together to choose what we're wearing."

Tyran just shook his head. "I don't care what I wear. I don't even want to go to that dance."

Lammat laughed and playfully slapped Tyran on the back. "Oh, come on, Tyran. We've got to pick out our outfits for the dance at some point! And who knows, they might even use some magic to help us choose." He gave Tyran a cheeky smile. "You wouldn't want to end up accidentally picking a dress, would you?" he joked.

Tyran just frowned at him, then let out a sigh. "Alright, let's just go and get this over with."

With Lammat's laughter leading the way, we set off. I wasn't sure where we were going, but Lammat seemed confident. We navigated through several corridors until we joined a small line of people waiting to enter a room at the end of a hallway.

As we approached, their lively chatter became more

distinct, a mix of disappointment and excitement bubbling among those who hadn't made it to the final round of the exams. Despite not advancing, their enthusiasm for the dance and the spectacle of the final events was undiminished.

"I can't wait until the final round," a short, stumpy boy exclaimed with an eagerness that filled the space around us.

"I know what you mean," a girl nearby responded, her voice tinged with excitement. "I can't believe they're letting us watch for free. A lot of the adults have to pay…"

Their conversation continued, a shared anticipation for the upcoming events creating a sense of camaraderie among the group. It was a reminder of the communal spirit that pervaded the training complex, a bond forged through shared experiences and challenges.

As their conversation drifted off, I turned to Tyran, curious. "So, have you thought about what you're going to ask for, clothing-wise?"

For a brief moment, Tyran seemed as though he might not respond, his gaze distant. But then he faced me, a hint of uncertainty in his eyes. "I don't know what my choices are," he admitted, his expression tightening as if a sudden thought had gripped him.

Lammat's laughter cut through the momentary tension, his confidence reassuring. "Don't worry, Tyran, I've been through this a few times. I can guide you." He stepped forward, positioning himself as if about to reveal some grand secret, then turned back to address us. "The Eulis will present what they think suits you best initially. From there, we can tweak and adjust to our liking." He glanced between us, his smile encouraging. "Simple enough?"

I nodded, just as a short, balding man appeared at the doorway, beckoning us inside. We followed him into a room that seemed to pulse with an ancient, mystical energy. The air was thick with dark green smoke, swirling around us, emanating from pink candles that lined the walls. Golden patterns adorned the surfaces, casting the room in a glow that felt both warm and inviting.

"Hello, come in, come in," the man sang out, his voice carrying a jovial tune. He gestured grandly for us to enter further, his green robe fluttering with the movement. "What can I do for you, gentlemen?" His head tilt sent a cascade of fabric rippling down his attire.

I couldn't help but pause at his address. "Sorry, did you just call me a gentle man?" The words slipped out before I could stop them.

His grin broadened, amusement sparkling in his eyes. "Yes, I did, sir." I returned his smile, opting to keep any further comments to myself.

When he inquired about our preferences, we all hesitated, unsure of where to begin. "It's probably best if you give us a selection first," Lammat suggested, the voice of experience guiding us.

"Okay," the Eulis agreed, stepping closer with an air of excitement. "Before we proceed, I must ensure everyone is comfortable with the process of changing your attire." Tyran and I instinctively recoiled, but the Eulis hastened to reassure us. "Don't worry, it's an instantaneous transformation, entirely magical in nature." His assurance coaxed us to relax, and we collectively nodded our consent.

"Great, then let's start with my personal favorite," he declared, his enthusiasm infectious as he prepared to unveil his magical wardrobe to us.

With a swift snap of his bony fingers, the Eulis initiated the transformation, and I immediately felt the fabric of my clothes tighten around me. Glancing down, I was taken aback by the drastic change; my attire had morphed into a black suit, adorned with unusual leather straps that crisscrossed my chest and knees. My shoes, now polished to a reflective sheen, caught the flickering candlelight, adding an unexpected elegance to my new look.

Lammat, caught up in the moment, was twirling on the spot, trying to get a full view of his transformation. His movements were fluid, almost dance-like, as he examined the intricacies of his outfit.

Tyran, however, seemed far from pleased with his new ensemble. Standing stiffly, with his arms awkwardly extended, he shot a discontented frown at the Eulis. "I don't like it," he declared, his tone devoid of any pretense.

The Eulis laughed, a sound that seemed to resonate with understanding rather than mockery. "That's fine, it's what I expect from a first attempt. How about you two?" he inquired, his gaze shifting between Lammat and me.

Lammat paused his self-inspection and turned his attention to me. "Hmmm, I don't think that suits you, Liam... maybe you should try something... brighter," he suggested, his critical eye assessing the suitability of my attire.

At the Eulis' next finger snap, I felt another wave of transformation wash over me. My outfit shifted once more, this time into a grey suit with notably broad shoulders that lent the ensemble an air of distinction. The material was softer, and more forgiving than the previous outfit, caressing my skin with every movement. The stark contrast to the restrictive feel of the initial suit was a welcome relief.

I moved about, testing the fabric's responsiveness to my actions. "Yeah, I think I quite like this," I remarked, appreciating the newfound freedom of movement. "It's very easy to move around in."

Lammat stepped closer, eyeing my attire with a thoughtful gaze. "I don't know, what if you make the clothes completely white?" he proposed, his creative input steering the direction of my final look.

The Eulis, ever amenable, chuckled at the suggestion and snapped his fingers once again. The transformation was instantaneous, and I looked down to find myself clad in an all-white suit that seemed to radiate a subtle luminescence. The outfit was not only visually striking but also exceptionally comfortable, the fabric moving with me as if it were a second skin.

"Wow," I couldn't help but express my admiration for the Eulis' craftsmanship. "I feel comfortable in this! I think I'll wear this tonight!" The decision felt right, the outfit reflecting a blend of my preferences and the magical touch of the Eulis.

Lammat's approval was evident as he watched the transformation, a satisfied grin spreading across his face. "Yes, I thought you would," he remarked.

The Eulis' laughter filled the room once more, a light-hearted sound that seemed to bounce off the walls. "Of course, your Highness."

His words caught me off guard, and I couldn't help but react. "Wha... what do you mean?" The sudden reference to royalty sent a jolt of surprise through me, and I couldn't help but wonder if he was somehow aware of my true identity.

The man waved off my concern with a chuckle, his demeanor still playful. "Only two types of people are permitted to wear white to social gatherings here, and those are Guardians and Royalty. Are you either of those, young man?" His question, though rhetorical, prompted a hesitant shake of my head.

With another laugh, he conceded, "Very well, sir, let's go back to that grey one then." Lammat, catching my eye, offered a reassuring smile and an eye roll, as if to say, "Don't worry."

Meanwhile, Tyran's patience seemed to be wearing thin, his discomfort with his current outfit evident. "Can someone please change me out of this?" he grumbled, his arms still awkwardly extended, his frown deepening by the second.

The Eulis, seemingly amused by Tyran's plight, chuckled. "Oh, I'm sorry, I nearly forgot about you." With a flick of his fingers, our outfits transformed once again. This time, both Tyran and I found ourselves dressed in the grey uniforms that had previously adorned me.

I glanced over at Tyran, taking the opportunity to assess the uniform's appearance on him. The dark grey fabric draped elegantly, complementing his frame in a way that seemed both practical and stylish.

Tyran's reaction, though subdued, hinted at a grudging acceptance. "It'll do," he conceded, his voice carrying the faintest trace of satisfaction. "Okay, you can remove them now."

Lammat, unable to contain his amusement, let out a giggle at the exchange. Tyran's gaze shifted to him, a mixture of irritation and resignation in his eyes. "You can give me my clothes back," he corrected, his tone slow and deliberate, the disdain barely masked by his controlled demeanor.

The Eulis' chuckle resonated through the room once more as he gestured towards Lammat. "You, sir, are number twelve, and you two," he directed his finger at Tyran and me, "are both number fours. Just mention these numbers when you come to the dance tonight, and I'll have your outfits ready." With a snap of his fingers, our transformed attire vanished, replaced by the clothes we had walked in with. "Please exit through this door," he instructed, guiding us to another doorway, "so I can welcome the next group."

We expressed our thanks to the man as we exited, stepping through the doorway he had indicated. The transition was disorienting; one moment we were in the Eulis' chamber, and the next, we found ourselves back in our room. Veyra was there, perched on her bed as if no time had passed. Curiosity got the better of me, and I swung the door open again, only to be greeted by the familiar corridor outside.

Tyran couldn't help but chuckle at the situation. "A fixed teleportation spell, huh? Very clever. Didn't even notice the transition."

Lammat, ever the analytical one, added, "Must've been combined with an illusion spell to mask the change. Quite seamless."

I could only nod in agreement, still processing the clever magic at work.

Veyra greeted us with a cheerful, "Hi, boys," waving from her spot on the bed. "Took me a moment to realize where I was too. Those Eulis' really know their stuff."

Lammat, seemingly still exhausted, collapsed onto his bed with a heavy sigh. "Yeah, they're capable of some amazing things," he murmured before closing his eyes, seeking a moment's respite.

I made my way towards my bed, glancing back to see Tyran still fascinated by the doorway, his fingers gently tapping against the wood. Lammat, half-asleep, addressed Tyran without opening his eyes, his words a rapid-fire stream. "Hey, Tyran, don't mind me, just trying to get some sleep."

"Okay," Tyran replied, his attention still fixed on the doorframe as he continued to tap on the wood, seemingly intrigued by its construction or perhaps the magic that had just transported us.

Veyra chuckled, a light-hearted sound that brought a sense of normalcy back to our unusual morning. "Did you all get your clothes sorted out okay?" she inquired.

"Yeah, we did. How about you?"

She beamed, a look of satisfaction on her face. "I think so. Just need to remember my number—fifteen. Remind me later, would you? I'm bound to forget."

I nodded. "So, what exactly happens at this dance? I mean, beyond the obvious, I have no idea what to expect."

Her response came with a touch of surprise. "You've been to dances before, haven't you? With all the events you must've attended…"

I sighed, the reality of my fragmented memories casting a shadow over the moment. "None that I remember," I admitted, the weight of forgotten experiences briefly dampening my spirits.

Then, as if struck by lightning, a thought jolted me upright. "The drawing of my parents dancing! I left it in the gravity room!" The panic in my voice was clear, the fear of losing such a precious item overwhelming.

Veyra's reaction was swift and reassuring. She rolled off her bed and rummaged through her bedside drawer, retrieving not only the cherished drawing but also Ding's note. "I found these on the floor in the gravity room and picked them up to keep them safe," she explained, her actions underscoring the bond of friendship that had formed among us. Handing them to me, she added, "I meant to give them to you earlier, but you were still out when I turned in for the night." She grinned, aiming a thumb at Lammat. "Likely why he's still tired."

Gratitude washed over me as I accepted the items, their return bringing a sense of relief. I studied the drawing once more, noting my father's attire, which, now that I looked closer, did seem likely to have been white, aligning with the Eulis' comments about royalty and guardians. "I must have been to many such events," I mused, allowing myself a moment of reflection. "Maybe one day, those memories will come back to me."

Veyra sat next to me on the bed. She nudged me gently, a silent gesture of reassurance. "Don't worry about tonight, you'll do just fine," she said. She took a moment to gather her thoughts before painting a picture of what the evening might hold. "We'll be in a large room somewhere in this complex. It'll probably be dimly lit, and there'll be musicians there to provide live music."

"Do I have to dance?"

"That's up to you," she answered. "Some will dance, while others might prefer to just sit and chat."

"I think I'll be in the latter group," I admitted, already feeling more at ease with the idea of being an observer rather than an active participant.

"Me too," she agreed.

"Apart from the dance with Joren," I added.

Veyra looked at me from the corner of her eye. "You're not going to let that drop, are you?" I grinned, and she continued. "I suppose one dance won't hurt me."

Tyran's interruption redirected our attention. "Veyra, come help me..." he called out, his voice echoing with frustration and curiosity.

Veyra promptly stood and approached him, her

expression shifting from amusement to concern. "What do you need me to do? Actually, what are you doing?" she inquired, her tone a blend of curiosity and caution.

Lammat, roused by the commotion, sat up, watching the exchange with interest. Tyran cleared his throat. "Where would they put the charm?" he wondered aloud, his gaze fixed on the doorway.

Veyra ran her hand across the top of the doorframe, her fingers searching for any sign of the charm. "This would be the logical place for it, but I can't find anything. It's not visible… Why are you so interested in it?" she asked, her brows furrowed in thought.

Tyran's response was slow, his mind seemingly elsewhere. "I've never seen a teleportation charm up close. I thought it might be interesting to study it."

After a brief examination, Veyra stepped back, her hands on her hips in a gesture of resignation. "I'm afraid I'm not the best person to ask about magic. I can't seem to find it, and even if I could, I'm not sure I'd understand how it works. They may have disguised it with an illusion, or maybe it's hidden in plain sight."

Lammat let out a groan. "Have either of you considered that it might be the doorframe itself?"

Tyran, caught off guard by the idea, hesitated for a moment before grasping the frame firmly in his hands.

Curiosity drew me closer to the unfolding scene. Veyra, with a note of caution in her voice, turned to Tyran. "If it is the doorframe, then you know you can't do anything with it while it's still attached to the—"

"Alright, hold on," said Lammat, standing up. "Before you go ripping that off the wall, let's go to a different room." He grinned. "Maybe we can rip Kai's off instead."

Tyran reluctantly paused, then opened the door and left with Lammat.

As the door closed behind them, I turned to Veyra as she walked back over to me. "I haven't had the chance to talk to

Tyran today. Do you know if he was alright after yesterday?"

Veyra offered a look of mild disappointment at my suspicion. "It's strange, you seem really close to Lammat and Naya, even Joren, but not Tyran."

"He's not exactly the easiest person to get to know."

She nodded. "Yeah, I get that. I never knew him as a kid," she continued, "but there were stories about his family. How Tyran, the son of the legendary warrior, had no interest in fighting." She gestured towards the door. "He's had to work hard for everything he's achieved since his father passed. While some of us have been training from a young age, Tyran only began to seriously train when he was ten. Yet, look at how far he's come."

"I don't understand," I said, "what does that mean?"

"Him wanting to fight you yesterday, that was him trying to push his limits against you, someone he knows he can't beat." She shook her head. "But you were more interested in pushing your own limits, rather than helping out a friend."

"A friend? He punched me just to see if I could heal!" I countered.

She laughed. "I never said he was a good friend."

"And he left us to team up with Kai during the third exam," I added, still trying to piece together Tyran's actions.

Veyra leaned in, her voice tinged with a hint of exasperation. "You mean the exam where teams were limited to three members?" She scrutinized my bewildered face, waiting for the realization to dawn on me. "What was he supposed to do, Liam? Force you to choose between him, Naya, and Lammat?" She shook her head, clearly disappointed by my lack of insight. "He knew he wouldn't be the one you'd pick, and you know it, too," she said, her sigh heavy with resignation. With a soft punch to my shoulder, she added, "Look, Tyran might make mistakes, but he's not malicious. He can be as dense as you sometimes."

I couldn't help but smile at her candid assessment. "You two have become pretty good friends, haven't you?" I observed, noting the rapport that seemed to have developed between them over the past few days.

Her smile broadened, a twinkle in her eye. "Ever since the start of the exam, there's been talk comparing me and Tyran. We do share a lot in common, and sparring with him has been incredibly useful for both of us. We've learned a great deal from each other," she confessed, her admiration for Tyran's skills evident in her tone. "And I think he's trying to share things with you, too."

"That's why he wanted to fight me?"

"He's not an idiot, he knows you can copy everything he does. I imagine that's his way of trying to teach you things and learn from you at the same time."

"Then why doesn't he just say that?"

"Pride," Veyra said simply before walking over and settling back onto her bed. "If I were you, I'd try to smooth things over today. He's a good guy, but he doesn't know how to show it."

With that, she closed her eyes, quickly finding solace in sleep. I remained seated, contemplating the vast potential of the spells I might have learned from Tyran without even realizing it.

CHAPTER THIRTY-SEVEN
Between Bonds and Burdens

After sitting in thoughtful silence for a while, pondering over Veyra's words and Tyran's actions, I felt a sudden urge to find Tyran and perhaps understand his perspective firsthand.

As I reached out to open the door, it swung open before I could turn the handle, revealing Leana standing on the other side. She was caught mid-motion, her arm raised as if she were just about to knock. The surprise on her face mirrored my own, a momentary pause hanging between us as we processed the unexpected encounter.

Leana quickly lowered her arm, a hint of embarrassment flashing across her features before she composed herself. "Oh, Liam," she said, her voice carrying surprise and relief. "Looks like I caught you just in time."

"Me?" I responded, my surprise evident in my voice.

Leana nodded, a slight smile forming. "Kai's gone off to train on his own for once, and for the first time in what feels like ages, I've actually got a moment to myself."

"I was just on my way to find Tyran," I said, stepping out into the hallways and closing the door behind me so we didn't disturb Veyra.

Her face lit up. "Do you mind if I come with you? It'd be nice to have some different company for a change. I've been with Kai all week, and after the… well, after the disagreement between him and Veyra, and you switching rooms…" Her voice tapered off as she mentioned the conflict, a shadow of discomfort crossing her expression.

In that moment, it dawned on me that I hadn't considered how Leana might have been feeling through all the recent events. Each time I saw her with Kai, there was a subtle hint of reluctance in her demeanor, a lack of enthusiasm that I hadn't fully acknowledged until now. Despite this, she always stuck by his side, a constant presence in his shadow.

"Why did you stay with him, though?" I asked. "Why not join us in this room? Lammat referred to you as Kai's bodyguard. Is there a hint of truth to that?"

Leana let out a laugh, one that carried resignation and amusement. "That's exactly what I feel like sometimes—a bodyguard," she admitted, her laughter fading into a more serious tone. "But the truth is, I have to stay with him. Kai's not just a friend or a teammate; he's my twin brother."

Her revelation added a layer of complexity to her relationship with Kai that I hadn't considered. The bond of family, especially between twins, held a depth of loyalty and duty that went beyond mere friendship or alliance. It was a connection that demanded her support, even in situations where she might have preferred otherwise.

"Oh, sorry about that," I said without thinking.

Leana laughed, then gestured down the corridor and we started walking. "I'd love to tell you that he's not as bad once you get to know him, but…"

I nodded, not knowing what to say. As we walked down the corridor, the silence between us felt like a space waiting to be filled with conversation. Leana seemed to sense this too and, after a moment of contemplation, began to speak again.

"Our father had very traditional views on training. He believed in practical, hands-on experience." She paused, her gaze distant as if she were visualizing the scene she was about to describe. "I remember this one time, our father had arranged for Kai to spar against some of the servants. They were reluctant participants, but they had little choice in the matter."

I listened, intrigued by this glimpse into their past. It was unusual to have what was essentially a stranger open up so readily. I imagined she must have been wanting to get this off her chest for a while.

"Kai was always gifted with elemental magic, even as a kid. During those spars, he'd use his abilities to restrain them, pulling vines from the ground as though they were limbs under his control. It was both fascinating and terrifying to watch," she continued.

"The servants couldn't fight back, not against Kai's magic. My father always felt pride when he watched, but I couldn't feel anything but worry." She met my eyes, offering a weak smile. "Worried about the intensity in his eyes, even then."

"I don't have any brothers or sisters," I shared, "but it still seems like you two really care for each other. I mean, you wouldn't be looking out for Kai as much as you do if you didn't. Remember when Lammat had Kai by the finger? You looked like you were ready to jump in and take on Lammat yourself, despite knowing full well how strong he is."

Leana sighed, a hint of a smile on her lips as she remembered the moment. "Yeah, I don't have a choice in the matter. I can't just stand by and let anything happen to him. Kai's going to be taking over our... family business in the future, after all."

"Why isn't that something you're considering? Taking over the business, I mean," I asked, genuinely curious about the dynamics of their family's succession plans.

Her response was straightforward, tinged with a hint of resigned acceptance. "Because I'm female." I expected her to continue, but she simply shrugged. "That's just how it is in our family."

I couldn't hide my disbelief at such an outdated notion. "That's stupid," I blurted out without thinking.

Her laughter at my reaction was light and genuine. "Yeah, it might be, but it's the reality we live in. We just have to make the best of the hand we're dealt, right?"

Leana's words lingered in the air, prompting me to reflect on my own circumstances. The hand I'd been dealt was no less challenging: the Prince of a murdered King, my memories stripped away, leaving me with more questions than answers about my past and my identity. These were burdens I tried to carry silently, choosing not to share with Leana at the moment. The weight of my lineage and the mystery of my lost memories were mine to bear alone.

As we walked, Leana's train of thought took a lighter turn. "I sometimes wonder how different life would have been if I'd had a sister instead of Kai," she mused with a chuckle. "Can you imagine? What would my father have done then?"

Her laughter was infectious, and for a moment, it eased the heaviness of my contemplations. Her hypothetical question hung in the air between us, a brief escape into a world of 'what ifs.'

Then, turning to me, she asked, "What about you? Would you have preferred a brother or a sister? And would you want them to be older or younger than you?"

The question caught me off guard, inviting me to consider a different kind of life, one with siblings and the dynamics they bring. For a moment, I allowed myself to entertain the idea, to imagine the companionship, the rivalries, and the shared experiences that come with having a brother or a sister. It was a rare opportunity to ponder a simpler aspect of life, untouched by the complexities of my royal birthright and the shadows that haunted my past.

The sudden, unbidden memory of Jessara, the young girl I encountered in the Tekka's dream world, brought my steps to an abrupt halt. How much time had passed since our last encounter? Was there still a sliver of mana connecting me to her room in the hospital?

Leana's voice, tinged with concern, broke through my reverie. "Is everything okay?" she asked, her eyes searching mine.

"I'll look for Tyran later," I said, a decision forming in my mind. "Actually, would you like to come with me to meet a friend?"

Her confusion was evident, but she nodded, trust outweighing her uncertainty. "Sure," she agreed, though her voice carried a note of hesitance.

As she nodded, the familiar sensation of mana wrapping around us took hold, and the world around us rippled and distorted.

In the blink of an eye, the hallways of the school faded away, replaced by the stark, clinical environment of the hospital.

Leana's astonishment was visible, her gaze sweeping over the new surroundings with wide-eyed wonder. "Wow!" she said. "Sorry, that was my first teleportation. I thought we were walking here." She looked around at the many occupied beds that surrounded us. "Where are we?" she asked.

I led her over to a nearby window and pointed to the large dome of the school. "We're not too far away," I answered. "I can take us back now if you want?"

Leana smiled, shaking her head. "I haven't met your friend, yet."

I looked over to Jessara's bed, then deflated when I saw it empty. "Looks like she may have gone home," I said. I walked over to her bed, taking hold of its frame. "Shame…"

"Liam?" I turned around, to see Jessara standing in the doorway, holding the hand of the Tekka. Her eyes were wide, and her mouth was wide open in surprise.

My spirits lifted instantly. "I thought you'd gone home!" I exclaimed, unable to hide my delight as I approached them. Turning to the Tekka, I added, "I hope it's okay that I came to visit."

Although he smiled, he looked almost as stunned as Jessara. "No, that's fine, Liam… but, how did you get here?"

"I… sort of… learned how to teleport," I said quietly.

His eyes narrowed, and he looked past me. "Leana, right?"

"Uhh, yes, Sir," she said, quickly stepping beside me, looking flustered.

"Could you help Jessara to her bed? I'd like to have a quick word in private with Liam."

"Oh, of course, Sir." Leana crouched down, offering a hand toward Jessara. "Hi, I'm Leana. It's nice to meet you! I'm a friend of Liam's."

Jessara smiled, not hesitating to take Leana's hand. "Are you his girlfriend?"

Leana laughed, standing up and slowly leading Jessara to her bed. "No, just friends."

As Leana and Jessara engaged in their gentle banter, I turned my attention back to the Tekka. "How is she-" I met eyes with him and was instantly plunged into darkness. The world twisted, turned, flipped upside down and I landed with a bump, falling over backwards.

I quickly sat up, finding myself facing the Tekka through metal bars. "Sorry about this, Liam," he said, his voice carrying a hint of regret as he approached the barrier between us. "Just need to confirm you are who you say you are."

Confused and slightly alarmed, I asked, "What are you doing?"

He posed a question in return, "Do you know where you are?"

Glancing around, the realization dawned on me. I was in a cave, and beyond the bars, I could see a forest stretching out. "Yeah, I'm in one of your criminal cages," I acknowledged, rising to my feet. "But why?"

His next words struck a chord of concern. "Sixteen-year-olds don't just learn how to teleport in a couple of days... unless they're Crossers."

"You're wrong. I'm not a Crosser. I'm a Goud."

"A Goud?" He seemed skeptical.

"I transformed yesterday," I explained. "I even had the blue hair to prove it."

His laughter was incredulous. "You expect me to believe

you transformed naturally?"

Intent on proving my point, I began to focus, attempting to push out mana, only to remember the limitations imposed by his world. "Of course, I can't… because you've made it so only you can perform magic here."

His warning was clear, "If you think I'm going to let you do magic here, you're mistaken."

That's when I decided to confront him with what I knew. "Why don't you tell people you're Eulis?" His reaction was immediate, a mix of surprise and caution. "There are so many stories about you… Why the secrecy?"

Eulis, now revealed, took a step back, his demeanor shifting. "How did you learn teleportation?"

"I copied it," I said, my frustration growing. "And not just that. I've copied this dream spell, energy beams, mana orbs, illusions… Did you know I can now walk up a tree?" I let out a laugh before meeting his eyes. "I've retained the Crossers' ability to mimic."

"So you *are* a Crosser," he concluded.

"No, I'm not. I just kept their copy ability after you turned me back into a Minor," I clarified. He continued to look at me, as though still unsure I was who I said I was. "Why didn't you tell me about my bloodline magic? That I could heal?"

His surprise was evident. "How did you…?"

"Apparently the back of my skull caved in, but…"

"The medics said that was an error. The junior medic made a mistake."

I shook my head. "According to Tyran, I should have died."

"The bloodline magic is triggered by near-death experiences," he admitted, a look of realization crossing his face. Eulis's demeanor softened, and the bars that confined me disappeared. "Jessara… you healed her?"

A smile, born of pride, blossomed on my face. "I wasn't even aware of it at the time. My control over this ability is nonexistent; it's as if simply touching triggers it. It must have occurred when—"

"When you hugged her…" He paused, glancing up at my hair. "You really turned into a Goud?"

I grinned. "Yeah. I was really worried that my hair would stay blue forever."

He gestured for me to leave the cave. "Sorry, Liam."

Shaking my head, I aimed to dispel his suspicion with a firm gesture. "I'm not a Crosser. However, keeping their ability seems to have unintentionally alarmed all of my friends. I'm pretty sure Joren is utterly convinced I'm some sort of god."

His laughter, rich and unguarded, briefly filled the air before his expression sobered. "How did you figure out I was Eulis?"

With a light shrug, I shared the simple realization. "You told me you were the only Eulis capable of removing my crest at the time." A chuckle escaped me, finding humor in the truth. "Eulis was the only Eulis at that time. Why did you name the faction after yourself?"

Eulis's response came with a playful eye roll. "I didn't choose it. It started with people saying 'Do it like Eulis', and it soon just became its own word. The more I fought against it, the more it seemed to stick." A smile then softened his features, "So, you knowing about your healing magic, does this mean your memories have come back?"

I responded with a gentle shake of my head. "No. I've had the odd spell trigger something in me, like Veyra's dream spell, and the other pieces I've read about in the library." I reached into my pocket, hoping, but still surprised to find the drawing of my parents dancing had also made it into this world. "I found this."

Eulis sighed, his tone carrying a blend of admonition and understanding. "You know the pages are meant to stay in the books, right?" Taking the page from my hand, he gestured for me to follow him, and we started to walk through the forest. "Those are certainly your parents," he confirmed with a reassuring smile. "I never met your mother, but your father often kept a picture of her, too."

As Eulis handed the page back to me, I breathed in deeply. The air was filled with the earthy scent of moss and the distant sound of birdcalls. Although this world was but a dream within Eulis's mind, I couldn't help but find it comforting.

"What made you come back?" Eulis asked, his voice breaking the comfortable silence that had settled between us. "Just to check up on Jessara?"

I pondered his question, my fingers absently tracing the edges of the paper now returned to my possession. "That was the original plan," I confessed, the pieces of the puzzle slowly fitting together in my mind. "But then it dawned on me—how Jessara was healed. It made me think… maybe I could help heal the others too."

For a fleeting moment, a spark of excitement lit up Eulis's eyes, quickly dimmed by a shadow of concern. He sighed, a sound that seemed to carry the weight of the world. "As much as that idea holds promise," he began cautiously, "if word got out about your healing abilities, it could attract unwanted attention."

I frowned, recalling Lammat suggesting the same thing. "What's the harm in people knowing?"

Eulis stopped in his tracks, turning to face me fully. The seriousness in his gaze was unmistakable. "Crossers, Liam. They still exist in this world. After Zeipher's defeat, some were hunted down, but many vanished into the shadows. If you can't control your healing, it would only take one scratch from them to steal your gift."

"What if I kept training? What if I-"

"What if they kidnapped your friends? Threatened to kill them unless you healed in front of them?"

His words hung heavy in the air, a stark reminder of the delicate balance of power in our world. The serene beauty of the forest suddenly felt like a thin veil over the lurking dangers beneath, a stark reminder that every action, no matter how well-intentioned, could have far-reaching consequences.

As we crested a hill, the foliage gave way to reveal a sprawling view of the settlement below. The cluster of homes, intertwined with winding paths and the occasional flicker of activity, painted a picture of a tranquil life. I paused, taking in the sight, the idea of reuniting with familiar faces ignited a spark of excitement within me. "Do you think I could go down and say hello to the others?"

Eulis shook his head, his expression firm yet not without understanding. "Once you're there, the urge to heal will be overwhelming." His gaze swept over the settlement, where life unfolded in its intricate dance of daily routines and relationships. "These people have found happiness, Liam. They've built lives, friendships, even love. Like it or not, this is their life now."

I felt a stir of frustration, the limits of my situation pressing in. "But shouldn't I have the say in who I heal or not?"

Eulis stepped closer, his hands gently grasping my arms, anchoring me to the moment with the sincerity in his eyes. "And where does it end, Liam? Would you then journey to the next town, to their hospital, and heal every soul within? Would you traverse the globe, a nomad bound by the endless path of healing?" His voice softened, the gravity of his words underscored by a note of compassion. "For now, you have one paramount duty—pass the exam. Once you ascend to the throne, the world is yours to mend, and no one, not even I, could stand in your way. But until that day, Liam, I must implore you to heed my guidance."

Frustration bubbled up within me, a torrent of confusion and disbelief. "So, passing some exam is more important than helping these people right now? That's absurd! Why am I even participating in this exam?"

"It was your father's wish," Eulis replied, his gaze lingering over the tranquil settlement below us.

"What?" The revelation jolted me, a piece of the puzzle I hadn't anticipated.

"To claim the throne, you need the backing of a faction, and they'll only accept a transformed ruler. It's the law of the land," Eulis explained with a nonchalant shrug. "Don't blame me, Liam. I didn't choose this for you."

"That makes no sense," I protested, the pieces not fitting together in my mind. "You made me take the exam the day after I woke up!"

Eulis sighed, a weariness seeping into his voice. "Lylackia has been leaderless for six years, Liam. Your only glimpse of governance was D'wan Ma'hal. Factions at each other's throats, businesses discriminating against individuals based on their magical abilities or even their appearance."

Memories of Ding pointing out the insignias and the exclusion they represented flashed through my mind, a stark reminder of the divisions that fractured our society.

"I would've been content living in obscurity, away from the turmoil. But our country is on the brink of collapse. If our enemies sense our weakness, there might not be a Lylackia to save," Eulis continued.

He turned to face me, his expression somber yet tinged with a glimmer of hope. "Your awakening... it was a ray of light in these dark times."

I swallowed hard, the weight of his words settling on my shoulders. "But after the transformation... I'm a Goud now."

Eulis nodded solemnly. "And with that power, do you feel prepared to ascend the throne?" His question hung in the air, a challenge not just to my identity but to the very essence of my destiny.

My response came as a whisper, fraught with uncertainty. "No."

"No," Eulis echoed my sentiment, his tone firm yet not without a hint of encouragement. "But think back to where you were just a week ago. Lylackians have always revered strength and prowess. Demonstrate your abilities in tomorrow's final challenge, and you might just secure the allegiance of every faction."

"But what if I fail?"

To my surprise, Eulis chuckled, a sound that seemed out of place amid the gravity of our conversation. "Frankly, I had my doubts about you even clearing the first exam."

I couldn't hide my astonishment. "What?"

"When news reached me of you getting knocked out, I was convinced that was the end of it. I planned to regroup, focus on intensive training, and aim for next year's exam. But you, Liam, you defied those expectations at every turn."

His words stirred a pride and defiance within me. "Yeah, but that's only because of my unique abilities to heal and mimic magic!"

Eulis fixed me with a penetrating gaze, his next words carrying the weight of undeniable truth. "Your strength, your resilience—that's what will rally the factions behind you tomorrow."

At that moment, amidst the towering trees, the enormity of the task before me became clear. It wasn't just about showcasing my abilities; it was about proving my worthiness to lead, to embody the strength and courage that defined our people. Eulis's faith in me, unexpected as it was, ignited a newfound determination to face the final challenge not just as a contender, but as a leader poised to unite Lylackia under a single banner.

"Let's head back," I suggested, casting a final, lingering glance over the serene landscape of the settlement nestled below us.

"As you wish, Your Highness," Eulis replied with a hint of formality, his hand resting reassuringly on my shoulder.

In the blink of an eye, the scenery shifted, and the familiar confines of the hospital room enveloped us once more. I turned to see Leana gently assisting Jessara back into the comfort of her bed, their laughter a balm to the weariness of my spirit.

"You know," Leana began, her voice tinged with mirth, "Liam and I were talking about wishing we had sisters, and his thoughts immediately turned to you."

Jessara's reaction was instantaneous, her nose wrinkling in distaste. "That's gross!"

Leana gave a loud surprised laugh. "And why, pray tell, is that so appalling?"

"Because Liam can't possibly be my brother," Jessara declared with the certainty only a child could muster. "I've decided I'm going to marry him when I grow up."

Leana's gaze shifted to me, a playful grin dancing on her lips. "Is that so? Well, I must admit, he does have a certain charm."

Caught up in their banter, I couldn't help but join in with a chuckle. "So, Leana, are looks a priority for you?"

She paused, her eyes appraising me with a newfound seriousness before a smile softened her expression. "No," she said at last. "They're merely an added perk."

Leana, Jessara, and I shared a few light moments, the room alive with Jessara's giggles and wide-eyed wonder. I couldn't help but laugh when, after listing my array of new abilities, it was my casual mention of walking up a tree that captured her imagination the most. Out of everything, this simple trick seemed to dazzle her, her laughter and disbelief echoing around the room, a bright spot in our conversation.

However, our light-hearted banter was gently interrupted by Eulis, who suggested it was time for Jessara to rest. "Jessara's had quite a day," he said, his voice laced with a soft concern.

I nodded, understanding the need for balance. Bidding farewell, I hugged Jessara, promising to share more stories next time. I exchanged a grateful nod with Eulis, before teleporting with Leana back to the school.

The instant we materialized, a ripple of surprise swept through a group of teenagers nearby. Their expressions mirrored the jolt one might feel witnessing the sudden appearance of two people out of thin air.

As the initial shock faded and whispers began to weave

through the group, I took a moment to observe them more closely. Their presence here, coupled with the anticipation and slight unease in their demeanor, led me to piece together their story. These were likely the students who hadn't made it through the exams, back at the school for the dance.

This sparked a realization in me, a sign that others, including Naya and Joren, might have returned as well. With this thought, a strong desire to find them surged within me.

Amidst these reflections, I was taken aback by the sudden warmth of an embrace. Leana unexpectedly pulled me into a hug that seemed to convey a multitude of emotions— relief, gratitude, and perhaps a shared joy. "Thank you, Liam," she said, her voice warm with genuine appreciation. "I haven't had this much fun since I got here."

Caught slightly off guard by the warmth of Leana's embrace, I did the only thing that felt natural at the moment—I patted her on the back, a simple gesture that somehow felt like enough. "You're welcome," I managed to say, my voice steady despite the whirlwind of emotions.

As she stepped back, her smile was like a beacon, bright and reassuring. "Come on," she urged, her eyes sparkling with determination and excitement. "Let's go find Tyran again. This time, no distractions…" She paused, a mischievous glint taking hold. "…Unless you have more adorable children who wish to marry you that I should meet."

Her jest drew a laugh from me. "You wouldn't happen to know where he usually hangs out, would you?"

She shook her head, her blonde locks swaying gently with the motion. "No, sorry," she apologized, her tone genuine. "But, you know, most people usually end up in the canteen. How about we start there?"

It made sense, and I found myself nodding in agreement. The canteen, with its constant buzz of activity and the lure of food, was indeed a likely gathering spot. Plus, it seemed a promising place to possibly run into Naya and Joren as well. "Good idea," I affirmed. "Let's head there."

CHAPTER THIRTY-EIGHT
One Month

As soon as we stepped into the busy canteen, a voice pierced through the din, anchoring my attention. "Liam!" The familiar call had me swiveling towards the source, only to find Lammat rising from a table in a grand gesture of recognition. At the table were Tyran and… my heart skipped a beat… "Naya…" I found her name escaping my lips in a whisper, barely audible above the chatter.

Naya turned; her golden hair, now neatly tied back, did nothing to dim the brilliance of her presence. As her gaze locked with mine from across the room, the warmth of her smile bridged the distance between us, her blue eyes sparkling with an unspoken joy.

"Oh," said Leana. "Your date for the dance?"

Before I could respond, an unexpected sensation—three distinct jabs—pulled my attention away. I turned to find Joren, his arms extended in a peculiar gesture, an expression of intense concentration on his face. "Interesting. Still no effect," he mused, seemingly perplexed.

The moment was swiftly followed by an exclamation from Calia, who sprang up from a nearby table, her eyes wide with apology and sibling exasperation. "Sorry, Liam!" she exclaimed. "He's been practicing that for the past few days." Rubbing her arm in a gesture of shared discomfort and a playful roll of her eyes conveyed the less-than-enjoyable experience of being Joren's test subject.

I greeted her with a smile. "Hi, Calia. You alright?"

"You mean after you made me fail the exam?" The sharpness of her words was quickly softened by a smile, revealing the light-hearted nature of her accusation. "Yeah, I've been fine. Just wish Joren hadn't failed so soon though."

Joren's dry retort, "I have a very supportive sister," was met with Calia's equally sardonic, "I'd have loved to have a longer break without him."

I gestured towards their modestly sized table. "Why are you sat over here?" I asked, hinting at the larger gathering around Naya.

Calia's playful punch to Joren's arm underscored her earlier suggestion. "I tried to tell him that, but he didn't want to be a bother."

Leana stepped forward. Offering a shy wave towards Calia, she introduced herself with a soft, "Hi, I'm Leana."

"Hi, I'm Calia. Pretty sure you've met Joren."

Leana nodded. "Yes, I have," she said. "Good to see you again."

I glanced at the trays on their table, still brimming with the remnants of their meal. "Come on, pick them up. Let's go say hi to the others."

Without hesitation, Joren grabbed his tray, his mind still tangled in the web of his failed experiment. "I can't believe that didn't block your mana!" he muttered, prodding my arm as if seeking a hidden switch that would explain the anomaly. "All that effort and mana, just gone. It'll take me ages to replenish it."

His frustration drew a chuckle from me, prompting me to gently shake off his probing hand. "Exactly how much mana did you burn through for this?" I asked, half-amused, half-concerned.

"A lot!" he replied with a shake of his head. "Whatever Lammat did to you, his blocks had some effect, but mine? Might as well have been a gentle breeze for all the good they did."

I offered a simple explanation, hoping to ease his bruised ego. "Lammat's got a deep well of mana to draw from. Remember, he's got years on us."

Joren's brow furrowed, his competitive spirit unassuaged. "Still, hard to believe he managed to beat you."

As we neared the larger table, Joren and Calia seamlessly integrated, selecting their seats among the familiar faces. It was then that Leana's grip tightened on my arm, a hesitancy in her posture. "I think I'll head back to my room," she murmured, her smile not quite reaching her eyes.

Surprised, I stopped, turning to face her. "What? Why?"

Her smile persisted, a veneer over the unease. "It's just… with all your friends here, I wouldn't want to intrude."

I couldn't help but find her concern unfounded, almost laughable in its modesty. "Don't be ridiculous," I insisted, my tone both firm and inviting. "You're more than welcome to stay. Besides, this could be a great chance for you to make some new friends."

I slid out the chair adjacent to the unoccupied one next to Naya, capturing Leana's gaze until she finally relented with a blush coloring her cheeks. "Hi, everyone," she offered softly as she sat down.

The group welcomed her with open arms and warm smiles, all except Tyran, who instead exchanged a silent, understanding nod with me.

"Hiya," Naya murmured under her breath, a gentle greeting that felt like a secret shared between friends.

"Hi," I responded, my smile broadening. "I'm sorry I couldn't beat Lammat."

Lammat, with a mouthful of food, waved a dismissive hand. "Already tried to say sorry, Liam," he mumbled between bites.

Naya shook off the concern with a light-hearted shake of her head. "Don't fret over it. I've already exacted a little revenge on his meal," she confided, her eyes twinkling with mischief.

Lammat halted, a piece of food suspended in his mouth, shock written all over his face. The table erupted into laughter, a unified chorus of amusement at the jest.

"There's always next year," Naya added optimistically, brushing off the moment with a forward-looking cheer. "I'll get more training in, and will try again."

"So, where's Veyra?" Joren inquired, glancing from me to the door.

Calia groaned, dropping her head in mock despair. "Oh, gods, if I have to hear about Veyra one more time…" she complained, her voice dripping with playful annoyance.

I couldn't help but chuckle. "She's resting. She's got this big dance event coming up, and it's all she can talk about."

Joren's lips curled into a rare smile, an expression that seemed foreign on his usually blank face.

"Isn't Kai joining us?" Lammat asked, his gaze briefly flickering to Leana before settling back on the group.

"I don't think so. He headed off for some training," answered Leana.

"By himself?" Lammat let out a whistle, clearly surprised. "That's a first, isn't it?"

Joren's posture suddenly straightened, his usual stoic demeanor giving way to an unmistakable air of excitement. Curious, I swiveled in my chair, following his gaze to the entrance of the canteen. There, making her way towards us with a confident stride, was Veyra. Her presence seemed to fill the room, drawing eyes from every corner.

Calia, catching onto Joren's barely concealed enthusiasm, couldn't resist a playful jab. "Oh gods, here she comes, here she comes!" she teased, her voice dripping with exaggerated drama, seemingly mimicking what she imagined was going through Joren's mind. Just as she brought a forkful of food to her mouth, Joren retaliated with a swift poke to her shoulder, causing her arm to momentarily lose its strength. The fork clattered against the table, its contents spilled.

"Great…" Calia muttered, her annoyance softened by a

resigned sigh.

"You deserved it," Joren whispered back.

"Yeah, I know…" Calia conceded, her tone glum as she switched to using her left hand to pick up the fork.

Veyra, seemingly unfazed by the minor commotion, circled the table to claim an empty seat beside Tyran. "I wondered when you'd all be back," she said, her voice carrying a casual warmth. She nodded towards Naya, "Hi, Naya," before turning her attention to Joren, a playful glint in her eye. "Looking forward to our dance?"

Joren, caught off guard by her directness, could only respond with widened eyes and a sheepish grin. "I knew you knew I beat you," he managed, his smile broadening.

"One dance," Veyra reminded him with a chuckle.

Seeking to shift the conversation to a lighter note, I asked Veyra, "Sleep well?"

She nodded, her demeanor relaxed. "I did, yeah! Didn't mean to fall asleep that quickly, sorry."

"It's fine. You must have needed it."

Veyra sighed, a hint of regret in her voice. "I was hoping to get a bit more training in before this evening, but I doubt there's time."

"Actually, Liam," said Tyran, leaning across the table slightly. "I wanted to talk to you about that."

My interest sparked, I leaned in as well. "Yeah, I was hoping to do some training with you today, too."

Tyran leaned closer, his voice dropping to a whisper that seemed meant for only Veyra and me. "That spell the Tekka showed you," he said, his eyes flickering with a hint of intrigue.

"You mean the—" I began, but he cut me off with a quick nod.

"Yeah, the one you showed Veyra." Veyra, who had been straining to listen despite sitting right next to him, also leaned in closer. "Do you think you can use it on me?"

I frowned, puzzled by the sudden request. "When?" I

asked.

"Now," Tyran replied, his voice still low but firm.

Veyra's excitement was clear as she gasped, "Oh! Yeah! Use it on me, too!"

Naya, who had been following the conversation finally voiced her bewilderment. "What are you talking about?"

Veyra, with a reassuring smile, reached out to tap Naya's hand. "Don't worry, it's just some last-minute training," she said, trying to allay any concerns.

Tyran's gaze locked with mine, a silent question hanging between us. "So?" he pressed.

I glanced around the table, noticing that Calia, Joren, Lammat, and Leana were deep in their own discussions, oblivious to our cryptic exchange. Turning back to Tyran and then to Veyra, I took a deep breath and closed my eyes.

When I opened them again, the familiar expanse of the large white void surrounded us. The transition was seamless, as if the bustling canteen had simply melted away.

Tyran surveyed the vast emptiness with a hint of surprise. "You haven't used this place?" he asked, his voice echoing slightly in the void.

I shook my head, the sense of underutilization settling in. "Veyra was the last person to use it," I admitted, feeling a sense of anticipation and uncertainty about what Tyran had in mind for this impromptu session.

As Tyran glanced around, he finally broke the silence with a curious question. "What's the time dilation in this place?"

I paused, not quite catching his drift at first. "You mean, how much slower is time here compared to the real world?"

Veyra, with a hint of excitement in her voice, jumped in. "Last time I was here, it felt like an hour passed in here for every minute outside."

I gave a noncommittal shrug, still trying to wrap my head around the concept. "I'm not really sure. When Veyra was here, I tried to balance the times out. An hour in here for a minute outside was the fastest I could manage."

"I was thinking the opposite, actually."

I was puzzled. "You mean, you want time to go even slower in here?"

"How slow do you think you can make it?" he asked, his tone serious.

I hesitated, the uncertainty clear in my voice. "I really don't know. I'm not entirely sure how it all works."

Veyra cut in. "Tyran, you haven't seen what Liam can do. What if he makes it so slow that one minute outside turns into a year in here?"

"One month," Tyran stated firmly, his gaze piercing through me.

"A month?" Veyra echoed, surprise evident in her voice.

Tyran's resolve was clear. "I didn't ask for you to join me. I just want more time to train, and this seemed like the best way to do it."

I was starting to feel the weight of their expectations. "I'm not sure I can make it exactly a month," I admitted, the worry creeping into my voice.

Tyran's confidence in me was unwavering. "I think you can, Liam. You might not realize it, but magic seems to come naturally to you."

Veyra added with a slight tease, "Oh, he's aware of his strength." Her words, though playful, carried a tone of respect for my abilities.

Tyran's display of power was both impressive and unsettling. As he launched a beam into the void, I watched, counting the seconds. Five... ten... twenty seconds. Veyra expressed her admiration. "Wow, you can do that for a long time!" she exclaimed.

Tyran, however, wasn't as impressed with himself. "That's because this world revolves around Liam," he pointed out, summoning a dagger with a casual flick of his wrist. The demonstration that followed—a quick slice on his thumbs and an instant healing—underscored his point. "This," he said, touching the healed wound, "is useful, but having unlimited mana will be an issue."

His next words took me by surprise. "Having control over this world is new to me, as is the ability to perform magic."

I offered a solution, albeit hesitantly. "I think I can adjust the rules here, but you'll have to be clear about what you need."

Tyran's response was swift and decisive. "Just aim for realism. I don't want endless magic, but I'd like to keep the healing aspect."

Veyra chimed in, "And we should need food and drink, too."

Her comment seemed to seal her decision to stay, prompting a grin from Tyran. "So, you're staying for the month?"

"But you don't need to eat or drink here," I said.

"One month, right?" Her gaze flitted between Tyran and me, seeking confirmation. "Going without needing to eat and drink for that long is likely to cause issues when we come back."

The gravity of what they were asking began to weigh on me. "Guys, I don't know if-"

"It'll be fine, Liam," Tyran reassured me. "We can't die in here, and in the real world, it'll barely be a minute."

Veyra's laughter broke through my apprehension. "Imagine us, just staring blankly at you for a minute. That'll be an interesting sight."

"Can you do it?" Tyran pressed, his gaze fixed on me.

I inhaled deeply, feeling the weight of Tyran and Veyra's expectations pressing down on me. My thoughts raced, sifting through every scrap of knowledge I had accumulated from countless hours spent with my nose buried in books, every intricate drawing I had pored over, and every vivid memory I had of Eulis's dream world. With a mixture of trepidation and determination, I focused my mind and reached out to the fabric of the void around us.

At first, a gentle rustling whispered through the stillness as thin blades of grass began to pierce the ground beneath our feet. The sprouts multiplied rapidly, weaving a lush carpet of vibrant green that stretched endlessly into the horizon. It was like watching a wave of life washing over a barren beach, transforming the void into a meadow in mere moments.

Next, I turned my attention to the trees. I envisioned towering giants, their trunks thick and sturdy, rooted deeply in the fertile ground of our new world. One by one, they burst forth from the soil, their growth accelerated by the magic at my command. The branches reached ambitiously for the sky, unfurling leaves that shimmered in the nonexistent sunlight, creating a canopy that danced with shades of green and gold.

As the forest took shape around us, I felt the need for water—a river to nourish this burgeoning ecosystem. With a flick of my intent, the ground before us trembled slightly, and then, with a sudden gush, a river sprang to life. It carved a winding path through the meadow and forest, its clear waters rushing with a lively chatter. The river's course acted as a natural barrier, gently nudging Tyran and Veyra onto one bank while I remained on the other, as though emphasizing their newfound independence in this world.

The air itself seemed to awaken next, filled with the calls and songs of birds that had not existed moments before. They materialized from thin air, a flurry of feathers and flight, adding a layer of sound that was both serene and lively. Their melodies intertwined with the rustling leaves and flowing water, creating a symphony of natural harmony.

Finally, I summoned the deer. With a subtle nudge of my will, they appeared at the forest's edge, graceful and alert. At the sight of us, they bounded away, their elegant forms a blur of motion against the backdrop of trees and grass. Their presence added a sense of wildness and freedom to the landscape, a reminder of the untamed beauty of nature.

Veyra's eyes widened as she took in the expansive world around us. "Wow..." she breathed out, her gaze wandering over the lush meadows, towering forests, and the vibrant river that cut through the landscape. "I thought my cabin was impressive."

Tyran furrowed his brow in wonder. "How large did you make this place?"

I scratched my head, a bit embarrassed by the lack of a concrete answer. "Well, I wasn't exactly sure when to stop... so I didn't really put a limit on it."

His eyes grew wide with astonishment. "You created an infinite world?"

I hurried to clarify. "Not exactly infinite. When it seemed big enough, I made it loop back on itself." I pointed upstream. "Head that way, and you'll find yourself at a mountain. And if you go downstream," I gestured in the opposite direction, "you'll reach a beach."

"Is mana still limitless here?"

I shook my head, firm on this decision. "No, your mana pool will stay as it is now. It won't increase in here."

Veyra let out a small sigh, understanding the reasoning but clearly finding it a touch inconvenient. "It's a bit of a nuisance, but I see your point. Having more mana here and then returning to the real world with less would be disorienting."

The concern for their well-being nudged at me again. "Are you both really okay with staying? It might feel strange returning to reality, especially with the dance and everything."

Tyran's grin was a mixture of mischief and relief. "The longer I can delay attending that dance, the happier I'll be."

Veyra and I shared a laugh, but then she grew thoughtful. "I don't know... I was kind of looking forward to seeing Joren again."

I took a moment to ensure they were certain. "Alright, if you're sure about this." Lifting my hand, I bid them farewell. "See you in a month."

With a subtle gesture, they disappeared from my sight, yet I couldn't bring myself to leave just yet. Instead, I moved myself to the peak of the mountain I had mentioned, taking a moment to survey the vastness of my creation.

As I stood there, the air beside me shimmered, and a perfect duplicate of myself appeared, offering a reassuring smile and a nod.

Closing my eyes, I allowed the serene landscape to fade from my vision. When I reopened them, I was back at the canteen table. Across the table, Tyran and Veyra were still sitting, their bodies present but their expressions distant.

Naya's concerned voice broke through my reverie. "Everything okay?"

I nodded, a genuine smile breaking through. "I've missed you," I said, the weight of the adventure I had just set in motion for Tyran and Veyra still lingering in my thoughts.

Naya's expression held a blend of frustration and regret as she spoke, "I tried to see you, but they asked us to leave immediately, saying it was policy or something." Her words trailed off, hinting at the disappointment that lingered behind her calm demeanor.

Calia leaned in, her eyes scanning the group before her. "So it's just the six of you in the final?" she inquired.

Leana nodded in confirmation. "Is it normal for so few to get this far?" she questioned, her voice a soft murmur that carried the weight of her curiosity.

With a laugh that resonated with warmth and disbelief, Calia responded, "No, that's far from normal."

Joren directed his gaze towards me, making me feel as though his next words were meant mainly for my ears. "The final exam tends to be the same each year," he began, his voice steady and clear. "A fight between all of the examinees."

Leana and I, caught off guard by the revelation, voiced our surprise in unison, "At the same time?"

Joren's frown, directed at Leana, hinted at his perplexity. "Where are you from?" he questioned, before clarifying, "No, not at the same time. It'll be a one-on-one fight. Everyone just has one fight each. It doesn't matter if you win or lose."

"I reckon they should have the winner stay on, and have the fights continue until one winner is remaining," added Calia.

Joren's response was tinged with humor, "You would say that." He then turned in his seat, aiming his next question at Veyra. "Who would you choose to fight?"

The room's attention swiveled towards her, with Tyran and Veyra's gazes piercingly focused on me. The moment hung heavy. I quickly glanced between them and Joren, wondering if I should pull them out early.

Joren's laughter broke the tension, "I should have known you'd choose Liam."

"Do we get to choose?" The question slipped from my lips urgently, trying to distract them.

Joren's head shake was gentle, yet firm. "No, it's usually random."

Calia once again added her thoughts, "Which is another shame. Much better if they pit fighters against those that might make a good match."

Leana's voice, barely a whisper, reached only my ears, "So long as I don't have to fight Kai, I'm happy." She smiled up at me. "No idea what'll happen if I'm forced to fight him."

"You'll win," I said with a smile.

My eyelids fluttered shut, only to lift and reveal the familiar yet ever-mystical dream world that awaited me. There I was, by the river, its gentle flow whispering secrets only known to this realm. A quick scan of my surroundings revealed no sign of Tyran or Veyra, prompting a sense of urgency within me. I felt a pull, an inexplicable tug further down the river, and I allowed it to guide me.

As the trees blurred past, a sense of displacement washed over me, until I found myself standing next to a log cabin. It bore a resemblance to the one Veyra had envisioned in her dream, yet lacked the same finesse in its construction. A sudden crash jolted me from my observations, drawing my attention to a tree that toppled and rolled to the ground with a heavy thud.

Tyran emerged from the settling foliage, his figure commanding as he began to strip the branches from the top of the fallen tree. He paused, his actions halting as his gaze met mine, and he raised a hand in greeting before resuming his task without missing a beat.

Approaching him, I called out, "Hey! Hope I wasn't too long."

Tyran's laugh, rich and welcoming, filled the air as he continued his work. But then, a pause, a moment of hesitation as he looked up at me with a newfound intensity. "Wait... are you the real one?" The question hung between us, charged with an undercurrent of uncertainty.

"Tyran?" My response was automatic, laced with confusion.

"Veyra!" Tyran's voice boomed, cutting through the quiet of the dream world. "Liam's back!" His excitement was clear, infectious even, but it did little to quell the growing unease within me.

"Tyran... how long was I gone?" My question was tentative, dreading the answer that might follow.

"Long enough..." Veyra's voice, calm and steady, floated towards me.

Turning, I inhaled sharply, my gaze locking onto Veyra who stood before me, gently bouncing a small bundle of cloth in her arms. The silhouette of a baby, so real and immediate in this dreamscape, sent a jolt of fear through me.

"Oh gods..." The words escaped me in a breath. My eyes darted from Tyran to Veyra, then to the baby, and back again, trying to piece together the impossible.

"It's been three years, Liam," Tyran's voice broke through my stupor, his hand resting briefly on my shoulder as he passed by. The weight of his words, 'three years,' anchored me to the spot, disbelief coursing through me.

"Three years!? Oh, no... I'm so sorry, I thought—" My apology, heartfelt and frantic, seemed inadequate against the stretch of time that had passed.

"We named him after you," Veyra's voice was soft, carrying a warmth as she stepped closer. "Come on, little Liam, come meet your—"

My heart, already a frenzied drumbeat in my chest, seized at the sight of Veyra stumbling over the branches Tyran had stripped away, her arms flailing in a desperate attempt to regain balance. Instinct took over, propelling me forward to catch the falling bundle… only to grasp at empty cloth.

"Wha…?" Confusion laced my voice, a single syllable that hung in the air as Tyran and Veyra's laughter, rich and full of mirth, enveloped me, dispelling the tension with the revelation of their playful deceit.

"That was totally worth it!" Veyra couldn't contain her glee, her laughter still echoing around us.

"I'm surprised I kept a straight face," Tyran admitted, a hint of pride in his voice.

"Told you he'd fall for it," came a voice from behind me, and turning, I was met with the sight of my own double, grinning ear to ear as if he'd just pulled off the greatest prank.

"Why would you do that?" I managed, my voice shaking with bewilderment and a faint trace of irritation, my heart still racing from the shock.

A sharp, strangely familiar thud in my arm redirected my attention to Veyra. "You deserve it, Prince! We said one month! It's been two!"

"Two?" My confusion deepened as I looked from Veyra to Tyran, who confirmed with a nod. Turning to my copy, I pressed, "You were meant to pull them out if there was a problem!"

My double simply shrugged, his grin never fading. "I tried!" he defended. "Turns out you and I have different heads. We're inside yours, and not even I can get out."

Veyra's laughter rang out again, light and carefree, as she reached out to reclaim the cloth from me. "We've been looking forward to doing this for weeks now."

"You still in the canteen?" Tyran's question brought me

back to the reality waiting outside this dream.

"Yeah! It's probably been less than a minute!" The absurdity of time's flow here versus the real world struck me. "Joren tried to talk to you, and all you're both doing is staring at me."

Tyran's laughter joined Veyra's, a sound I was starting to associate with their shared amusement at my expense. "Yeah, the canteen probably wasn't the best place to do this."

Seeing Tyran like this, his usual brooding demeanor replaced by this light-hearted jest, was jarring. "But you're both okay, right?" The concern in my voice was genuine, needing assurance beyond their playful antics.

They nodded, their smiles reassuring. "As I said," Tyran responded, "anything to avoid that dance." The relief in knowing they were alright did little to settle the whirlwind of emotions their prank had stirred within me.

Veyra, with a flick of her wrist, casually tossed the cloth aside and placed her hands firmly on her hips, turning to face me with a decisive look. "Alright, send us back."

Tyran joined her side, his movement easy and familiar as he draped an arm over her shoulders, a gesture of camaraderie and shared experiences. "Thank you for the holiday, Liam. We've both learned a lot." The warmth in his voice and the closeness they now shared made me pause, reflecting on the evolution of their relationship right before my eyes.

With a deep breath, I gathered my focus and, with a slight push of my will, their images dissolved into the fabric of the dream, leaving me alone with my duplicate.

Facing him, I couldn't help but scrutinize his every feature, searching for any hint of what I should do next. "What do I do with you?" I asked, the question hanging heavily in the air between us.

My copy met my gaze with a knowing smile. "I know it's your instinct to dismiss me, you know, absorbing mana being as painful as it is… but right now, in this world… there's no pain at all."

His words piqued my curiosity. "Do you want to stay here?" I inquired, uncertain of his desires.

He laughed, a clear, resonant sound that cut through the tension. "Gods, no. I want you to absorb me." His smile broadened, a hint of excitement in his eyes. "I think you'll be interested in the result."

Extending his hand towards me, I hesitated for only a moment before taking it. As our hands met, his form began to dissolve into smoke, swirling and coalescing into my fingers. The sensation was foreign yet strangely exhilarating as I felt it course through me, a rush of energy flooding my senses.

The memories came in a cascade, vivid and immersive. I saw through his eyes as he watched Tyran and Veyra laboring over the log cabin, their determination forging something tangible from foraged logs. I experienced the solitude of camping out in the mountains, a self-imposed exile to avoid disturbing their training, feeling the crisp mountain air and the vastness of the night sky enveloping me. I recalled the moment I realized my mana didn't regenerate in this world, prompting a desperate need to learn how to absorb mana after I'd used it.

The memory shifted, and I was stood by the cabin, revealing myself after a month, my intentions to bring them back thwarted by an unexpected failure. The ensuing panic and worry weighed heavily on my chest as I faced the consequences of my actions.

The moment the three of us sat beside a campfire, each adding a piece of the puzzle to the scheme with the fabricated baby. The tears running down our cheeks as we laughed.

As the memories settled, I was left with a profound realization. Two sets of memories now resided within me, each as real and tangible as the other. The casual conversations in the canteen, interspersed with laughter and light-hearted banter, contrasted sharply with the two months spent in the dream world, a period marked by learning, growth, and friendship.

The duality of these experiences, both rooted in reality yet vastly different in their implications, left me reeling, struggling to reconcile the weight of what I had just absorbed.

I looked at the cabin, and smiled, deciding to leave it as it is, before closing my eyes once again and returning to the canteen.

"I seriously doubt it," said Leana, her eyes twinkling with mirth.

Her sudden words caught me off guard, and I couldn't help but startle slightly. "Doubt what?"

She exhaled deeply, a mixture of resignation and humor in her voice. "That I'd ever outdo Kai," she admitted. "But really, there's no use fretting about it beforehand, right?"

Amidst this, Tyran's voice, warm and genuine, reached out across the table. "It's good to see you again, Naya."

Naya, taken aback, could only muster a confused, "What?" Her gaze locked onto his, searching for an unspoken meaning.

The room's atmosphere shifted when Veyra sprang from her seat, her enthusiasm uncontainable. She rushed to Joren, her arms enveloping him in a tight embrace. "Joren!" she exclaimed, her laughter echoing. "I'll dance with you as many times as you want tonight."

Joren's reaction was more subdued, his lips pressing into a thin line as his eyes sought mine. "Confused," he murmured.

CHAPTER THIRTY-NINE
A Dance of Light and Shadows

As Tyran, Lammat, and I crossed the threshold into the dance hall, I couldn't help but be engulfed by the lavish scene. The hall, a cavernous space of splendor, was alive with the rhythm of the dance. Couples swirled on the glossy floor, their elegant forms a whirl of shadow and light. The ceiling arched above us like the inverted hull of some great ship, its timbers dark against the soft illumination of the chandeliers, which cast a honeyed light over the revelers.

The windows, grand and reaching to the heavens, displayed a false yet convincing starry night, a triumph of artifice that brought the grandeur of the cosmos indoors. I admired the cleverness, the way the artificial sky lent an air of endless possibility to the evening.

The drapes, grand sweeps of fabric, billowed gently from the walls, their movements a silent dance to the melody of the strings and keys. I watched the musicians, their fingers deft and sure, as they poured their souls into the music that commanded the flow of gowns and the step of polished shoes.

At a table, the flicker of candlelight caught my eye, casting a warm glow on the faces of those seated around it, drawing them together in a circle of intimacy amid the grandeur.

I searched the crowd for Naya, a thread of excitement woven through my nerves. She wasn't in my immediate line of sight, but the anticipation of finding her here, among the dancing figures and beneath the simulated stars, quickened my pulse.

I took a step, ready to delve deeper into the sea of dancers, when my name sliced through the orchestral swell behind me.

"Liam!"

The voice, unmistakably Veyra's, was laced with an excited urgency. I turned, a laugh escaping me as I found her waving at me from the doorway, her eyes alight with anticipation.

I met her with a smile. "Your number is fifteen."

With a grin, she repeated the number to the Eulis tailor standing like a sentinel by the door. He snapped his fingers with a flourish, and the air around Veyra hummed with a silent energy.

Her outfit began to quiver and ripple. It was as if a thousand tiny creatures of silver light were waking from a slumber, crawling over one another to craft a new form. The fabric shimmered and shifted, the seams and stitches dissolving into a fluid dance of transformation.

The new gown was breathtaking, it clung to her like a second skin, a sculpted marvel that hugged every curve and contour of her figure. It was as though she was draped in a cascade of silver scales, each one catching the light and throwing it back, creating an illusion of liquid motion. The scales seemed almost alive, moving with her body, enhancing her every movement with a play of light that was mesmerizing.

The dress tapered in as it neared her waist, accentuating her silhouette, before flaring out slightly and falling to the floor in a subtle echo of the dancers' twirls around us. The entire transformation was a silent symphony of elegance and innovation, leaving those nearby watching in awe. Veyra, now a vision in sculpted silver, gave a small twirl, her laughter mingling with the soft exclamations of the onlookers. The tailor nodded, his work complete—a stunning assemblage of art and magic.

I watched the final glimmer of transformation settle over Veyra, and couldn't help but be impressed. "You look amazing," I told her, and I meant every word.

She nodded, a playful confidence in her smile. "I know, right?" she laughed, the sound bubbling up from her with genuine delight. "I never wear stuff like this."

Just then, Tyran approached, a figure of quiet strength. He offered his arm to Veyra, and with a grace that seemed to match her transformed attire, she accepted. Together, they navigated through the throng of guests to a table set apart from the dance floor.

Beside me, Lammat nudged my arm, his brow furrowed in mild curiosity. "Why are they suddenly so friendly?"

I chuckled, the sound mingling with the notes of the live music. "I'll let them tell you," I said, my gaze following the pair as they settled into the soft candlelight of the table.

Lammat nudged me, a teasing edge to his voice. "Seen her yet?"

"Who?" I played along, knowing full well who he meant.

He rolled his eyes. "Naya, who else?"

I scanned the crowd once more, the sea of faces blurring into a tapestry of anticipation. "Not yet," I admitted.

Lammat glanced at a grand clock that presided over the hall. "She's probably not here yet. The night's only just begun, after all." His gaze followed mine as I took in the room once more.

"Yeah, and I haven't seen Joren or Calia either. Maybe they're all arriving together," I mused aloud, the thought bringing a new wave of anticipation.

He sighed, then in a playful mimicry of Tyran's earlier gesture, offered me his arm. "Shall we?" he asked, a wry smile on his lips.

Laughing, I linked arms with him, and together we made our way over to the table where Tyran and Veyra sat in quiet conversation.

"You two make a beautiful couple," Veyra teased as we approached.

Lammat, playing his part to the hilt, held a chair out for me. "After you, my dear."

But I wasn't about to be outdone in this game of chivalry. With a flourish, I pulled out a chair for him. "No, no, I insist!"

I felt the seat move, and looked down to find Joren, slipping into the seat I had just offered to Lammat. "Thanks!" he said with a grin, oblivious to the little play we had just enacted.

When Joren settled into the chair with his easy thanks, a thought struck me like a chord – if Joren was here…

As I turned around, the sight of Naya standing before me momentarily stole the breath from my lungs. Her gown was beautiful, enveloping her in a spectrum of soft pinks that seemed to have been plucked right from the heart of a blooming rose garden. The dress graced her form, the upper portion fitting perfectly, showcasing an artful balance between elegance and comfort. It was richly adorned with an intricate pattern of roses and leaves that spiraled across the fabric, each stitch a testament to the skilled spell that had crafted it.

The skirt of her dress was a masterpiece in its own right, falling in generous, sweeping folds that promised to sway with every step she took. The roses that embellished the skirt were so vivid and detailed that they almost seemed real, as if at any moment, they might release their fragrance into the air.

Naya's hair cascaded in waves of gold, framing her face with a softness that accentuated the vibrant blue of her eyes. Tucked into the curls were delicate roses that matched those on her dress, creating a harmony between her hairstyle and gown. And, resting just above the neckline of her dress, was a necklace with a gem that caught the light, its glow a quiet echo of the life and color that surrounded her.

At this moment, with the grandeur of the hall as her backdrop, Naya was not just a guest at the ball but the embodiment of its very essence—a blend of beauty, grace, and a touch of the magic that the night promised – and all I could say was, "Wow, Naya."

"Gods, Naya. Way to put me in the shadow!" said Veyra with a smile.

Joren's words were immediate. "Idiotic," he muttered, as he turned towards Veyra. "You still have my eye."

Seizing the moment, Veyra stood, her hand finding Joren's as she pulled him from his seat with a playful tug. "I'll pretend you didn't call me an idiot, and instead reward you with our first dance," she declared.

Joren offered no resistance, allowing himself to be led to the dance floor by Veyra, his usual stoic demeanor momentarily set aside. They moved together, becoming a part of the dance hall's living flow.

I turned back to Naya, struggling to find words equal to the moment. "How... you look..."

Tyran's subtle throat-clearing cut through my fumbling attempt at speech. His glance flicked from me to the chair Joren had just vacated, a wordless cue. "Oh!" I exclaimed, hastening to be the gentleman. Grabbing the chair, I slid it out smoothly for Naya. "Please, sit," I said, a bit too eagerly, perhaps.

Naya eased into the chair with the grace of a summer breeze, the skirts of her dress whispering against the floor. Once she was settled, I gently pushed the chair in, closing the space between her and the table. I then walked around and, without any ceremony, took Veyra's recently vacated seat.

Lammat gave an exaggerated sniff. "Jilted already..." His eyes twinkled with humor as he clapped his hands together. "Don't worry, I move on fast." And with that, he sank into the chair he had initially pulled out for me, a final act in our little comedy of manners.

Naya's voice, tinged with a hint of vulnerability, broke the momentary silence. "I was worried it was a bit too much," she admitted, running a hand down her dress.

Looking at her, I couldn't imagine anything more perfect. "Really, you look amazing," I assured her sincerely.

Then, with a touch as light as the petals on her dress, she reached over and traced a finger across my chest. "I half expected you to be wearing white," she mused, her eyes playful. Her eyes shot wide and she turned abruptly towards Tyran and Lammat. "Oh, I mean…"

They both wore expressions of confusion for a mere moment before the pieces clicked into place. "Oh," Tyran echoed with a newfound understanding. "Prince."

Lammat nodded, adding, "Yeah, we already know."

Naya's cheeks colored slightly, a whisper of pink that matched her dress. "Sorry, I really should be a little more careful about stuff like that."

Lammat shrugged, brushing off her concern. "It's fine, I tried to get him to wear white, but the Eulis wouldn't allow it."

With an easy smile, Naya turned back to me. "Oh well, you look great. Very handsome."

The conversation hung in the air for a moment before Tyran's blunt inquiry cut through. "So what are you two?"

Naya's laughter was a light note amid the heavy question. "I honestly don't know. We'll have to see how things go after the exam."

Lammat leaned in, his whisper theatrically loud, "Don't trust her, Liam!" He wagged a finger mockingly. "She's only in it for the status!"

But Naya was quick with her retort, swatting Lammat playfully. "Don't say things like that!" She turned to me, her eyes sparkling with mirth. "I'll have you know we kissed long before I found that out!"

Lammat's laughter rang out, unguarded and genuine. "Good lad."

Naya let out a sigh, her gaze sweeping over our little group. She leaned in my direction, the distance closing as she settled into the moment. "Look at us four, the original team back together." Her voice wavered slightly, a tremor of nostalgia or perhaps uncertainty. "I wish I were there with you in the final exam, but if anything, this exam has taught me that

I certainly need more training. You three were so far ahead of me...” she trailed off.

Tyran’s response was immediate, his head shaking in mild dissent. “I fought you, you held your own,” he insisted, his tone brooking no argument.

But Naya countered with a playful firmness. “No, you fought me and Joren, at the same time. You’re the one who held their own.” Her expression shifted then, a spark of mischief igniting in her eyes as she leaned across the table toward Tyran. In a swift, unexpected move, she gave him a soft slap on the cheek.

“What was that for?” Tyran asked, his surprise evident.

Her laughter followed, light and teasing. “For breaking my arm in our first battle!”

Tyran’s demeanor turned bashful, an awkward smile tugging at the corners of his mouth. “Yeah, sorry about that. In my defense, that kick was aimed at Liam. Did you expect me to stop just because you jumped in front of it?”

I was about to respond to the playful banter when I noticed Tyran’s attention shift. His gaze lifted and focused on something beyond our group. Curious, I turned to follow his line of sight and saw Leana standing a dozen paces away. She was in a glossy, green dress, her eyes on the dancers as her fingers nervously twisted together.

I turned back to the table. “Shall we invite her to join us?” I suggested, but Tyran was already one step ahead.

He stood, his eyes still locked on Leana with a kind of intent focus. “I have a better idea,” he said, and without another word, he made his way over to her.

I couldn’t help but smile as I watched them talk, the easy confidence of Tyran’s posture speaking volumes. But then Naya’s voice brought me back to the moment. “Would you like to go and get a drink?” she asked, her eyes bright with the suggestion.

I nodded, my gaze lingering on Tyran and Leana for just a second longer before turning to Lammat. “Would you mind holding the table for us? And can I get you a drink while I'm up?"

Lammat leaned back in his chair, his hands clasped behind his head in a picture of relaxation. "I'm fine, thanks," he said, and then with a reassuring nod, he added, "Don't worry about the table. I've got it covered."

We weaved through the crowd, the rhythmic pulse of music guiding us toward a long, polished wooden bar that stood sentinel at the edge of the dance floor. Our fingers were intertwined, a silent acknowledgment of the connection between us as we approached the barkeep, who was leaning comfortably against the sturdy structure.

"What can I get you?" he asked, his voice a buoyant note amidst the symphony of festivities. The bartender's cheeks were flushed a merry shade of red, likely from sampling his own wares, and his eyes sparkled with a mirth that seemed to be enhanced by the rosy tint of bloodshot veins.

"A drink, please," I said.

"Yes... which drink?" He arched an eyebrow.

Naya quickly chimed in before I could flounder further. "Suji please... could I have it in a glass, if possible?" Her request was met with a brisk nod as the bartender ducked below the bar. When he resurfaced, he had a glass and a bottle labeled with the distinctive script of a Suji brew. With a practiced hand, he filled the glass to an appropriate level.

"And you, sir?" he turned his attention to me.

A name popped into my mind, a hunch that felt right. "A glass of Crestberry, please." The words slipped out, carried by a faint hope.

The bartender paused, his motion stilling as he gave me a long, appraising look, mildly impressed yet edged with surprise. "Crestberry, hey? Sorry, son, but we don't serve that kind of luxury here."

My confidence faltered, words tripping over themselves in a rush. "Uhh, okay, then can I have—"

"He'll have a Suji, too, but in a bottle," Naya interjected

smoothly, saving me from my fluster.

"Another Suji, coming right up. Hold on a moment," the bartender said, his cheer undimmed by my blunder. He slid Naya's glass across the bar with a gentle push, the liquid inside catching the light like liquid topaz. He then grabbed another bottle, popped it open with a flick of his wrist, and handed it to me. The cool surface of the bottle was a welcome contrast to the warmth of the room, and I nodded my thanks.

As we took our drinks, Naya's brow furrowed slightly in curiosity. "Crestberry?" she echoed, the word unfamiliar and intriguing on her tongue. "What is that, exactly?"

I took a sip from the bottle, the cool Suji refreshing against my lips before answering. "Honestly, I'm not sure. When he asked what I wanted, the word just... came to me. Like it was something I knew I liked, even though I can't remember having it."

Naya considered this for a moment, her gaze thoughtful as she took a delicate drink from her glass. "Maybe it's a favorite of yours. You know, from before." Her eyes met mine, a flicker of something deeper passing between us. "From before all this," she gestured vaguely, encompassing the grandeur of our current lives.

A smile tugged at my lips as I pondered the possibility. "Could be. It feels right, like a distant memory that's just out of reach." I took another drink, letting the flavors of the Suji mingle with my thoughts.

Naya's eyes brightened with a look of excitement. "Why don't we make finding a bottle our little project after the exam? If it's as special as it seems, it would be the perfect way to celebrate," she declared with a playful raise of her glass.

I clinked my bottle against it, the sound crisp and clear. "It's a deal then. After the exam, we'll find out if Crestberry is as good as my mysterious hunch claims it to be." The future, with all its uncertainties, suddenly seemed a little brighter with that simple plan in place.

After finishing our drinks we returned the glass and bottle

to the bar. The bartender gave us a nod of appreciation as we stepped away, turning back to his array of bottles and glasses with the practiced skill of someone who thrives in the lively atmosphere of the dance hall.

As we moved back toward the throng of dancers, the band on stage transitioned from one song to another. The upbeat tempo giving way to a slower, more tender melody. The shift in music felt like an invitation, one I found myself eager to accept.

Taking hold of Naya's hand, I offered a smile, half playful, half earnest. "Excuse me, miss," I began, the words laced with a hint of formality, "Would you be interested in dancing with Prince Lexis, the future King of Lylackia?"

Her laughter was a melody all its own, clear and joyful. "No," she said, her smile broad and eyes shining.

"Oh, I—"

"No titles, no white outfits, no fanfare… just you." With that, she led me by the hand to the center of the dance floor. To my surprise, the space around us filled quickly with other couples, drawn by the music's gentle call.

As I took in the scene, Naya sought to capture my attention, a task she accomplished with ease as I finally turned back to her. Her hand found mine, guiding it to rest on her waist. The unexpected contact made me jump slightly, but her laughter and the reassuring nod that followed eased any nerves. Her other hand rested lightly on my shoulder, and she clasped our free hands together, extending them to the side. Our eyes met, and for a moment, time seemed to stand still. There was no need for movement, no rush to join the dance. Just the two of us, lost in a moment of connection.

"What do we do now?" My voice betrayed a hint of anticipation and uncertainty, prompting me to clear my throat in an attempt to steady it.

Naya's smile was a beacon in the soft light. "Now we dance," she said simply.

And so we did. The world around us faded into a soft

blur, the music a gentle wave that carried us. Naya rested her head against my chest, and in that moment, everything felt right. She looked up at me, her expression one of serene beauty, and I couldn't help but think how peaceful, how perfect this moment was. It was like stepping into a dream, one I never wanted to wake from.

As we swayed gently on the dance floor, a memory flickered across my mind—a drawing of my parents, locked in a dance that seemed to mirror our own. Could they have danced in this very spot, I wondered, at a similar age when their love story was just beginning? The thought of it, the continuity of past and present, added a layer of depth to the moment. I found myself thinking about what the future held for Naya and me.

Looking down at Naya, something within me shifted, a realization crystallizing with every beat of the music. "I think I'm falling in love with you," I confessed, the words slipping out in a breath, a whisper meant only for her.

Her response was immediate, her smile radiant. "Oh, Liam. I fell for you the moment I saw you injured."

That wasn't quite the backdrop I had imagined for a confession like this. "Not quite as romantic a moment as I'd hoped this would be," I replied, a hint of amusement in my voice.

Naya's laughter was a melody that filled the spaces between us. She rapped her knuckles lightly on my shoulder. "I mean, after I found out what you did for me, what you did for everyone, and me seeing what happened to you... I realized even though I barely knew you, I had never been so worried about anyone like that in my entire life."

"Well saved," I said, a smile playing on my lips. Leaning in, I kissed her, sealing the moment with a promise of the many chapters yet to be written together. Our kiss was a testament to the journey we had embarked upon, one that was just beginning under the soft glow of the dance hall lights.

As the melody enveloped us, a harsh sound pierced the

tranquility of the dance floor—shouting. I instinctively turned toward the source, releasing Naya's hand to allow her to see the unfolding drama.

Kai was at the center of the commotion, his grip tight around Leana's wrist, pulling her across the dance floor with an aggressive disregard. Tyran was right on their heels, his concern evident in his quick steps.

Suddenly, Leana's voice cut through the noise as she shouted something indiscernible, yanking her arm free from Kai's hold with fierce determination. In a reflexive and shocking response, Kai spun around and backhanded her, sending her tumbling to the ground.

I hadn't fully registered the motion, before finding myself standing between Kai and Tyran, one hand pressing against Tyran's chest to hold him back, while my other hand was unexpectedly holding Kai up by his collar, suspended in the air.

I turned to Tyran, my voice steady, "Forget him, see to Leana."

Tyran, his anger clear but controlled, pointed a finger at Kai. "I'll see that you pay for that," he spat before turning his attention to Leana, crouching down to offer her assistance.

Surrounded by the sudden commotion, my calmness surprised me. I took a moment to look around and noticed Veyra, Joren, and Naya had quickly formed a protective circle around us, their focus sharp on Kai. They were tense, clearly ready to step in if the situation escalated. Their unified stance was a clear sign of their readiness to protect one of their own, showing strong support without hesitation.

"Put me down right now!" Kai's demand sliced through the tension.

"Do what he says, Liam." Turning, I saw Eulis standing beside us, his white suit blending with his white hair, embodying the calm authority he was known for. "He's made no friends in this exam. One of you will have your chance tomorrow."

Without a word, I released my grip, and Kai awkwardly caught himself, barely avoiding a fall. He stepped threateningly close, but I remained unshaken, meeting his glare with a steady gaze. It was then that Eulis intervened, his hand landing firmly on Kai's shoulder. "Don't be an idiot, boy. I think you're done for the day."

Kai's eyes remained locked on mine. "Filthy Lylackians," he spat.

In an instant, the two of them vanished, leaving a ripple of whispers in their wake. I couldn't help but smile, curious about where Eulis might have taken Kai.

Turning back to Naya, I draped an arm around her shoulders. "Thanks for having my back," I said, gratitude warming my words. My gaze then swept to Joren and Veyra. "Same for you two." It was then I noticed their intertwined hands, and offered a smile.

As I scanned the room for Leana, I saw her being gently guided to our table by Tyran. Making my way over, I noticed that our group had grown: Lammat was still in his seat, but now Calia had joined him, her dress a deep shade of dark orange that complemented her fiery red hair perfectly, adding a warm glow to our corner of the room.

"Thanks for looking after the table," I said to Lammat as I approached.

He rolled his eyes in mock frustration. "Last time I do that for you! I missed out on all the fun!"

"You okay, Leana?" asked Naya, gently.

Leana managed a nod, her expression still a bit shaken but grateful for the concern.

"What happened?" I asked.

Tyran answered, his voice carrying a hint of frustration. "He didn't like me dancing with her," he said, nodding towards Leana.

The table fell into a thoughtful silence. It was Calia who broke the quiet, her curiosity piqued. "Why would he react like that? Just for dancing?"

"Kai? The boy's insane," answered Lammat.

The conversation meandered, with each of us chipping in our thoughts and feelings about what had transpired. Despite the tense start, our collective resilience turned the conversation towards lighter topics, gradually restoring a sense of normalcy.

Eventually, Lammat suggested a change of pace. "You lot should head back to the dance floor. This might be the last time you're all together like this."

The suggestion was met with nods of agreement. Veyra and Joren paired off, a silent understanding between them. Tyran offered his hand to Leana, a protective gesture that she accepted with a small smile. I reached for Naya's hand, eager to return to the dance and the promise of the evening before us.

Lammat found himself being playfully dragged onto the dance floor by Calia. Her vibrant energy and his reluctant amusement were a sight to behold as they joined the rest of us.

The arrival of Joren and Calia's parents added an unexpected warmth to the evening. Merchants by trade, they had woven their way through the vast expanses of Lylackia, making a rare stop to spend time with their children. Glancing around, I couldn't help but notice the room had filled with a mix of generations, all basking in the gentle buzz of conversation and anticipation for the morrow's festivities.

A ripple of amusement spread among us as Joren, with an eagerness that bordered on insistence, coaxed Veyra from her perch. Despite our collective tension over the bold move, Veyra's response was nothing short of graceful, her greeting to his parents brimming with warmth.

Later, Joren guided his parents through the gathering to where I stood. The introduction was laced with mystery, as he implored them to take a good look at me, hinting at a shared future to which only he held the key.

As the music enveloped us once more, the night seemed to reclaim its magic, transforming the earlier altercation into a distant memory. Surrounded by friends, the evening blossomed into a vibrant celebration of our connections and the collective strength we had discovered within each other. It was indeed a night to remember, a testament to the bonds we had forged and the shared journey that had brought us to this pivotal moment.

However, the reality of the exam's rules soon loomed over us, dictating that examinees and guests were to be separated. Leana, Lammat, Tyran, Veyra, and I, having all navigated the challenges of the exam together, found ourselves in a rare moment of unity, sharing the same room.

Before we settled into our shared quarters for the night, the time came for farewells, a moment made poignant by the understanding that Joren, Calia, and Naya, who had to leave, would be missed. Joren and Veyra, in particular, seemed to struggle with their goodbye, their connection making the separation harder to bear.

Amidst this, my goodbye to Naya was laden with an unspoken depth, our hug lingering, a silent promise hanging between us. Letting go was a challenge, underscored by the absurdity of our imminent reunion during tomorrow's final exam. Yet, as we each embraced in turn, the solidity of our friendships offered a soothing balm against the sting of temporary separation.

With that, we turned in for the night. The shared space became a quiet reflection of the day's events and the connections that had grown stronger among us. It was a fitting end to a day filled with both trials and triumphs, leaving Kai and any lingering tensions far behind us.

CHAPTER FORTY
The Final Exam

Walking down the long stone corridor, a bright light at its end beckoned me forward. Around me, the air was filled with a rhythmic beat—two small thuds followed by one large thud. Bang bang boom! The sound echoed off the walls, both ominous and exhilarating.

Beside me, Lammat kept pace. "What a sound, right?" he remarked, a hint of anticipation in his voice.

"What is it?" I asked, drawn in by the unfamiliar rhythm.

"Our audience," he replied, a smile in his voice.

As we continued, the corridor opened up into a vast space that took my breath away. Before us lay a fighting arena, grand and alive with the anticipation of the crowd. It was a circular coliseum, its staggered seating rising into the shadows, packed with hundreds of spectators whose cheers filled the air as we emerged.

At the heart of the vast arena stood the imposing fighting platform, a massive square stage spanning nearly one hundred paces in each direction. Its surface, a meticulously arranged mosaic of immense concrete blocks, exuded an aura of implacable solidity against the backdrop of the circular seating tiers that surrounded it. A narrow walkway encircled the elevated platform, separating it from the spectator stands.

At each corner of this platform stood a hooded Eulis, garbed in green and facing the center of the arena. Their presence, silent yet imposing, added an air of solemnity to the charged atmosphere.

Standing at the edge of the central platform, I took a moment to absorb the scene. The roar of the crowd, the imposing structure of the fighting platform, and the vigilant watch of the hooded Eulis combined into a moment I knew I would never forget. It was here, in this arena, that courage, skill, and determination would be tested under the watchful eyes of hundreds.

Although I was told I had already passed due to my transformation, a bigger test awaited me. I needed to prove to the citizens of Lylackia that I was capable. I had to prove to them that I was a Goud. That I was a King.

As I was soaking in the atmosphere of the arena, Veyra suddenly spun around me, her movements graceful and deliberate. She took my arms, guiding me to turn toward a specific section of the crowded stands. "Look," she whispered, her excitement barely contained.

Following her gaze, my eyes found Naya, Joren, and Calia among the sea of faces. Their presence sparked a surge of warmth within me, and together, Veyra and I waved enthusiastically, our spirits lifted by the sight of our friends.

Just then, a voice emerged close to my ear, pulling my attention away from the stands. Turning, I found myself face-to-face with Kai. "Who are you looking to fight?" he asked, his tone casual, almost indifferent.

I studied him for a moment, taking in every detail—from his black hair, and the depth of his brown eyes, to the green vines that always seemed to embrace him.

"You're the only one I'm yet to fight," I finally said, my voice steady, despite the whirlwind of thoughts racing through my mind.

"That would be a waste of both our time," Kai retorted quickly, a flicker of resignation in his eyes. "We both know I wouldn't beat you."

I paused, considering his words. "For what it's worth, I

wish you luck. If we do need to fight, let's both give it everything we've got."

"Are you Lylackians always this self-righteous?" He couldn't help but smile, though it appeared to be tinged with disappointment.

I laughed softly, the tension between us lightening. "I keep forgetting you're not from around here. Tal-Set Elemental, right?"

At that, Kai's smile vanished as quickly as it had appeared. "Right," he said, his voice carrying a mix of emotions before he turned and walked away, leaving me to ponder the encounter.

The air in the arena seemed to thicken with anticipation as the Minor, Eulis, and Goud examiners from the prior rounds, stepped into view. Their entrance was not just a mere arrival; it was a proclamation, a heralding of the culmination of all our efforts and trials. The Minor, with a presence that commanded attention, gestured expansively towards us, a clear signal that the moment we had all been waiting for, and perhaps dreading, had finally arrived. It was time for the six of us, the remaining contenders, to take our places on the central stage, the arena of our final challenge.

We moved almost in sync, propelled by a mixture of adrenaline and resolve. Each of us took that leap onto the raised platform, an ascent that felt like crossing an invisible threshold from the ordinary into the realm of the extraordinary. As we gathered atop the stage, we instinctively formed a line, our positions marking the beginning of the final act in this rigorous examination.

Stationed between Lammat and Leana, I could feel the pulse of shared determination vibrating through us. Lammat, though outwardly calm, had a look of focused intensity, his eyes scanning the crowd. Leana, for her part, appeared nervous, frequently playing with her hands. The contrast between them, between all of us, was a vivid reminder of the diverse paths that had led us here, to this point of convergence.

It was as if the air itself was charged with the collective hopes, fears, and dreams of not just us, the examinees, but also of the spectators who filled the stands, their eager faces a sea of anticipation. This wasn't just another test; it was the definitive trial, one that would demand everything we had to give and perhaps a little more. The realization that every step, every decision from here on out, would be scrutinized, magnified the gravity of the situation, binding us together in silent solidarity as we awaited the commencement of the final ordeal.

Lammat leaned closer, his voice barely above a whisper. "There are more eyes here than I expected. You can't risk healing."

I frowned, the concern evident in my voice. "What if I get hit? I can't just turn it on and off like a switch."

His gaze swept over the crowd, assessing. "If a single Crosser manages to copy that ability, we're all in trouble."

The mention of Crossers sent a shiver down my spine. "You think there are Crossers here?"

"I'd stake my life on it," Lammat said, his tone grave. "Where better to learn spells than in an exam designed to show them off?"

A cold fear took hold of me. Every spell I cast, every technique I revealed on this stage, could potentially arm an enemy with new capabilities.

"Hey!" Leana's voice cut through my preoccupation with the crowd.

"Hi," I responded, briefly pausing my futile attempt at scanning for potential Crossers among the sea of dark-haired spectators. I had lost count well beyond twenty.

Leana chuckled, her laughter light and easing the tension for a moment. "You look more worried about this exam than you did for the second one." Her hand found my shoulder, a comforting weight. "This will be easy for you."

Just then, the Minor examiner stretched his arms out

before speaking. His voice filled the arena, commanding, loud, and clearly magically enhanced. "Fellow Lylackians! Welcome to the 70th annual Crest exam."

The response from the crowd was electric, a wave of cheers and applause washing over us. My eyes caught Naya in the throng, standing and waving energetically at me. Her enthusiasm was infectious, drawing a smile from me despite the nerves.

The Minor examiner pressed on, "Although this year's final will be smaller than most, it's sure to be thrilling!"

At that moment, the Eulis examiner snapped his fingers, and, with a flourish, a silver bowl materialized at his feet.

"Guess you just learned a new spell," Lammat muttered beside me. "See what I mean? A Eulis examiner should be smarter than revealing magic like that."

The Eulis lifted the bowl for all to see. "In this bowl," he announced in an equally booming voice, turning towards us, "are orbs that will determine who will be competing against whom."

"Before we choose our first two fighters, I'll explain the rules," announced the Minor examiner, his voice echoing across the arena, ensuring every ear was tuned to his words. The air hung heavy with anticipation as he began.

"One. Fights will be exclusively one-on-one," he declared, emphasizing the personal duel nature of the upcoming confrontations. The notion filled me with a stark realization of the isolation within the ring—just me against another, in front of all these people.

"Two. There are three paths to victory: surrender, being forced out of the ring, or death. If you're in danger of dying, I urge you to surrender or exit the ring. While taking a life is permitted, should your opponent be incapacitated, you should eject them from the ring to secure your win." The severity of these options weighed heavily on me. The allowance for death underscored the brutal reality of what we were stepping into.

He took a moment to let the information sink in before

continuing. "Three. Weapons are allowed. Should your style of combat include weapons, you are welcome to use them." I wasn't aware of anyone using weapons, but the idea of being cut by daggers immediately worried me.

"Four. All magic is permitted. We have protective barriers around the stage to shield the spectators from any mana attacks. This is your chance to showcase the full extent of your capabilities." Normally, this would be where I'd feel at ease, ready to display the breadth of my magical skills. However, the fear of revealing too much, of a potential Crosser in the audience learning and copying my abilities, left me questioning how much I dared to use.

"And five," he concluded, "there will be no time limit. Battles will last until a clear victor emerges." This was the only rule that didn't immediately send a wave of panic through me. Perhaps endurance could be my ally if I played my cards right.

"Remember, it's entirely possible to win the battle but fail the exam. Saying that, it's also possible to lose the battle, yet still pass." He gestured towards the crowd, "Impress them, and you'll soon be in the faction of your choosing." With a final clap of his hands, he signaled the end of the briefing. "And now, with that out of the way, let's find out who our first combatants are."

The anticipation in the air thickened as the Goud examiner stepped forward, his hand delving into the silver bowl. Our eyes met for a fleeting moment; his nod and smile felt like a silent encouragement. He withdrew a golden sphere, lifting it high for all to see before making a show of presenting it to the audience. Their attention was rapt, a collective breath held in anticipation.

"They certainly drag this out, don't they?" Lammat's mutter broke the tense silence between us, a momentary distraction from the suspense.

Without warning, the Goud tossed the sphere into the air. It soared, striking the ceiling, and shattered into hundreds of sparks of golden light. The spectacle was mesmerizing, the fragments of light dancing in the air before they began to coalesce, merging back together in a display of magical prowess to form a familiar face—Lammat's.

"Kinda wish they dragged it out a little longer, now," he lamented, a note of resignation in his voice as his shoulders slumped.

"Looking good!" Leana chimed in, craning her neck to get a better view past me, her tone light and teasing.

"I look forward to seeing your giant head up there next to mine," Lammat shot back, though his gaze remained fixated on the magical visage above.

The Goud examiner delved into the bowl once more, and I couldn't help but think that facing off against Lammat might be in my favor. He knew me well enough to avoid causing serious injury, and given our mutual concern about revealing too much to potential Crossers, he'd likely stick to physical combat.

The crowd's anticipation built into a tangible hum, growing louder as the Goud retrieved another sphere and displayed it. The noise reached a peak, exploding into cheers as he threw the sphere upward, where it shattered against the ceiling. Sparkling fragments danced in the air before coalescing into the face of Veyra, her image now floating beside Lammat's, overseeing the arena.

"Figures I'd end up going against the only person who can beat Liam," Veyra quipped from her spot in line, her voice carrying jest and challenge. "I'm going to love this!"

"We have our first match! Please will the other examinees step off the stage," announced the examiner. As they led the way, we began to file off, leaving Lammat and Veyra alone in the spotlight.

Just as I started to move, Lammat grabbed my arm, pulling me close enough to whisper. "Liam, during your match, just transform then walk off the stage. That'll be all you need to pass." His advice, quick and clandestine, offered an unexpected yet intriguing strategy.

With a nod of understanding, I stepped away, trailing behind Kai. As I passed Veyra on my way off the stage, I couldn't resist emulating her signature move, playfully punching her in the shoulder. "Have fun!" I said, injecting a bit of levity into the moment.

She returned the gesture with a wide grin. "Easy."

When I reached the edge of the stage, my gaze briefly met that of one of the Eulis stationed at the corner. Though his eyes were hidden, I sensed our gazes lock. Offering a small smile, I jumped down to the lower level.

The necessity of having four Eulis' around the arena piqued my curiosity, a thought that was still on my mind when Leana landed beside me. In response, the Eulis' arms lifted in unison, and a shimmering green barrier sprang to life, encircling the stage.

I stepped aside for a clearer view, assuming that all four were responsible for this impressive mana shield.

"What are they doing?" Leana's question broke my contemplation.

Tyran, who had approached to watch the spectacle, explained, "Those are mana shields. They're designed to allow physical objects through but block any mana-based attacks, protecting the spectators. Looks like each Eulis is maintaining one shield while strengthening another."

"Wouldn't that need a lot of mana?" I wondered aloud.

"Absolutely," Tyran confirmed. "These Eulis' are among the most powerful. Their ability to conjure and sustain these shields speaks volumes of their mastery over mana."

"Come on, you can't see from down there," the Goud examiner remarked, his voice pulling me from my thoughts as he began to ascend some stairs nestled among the crowd. We followed his lead to a small, empty row of seats on the lower level, taking our places with a clear view of the arena. I found myself seated between Kai and Leana, the three of us among the spectators now, our roles momentarily shifted from participants to observers.

The crowd's enthusiasm didn't wane; their cheers and applause crescendoed as Lammat and Veyra took their positions in the center of the stage. Each received a respectful hand on their shoulder.

"Don't go easy on me, alright?" Veyra's voice, amplified and echoing through the arena, broke through the din. Realizing her words were broadcasted for all to hear, she quickly covered her mouth, her eyes scanning the crowd in surprise. "Wait, can I hear myself? Can they hear me?"

"Looks like it," came Lammat's resonant reply, his voice also echoing around us.

"Right… Oh, well." Veyra shrugged off the mishap and turned her attention to a specific section of the crowd. "Hey, Joren! You'd better be cheering for me!" she shouted with confidence.

Joren's response, though unamplified and faint from our distance, carried the warmth of their bond. "You're probably going to lose, but I love you anyway!" he called out, standing and waving in support.

Veyra, unable to catch his words, simply blew him a kiss before refocusing on Lammat. "Alright, ready when you are."

"I'm always ready," Lammat responded, though his gaze lingered on the crowd for a moment longer before settling on Veyra.

The tension in the arena spiked as the Minor's voice cut through the anticipation. "Let match one, begin!"

Both stood still, simply watching each other, before Lammat began to tilt and topple to the side. Suddenly, just as though it looked like he was about to fall over, his image streaked, and he transitioned to pure speed. Lammat, now little more than a blur started to circle. "Come on, Veyra, you not going to strike?" His voice, laced with challenge, echoed across the arena.

"You're running in circles. It's too easy to predict," Veyra replied calmly, her voice steady despite the whirlwind around her.

"Good point," Lammat conceded, and almost instantly, his movements became erratic, zigzagging across the floor in a pattern that defied prediction.

"I can't even track him from back here," Leana admitted, concern edging her voice. "I'm only catching glimpses, but it's like there are multiple of him down there."

"No," Tyran interjected, his analysis cutting through the confusion. "There's just the one. He's just retracing his steps, creating afterimages."

Curious, I turned to Kai. "Are you able to track him?" But he remained silent, his attention wholly absorbed by the spectacle, his eyes darting back and forth in an attempt to keep up.

"Do you think Veyra can see him?" Leana's question hung in the air, ripe with anticipation.

In a moment that felt like a direct response, Veyra surged into action. She dashed forward with astonishing speed, launching a powerful kick. But Lammat dipped low, attempting to grasp her standing leg, only for Veyra to deftly lift it, spinning away from his reach with grace.

The moment her feet met the floor, Veyra also turned into a blur, mirroring Lammat's movements. She darted across the arena, her movements creating a dizzying spectacle that rivaled Lammat's own display.

"Woah!" I said. "When did she get that fast?"

"Yesterday," Tyran replied simply, a smile on his face.

The crowd erupted in cheers and gasps, thoroughly captivated by the exchange. The match had transformed into a mesmerizing dance of speed, strategy, and agility, with Lammat and Veyra pushing each other to the limits of their abilities. As they moved, they blurred the line between combat and art, their duel a testament to the depth of their skill and the intensity of their training.

Suddenly, everything halted as quickly as it had begun. Lammat stood still in the center, his stance relaxed, with his arms hanging loosely by his sides and his head bowed.

Behind him, Veyra had one hand gently placed around his neck. A brief flicker of confusion crossed her face as she glanced around at the audience and then noticed me. "Guess you didn't tell him after all," she commented.

Circling Lammat, Veyra crouched to inspect him closer. After a moment of contemplation, she again looked my way, an expression of uncertainty shaping her features. "Uhh…"

The realization hit me, and I laughed, understanding the clever tactic Veyra had employed. She had put Lammat to sleep, a technique she hadn't utilized during their last encounter in the third exam. It was a move so unexpected that Lammat was completely unprepared for it.

Effortlessly, Veyra lifted Lammat onto her shoulder and carried him to the edge of the stage. With great care, she then removed him from the platform, gently lowering him to the ground.

"Veyra wins the first match!" the Minor examiner's voice boomed across the arena, declaring the outcome of their bout.

Without wasting a moment, Veyra jumped down, positioning herself between Lammat and the stage and sitting him up to face her, swiftly waking him with a few light slaps to his face.

As this unfolded, the Minor and Eulis Examiners reclaimed the center stage, preparing for the next match. From my position, I couldn't see Lammat's reaction as he came to, but I imagined Veyra, with her voice no longer amplified, likely teasing him about her victory. With no fighting taking place on the stage, the Eulis' lowered their arms, dropping the four shields.

"Congratulations, Veyra!" the Minor exclaimed, his voice echoing with genuine admiration through the arena. Meanwhile, the Eulis, still holding the silver bowl, reached inside to select the next sphere, signaling the continuation of the ceremony. "We will now determine the final two battles. Our first combatant will be…"

My gaze shifted between Kai, Leana, and Tyran,

contemplating which of them I might prefer as my opponent. Kai's approach would likely be aggressive, aiming for a quick incapacitation. Leana remained somewhat of an enigma, her capabilities and strategies less known to me. And Tyran, after his extended period in the dream world, was a wildcard. His skills could have evolved in unpredictable ways, much as Veyra's speed had impressively increased. What secrets had he unlocked during his time away?

The sound of shattering glass drew my attention upwards. The ceiling was aglow with scattering golden light, yet, as the fragments began to coalesce once more, a sense of excitement bubbled within me. I couldn't help but grin at the sight of my own enlarged visage looking down upon the arena.

CHAPTER FORTY-ONE
The Echoes of Power

"Vodshkri'kav…" Leana's whisper, barely audible, caught my attention as we both gazed at our faces projected onto the ceiling.

"What was that?" I asked, curious at the unfamiliar words.

"Old family saying," she replied with a muttered breath, her eyes not leaving the giant visages above us. "Basically means… damn."

My attention shifted as the Minor examiner gestured toward us, signaling it was our turn. "Come on, looks like they want us now," I noted, feeling anticipation and apprehension for what was to come.

As we descended the small set of stairs leading to the arena, Leana threw a playful glance over her shoulder. "Go easy on me, will you?"

The irony of her request sparked a brief laugh between us. "I was going to ask you the same thing," I admitted, though my tone carried a hint of seriousness. Catching up to her, I placed a gentle hand on her shoulder, stopping her in her tracks. "I'm not joking," I confessed, my voice tinged with unease. "I… sort of… can't risk taking any damage in our fight."

"What?"

"So my only options are for you to agree to not damage me, or for me to go all out to end the fight as quickly as possible," I explained, laying out the stark choices before us.

Leana faced me, stepping closer, her expression a mixture of apology and determination. "I'm sorry, Liam, I really am, but I need to pass this exam." Her gaze drifted past me to Kai, who was watching silently. "Something tells me he isn't going to be able to beat Tyran, and he's going to look like an idiot trying, so that just leaves me."

"So you're going to try to beat me?"

She shrugged. "I don't have a choice."

The weight of her words settled between us, heavy with the implication of what was to come. "One minute," I offered, a compromise that felt both risky and necessary.

"One… what?"

"I'll give you one minute, but that's all I can risk. Come at me with everything you have, but after that minute, I'll end the match." My declaration hung in the air.

"You don't think I can beat you before the first minute?"

"Honestly, no, but that's all I can give you." My response was straightforward, rooted in the stark reality of my situation rather than any desire to belittle her capabilities.

"Not sure I like this arrogant side of you, Liam," she retorted, the lightness in her demeanor fading.

"I'm sorry… but after one minute, you'll understand that it's not meant as arrogance." My words were an attempt to convey the urgency and necessity of my strategy, not to boast.

"Right…" Skepticism laced Leana's voice, but she didn't dwell on our exchange for long. Instead, she launched into a backflip, a fluid motion that saw her transitioning mid-air into a cartwheel. Her hands found purchase on the edge of the arena's platform, about two meters above us, supporting her entire body for a brief, breathtaking moment before she completed the rotation and landed gracefully on her feet atop the platform. Her grin, wide and confident, was a silent but eloquent declaration of her readiness and agility.

I couldn't help but roll my eyes at our contrasting approaches—hers, elegant and showy; mine, dictated by the limitations I faced. As much wanted to copy Joren and fly up onto the stage, I knew my constraints all too well. With a resigned sigh, I opted for a straightforward jump, vaulting over Leana and landing squarely in the center of the platform, ready to face whatever came next.

"Our second match will be Liam versus Leana," the Minor announced, his voice resonating with authority. "Examinees, are you ready?"

"Sure," came my terse reply.

"Ready," Leana said, her tone firm and determined.

"Then let match two… BEGIN!"

As the word "BEGIN" echoed through the arena, I steeled myself for the minute ahead, aware that every second would count. The challenge wasn't just about facing Leana; it was about navigating the fine line between demonstrating my skills and protecting the secrets that could not be exposed. The battle ahead promised to be as much a test of strategy and restraint as it was of combat prowess.

"Sixty…" Leana wasted no time. She swept her hand through the air, summoning a series of energy balls that hovered menacingly before they shot toward me in unison. I dropped into a backbend, feeling the rush of air as the orbs passed inches above me. My hair grazed the floor, a physical reminder of how close the attack was. With a swift motion, I was back on my feet, eyes locked on Leana, ready for her next move.

"Fifty…" Her attacks grew more aggressive. This time, Leana conjured a wave of energy, sending it crashing towards me like a tidal wave. I had to sprint, circling the perimeter of the platform, using every bit of my physical agility to stay ahead of the onslaught.

"Forty…" The intensity in Leana's eyes was unmistakable. She launched a volley of sharp energy projectiles, their speed and precision forcing me into a series of rapid, evasive maneuvers. Each leap and dodge was a desperate bid to stay unharmed.

"Thirty…" She created a massive energy construct, a beast that roared and charged at me. Without magic as an option, I relied on sheer speed, darting away at the last possible moment, feeling the heat of the creature's energy as it exploded against the green energy walls, the force of the impact a testament to Leana's growing frustration.

"Twenty…" The attacks became a blur of motion and energy, Leana throwing everything she had at me. An onslaught of energy blasts rained down, each explosion rocking the platform. I was running, jumping, barely keeping ahead of the devastation, each explosion lighting up the arena as they collided with the Eulis' barriers.

"Ten…" The final countdown began just as Leana unleashed her most powerful attack yet, a concentrated beam of energy that seemed to cut through the air itself. With no options left, I threw myself to the ground, the beam passing so close I could feel its heat. As it struck the barrier, the arena was illuminated in a blinding flash of light.

"Zero…"

I tapped into the core of my power, feeling it stir like a hurricane bound within the confines of my soul. As I released this force, blue energy erupted from me, not just as a glow but as a tempest, a wild, swirling vortex of power that radiated outward with ferocious intensity.

The air around me transformed, whipped into a frenzy as the energy expanded. My clothes and hair were caught in the tumultuous wind, flapping and twisting as if caught in the grip of a relentless gale. The ground beneath my feet seemed to tremble with the sheer force of the unleashed power. Debris began to rise, chunks of concrete caught up within the energy itself. This wasn't just a display of energy; it was a declaration, a manifestation of my will made visible in the swirling chaos of wind and light that surrounded me.

Leana, amid this chaos, attempted to resist the gale-force winds that I had summoned. She clawed at the ground, her efforts to anchor herself a testament to her resolve. But the power was relentless, prying her free from her grip and propelling her towards the edge of the arena.

The moment she was caught by the tempest and began to be forcefully expelled from the ring, passing through the green energy barrier with an explosive burst of light, I realized the potential consequences of my actions. Without hesitation, I propelled myself after her, moving with a speed and urgency I hadn't known I possessed.

Catching Leana in midair was instinctual; ensuring her safety, my only priority. As we hurtled towards the stone stairs just beyond the barrier, I positioned myself to absorb the impact. My feet hit the stone steps with precision, the force of our descent causing the stone beneath us to crack under the impact.

With Leana still in my arms, I carefully set her down on solid ground, away from the damaged steps. The violent storm of blue energy that had raged around me dissipated, leaving behind a sudden, stark calm. The air, once charged with the raw force of my transformation, now lay quiet, as if holding its breath in the aftermath of our dramatic descent.

"So, it turns out I didn't have a chance after all," she admitted. Her hand reached out, touching my blue hair that still whispered with the remnants of the storm's energy. "I like it."

Shaking my head slightly, I let the transformation fully recede, feeling the extraordinary power ebb away as if it were a tide going out. The cracked stairs beneath our feet served as a physical reminder of the intensity of the moment we had shared.

"Wow! Did... anyone catch what happened?" The Minor Examiner's voice echoed with a mix of astonishment and curiosity, momentarily silencing the murmurs of the crowd. The Goud Examiner approached him, leaning in to whisper something, then retreated to his seat with a nod.

"It appears that our winner is Liam, but not only that, he is the first guaranteed to pass due to a NATURAL transformation!" The announcement sent a ripple of gasps, mutterings, and a smattering of applause through the audience. "That's right, this marks the first natural transformation in years. Congratulations, Son!"

A wave of loud cheers filled the arena, and I glanced up to see Naya, Joren, and Calia on their feet, their faces alight with excitement and pride. With the match behind me, I gestured for Leana to follow, and we made our way over to join our friends.

As we approached, some spectators slid further down the seating, making room for the two of us.

"When did you transform?" Joren asked, his voice brimming with excitement.

"A couple of days ago," I replied. "Back in the gravity room."

"They have a gravity room here?" Calia echoed, her surprise momentarily overtaking her. "Oh, also, congrats on your win," she added quickly, her tone sincere.

"You were amazing, Leana!" Naya exclaimed, standing up to give her a small hug as we took our seats.

"Thanks!" Leana responded, her smile bright. "I'm glad I wasn't the only one who didn't know Liam could transform."

"Why didn't you just transform then forfeit?" Joren's question cut through the celebratory atmosphere. "That way, you'd have passed, and Leana would have won."

I shook my head, reflecting on my decision. "Originally that's what I was going to do, but I didn't think it was fair on Leana. I saw her fight in the third exam, and she deserved to showcase her skills."

"That's why you gave me a minute?" Leana's voice was tinged with realization, looking for confirmation.

I shrugged, a gesture that conveyed my intentions without the need for many words. "I didn't mean for it to be mere charity." The minute was my way of balancing the scales, giving her a fighting chance while still adhering to the constraints of my situation.

"No, I'm not upset. I appreciate it. Now at least there's a

chance I will also pass," Leana responded, her tone laced with gratitude and a newfound determination.

"With how few finalists there are this year, I feel you're almost guaranteed to pass," I added, trying to bolster her spirits with a dose of optimism.

"I hope so…" Leana's voice trailed off, her eyes fixed on a distant point as she seemed to contemplate the possibilities that lay ahead.

"Finally, our last match of today's event. Tyran versus Kai. Will our two combatants please step onto the stage?" The Minor's announcement redirected everyone's attention to the impending showdown.

"Anyone know where Veyra is?" Joren's inquiry pulled me from the anticipation of the next match. I glanced around, my eyes quickly locating Veyra and Lammat engaged in a deep conversation, seated close together in the lower levels. "Down there, with Lammat," I pointed them out.

"Can you believe she beat him?" Naya's question was laced with surprise and admiration. "Did he let her win?"

I shook my head, dispelling the notion. "I don't know, I don't think so. I never told him about her ability to put people to sleep." Still, it was true; Lammat's defeat was as much a surprise to me as it was to everyone else.

"That's my girl!" Joren couldn't contain his excitement. "I knew she'd have a plan put aside for him. I wondered why she didn't use it in the third round."

"Honestly, I'd kind of forgotten about it," I admitted, a sheepish grin crossing my face as I rubbed the back of my head.

Amid our conversation, Kai's voice cut through the arena, bold and confident. "I'm going to look forward to this."

Our attention snapped to the stage, where Tyran responded to Kai's grandstanding with a mix of amusement and exasperation. "Showing off for the crowd? Really?" He gestured towards the seats where they had been sitting together moments before. "I've been sat with you for ages! You wanted to wait until your voice was amped first?" His shrug was theatrical, dismissive of Kai's antics.

Leana's reaction was immediate; she buried her face in her hands, her voice muffled but clear. "Idiot," she muttered.

"How do you know him?" Naya asked, bluntly.

Leana seemed momentarily taken aback before answering Naya's question. "He's my brother."

"Oh gods," Calia chimed in, her voice tinged with sympathetic humor. "Brothers are the worst."

Leana's laughter, light and genuine, filled the space between us. "They can be, yeah." Her words, shared in camaraderie, underscored the complex web of relationships that intertwined through our shared experiences. It offered a moment of levity before the tension of the final match resumed its grip on the arena.

"BEGIN!" The Examiner's command reverberated through the arena, drawing all eyes to the central platform where Kai and Tyran stood ready.

Without a moment's hesitation, both combatants moved in unison, their fists crashing down into the concrete, a testament to their power as the ground beneath them shattered. Kai made the first move, swiftly pulling out two rocks and hurling them forwards. Tyran was already two steps ahead. He tore up an entire slab from the platform, wielding it both as a shield to deflect Kai's initial assault and then as a weapon, hurling it like a giant blade straight back at Kai.

The slab spun through the air, a deadly projectile on a collision course with Kai. Yet, at the last possible moment, a large, thick root erupted from the ground in front of Kai, catching the slab with a flexibility that belied its strength. With a deft side-step, Kai avoided the counterattack as the root swung the slab back towards Tyran with a forceful whip.

Tyran's attempt to dodge was thwarted by an ambush of small roots bursting from the ground, ensnaring his movements. He dodged most, but one managed to latch onto his leg.

"Oh no!" Naya's exclamation was filled with concern as

she squeezed my hand tightly.

With a swift motion, Tyran extended his arm, and the air before him shimmered with energy. The slab split in two, narrowly missing him as he executed a backbend, mirroring my own dodge from earlier. The top half whisked over his nose, the bottom half grazing the ground beneath him.

"Gods, that was close!" Joren's voice was a mixture of awe and relief.

Tyran quickly aimed two fingers at his ankle, flicking them in an attempt to cut free from the small root. Despite the air shimmering with his effort, the vine remained stubbornly intact, tripping him as he tried to step away.

"Not going to be that easy," Kai declared, a hint of determination in his voice.

Undeterred, Tyran launched a series of energy balls across the platform. Kai navigated the barrage with impressive agility, his movements a dance of avoidance. Yet Tyran was not finished. Clasping his wrist, he unleashed a powerful beam of white light, targeting Kai directly.

Kai responded just in time, crouching low as three thick roots burst forth, further ravaging the already torn concrete. The beam hit the roots squarely, causing them to shudder under the intense energy, yet they held firm, protecting Kai from the brunt of the attack.

The roots that had shielded Kai slowly receded into the ground, revealing him standing upright, arms folded across his chest with an air of finality. "That's this fight over," he declared, his voice ringing with confidence.

"What? What happened?" Calia's confusion mirrored the growing uncertainty among us.

Joren's response was a quiet shake of his head, directing our attention back to the platform. "Look at Tyran."

"What are those?" Naya's question hung in the air as we all focused on the scene unfolding before us.

Tyran appeared trapped, a network of tiny roots ensnaring his entire body. His legs were rooted to the floor, immobilizing him completely. To our astonishment, the energy beam he had unleashed seemed to have backfired, with the roots taking advantage of the moment to bind his arms together as well. Despite Tyran's visible efforts, straining against the bindings, the roots held fast, unyielding.

"What's going on?" I couldn't help but voice the question that I felt lingered in all our minds. "Why can't he free himself?"

"I… don't know…" Joren's reply came.

Kai's laughter cut through the tension, a sound of triumph and vindication. "I've been looking for a chance at revenge ever since you knocked me out in the first exam." His words revealed a depth of planning and patience, a long-held grudge that had found its moment of retribution.

"Just take the win, Kai," Leana whispered under her breath, her hands pressed together, her eyes shut tight.

"What are these things?" Tyran's voice, filled with confusion and frustration, echoed off the arena walls, his gaze fixed on Kai for an explanation.

Kai paused, a brief moment of contemplation crossing his features before he responded. Leana's lips continued moving silently. "Nah, sorry, I'll have to keep that a secret I'm afraid," he finally said.

Leana exhaled a sigh of relief at his response, a subtle tension leaving her body.

"Leana?" I turned to her, puzzled by her reaction. "What's going on?"

She jumped slightly, leaning away, caught off guard by my question. "The rules say we're allowed to use weapons, right?" Her response seemed tangential, yet laden with unspoken implications.

"What are they?" I pressed, seeking clarity.

"I… I can't tell you…"

Meanwhile, Tyran made another attempt to free himself, his foot starting to drag through the concrete, pulling against the tenacious grip of the roots.

"Ah, ah ah!" Kai's admonition was playful yet firm as he quickly closed the distance between them, landing a punch directly on Tyran's nose. The sound of the impact was sharp, a clear crack that resonated through the arena. Tyran's body swayed, seemingly on the verge of falling, but the vines held him upright, a grim parody of support.

"The rules state if the opponent is immobilized, you should remove them from the ring to claim victory," the Minor Examiner interjected, his voice carrying the weight of the regulations governing their combat.

"Should!" Kai echoed with emphasis, placing both hands on his hips in a theatrical gesture. "Not must, but rather I should remove them from the ring to claim victory." His laughter filled the arena, a stark contrast to the tension of the moment. "He's immobilized right now, sure, but the moment I release him to try to move him—" In a sudden move, Tyran's arm lunged toward Kai, prompting another round of wild laughter from Kai. "See? Much easier if I just finish him off once and for all."

The arena fell into a hushed silence, punctuated only by Tyran's screams that reverberated off the walls. At that moment, driven by a sense of urgency, I stood up and leaped, landing on the lowest level with a single-minded determination.

"Umm, no interference from the audience, please!" the Minor Examiner's voice rang out.

"You think I care?" My response was blunt, fueled by the need to intervene. I charged forward, expecting to pass through the barrier, only to find it solid. Colliding with it, I slid down, landing awkwardly at the edge of the arena, right next to one of the Eulis maintaining the barrier.

Naya landed beside me, her focus immediately on the Eulis. "Drop the barrier," she demanded, her voice carrying a weight of authority.

Peering through the barrier, my attention was snared by Kai, who waved at me with a grin that bordered on the inane. It was this gesture that brought my gaze sharply to his hand. At first glance, it seemed as though incredibly thin vines were extending directly from his fingertips, an eerie sight. But a closer, more discerning look revealed the truth: these weren't emanating from his fingertips at all. Kai was donning a glove on his left hand, intricately designed to mimic the appearance of slender, living vines.

These faux vines cascaded to the ground before slithering up Tyran's body with a sinister intent. As they wrapped around him, the distinction became alarmingly clear. Unlike the natural roots I had seen many times before, these tendrils tightened with an unsettling precision, cutting into Tyran's flesh and muscle with a cold, mechanical efficiency.

Frustrated and desperate, I threw a punch against the barrier, the impact sending a ripple through the air, but the barrier held firm. The Eulis beside us chuckled at our futile efforts, unmoved by the scene unfolding before us.

"Tyran!" Veyra's voice cut through the tension, her figure visible on the opposite side of the arena, pounding her fists against the barrier in desperation. "Don't give up! Use all your mana if you have to!"

As I glanced back at Tyran, I noticed he had managed to free one of his arms, despite the deep cuts that marred its surface, bleeding profusely. With a relentless determination, he fought against his restraints, his hand moving in a blur, slicing through the air and causing faint ripples around the entangling vines.

In a burst of resolve, I shifted into a Goud and launched a fierce punch against the barrier's unyielding surface. Simultaneously, another powerful strike resonated next to mine. Turning, I saw Lammat, his stance ready for battle beside me.

Obscured partly in shadow, the Eulis cast a glance our way, his deep voice laced with irritation breaking the momentary silence. "What are you doing? The barriers are impenetrable."

"Liam, Tyran's already done an energy beam..." said Lammat.

With a nod of understanding, I watched as Lammat quickly maneuvered to the Eulis' other side. Together, we channeled our energy into beams, aiming them directly at him. "You're kidding…" he muttered under his breath.

Undeterred, I responded, "There's more than one way to cut through this barrier." To my surprise, the energy beam that began to glow in my palm now shimmered with a vibrant blue hue, contrasting starkly against its usual white.

The tense air was suddenly pierced by Tyran's cough, which morphed into a series of chuckles. "You're right, Liam… Thanks for the idea," he called out, his voice carrying a note of triumph.

Kai's laughter rang out mockingly. "You're wasting your time!" he shouted. "These vines are unbrea—"

But his taunt was cut short. Tyran's arm shot upward, and the vines loosened as if acknowledging his command. Time seemed to freeze, elongating the moment before a scream shattered the silence. I watched, stunned, as Kai's severed hand spiraled through the air.

CHAPTER FORTY-TWO
The Cost of Power

Chaos unfolded in a singular, breathless moment. Kai, in disbelief, stared at his wrist, his actions bordering on the absurd as he attempted to reattach his severed hand, his screams piercing the air.

"Fool!" The Eulis beside us erupted in fury. With a swift motion, he dispelled the barrier, his hand glowing ominously as he hurled an energy ball at Tyran. Lammat intercepted the attack, deflecting it with a mere backhand. "What do you think you're doing?" he challenged.

"Try that again, and you're dead," Lammat warned, his posture unyielding as he positioned himself protectively in front of Tyran, eyes locked on the Eulis.

"Liam, heal Kai, now!" commanded the Eulis.

"I… what?"

Suddenly, Leana brushed past, her presence a whirlwind of concern as she reached Kai. "Oh my god, Kai, you're okay, I'm here!" Her words were a mixture of reassurance and shock.

"My hand! He cut off my hand!" Kai's scream was a raw expression of betrayal and pain.

Veyra and Naya moved to Tyran's side, assessing his wounds with grave concern. "Liam, he's bleeding a lot!"

Leana's gaze snapped to another Eulis on my left, her voice rising in desperation. "We had a deal!" she exclaimed. "Get us away from here!" Acknowledging her demand with a single nod, the Eulis turned away, mirroring the actions of his counterparts at each corner.

The atmosphere tensed further as the Minor began to speak, promising calm, only for his voice to abruptly vanish. The barriers around us, once imbued with a green hue, shifted to an ominous, transparent black.

Medics, in their haste to assist, leaped onto the platform only to collide with the new barrier, their efforts silenced by the magic that contained us. Standing up, I faced them, separated by the wall. "You need to let them through," I urged.

"You're not king yet, lad," the Eulis beside me retorted, his arms lowered but leaving the barrier intact.

Confusion swirled within me as the Eulis placed a comforting hand on my shoulder before pointing towards his counterparts, assigning them their charges with a brisk efficiency that left no room for questions. "Take the royals," he instructed one. To another, "Take him and Tyran," his finger now aimed at a different corner of the space. And finally, with a gesture towards the last Eulis, "Take the girls. I have Liam."

My mind raced as I attempted to piece together their intentions. "Wait, where are you taking us? To a medic?" I asked, the words barely leaving my lips before the Eulis' sprang into action, swiftly approaching their designated targets. A twinge of unease settled in as I observed the first Eulis firmly grasp Leana and Kai. 'Royals?'

"A medic?" The Eulis echoed my question, his tone dripping with a mixture of amusement and disdain. Around me, the world began to shift, people disappearing as if swallowed by the ground itself. A cacophony of thuds and desperate fists pummeling the barrier filled the air, beams of light assaulting the invisible walls from all angles. The air was thick with confusion and aggression. "No, Liam. Why would we need a medic, when we have you?"

Before I could process his cryptic words, reality seemed to fold in on itself, the arena's vivid chaos replaced by the oppressive darkness of a large, stone chamber. Kai's groans, distant yet piercing, were the only familiar sound in this new, unsettling environment.

A loud bang jolted me from my thoughts, the silhouette of the Eulis outlined against the dimness as he struck a stone table with frustration. Each impact was punctuated with curses, a raw display of emotion rarely seen from such a composed being.

The room was suddenly awash with the deep orange glow of ignited torches, their light unveiling the chamber's secrets. The stone surfaces, marred with scratches and indentations, spoke of desperation and despair. As my fingers traced the marks, the chilling realization hit me – they were not just marks, but the imprints of human anguish, etched into the stone by fingernails.

In the dimly lit chamber, tension knotted the air as Naya's voice broke the silence, her question echoing off the stone walls. "Where have you taken us?"

The Eulis, cloaked in uncertainty, paced the room, his movements betraying a glimpse of indecision. Abruptly, he halted, his decision made. With a swift motion, he seized me, dragged me toward Kai and Leana, and forced me into a kneeling position. "Liam, you need to heal him."

Lammat's protest sliced through the tension. "Don't do it, Liam!"

In a swift reaction, the Eulis spun, unleashing an energy ball towards Lammat, who deflected it effortlessly. The air crackled with power as Lammat conjured an energy ball of his own, poised to strike. "We both know you're not stronger than me right now."

The standoff intensified as the Eulis countered, his voice steady, "Kill me, and what do you think will happen to you?" The threat hung heavy between them, Lammat's resolve wavering as he dissipated the energy, the potential confrontation dissipating with it.

The Eulis' focus snapped back to me, urgency lacing his words. "If you don't heal him, we're all dead."

I sought reassurance in Naya and Veyra's presence, but found none. Their confusion mirrored my own.

"Don't look at them!" the Eulis barked, desperation creeping into his command. "Heal him, now!"

Leana's tear-streaked face sought mine, her silent plea almost swaying me. Yet, the dissonance within me grew. The oppressive magic of the black barriers, the undeniable wrongness of the situation—I couldn't comply. I shook my head firmly. "No."

A scream of frustration tore from the Eulis as he issued a grim command to another nearby, his finger pointed at Kai and Leana. "Take them both to the warehouse. Put him to sleep and do what you can to dress the wound. If I'm not there in fifteen minutes, take him home. They'll have something that will work."

With a gesture of resignation, the Eulis vanished with Kai and Leana in a blink, leaving a void in their wake.

"Right then, as you heard, we're now on a timer. You have fifteen minutes to teach me how to heal," he declared.

"Teach you?" My voice echoed the disbelief, mirroring the absurdity of the situation.

With a casual flick of his wrist, the Eulis summoned chairs from the very walls of the room. They aligned themselves with an eerie precision in the center, awaiting occupants.

"Each of you, sit down, now."

Tyran's muttered defiance, "Who do you think you are?" barely filled the room before Naya's confusion added to the mix, "Where are we?"

"I SAID SIT DOWN!" The command, bolstered by a surge of energy from the Eulis, left no room for resistance. The two other Eulis stood guard as we reluctantly made our way to the chairs. Naya sat first, followed quickly by Veyra, Tyran, myself, and Lammat. Once seated, the Eulis produced several strands of black string from his cloak, tossing them towards us. Like serpents awakened, the strings animated, binding us to our chairs with an unexpected ferocity, rendering us immobile.

"Going to be a bit hard to learn anything with us restrained like this, isn't it?" Lammat's tone was calm, betraying none of the tension that surely gripped him.

"We'll get there," the Eulis assured, a cryptic smile playing on his lips.

"Before or after you drop the hoods?" Lammat pressed, his gaze piercing.

At this, the Eulis chuckled, a sound that seemed oddly out of place in the grim surroundings. "Eager to skip ahead, are you? Fine." With a grace that seemed at odds with the situation, he revealed his face. The man who now stood before us, with his long black hair and neatly trimmed beard, was unexpectedly unfamiliar. His smile, though friendly, did little to ease the tension.

"Don't recognize me?" he probed, his eyes locking with mine. "How about now?" The transformation unfolded with an uncanny subtlety, his features shifting almost imperceptibly before my eyes. His brow deepened first, etching a narrative of wisdom and resilience into his forehead, while his nose broadened slightly, lending a familiar prominence to his profile.

"The man from the tavern..." The realization hit me like a wave.

"Hey, yeah! You got it! Good to see you again, lad!" His face once again shifted, back to his original. He pointed at Tyran. "He, however, knows exactly who this face belongs to, right?"

Tyran's reaction was visceral, his body trembling with barely contained rage as he glared at the man, his teeth clenched in a silent snarl of defiance.

"You'll not be able to break them, Tyran. How do you intend to kill me if you pull your own arms off in the process?" The man's taunt was cold, calculated to provoke.

Confusion and concern etched Veyra's face as she leaned in, seeking clarification. "Wait... who is this man?" Her gaze flitted between me and Lammat, seeking answers we didn't have.

"Release me," Tyran's voice was a low growl, his entire being radiating with anger and desperation. His eyes never left the man's face, a testament to a deep-seated animosity and recognition.

"Tyran, who is he?" Veyra's voice cut through the tension, her gaze darting between Tyran and the mysterious figure, seeking answers amid confusion.

The man, sensing the moment ripe for revelation, gestured towards the hooded figures beside him. With a dramatic flair, he lowered their hoods, revealing faces identical to his own, a trio of mirrors reflecting the same dark hair, the same beard, the same piercing gaze. "You can call me Zeipher," he announced, his voice carrying the weight of his newfound identity across the room.

"No..." Veyra whispered.

The atmosphere in the room shifted abruptly as the two replicas of Zeipher, with grim resolve, manifested black energy blades in their hands. Without a moment's hesitation, they turned the blades upon themselves, plunging them into their own stomachs. This act, stark and harrowing, was not a display of loyalty or a demonstration of power; it was a final, unsettling resolution to their existence. As their forms vanished, dissolving into dark smoke, the room was enveloped in a heavy silence.

Zeipher himself seemed to draw a deep, contemplative breath, a sigh that might have been mistaken for regret had his actions not spoken louder. Turning to Lammat, he offered a smile. "Still not quite your level, but certainly higher than all of theirs now."

"Why didn't you just dismiss them?" Lammat's question, voiced amidst the shock of the room, sought logic in the macabre display.

Zeipher's laughter, light yet chilling, filled the space. "I find this makes more of an impression," he explained, his amusement at the situation a stark contrast to the fear and tension gripping me.

"Liam!" Veyra's sudden call was a one of warning and desperation. In response, Zeipher's arm moved with a speed that belied his earlier contemplative demeanor, aiming a black energy ball directly at Veyra's face. "From now on, nobody speaks unless I ask them a question. Break this rule, and you will see blood."

The threat hung heavily in the air, a clear line drawn by Zeipher defining the new rules of engagement. Veyra's mouth snapped shut, her eyes wide with the realization of our precarious situation, her body shaking with a mixture of fear and indignation.

"You're Zeipher?" The name felt oddly familiar as it left my lips.

His response, wrapped in a light-hearted chuckle, was unexpected. "You know, you used to call me Uncle," he reminisced, a tinge of sadness lacing his words. "I've known you since you were born. Honestly, it breaks my heart to hear you've forgotten me."

"Stop it," shouted Lammat.

Without warning, Zeipher conjured a small black blade on his finger, pressing it into my shoulder with precision. The pain was sharp, yet I refused to give him the satisfaction of hearing me cry out. "I let Liam's slip of the tongue go by, for old time's sake, but nobody else, understand?" His gaze bore into mine. "I want to have a proper catch-up."

As quickly as it had appeared, he withdrew the blade, inspecting the wound with an almost clinical curiosity before a sigh escaped him. "I don't understand," he mused. "It's like your father all over again." He paced before us, his words painting a grim picture of past torment. "For years I'd see him heal everything from stubbed toes to paper cuts, but the day I *needed* to see it?" His gesture to my non-healing shoulder underscored the gravity of his frustration.

The revelation that I wasn't healing sparked a cascade of worry. Why wasn't I healing?

"I'd hoped Kai would have been some kind of incentive,

but who cares about that guy, right?" Zeipher's gaze swept over each of my friends before returning to me. "No, you need someone you care about." A snap of his fingers punctuated his words. "You see, with your father, he didn't have these connections. He wouldn't share the blood magic with me even if I threatened others. So, I just kept on hurting him, breaking him, cutting him, thinking he'd have no choice but to heal himself." He paused, a cold laugh escaping him. "But in the end, he proved me wrong."

His laughter grew darker, more deranged as he continued. "Honestly, I have no idea how long I was still cutting away before I realized he was already dead."

I summoned my energy, attempting to break free from the restraints, but the moment I did, I felt the energy drain from me. The more I channeled, the weaker I became.

"You're wasting your time," Zeipher remarked casually, nodding towards the black string. "Saddul technology. Absorbs mana and isn't affected by it. Can't even pick them up with telekinesis." He then leaned closer to Tyran, tracing a finger along one of his wounds. "Same thing Kai used in his fight. I acquired some from Saddul the other day, promising to use them to help Kai pass the exam. Didn't expect the idiot to try to kill anybody with them, though." Turning back to me, he concluded, "See, this is why Saddulians are so dangerous."

"Kai... is from Saddul?"

"And his sister, too!" Zeipher's smile widened as he divulged more. "She had quite the thing for you, I must say. Prince and Princess of the royal family." Standing, he exhaled a long sigh. "See, we had a deal. I discovered they were here, confronted them, and figured out their plan. You figured it out too, right, Lammat?"

My gaze shifted to Lammat, who met Zeipher's revelations with a stern glare. "Yeah," he confirmed. "They wanted to learn how we break the seals to artificially create Gouds and Eulis'."

Zeipher's nonchalance was unsettling. "I figured it wasn't

a big deal. They'd return to Saddul with their changed crests, they'd then have them examined, studied, blah blah blah. What's the harm, hey?" His laughter, though brief, was laced with a dark amusement. "With any luck, they'd remove the crests, turning both kids into vegetables."

Without warning, his arm moved with lethal precision, gripping Tyran's leg. Five black blades formed at his fingertips, plunging into Tyran's flesh. "But then this one goes and cuts off his hand! How do you think the King will react knowing we dismembered his son?"

"Stop it!" The urgency to intervene, to heal Tyran, surged within me, a futile effort against my restraints.

Zeipher's tone shifted, to one of frustration. "You think I'm doing this for fun, Liam? You think I enjoy this?" He turned away, a gesture that seemed to close off the conversation. "They've been watching us, waiting to attack us for years. Waiting until their special technology is ready." From his cloak, he produced a small metal cylinder, a device that seemed innocuous yet ominous in his hands. "They don't seem to understand that we're already powerless to stop even something as small as this."

"We now have less than ten minutes for you to teach me how to heal. Four friends are going to help me. I will make them bleed, I will bring them to you, and you will heal them. If you don't, I will leave them to bleed out."

Suddenly, Veyra's voice pierced the heavy air. "Liam, don't fall for it! Lammat is one of Zeipher's clones!"

Her words were barely out when Zeipher's response cut through the air—a dark beam launched from his fingertip with lethal precision. My heart seized, expecting the worst, only to find Veyra unscathed. Confusion reigned for a split second before a harrowing cough drew our attention to Naya, her form collapsing, blood blossoming across her clothing in a stark, terrifying contrast.

Desperation clawed at my throat. "No… Please, no… Naya… I'll heal her, just… let me heal her," I pleaded, my voice breaking under the strain.

Zeipher, his features a mask of cold indifference, seemed to consider my plea. Yet, it was clear his actions were not born of compassion but a calculated manipulation. Dragging Naya's chair closer, he positioned her before me as if she were merely a pawn in his cruel game, a tool to test my abilities—or their absence.

With a flick of his wrist, he released one of my bindings, a cruel semblance of mercy that allowed me just enough freedom to reach for Naya. My hand shook as I extended it towards her, the air between us charged with a silent, desperate hope. But as my fingers brushed against her skin, the reality crashed down with suffocating force—there was no familiar surge of energy, no warmth of healing power flowing through my veins. It was as if my very essence had been drained, leaving me powerless and defeated.

Zeipher watched carefully, his impatience tangible. When it became evident that no miracle would occur, he snatched Naya away, returning her to the line, a growl of frustration escaping him as he paced like a caged beast, wrestling with his next move.

"What am I going to have to do to get you to heal?" he muttered, more to himself than to me. The semblance of a twisted idea seemed to take hold, and he paused, the gears of his mind turning towards a new, macabre form of motivation. "Alright... how about a show of good faith? How about I let one of your friends go?"

The suggestion struck like a lightning bolt, a perverse offer amid our torment. "Naya!" I shouted, clinging to a shred of hope, desperate to save her from this nightmare.

His laughter, devoid of any warmth, was a chilling reminder of his control over our fates. "Don't be stupid!" he taunted. "I'm not going to release the one you care for most." His gaze swept over us, calculating, as he deliberated over his next move with a cruelty that seemed to entertain him. "How about Tyran? He barely seems like your friend. No point in threatening Lammat anymore, right? So that just leaves Tyran and Veyra."

Each word from Zeipher twisted the knife deeper, a vile game where the stakes were the lives of those I held dear. The choice he presented was a torment in itself, a sadistic test of my resolve and the value I placed on each of my friends' lives.

I lowered my head, the weight of the decision anchoring me to the spot. "Okay, take Tyran." When I turned to look at Tyran, there was an unspoken exchange, a moment where his gaze bore into mine. Though words remained unspoken, I felt a surge of something akin to gratitude emanate from him. Despite the dread that filled me, I managed a small, reassuring smile and nodded, hoping to convey a silent message of solidarity.

"Alright, despite the fact that he's the reason we're now in this mess," Zeipher mused aloud, his steps measured as he approached Tyran. His hand reached for the restraints, his voice trailing off into contemplation. "It would have taken months for them to figure out the seal unlock can't be reverse-engineered. But now, what are my options? Kill them? Guaranteed war. At least with the severed hand, there's a chance that—"

The moment Tyran was freed, the air charged with an electric tension, a scream tearing from his lips as he launched at Zeipher with a force born of desperation and rage. A brilliant flash of blue light enveloped Tyran, his hair igniting into a luminous aura, energy crackling around him like a storm. Zeipher, caught off guard by the sudden onslaught, retaliated with dark blades, but Tyran, now transformed and alight with fierce blue energy, dodged with ease.

The moment their bodies collided, the force of their impact sent them careening into the far wall, a maelstrom of unleashed fury and raw energy. Tyran's arms, animated by a sudden surge of power, wrapped around Zeipher's neck with a ferocity that left no doubt of his intentions. His fingers dug in, muscles tensed to the brink as if he sought nothing less than to tear Zeipher's head from his shoulders. The air around them crackled with the electricity of Tyran's transformation, his hair ablaze with a radiant blue light that seemed to fuel his resolve.

As they grappled, the struggle between them was not just physical but a clash of wills, a testament to their respective strengths and determination. Tyran, empowered by a newfound force, seemed unstoppable, his grip tightening with every second that passed. Zeipher, caught in the vice-like hold, fought back with a desperation that matched Tyran's intensity, his dark blades flailing in a futile attempt to gain the upper hand.

However, Tyran's dominance was undeniable. With each passing moment, he managed to maneuver Zeipher beneath him, pinning him to the cold ground with a weight that spoke of finality. His knees dug into Zeipher's back, anchoring him in place, as Tyran's hands continued their relentless pursuit, his entire being focused on the singular goal of ending Zeipher's threat once and for all.

"Do it, Tyran!" Lammat's voice echoed across the room, a call that seemed to further ignite Tyran's determination.

At that moment, Zeipher's eyes found Lammat's, and an unexpected change occurred. The fear and concern that had momentarily flickered in his gaze gave way to a disturbing sense of joy, a twisted excitement that seemed entirely out of place. His laughter, choked yet unmistakable, filled the air as he managed to reach into his cloak, drawing forth the metal cylinder once again. With a deliberate, strained motion, he twisted the end. The device came alive, a circle of lights illuminating its surface only to begin extinguishing one by one, a countdown of unknown consequences starting before our eyes.

Lammat's warning cut through the chaos. "Oh gods, Tyran! That thing's going to explode!"

Tyran's eyes snapped to the metal device, a moment of calculation flashing across his face, even as his hand stretched toward it, refusing to release Zeipher's neck.

"I told you," Zeipher gasped between choked laughs, "Not even telekinesis… can move these things…"

"Then we die together," Tyran declared, his voice steady.

"Don't be… an idiot, I'm not going to kill myself!" With a swift motion, he hurled the device through the air, aiming it towards us.

In an instant, the world seemed to tilt on its axis. I was catapulted from my spot, my body hurtling towards Veyra and Naya with an unstoppable force. It was only when I twisted in mid-air that I caught sight of Lammat. His leg was extended from a forceful kick, the realization dawning on me then—that it was Lammat's desperate act that had sent us flying. Our bodies knocked into one another and then, with the momentum of our combined weight, we were all sent crashing into the wall.

From this jumbled vantage point, I saw Lammat collapse, still tied to his chair, his effort taking its toll as he slumped to the ground. The device, now ominously beeping, rolled to a stop close to where he lay.

"Keep going, Tyran!" he managed to yell.

"Lammat!" Tyran's response was laden with a complex mix of emotions—anger, desperation, and an underlying thread of respect.

"Don't worry about me, boy! Just finish him off!" From the ground, Lammat issued his encouragement, his focus solely on the greater threat at hand, his own peril forgotten.

As I struggled to regain my bearings, Naya's pale skin and blue lips caught my attention, her eyes locked on mine, a silent plea for help as her condition worsened. Turning my gaze back to Lammat, I caught his eye, his expression one of peace and resolve. "Go be the King I always knew you could be!" His smile was both heartbreaking and inspiring.

Tears blurred my vision as I whispered, "Lammat…"

Tyran, cloaked in a sudden flash of blue, materialized with startling immediacy. He dropped into a crouch, snatched up the device, and with a fluid motion, spun on his heel.

Propelling himself back towards Zeipher, he moved with such speed that his form blurred, a vivid streak against the dim background. With the device firmly in grasp, he extended his arm, launching it towards its intended target. The moment his fingers released it, time itself seemed to pause.

My senses were overwhelmed. The air was filled with a loud crack, immediately followed by an intense white light that swallowed everything in sight. A persistent ringing invaded my ears, a flat, unyielding tone that seemed to resonate with the shockwave.

A few moments passed before I was lifted from the ground. I felt an odd sensation of weightlessness as my chair and I were gently placed back onto the floor. My attempts to blink away the blinding light were futile; all I could perceive was an endless expanse of white. A hand tenderly brushed my hair, then proceeded to examine my shoulder with a careful touch.

"Hello?" My voice echoed back to me, sounding hollow and far away. A muffled response came, indecipherable, lost in the ringing that filled my ears. "I can't hear you!" I tried again, louder, straining to break through the silence that enveloped me.

Laughter pierced the veil of my disorientation, and slowly, a silhouette materialized from the white. "No need to shout, Liam. I can hear you just fine." As my vision gradually cleared, Lammat's face came into focus, a reassuring sight that brought a small smile to my face. A hand landed on his shoulder, and I looked up to see Zeipher looming over us. "Those things pack a punch, don't they?"

My heart sank at his words. "Where's Tyran?" The question hung heavy in the air.

"Behind you," Zeipher's voice was cold, devoid of empathy. "Also, to your right, and a bit to your left. It's probably best not to look. There's not much of him left." The urge to turn was immediate, but my body wouldn't comply, leaving me with a view of Veyra and Naya still on the floor—

Veyra struggling against her restraints, while Naya lay motionless.

"You coward!" Anger flared within me as I glared at Zeipher.

"A coward? Me? That's the last word I'd use to describe myself." His tone was smug, self-assured.

"You threw that device at us…"

"… knowing that Tyran would release me to save you." He shook his head, a gesture of mock disappointment. "That's not cowardice. That's intelligence, something our mutual friend here has an abundance of."

My gaze shifted to Lammat, confusion and betrayal swirling within. "What Veyra said… that you're a copy of Zeipher. Is that true?"

The pause that followed was heavy, laden with unspoken truths. Lammat swallowed hard, his eyes meeting mine before he gave a solemn nod.

Zeipher's movements around us were deliberate, his presence looming as we sat restrained. The gentle touch under my chin forced my gaze upwards, though I resisted giving him the satisfaction of making eye contact with Lammat. His laughter, devoid of warmth, echoed mockingly in the charged air.

"Liam…" said Lammat.

Zeipher's voice dropped to a whisper, his words carrying a weight of revelation. "He was the first one I created, you know. That means he has half of my strength. Half of my *complete* strength." The proximity of his confession felt invasive, his breath almost on my ear. "You know, I hate to admit it, but right now, he's stronger than me. When I formed him, my power was also halved. As you know, there's still one clone left, trying to help the Saddulian Royals, so… halved again." His laughter resumed, a sound that seemed to dance with derision. "Time's already run out, so he's probably already taken them home."

"Then you failed," Lammat interjected, his voice steady.

"I failed?" Zeipher's retort was sharp, a challenge. "WE FAILED! Stop trying to pretend you're not me! How could anyone change as much as you have? What happened to you that triggered this!?"

"I thought I saw Liam die."

I looked up at him. Lammat's admission was a whisper of vulnerability. His smile, small and resigned, was a brief reprieve from the tension. "After I saw you in the tavern, I knew it had to be you. Older, yes, but when you told me your name, it confirmed my suspicion. That's when I was created to follow you, Liam."

"Why?" The question escaped me, a plea for understanding amidst the revelations.

"Because we finally had a way to learn how to heal again," Zeipher interjected, his tone suggesting layers of unspoken plans and manipulations. "We didn't expect your father to die so easily, so planned to move on to you, but that's when Tylak, Meltek, and Eulis appeared."

Lammat's laugh, in response, carried a note of irony. "Who knew Eulis could control time?"

"Six years, I was trapped there." Added Zeipher. "The sun, flashing across the sky. I ran, and although it felt like seconds, it still took six years to escape the spell's radius."

Confusion clouded my thoughts as I tried to reconcile the stories Lammat had shared with me. "I don't get it..." The words barely left my lips, my mind grappling with the discrepancies. "The stories you told me... you said you trained with me when I was a child... that your father beat you when you found out the royal bloodline magic..."

Zeipher's response was a laugh, loud and devoid of any warmth. "You used *that* story? Talk about a good lie!" His arm draped around Lammat's shoulder in a gesture that feigned camaraderie but felt sinister. "No, a boy did find that out, one of the servant's children, I think. He told his father, who was meant to tell me, but instead decided to keep it a secret." The smile that followed was chilling. "My job was intelligence... so it wasn't long before I found out."

"What happened to the boy?"

"What do you think happened?" Zeipher's casual cruelty was on full display as he mimed a slit throat. "I followed the law."

"Monster…"

"Monster? Liam, who do you think wrote the law?" His retort was swift, a twisted justification for his actions. "I did only what your father told me to do, nothing more, nothing less. If I'm a monster, it's because he turned me into one!"

"Yet you still betrayed him in the end!"

"Because he was a fool!" The venom in his voice spiked. "I showed him pictures of a desert turned to glass, and he just shrugged it off. I brought him early prototypes of these explosives and demonstrated how they resisted our mana, and still, he did nothing!"

In a sudden burst of fury, Zeipher cast Lammat aside as if he weighed nothing, turning his ire towards me. Gripping me by the collar, he lifted me, along with my chair, his face inches from mine, his eyes burning with a mixture of rage and betrayal. "Your father was more interested in courting, dining, dancing, playing King!" Each word was punctuated with a spit of contempt. "Who do you think looked after you? Me! Who do you think taught you about the world? Me! Who do you think cared for you? ME!"

"Alright, that's enough." The tension broke with Lammat's intervention. He stood, his restraints discarded with an air of ease. "You're done, now."

"What the… How did you…?" Dropping me, the shock in Zeipher's voice gave way to action as he thrust his hand forward, expecting his usual dark energy to lash out. But nothing happened. His confusion deepened, "What?" echoing his disbelief. Refusing to accept this failure, he aimed a finger, attempting another attack, the kind that had previously struck Naya. Yet, once more, there was no effect.

"I'm afraid you're already beaten," Lammat announced

calmly, his hand gesturing nonchalantly. As he did, my bindings began to unravel, drifting through the air with an elegance and fluidity reminiscent of fish gliding through water. "This is a useful little skill I picked up from Liam only yesterday."

In a desperate bid to regain control, Zeipher lunged at Lammat. However, the moment his feet left the ground, his advance halted abruptly, and he found himself suspended in mid-air, spinning helplessly. "What...? How are you doing this?" he demanded, his voice laced with incredulity and a growing sense of defeat.

"My job was to keep an eye on Liam until I learned how to heal, right?" Lammat's gaze met mine as he placed a comforting hand on my shoulder, anchoring me in the unfolding chaos. "I finally succeeded at my task the first time you transformed in the gravity room." His smile seemed almost nostalgic. "Apparently, that was a wonderful evening."

"Apparently?" My confusion was evident, struggling to piece together the implications of his words.

With a soft chuckle, Lammat clarified, "That was one of my copies, you see. He came back to me, told me about your body breaking and healing during your transformation, about you two training in the forest for hours afterward..." His voice trailed off into a sigh, heavy with unspoken emotion. "Usually, I would merge with my copies to share our knowledge... But this copy... he insisted I dismiss him."

"He what?" Zeipher's shout pierced the tense atmosphere, his disbelief echoing our own. "You learned how to heal? You had the power of a god, and you threw it away?"

"His blood magic isn't for a god, and it certainly isn't for people like us!" snapped Lammat. "It's for people like Liam." His gaze turned away from Zeipher, who remained trapped in his involuntary aerial dance, settling onto me. "I've had so many opportunities to copy it, but I've always chosen not to."

"Then you're a fool!" Zeipher spat, the insult tinged with desperation.

"You're right," Lammat conceded, his tone reflective.

"You and I, we're both fools. Liam was a Crosser, but he learned to be good again. He proved that it was possible for me to do the same."

"You're nothing but a copy! A poor imitation! You think you're better than me? A week ago we were the same person!"

"The difference between us," continued Lammat, "is that while you've been hiding… while you've been killing… while you've been plotting…" he stepped closer to Zeipher. "All this time… I've been learning."

"What do you think you're going to do to me? Trap me in here forever? Kill me? Do that, and you die, too!"

Lammat nodded. "I'm ready to die for what I've done." As he spoke, the space around us shimmered, morphing to reveal me in the arena, locked in a confrontation with Leana. Blue flames filled the arena, pushing against the green barriers that surrounded us. "Besides, look at that power. He's already surpassed me. He doesn't need me anymore." The scene shifted, focusing on one of the Eulis' in the corner, capturing Zeipher's expression. "And look at that fear. You know he can beat you."

My attention was torn from the illusion, turning back to Lammat. "This is a dream world…"

Lammat's smile was one of confirmation. "Copied it from you yesterday when you pulled Tyran and Veyra into that world of yours." He paused, a thoughtful expression crossing his features. "I wonder how many more abilities you've managed to keep from me. Wish you'd shared this one with me sooner, I'd have liked to have had more time to make the dream look like the room we were held in." As he spoke, the room faded away, leaving us in a white void.

"Does this mean Naya and Tyran are okay?"

Lammat shook his head, his expression somber. "No, I'm sorry. I had to pull you and him in at the same time; otherwise, he might have copied the spell and realized my plan. I've slowed things down as much as I can, but Liam… Neither of them have much time left."

The weight of his words was crushing. "Are we still restrained in the real world?"

Lammat's nod confirmed my worst fears. "You probably don't have time to save both of them."

A spark of hope flickered within me. "I could teach you how to heal! You could heal Tyran while I heal Naya."

"After all this?" He smiled at my suggestion, a gesture tinged with melancholy. "No, Liam. I meant what I said. I can't learn how to heal." His attention briefly shifted to Zeipher, still floating helplessly above us.

"What makes you think you'll suddenly be able to heal anyone?" said Zeipher, laughing.

"You still haven't figured it out?" asked Lammat.

"What? He can detect Crossers? He knows when someone's trying to copy it?"

Lammat shook his head. "No. Bloodline magic isn't a secret by choice but by design. So long as Liam knows someone is trying to copy it, he can't do the spell." He turned to me. "That's why, no matter what we did to the King…"

I stood back, looking at Lammat and Zeipher stood together, then nodded. "Let me out!" Suddenly, I was back in Zeipher's room. "Veyra!" I called out, desperate for assistance.

She quickly stood, the restraints no longer binding her. "Why did they suddenly stop?"

"I need you to untie me!" My bindings had loosened but were stubbornly knotted.

"But what about…"

"He's in the dream world, hurry!"

Without hesitation, Veyra sprinted to my side and swiftly untied my bonds. As soon as I was freed, I conjured a duplicate of myself and hurried to Tyran. The sight of him was startling. He had lost his right arm and the lower half of his left leg, and his face bore fresh, pink scars from his recent ordeal.

Kneeling beside him, I gently placed my hand on his shoulder, initiating the healing process. A familiar sensation of warmth and energy coursed through me, extending into his body. I watched, hopeful, as his skin began to knit together at the edges of his wounds. Focusing intently, I tried to will his arm and leg to regenerate, but the magic faltered; the skin merely sealed over the ends of his injuries, leaving smooth, unblemished surfaces where his limbs should have been. Despite a second attempt, the outcome remained the same—no regeneration, just closure.

Tyran's eyes slowly opened, and he laboriously sat up, taking in the extent of his injuries. His gaze drifted to where his right arm once was, then lifted to meet my eyes. A faint smile touched his lips, a bittersweet acknowledgment of the situation. "Guess you can't heal other people's limbs," he remarked, his voice tinged with resignation and gentle humor.

"I'm so sorry," I responded, my voice barely above a whisper, laden with a deep sense of sorrow and inadequacy.

"No, no! Please!" The urgency in my copy's voice echoed as I spun around, only to see him kneeling before Naya, desperately shaking her, trying to rouse her.

I rushed to her side, my feet barely touching the ground, heart hammering against my chest. Dropping to my knees, I reached out, my hand trembling as it found hers. The warmth of her skin against mine was a stark, cruel contrast to the stillness within her. "She's still warm," I whispered, a sliver of hope threading through my voice. I closed my eyes, concentrating, channeling every bit of healing energy I could muster. Yet, the connection I sought, that tell-tale sign of life needing repair, remained elusive. It was as if my power, usually so responsive, now stumbled through darkness, finding no injury to mend.

My eyes, heavy with dread, moved to the wound on her chest—a vivid, brutal testament to the violence she had endured. It defied reason, defied my abilities. The realization dawned on me, cold and unforgiving, as I finally forced myself to look at her face. Naya's blue eyes, once vibrant with life, now stared emptily at the ceiling, her golden hair splayed out beneath her, a stark contrast against the cold, hard ground. A shiver ran down my spine, the gravity of the moment anchoring me to the spot.

Beside her, my double's anguish filled the air, a raw, heart-wrenching sound that seemed to echo off the walls. He gathered her into his arms, his grief manifest in the tightness of his embrace, the quiver in his breath. I wanted to hold her... I wanted to cry... Why did he get to?

A realization, heavy as lead, settled within me. The task of healing Tyran had been assigned to my double, leaving Naya's care in the more capable hands of the original.

Rooted to the ground, I struggled to draw breath, each inhalation a battle. My mind raced, piecing together the fragmented reality before me. My gaze drifted to Tyran, his presence like a shadow, his interest in the scene before him seemingly detached, almost clinical. I was the one who healed him... that meant... I was the copy.

I looked back to my original and watched as the tears ran down his cheeks. There was nothing I could do to help him. No words, no gestures... In that moment, he likely didn't even know I was there.

Turning, my gaze found Zeipher's mindless body, the accusation in my eyes as sharp as a blade. "You... did this..."

Lammat stood a short distance away, his form shaking with sobs, tears streaming down his face. He reached out towards Zeipher, and from his hand, dark energy surged, forming a sphere of pure blackness that shot down into Zeipher, reducing him to smoke.

Lammat's eyes fell to his hands before his knees buckled, bringing him to the ground. His body shook with sobs.

I made my way to him, each step heavier than the last. Kneeling before him, I met his eyes, my voice soft, yet unwavering. "He lied... He wasn't the one who created you... He wasn't the original."

Lammat's voice was a mere whisper. "No... He wasn't..." His eyes, filled with torment, flickered to Naya, then to the scene of my original's mourning. "I'm so sorry, Liam..." His voice was a murmur of regret as he ran his hands through his hair, the magic that altered his appearance beginning to wane, revealing his true self beneath the spell.

Zeipher's gaze found mine, a mix of defiance and resignation within. "I did everything I could..." His words, though simple, carried the weight of countless unspoken battles, a testament to the complex web of intentions and actions that had led us to this moment.

"You've done enough..."

He nodded, slowly looking up at my hair. "Black doesn't suit you, Liam."

I reflected his nod. "I know." Raising my hand to my head, I gathered my energy, focusing it into a singular point. Then, with a sense of finality, released it.

CHAPTER FORTY-THREE
One Final Transformation

Lammat guided me forward, his presence reassuring in the dimly lit corridor. Naya's body felt both light and unbearably heavy in my arms as I stepped through the doorway he held open, entering the base of a stone spiral staircase that wound upwards into shadow.

"This way," Lammat directed, gesturing towards the ascending path.

With each step, the weight of the moment and the burden I carried seemed to echo off the ancient stones. Glancing back, I saw Veyra, her strength evident as she supported Tyran, both following through the door that Lammat still held ajar. Tyran's nod of gratitude to Lammat was a small, yet profound acknowledgment of our intertwined fates.

"Where are we?" Veyra's voice, filled with a mixture of curiosity and concern, broke the heavy silence that enveloped us.

"The lower levels of the palace," Lammat explained, his voice echoing slightly in the stairwell. "That room was the examination room."

"Examination room?" asked Veyra.

"It sounds better than 'experimentation room'," Lammat admitted, the awkwardness in his tone betraying the discomfort of the truth. "It's where we brought any Crossers we managed to capture."

As we ascended, Tyran's question reverberated against the cold stone walls. "When did you figure out he was Zeipher?"

Veyra's reply was tinged with the clarity of hindsight. "During our fight. The moment I hit him with the sleep spell, his illusion vanished."

Lammat added, "The illusion vanishes the moment I sleep. I never slept in the dorms. I would just teleport somewhere else."

Veyra's admission was almost lost in the vastness of the staircase. "I didn't know who he was at first. I thought he was just some old guy trying to sneak into the exam." Her attempt at humor fell flat, the gravity of our situation leaving little room for laughter.

Reaching a landing, we found ourselves at a crossroads of sorts, a small hallway with doors on either side. The gentle flicker of candlelight from a chandelier above bathed the space in a warm, soft glow.

"Take the door on your right," Lammat instructed. "Wait, let me…"

Before I could react, Lammat's image materialized in front of me, his form flickering before becoming solid. He pushed open the right door, revealing a large room, bathed in light.

Entering the room was akin to stepping through a portal to a bygone era, a realm suspended in time yet touched by years of neglect. Two majestic staircases rose on either side, their grandeur somewhat dimmed by the accumulation of dust and the passage of time. Above, a once resplendent crystal chandelier dangled, its light now casting shadows that played across the wooden floors and the faded red carpet, which stretched the room's length like a weary traveler.

The once smooth white walls bore the weight of history with dignity, adorned with portraits in thick gold-plated frames. Each painting now muted by the dust of ages, their subjects gazing out from a past that seemed both splendid and remote. Grand marble pillars, standing as silent sentinels, reached for the high ceiling, their reflections upon the floor now blurred and distorted, as if even their grandeur could not escape the touch of time.

"This is the Grand Hall..." Tyran's voice trailed off as he took in the sight before us.

"Yes," Lammat confirmed with a nod, his eyes sweeping over the room that bore silent witness to a grandeur now faded.

"But... I don't understand. I thought the entire palace was under the influence of Eulis's spell," Tyran continued, his confusion evident.

Lammat shook his head, his finger tracing an invisible line from the palace's entrance, up the stairs, and along the corridor. "The spell's effect diminishes with distance from the throne room," he explained, tapping his foot on the red carpet beneath us. The carpet itself told a story of gradation; the end nearest the entrance showed signs of significant wear, while the far end was merely dusted with age. "The spell's reach has receded over time."

Veyra, looking out the main doorway, added, "We're within the spell's effect right now." Beyond, the sun's slow, but visible, descent over the sea marked the passage of time outside the spell's influence.

"We shouldn't linger here," Lammat urged, moving towards the entrance.

Tyran, his voice heavy, broke the silence that followed. "My father..." We all turned towards him, the question in his eyes mirroring the turmoil within. "Did you really kill him?"

Lammat looked at Tyran, his response measured, filled with the weight of memories. "I don't know." His eyes flickered with the pain of recollection. "He and Meltek were holding me down as Eulis cast the spell. When I realized what was happening..." He hesitated, his gaze drifting to Naya before returning to Tyran, "...I shot them both and fled."

"So, there's a chance they're still alive?"

"How much time has passed for them?" Veyra's question added to Tyran's.

Lammat positioned himself, a barrier to the staircase. "No," he stated, the finality in his voice brooking no argument. "The discrepancy in time means any attempt to reach them now would be futile. You need to leave." He turned, a silent command in his stance. "I'll attempt to rescue them…"

Stepping forward, I cradled Naya in my arms, offering her to Lammat. "I'll do it," my voice steady, resolute.

Lammat's eyes snapped up to meet mine, a storm of emotions crossing his face before he shook his head. "Liam, the risk is too great. With Saddul seeking vengeance, we cannot afford to lose you."

Veyra stepped up, "I'll go. I'm the only one not—"

"This isn't open for discussion!" My response left no room for debate. "Tyran, you're in no condition. Veyra, you need to help him get out of here. Lammat…" My eyes fell on Naya, her now closed eyes gave the appearance that she was simply sleeping. "Please, take Naya to her family."

Lammat, momentarily immobilized by the gravity of the task, met my gaze. "Liam… I…"

"I trust you," I said, the words a bridge over the chasm of uncertainty. "If an attack is imminent, we'll need every able fighter. I'm going to try to add another two to our number."

Accepting Naya from my arms, Lammat nodded, his steps retreating toward the doorway. "Follow the corridor, it leads to the large double doors." He momentarily stopped and stood beside Tyran and Veyra. "I'll come back for you."

A smile touched my lips, a silent acknowledgment of the bond between us. "I know." As I felt the transformation surge through me, the air vibrated with the promise of what was to come.

My gaze lingered on each of their faces, a silent question hanging in the air: How much time would elapse before our paths crossed again? With that thought heavy on my mind, I crouched, then propelled myself backward, executing a midair turn with the grace and precision Joren had instilled in me. A visceral roar enveloped me, a sound more felt than heard, as I surged down the corridor. My movement transcended mere walking; I was airborne, gliding through the space with the ease of a current sweeping through the ocean depths.

The journey to the double doors took but a moment. As I approached, I found them agape, welcoming me into the sanctum they guarded. I crossed the threshold, my momentum carrying me forward, my senses immediately cataloging the grandeur of the room's interior.

The throne room unfurled before me in an opulent display of royal majesty, its grandeur undimmed even in the face of the palace's general neglect. At the heart of the room, the largest of three magnificent thrones commanded attention, its imposing structure a testament to the power it represented. Directly in front of this central throne, a figure clad in white lay sprawled on the ornate tiled floor, his blonde hair framing his face in stark contrast to the regal backdrop.

To my left, the atmosphere was charged with a raw, desperate struggle for survival. A figure garbed in black, his consciousness flickering like a dimming candle, exerted every ounce of his dwindling strength in a grim display of determination. He was dragging another man by the collar, inching towards the promise of safety offered by the corridor. The man's method was as ingenious as it was heartbreaking— he had wedged a sword into the floor, using it as a makeshift anchor to pull himself and his companion forward. Around him, the spell that had cast the entire palace into a slow temporal dance seemed to hold him in its grasp as well, making his movements appear agonizingly slow and laden with effort. Every inch gained was a victory against the unseen force that sought to keep them rooted in peril.

Turning to my right, a grand window offered a view of the sky, where the moon's slow ascent was overtaken by the sun's rise, a magical yet unnerving cycle that spoke of the powerful enchantments at work.

I dropped to the floor, settling beside the two men, my hand instinctively reached out, touching theirs. The air seemed to quiver subtly around us, an almost imperceptible shift that felt like the world exhaling. The man cloaked in black reacted with a start, his movements abruptly aligning with the natural flow of time.

"Who are you?" His voice was ragged, tinged with pain and confusion, as blood trailed down his chin, staining his teeth a stark red. The question hung between us, loaded with the weight of our sudden and unexpected encounter.

Choosing to focus on the task at hand rather than his inquiry, I extended my hand once more, this time with a deep concentration. The man before me bore a significant wound across his stomach. As my fingers hovered over the injury, a familiar shiver of energy coursed through me, a tangible current of healing magic flowing from my palm into his flesh. His reaction was immediate; eyes widening in shock, he instinctively rolled onto his back, one hand flying to his abdomen as if to verify the reality of the sudden relief.

Meltek, witnessing this silent exchange, propped himself up to better observe. His gaze, sharp and blue, locked onto mine with an intensity that spoke volumes of his confusion and burgeoning hope. My attention, however, swiftly shifted to Tyran's father, whose condition was markedly more dire. The injury he sustained was catastrophic—a lung appearing to be completely severed, a challenge that tested the limits of my abilities.

With a renewed focus, I initiated the delicate process of reweaving the fabric of his being, my magic delving deep to mend the tear that threatened his life. The air around us charged with the silent power of the spell, a dance of energy and intent that sought to reverse the damage inflicted.

"Little... Lexis?" Meltek's inquiry broke the brief silence, his blue eyes locking with mine.

A smile found its way to my lips. "I'm getting you out of here," I assured him, even as his gaze shifted to the window, questioning the anomaly of our unaffected pace within the spellbound time.

His attention briefly shifted to the large window, through which the erratic dance of celestial bodies could be observed—day and night cycling with unnatural haste. "How are you countering the time charm?" Meltek's question was more than curiosity; it was a search for understanding the nature of the power that defied the potent magic at play.

I followed his gaze to the window, observing the slow progression of time within the room contrasted with the accelerated passage outside. "I don't know half of what I'm doing," I admitted. The truth was a simple acknowledgment of the extraordinary circumstances we found ourselves in, a moment where intuition and magic intertwined to challenge the very fabric of reality.

Tylak's gasp was sudden as he abruptly sat up, turning to face me with a look of urgent confusion. "What happened?" he queried, quickly patting his chest as if searching for answers through touch.

"We're leaving," I declared, my voice carrying the weight of our imminent departure. As I placed my hands on their chests, intending to teleport us away from danger, an unexpected resistance met my efforts. The spell didn't activate; it was as though an unseen force was blocking our escape.

With no time to ponder the spell's defiance, I acted on instinct. Clenching my hands, I grasped the fabric of their garments, and with a force born of necessity, propelled us upward. The sensation of flight enveloped me once more, the corridor's familiar contours rushing past in a blur as we sped towards the threshold of the palace.

Emerging into the open air, I didn't pause, soaring through the grand doorway into the expanse beyond. We hovered momentarily above the palace's icy approach, the chill of the air a sharp contrast to the warmth of the sun's rays that struggled to penetrate the enchantment's lingering shadows.

Below us, the city of D'wan Ma'hal stretched out, the lives and stories unfolding beneath the slow descent of the sun. Its golden light shimmered on the ocean's surface, a peaceful scene that belied the turmoil we left behind.

Hoisting both Meltek and Tylak into the air, I stretched my arms out, ensuring they faced me. "Are you both okay?" I inquired, concern lacing my tone.

"Yeah, I'm oka—" Tylak's response was cut short by a sudden gasp, his hands instinctively reaching for my arm as I momentarily loosened my grip. His attempt to grasp me faltered, his arms moving slowly and awkwardly to the side as they both remained suspended in the air before me.

A chuckle escaped me at his reaction. "Don't worry, I won't drop you, though I'd appreciate you not squirming around so much. This is hard enough as it is."

Tylak, regaining some of his composure, managed a quip. "What are you? Fifteen? Flying's a normal thing now?"

Shaking my head, I corrected him, "No, I'm sixteen, and this is actually my first time flying."

Meltek couldn't help but laugh at the situation. "Why the show? Why not just drop us outside the entrance?"

My smile widened at the question. "I wanted your reunion to be special." With that, I adjusted our formation, guiding them to either side of me as we floated above the ground. Below us, a small group of familiar faces looked up, anticipation and surprise mingling in their expressions.

Gently, I lowered us to the ground, our feet softly touching down.

"How can he not be a god?" Joren remarked, jest and awe in his tone.

Taking a moment, I surveyed the faces before me: Joren, Lammat, Veyra, Eulis, Tyran, and an unknown blond teen. Their expressions ranged from disbelief to joy.

"How long was I gone?" I asked.

"Nine days," Lammat's voice broke the silence, his words settling over us with a weight that seemed to make the air around us denser.

Eulis, with a visible tremble in his lips, stepped forward, his gaze flickering between Meltek and Tylak. "I thought you were dead," he admitted, the vulnerability in his voice drawing everyone's attention.

Meltek, eyeing Eulis with a look of confusion, took a moment before responding. "Nearly was, uhh..."

"Oh, uh, sorry..." In an instant, Eulis's appearance shifted, his features morphing to reveal his true self.

"Gods!" exclaimed Tylak, a note of surprise coloring his tone. "Little Eulis became a Guardian, too?"

"Good for you, friend," Meltek offered, his voice carrying a genuine warmth.

Without wasting a moment, Eulis advanced, gathering both men by the shoulders and pulling them into a brief, tight embrace. As quickly as he had closed the distance, he stepped back, turning his attention to the blond-haired boy and then to Tyran.

"You're kidding..." Meltek's disbelief was clear, his eyes widening.

The blond boy's laughter filled the space between them. "Hey, Dad."

"Tyran?" The name fell from Tylak's lips in a whisper of realization.

"Hi," he said, his voice breaking slightly. Despite standing upright, a subtle limp hinted at the challenges he faced, and his right sleeve, neatly folded back, served as a silent testament to his sacrifice.

The sudden impact against my chest was startling, and I found myself tumbling backward onto the snowy path, Veyra and Joren having collided with me in their rush. "I can't believe you're okay!" Veyra exclaimed.

"They gathered a team to come and save you," said Joren. "I thought it was a stupid idea, but wherever she goes, I go."

"Idiot," Veyra muttered affectionately, her embrace tightening around me for a moment.

As I regained my bearings, I noticed Lammat making his way over. He crouched, offering me a hand, which I gratefully accepted, allowing him to help me to my feet. There was a brief hesitation in his gesture before he embraced me, a strong pat on my back accompanying his words. "I knew you could do it," he said.

"Still took me nine days," I replied, pushing back slightly to look him in the eyes. The question that had been weighing on my heart finally found its voice. "Naya?"

His eyes dropped for a moment, a shadow passing over his face. "Her funeral was a few days ago... Her family..."

I shook my head, the grief a heavy cloak around my shoulders. "I understand..."

"Liam." The voice drew my attention, and I turned to find Tyran approaching, his movement marked by an unmistakable limp. He paused briefly before placing his hand on my shoulder, a gesture heavy with significance. "Thank you."

A smile found its way to my lips as I glanced over at Tylak. "I wish I could have done it sooner."

Tyran's laughter was light, carrying a sense of shared understanding. "Guess you had to transform into a Guardian first, right?"

My smile wavered, confusion seeping in. "What?"

The humor faded from Tyran's expression, replaced by a look of surprise. "You... you don't know?"

Joren's laughter broke through the moment, loud and disbelieving. "Nobody told him?"

My gaze dropped to my hands, noticing the absence of the familiar blue mana—or any mana, for that matter. "You mean—"

"You're a Guardian, Liam," Lammat interjected, his grin wide and encouraging. "You transformed just before you left us at the entrance."

Instinctively, I reached up to touch my hair, half-expecting to find some alteration, some sign of the Guardian I had supposedly become. But everything felt normal. Was I truly a Guardian now?

Eulis, detaching himself from Meltek and Tylak, made his

way toward me with a purposeful stride. "Liam, we need to discuss Saddul."

"They declared war?" The question left my lips without thinking.

He nodded, the gravity of the situation mirrored in his firm expression. "They demanded our surrender this morning. They've given us forty-eight hours to comply." He turned to look out at the ocean. "They already have ships at our borders."

The urgency of the moment settled over us, a tangible force that demanded action. "Then what do we do?" I asked, my gaze sweeping over the faces of those gathered, each one a pillar in the looming conflict.

"First, we crown you King," Eulis declared, his voice resolute.

My frown deepened, the title sitting uneasily with me, but before I could voice any objections, Lammat chimed in with a fierce determination. "And then, we go to war."

CHAPTER FORTY-FOUR
Epilogue

In the heart of an ancient forest, where the trees whispered secrets of old and the air shimmered with barely perceptible magic, Liam found solace. His days were spent among the towering pines and the gentle rustle of leaves, a simple but fulfilling existence. His log cabin, nestled at the edge of a clearing, stood as a testament to his dedication to the real and tangible. It was here, under the dappled sunlight that filtered through the canopy, that Liam busied himself with repairing a recent wound to his home—a gap in the roof that let in the rain and the chill of night.

"Why don't you just fix it with a wave of your hand?" Naya's voice broke through the peaceful hum of the forest, her figure emerging from the trees with a grace that belied her powerful presence.

Liam paused, his hands still on the wood he was cutting, and looked over at her with a smile that reached his eyes. "There's value in doing things the real way, Naya. It's not just about the result... it's about the effort, the process. It keeps me grounded."

Naya, ever curious and eager to understand, nodded thoughtfully. Without another word, she picked up the spare axe and joined him. The rhythmic sound of their axes striking wood became a melody of its own, harmonizing with the natural orchestra of the forest. Time seemed irrelevant as they worked side by side, their laughter and banter weaving into the fabric of the day.

As the days melted into each other, their shared endeavors brought a new rhythm to Liam's life. The cabin, with Naya's help, transformed. The roof was mended, stronger than before, and their combined efforts saw the clearing bloom with a vibrant array of flowers and herbs that Naya tended with loving care.

One evening, as they sat by the fire that crackled with a life of its own, casting warm, flickering light over their faces, Liam turned to Naya. The firelight danced in his eyes, reflecting the earnestness of his question. "Do you like this world?"

Naya's gaze met his, and in her eyes, he saw the depth of her contentment. "If you're asking if I'm happy, I am," she said, her voice soft but certain. "Here, with you, doing things the real way—it's more magical than any spell."

One evening, as the last rays of sunlight filtered through the leaves, casting a golden glow over their sanctuary, Liam noticed a shadow of pensiveness on Naya's face. They sat side by side on the wooden steps of their cabin, immersed in the tranquility of the forest. The air was filled with the scent of pine and the gentle crackling of the fire they had built in the clearing.

Liam turned to her, his voice laced with concern. "Your family?" he asked. "If you'd like, I could bring them into this world, just to see you."

Naya's gaze lingered on the flames, reflecting the complexity of her thoughts. After a moment, she shook her head gently, her expression softening. "That would be too hard on them," she murmured. "This world, as beautiful as it is, belongs to us. It's not their reality."

With a graceful wave of her hand, the air before them shimmered, and for an instant, the figures of her parents and brothers appeared, their smiles warm and eyes filled with love. The vision was so vivid, so real, that Liam could almost hear their laughter. But as quickly as they had appeared, they vanished, leaving a lingering sense of bittersweet longing in the air.

Naya turned to Liam, her eyes glistening with unshed tears, yet there was a strength in her voice. "I prefer my memories of them," she said. "They are perfect in my mind. Here, I can cherish those memories and keep them alive. They remind me of where I came from and who I am."

Liam reached out, taking her hand in his, offering silent support. He understood her choice, the delicate balance between holding onto the past and living in the present. Their world, woven from dreams and reality, magic and the mundane, was their sanctuary. It was a place where memories were treasured, where the essence of those they loved could be felt in every leaf and breeze.

Years wove themselves into the forest, each one leaving its mark upon the land and the two souls who had chosen it as their home. The cabin, once a solitary figure amidst the wilderness, had grown into a part of the landscape, as much a creature of the woods as the trees and the wildlife that frequented its clearing. Near the cabin, a lake had formed, its waters a mirror to the sky above, reflecting the ever-changing dance of nature.

On a day when the air was filled with the gentle warmth of late spring, Liam and Naya found themselves by the lake's edge, wrapped in each other's arms. They watched in silence as the sun cast its golden light upon the water, turning the surface into a canvas of shimmering light and shadow. The beauty of the moment, serene and undisturbed, was a testament to the life they had built together, a life of simplicity and depth, woven through with the magic of their love and the world they had created.

Liam, feeling the weight of the years and the joy of the moment, turned to Naya, his voice soft with emotion. "Are you happy?" The question, though asked many times before, held within it the entirety of their journey, a reflection of their past and the anticipation of all the moments yet to come.

Naya lifted her gaze from the water to meet his, her eyes alight with the peace and contentment that had grown in her heart over the years. "I am," she replied, her voice resonating with the truth of her words. "With you."

Their eyes locked, and in that look, they shared the unspoken memories of their years together—the challenges they had faced, the joys they had celebrated, and the quiet moments that had filled their days. Their love, a bond strengthened by time and experience, was as deep and vast as the lake before them.

As the sun continued its descent, casting the sky in hues of orange and pink, Liam and Naya remained by the lake, embraced in each other's arms. The world around them, a world of their own making, was alive with the magic of existence and the beauty of nature. They had each other, and in the reflection of the sun upon the water, they saw the promise of many more years to come, filled with love, happiness, and the simple magic of being together.

As seasons turned and years unfurled like leaves in the vast tapestry of time, Liam and Naya's world remained untouched by age, a realm where time itself seemed to bow to the magic that sustained it.

One day, as they walked hand in hand along the edge of

their lake, the surface of the water smooth as glass and reflecting the endless sky above, Naya's voice broke the silence, her words floating between them like the delicate petals of the flowers that now lined the shore. "How long has it been since I died, Liam?"

Liam's steps faltered, and he turned to face her, the weight of her question hanging in the air. He didn't answer at first, the complexity of their reality settling heavily on his shoulders. Naya nudged him gently, her gaze filled with an understanding that transcended words.

"In here," Liam finally spoke, his voice tinged with a mixture of awe and melancholy, "we're approaching forty years. But in the real world, it's only been seconds."

Naya nodded, a thoughtful expression crossing her features as she looked down at her hands, still young and vibrant. "Would you have made me Queen?" she asked, her voice soft but curious, a question that had repeatedly woven itself into their conversations over the years.

Liam smiled, the affection in his gaze warming her heart. "You always ask me that," he said, pulling her into an embrace and planting a gentle kiss on her forehead.

Her laughter rang out, clear and bright, echoing across the lake. "I know, but I like hearing your answer."

With a look of profound love and respect, Liam answered, "I would have been proud to call you my wife, Naya. And Lylackia would have been proud to call you Queen." His words were a balm, a reaffirmation of the depth of their bond and the strength of their love, a love that had created a world unto itself.

Naya's laughter faded into a contented sigh as she leaned into Liam's embrace, her heart full. As they gazed out over the tranquil waters of the lake, the silence between them was a reflective pause in the melody of their existence.

Naya's voice, when it finally broke the stillness, was gentle but laced with a resolution that startled Liam. "I'm ready to go," she said, her eyes still fixed on the horizon, where the setting sun painted the sky in hues of gold and crimson.

Liam turned to her, confusion and concern etching his features. "Go where?" The question hung between them, a fragile thread of hope that perhaps she meant something else, anything but what his heart feared.

Naya met his gaze, her eyes holding a depth of understanding and sorrow. "I've experienced everything real that life here has to offer. I can wave my hand and create friends and family, but they won't be real." She paused. "It's time for me to say goodbye, Liam."

Liam shook his head, denial and despair mingling in his response. "I'm not ready. I don't want to return to the real world." His voice was a whisper, a plea for more time, for the continuation of the dream they had lived for so long.

With a tenderness that spoke of years of love and shared memories, Naya kissed him. It was a kiss of farewell, of gratitude, of love that had blossomed and thrived in the most unlikely of circumstances. "I've wanted to leave for years now," she admitted, her voice barely above a whisper. "But I stayed for you."

Liam was speechless, the magnitude of her revelation rendering him incapable of response. The realization that Naya had lingered in this world, in this existence, not for herself but for him, was overwhelming. It was a sacrifice borne of love, a testament to the depth of her feelings for him.

As the last light of day faded from the sky, Liam and Naya stood together by the lake, the world around them a reflection of the journey they had undertaken. The magic that had sustained their world, that had allowed them to escape the realities of life and death, suddenly felt fragile, a delicate veil about to be lifted.

In the dwindling light, Naya's gaze, deep and oceanic, held Liam with an intensity that spoke volumes. "I think you're finally ready to move on with your life," she said softly, her voice imbued with a mix of sadness and resolve. "And I'm ready to say goodbye to mine."

Liam, overcome by the enormity of the moment, felt a tremor run through him. Tears, unbidden, traced paths down his cheeks as he leaned in to kiss her, a kiss that was a confluence of every moment they had shared, every laugh, every tear, every silent understanding. "I'm going to miss you so much," he whispered against her lips, his voice breaking with the weight of his grief.

She nodded, a small, sad smile touching her lips. "I'm glad I made such a good impression," she said, her humor a fleeting light in the gravity of their farewell.

Liam's voice was thick with emotion. "I'm sorry, if I hadn't kept you here…" His words trailed off, the unspoken blame heavy on his heart.

But Naya interrupted him, her voice firm yet gentle. "I'm not sorry. Not for a single moment." In her eyes, Liam saw not regret, but a deep, abiding love and the peace that comes with acceptance.

Their final declarations of love were whispered with a reverence reserved for the most sacred of confessions. "I love you," they said almost in unison, the words a balm to their aching hearts.

With one last kiss, a goodbye that held within it the essence of their time together, Naya vanished. The space where she had stood moments before now held nothing but the night air and the faint scent of the flowers that grew wild by the lake's edge.

Liam stood alone, the silence around him a stark contrast to the life and love that had filled his world just seconds ago. Naya's absence was a void, yet within him, the love they had shared burned bright, a beacon in the darkness.

As the stars blinked into existence overhead, Liam looked up at the sky, the universe stretching out infinite and majestic above him. In that moment, he understood the true nature of love and loss, of life and the passage of time. Naya had been his heart, his soul, and though she was gone, the love they had shared was eternal, a light that would never fade.

* * *

Lammat's hand pressed against the heavy wooden door, pushing it open with a gentle nudge. The hinges creaked softly, revealing the shadowy ascent of a tall spiral staircase, its stones worn by time and countless footsteps. Liam stepped through the threshold, his silhouette framed by the flickering light from the torches that lined the walls. With each step, the echo of his boots on the stone steps filled the air, a steady rhythm in the quiet.

In his arms, Liam cradled Naya, her form nestled against his chest. The dim light danced across her peaceful face, casting soft shadows that played with the gentle curves of her cheeks. Liam's gaze lingered on her, soaking in the serene beauty of the moment. A smile, tender and full, spread across his face. As they ascended, a single tear escaped from the corner of Liam's eye, tracing a solitary path down his cheek.

Thank you so much for taking the time to read my book.

I hope you enjoyed the journey!

If you could spare a moment to leave a review, I'd truly
appreciate it.

Your feedback helps more readers discover my work.

For updates on upcoming books, behind-the-scenes content,

and to join my newsletter, please visit my website:

ajfordbooks.com

Thank you again for your support!